Of Lies and Honey

DONNA NORMAN-CARBONE

Of Lies and Honey
Red Adept Publishing, LLC
104 Bugenfield Court
Garner, NC 27529
https://RedAdeptPublishing.com/

To my mother and my daughter

Part I

Harper
Oak Creek, Georgia, 2003
Chapter 1

"Harper Alexander." There it was, prominently displayed in gold lettering on a blackboard in the foyer at House Divine Real Estate. Next to it, "Wingate estate, 2.4," her most recent sale. Hunger to advance her career had propelled Harper to the top of the sales list. The other agents vied for the opportunity, but she got the nod from the owner because he'd recognized her ability to be both personable and shrewd.

Harper paid attention to detail. She seemed to understand what her customers desired most even when they didn't know themselves. She would welcome the buyers on move-in day with her signature touch: chilled Moët and fresh-cut flowers in a crystal vase. Everything would be perfect.

Always last to leave, Harper turned off the lights at the agency, set the alarm, and locked the door behind her to head home. She would need a good night's sleep before the big day.

The next morning, Harper woke to her husband, Gabe, shaking her shoulder, his voice raised in annoyance. "Babe, wake up."

She opened her eyes, aware that her alarm was blaring on her side of the bed. Gabe pounded his finger on the clock to make it stop.

Harper sat up quickly, or as quickly as she could with a five-pound baby in her belly. "Shit! I'm late." She was never late. She pivoted her body almost mechanically until her legs dangled from the side of the bed. "Wingate closing is today."

"I know." Gabe still sounded annoyed as he returned to bed and threw the covers back over himself.

There wasn't time for a shower. That was a fact. Instead, Harper looked in the bathroom mirror, tousled her ash-blond curls into place, and told herself, *This will have to do*. The compromises she was already learning to make as a first-time expectant mother.

She'd almost finished washing her face when a sharp pain crossed the bottom of what now felt like a honeydew melon protruding from her once-shapely figure. She grimaced, rubbing until it subsided, and called out to Gabe, "I had an awful sleep last night. Probably why the alarm didn't wake me."

Gabe grunted in response, and she looked back in the mirror at her seven-months-pregnant body. "I just want my body back."

Harper had taken the first five months of pregnancy to resign herself to becoming a mother—something she'd never thought she wanted. Not having children had been part of the unwritten marriage contract. They'd talked about it. Harper saw herself as a career woman and made sure she and Gabe were on the same page. However, their contraception didn't do its job, and after the second consecutive month of not getting a period, Harper faced her imminent fate. Gabe had received the news with caution, clearly delaying his own excitement, although it bubbled close to the surface. Harper knew he was waiting until she had accepted it.

Harper's mother, on the other hand, had flat-out brimmed with jubilation, reassuring her daughter by saying, "Sometimes life takes us in directions we hadn't imagined, but that are, in the grand scheme of things, right where we're supposed to be."

At first, Harper experienced trepidation about this theory until she felt a little flutter, like the brush of a butterfly's wings, inside her stomach. She had been in the office, about to make a copy of a contract, but she immediately stopped in her tracks and placed her hand on the hard bump beneath her too-tight skirt. She waited, conscious of her breath filling her lungs then rushing out. When the movement happened again, an unexpected smile crossed her face. She'd given in to the possibility that maybe motherhood was something to look forward to instead of fear.

Harper quickly dressed and made herself "publicly presentable"—fully made-up with every strand of hair in place, wearing a white linen maternity skirt with the over-thick elastic waistband to accommodate her growing stomach. She wanted so desperately to wear yoga pants, but she thwarted the desire for comfort in order to maintain professionalism.

Harper waddled down the stairs, put on the teakettle, and went into the back garden armed with scissors. She made her way down the sloped yard by the pond where they'd planted a garden just two years before when they moved to the four-bedroom mid-century house. With its eleven spacious rooms—one already decorated for the baby coming in just a few months—two garages, front porch, and sunporch, it was definitely an upgrade from their townhouse in Savannah. Working at a competitive real estate agency had allowed Harper to monitor the best finds.

Drawn first to the vibrant red cleome and purple aster, Harper clipped a few, keeping the stems long, and placed them gently into a wicker basket so as not to disrupt the petals. Next, she moved to the yellow wax bells, deliberating the length in comparison to the vase she'd bought and the already-cut flowers. *This will do.* She clipped some, then the white iceberg roses climbing up the trellis caught her eye. She'd almost missed them. *Yes, this is an especially important sale—white roses are a must.*

Just as she was about to snip a rose, a bee buzzed in front of her face and she pulled away, pricking her finger on a thorn. She jerked back then looked at the bubble of blood forming on her fingertip. After sucking on it to make it stop, she cut her roses, placing them with the other flowers in the basket. *Perfect. The buyers will love them.*

On a closing day, Harper always tried to arrive at the house precisely at the scheduled time to make her way in, leave a little housewarming gift, and disappear before the homeowners arrived. But because of her late start, she was rushed. Her mother's voice crept into her head again. *"Timeliness is next to godliness."* Harper was sure her mother had messed up the idiom, but had repeated it so damn much that she couldn't remember the original. "I know, I know," she said aloud, as if her mother were with her.

The expansive paved drive up to the Wingate estate wound near-endlessly through tall trees before opening to three acres of lush, manicured lawn. At its center sat a twenty-four-room turn-of-the-century stone mansion. The first time she'd driven the buyers to the property, the wife had gasped at the sight before even stepping foot inside.

Now, standing at the center of the kitchen, wicker basket full of flowers on the counter, Harper began to arrange them in the vase, priding herself that they came from her very own garden that she tended with great care. Gabe had once told her, "If you take care of this baby like you do your garden, he will be the happiest kid alive," in an attempt to assuage her trepidation over becoming a mom.

In another life, Harper could have been a florist with the way she enjoyed cutting and arranging fresh flowers. It put her in a Zen place. She started with the wax bells. *Tallest first.*

Then came the others and, as the finishing touch, the pungent roses. Just as Harper stepped back to admire the composition, she felt another sharp pain in her belly, stronger than before. Her hand moved immediately to her stomach, trying to rub it away to no avail.

Not now. I've got to get this done before the buyers arrive. As she pressed and rubbed, the sharp discomfort seemed to go deeper. But

Harper knew time was not on her side. Adrenaline coursed through her with the necessity to keep going. The vase was full of flowers and in need of water, so she needed to hurry. If it persisted, she would call the doctor later.

Just as she moved toward the sink, Harper saw it—a drop of ruby-red blood on the floor. She looked at the prick on her finger. *Has the wound reopened?* When she bent to look closer, she discovered a stain of the same color on her skirt and felt warm liquid let loose, pouring down her thighs.

Harper shrieked. The vase escaped from her grasp, smashing and scattering fragments of glass and flowers on the floor. The sound of the ocean rushed from one ear to the other. The room tilted, and...

Harper came back to consciousness slowly.

Her last memory was of falling. Sensing her overly dry throat, Harper forced herself to salivate and swallow. Her eyes struggled to open to slits but closed again when affronted by bright lights. *Where am I?*

Her eyes blinked several times as she slowly acclimated to the glare. While her vision was cloudy at first, Gabe's silhouette looking out of a window came into focus. Her body lay taut under tightly tucked sheets, and she processed her surroundings, a cold, sterile white room filled with gleaming steel equipment. *Hospital?* She heard muffled voices from a television, but even more pronounced was the deafening sound of monitors beeping next to her ear, which triggered awareness of the pull of IVs attached to her wrists.

How did I get here?

In that distinct moment, Harper discovered how empty felt when she realized the absence of the tiny life inside her, and she knew even before Gabe uttered the words or was able to wipe away her flowing tears with his shaky hand. Even her insides began to quiver as her breath quickened with sobs.

She knew they'd lost the baby, and she knew it was all her fault.

IN THE FOLLOWING WEEKS, a period of darkness shrouded all corners of Harper's life. Black funeral dress, tiny coffin. A barrage of people coming and going through her front door, a bounty of food she wanted to neither smell nor eat. The ringing phone, the whispering voices, the curtains drawn to keep the light hidden—at her request. Her mother, hovering over her. Her chest tightening until she couldn't breathe, like an elephant stood on it.

When the panic set in, which was not an unfamiliar feeling for Harper, she reminded herself to focus. On the crack in the paint where the ceiling met the wall—it had begun to settle. On the silver speck from the light hitting the glass of a picture frame just right where it rested on her bedroom dresser.

Soon she was given pills and water, followed by more pills and water—an attempt to quell the inconsolable pain that flowed through her veins like the blood that now separated her life from her daughter's.

Gabe had insisted upon giving the baby a name—Delilah Grace, because he was sure she would have been beautiful and perfect. Harper would have preferred for her to remain nameless. "Baby Alexander." She thought it would have made the loss more bearable somehow, while in naming her, their daughter would remain a tangible absence instead of an idea never meant to come to fruition. But how could she deny Gabe this last wish for their child?

Harper insisted on cutting the flowers for the baby herself, white lilies and white roses from her trellis to place at the stone after it had been mounted at the gravesite. A tiny little stone on top of a hill looking over a sea of monuments, all various shapes and sizes. At the grave, Harper bent to lay the flowers between the etched angel and the letters of her lost baby's name. When she stood back up, her legs wobbled and her hands shook. Gabe steadied her, drawing her close to him.

She thought the visit would give her closure, but it didn't.

Two months passed. The loss became part of her, physically and emotionally. It moved inside Harper the way Delilah once had. From that first moment, everything she thought she knew about herself changed.

Until Delilah, she hadn't wanted children.

The pregnancy had been a mistake. Gabe had always wanted kids—in fact, he made no secret of it—but he'd accepted early on that his marriage to Harper was more important when she told him, repeatedly, that she wasn't the one for him if he saw children in his future. She recalled the devoted look in his eyes when they stood at the end of a breezy pier on a Nantucket vacation when he'd asked her to marry him, when he pulled the blond curls from her face, tucking them behind her ears. "I can live without a family," he said. "It's you I can't live without." Tears had escaped from her eyes then, and her tightened chest had released; she'd finally found *the one*.

Harper blamed herself for their loss because she'd spent the first months of her pregnancy wishing it away.

ON THE BACK DECK OVERLOOKING a pond that stretched across the yard and down the hill, Harper watched the mallards, two of them, swimming and playing follow-the-leader. One dipped its head, and the other mimicked its behavior. One flapped its wings, and the other flapped wider. Together, they pumped their heads back and forth at one another.

Harper didn't crack a smile, although normally, she would have. Instead, she just watched, keeping her eyes on their every movement, wondering if their mirroring was some sort of mating ritual. It had been two months since the funeral, and she couldn't even begin to think of being intimate with Gabe again. Thoughts of them together inevitably led only to the vacancy she felt, the permanent hole inside.

In her hands, she held a sweating glass of water. She raised it to her lips. Behind her, the screen door creaked open, and two sets of footsteps followed.

"Harper." It was the saccharine voice of her mother, who had been visiting frequently. Her presence felt suffocating at times, but she was too numb to object.

During Harper's darker days, Gabe and her mother had disassembled the baby's nursery, packing up the baby bumpers, mobile, and sheets from the crib, leaving the crib bare. They'd stored everything in the room's closet. Each time she heard the two of them in there, those somber voices behind a closed door, Harper had taken another Xanax followed by a nap. Every time she passed by the room since then, the door was shut. She'd left it that way.

Harper didn't look up. It wasn't that Harper didn't hear her mother—responding would simply have taken far more energy than she could conjure.

She heard Gabe whisper, "This is what she does all day."

"Still no talk of work?" Concern was thick in her mother's voice.

Harper realized she had been of little company to Gabe. Perhaps he needed her mother's presence. The guilt gnawed at her, chipping away, all-encompassing, a Catholic trait her mother had passed on to her. If Harper could list all the times her mother had told her what she should do and how she should behave and how she should think, Harper could pave a trail of shoulds from the time she'd declared she didn't want children to the moment she fell in love with her "whoops" baby.

Harper's mother made her way to the empty chair beside her with only a small table separating them. Harper pasted on a flat smile. When she put the glass down, she wiped her hand on her smock shirt that hid the diminished bump Delilah had left in her wake.

Her mother wrinkled her brow, gazing at Harper. "What can I do for you?"

Harper stared at her mother. Through her.

She tried again. "Gabe tells me you aren't ready to return to work. It's been months, honey."

Lowering her head, Harper began picking at her cuticles.

"I thought we agreed this was the week," her mother continued. "Maybe just a little at a time. Something to get you out of this house."

You should move on. That was all Harper could hear. She sighed heavily.

"We're worried about you, darling. This was a devastating loss, I know."

Like an elastic band stretched too far, Harper's head snapped up. Her eyes seared into her mother's. "Do you? Really? I felt her moving inside of me. She was whole, Mom. She was mine." Her voice grew louder and more indignant with each word.

Her mother leaned in, placing her hands on Harper's knees as if she were really listening. Hearing what her daughter was saying.

But Harper knew the truth. "How could she be moving one minute and just... just..." She couldn't bring herself to say what she already knew.

The truth was that her baby was never meant to survive. Delilah's death was meant to punish Harper for not wanting a child in the first place. Each time Harper thought about her responsibility, her breath became jagged, so she took another Xanax, another nap. But like anything else dealt with by suppression instead of confrontation, that guilt would eventually resurface like a body buried at sea.

She contemplated confessing to her mother that she'd prayed early on in her pregnancy she would lose the baby—but she dismissed the urge after a moment. It passed, as it had so many times when those words were on her lips, ready to be revealed and possibly purge her of the weight of her guilt. Instead, she turned her attention back to the mallards, which had moved to opposite sides of the pond.

"There aren't any answers," her mother said. "I'd love to give you a full explanation, but there isn't one. Still, this doesn't mean you can't get pregnant again."

Can't or shouldn't? Harper wanted to ask. She already knew, deep down, that she shouldn't—or couldn't—put herself through it all again.

"But you have to take the first step, and that's getting back to your life," her mother went on. "It doesn't mean you'll stop mourning the loss of your daughter. You never will, but the grief will wane. I promise you that."

Harper looked up at her mother, who had folded her arms across her chest. *How can she promise me anything?* She'd never lost a child. She had two healthy pregnancies: first Ben, then herself.

Harper's mouth slacked as she questioned the plausibility of her mother's words, but then her mother reached over to lift Harper's chin. "I promise you."

But how can you promise me anything when you're the reason I didn't want to be a mom in the first place?

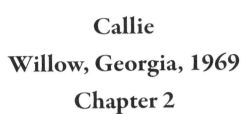

Callie
Willow, Georgia, 1969
Chapter 2

With one step down, Callie began to descend the grand mahogany staircase with the ruby carpet runner. The banister, garnished with tulle and white roses, extended out like open arms, inviting her in. As she moved, she wriggled her toes, cramped in satin pumps that came to a very distinct point. When she looked up, she noticed the crystal chandelier, as round as the table in the oversized foyer of Callie's home, hung with hundreds of tiny prisms that shimmered when they caught the light just right. Callie longed to lose herself in the light for just a moment, but the cramp in her shoes reminded her of the dull ache in her stomach.

The tempo of the band's music—strings and horns and a grand piano—heightened to a perfect crescendo.

Her father, waiting to escort her, held out his arm. Callie tucked hers through it. She looked up at him with the wide sapphire eyes of a seventeen-year-old on the cusp of a turning point in her life. Her father understood, and he clutched her arm to his waist as if he wasn't ready to let go. Her knight in shining armor. His little Cinderella was growing up, and this night was tangible proof of it in ways that she knew he couldn't yet fathom. He looked down at her with a melancholy expression quickly glossed over by an assured smile. Beads of sweat pooled at Callie's hairline.

The notes to the music dipped. This was their cue to begin the walk down together, slow and choreographed, the way they'd rehearsed it. They moved, and she felt the swish of the crinoline beneath her satin dress.

Hundreds of eyes watched.

Callie's heart should have fluttered. She had dreamed of this day, her debut, for as long as she'd had memories. She'd always imagined gardens of beautiful June flowers and dainty white dresses and blush nail polish, the giggles of a gaggle of girls coming out for the first time, being introduced to society, and of the debutantes' princes, at the ready to whisk them away in dances and fairytales.

Everything should have been perfect. Was perfect.

As the chair of the debutante ball for seven years running, Callie's mother, Evelyn Sebastian, had made sure of it. She left no room for error, not an inch. Delegating tasks, supervising every bullet point on her list, and checking off every detail—these were her specialties, and this year, even more than others in the past, promised to be her pinnacle.

Evelyn Sebastian's daughter is finally making her debut. Callie could hear the whispers now, and she could picture her mother's smug reaction. All the papers had written about it. All the high-society women in Willow, Georgia, were talking about it. And Evelyn wouldn't have had it any other way.

As Callie neared the bottom of the steps, she couldn't see her mother, but she imagined Evelyn sitting at the head table on the dais: a wax-like thin, straight smile, no teeth—that would be far too overt—back straight, nose poised and tipping the air, hands clasped on her lap. But even if Callie had seen her mother, she wouldn't have made eye contact. She knew Evelyn could read her like a book. She would see in Callie's eyes that this was the last place Callie wanted to be.

Blocking Callie's view was the row of posh young men standing across from the debutantes who had already taken their places. Her dad drew his elbow in toward his body, giving Callie's arm a squeeze. When she looked up at him, his adoring eyes met hers. He smiled and whispered, "Are you ready, princess?"

The master of ceremonies announced in a melodic voice, "Calista Eve Sebastian, escorted by her father, Asa Sebastian, owner and CEO of Sebastian Oil."

Asa leaned over and kissed the top of Callie's forehead. "This is your night." Callie thought she detected a tear forming in the corner of his eye, but that couldn't be. She had never once seen him cry.

Callie nodded ever so slightly to her father, and he released her arm at the same time she pulled away. A wave of guilt tugged at her. This *would* be her night, but not in the way her father imagined, not in the way Evelyn had so feverishly planned. Callie pasted on a fake smile, feeling the gloss of Vaseline on her teeth, a trick she'd learned in etiquette class to make them gleam.

She joined the other debutantes who had preceded her, all having already walked down the stairs with their fathers. They stood in line with perfect posture, heads held high, toothy gums exposed. Callie knew every single one of these girls. Together, they had attended private school, summer camp, dance lessons, etiquette classes, and countless social events. Evelyn had referred to them as an "elite class of young women."

As a young girl, Callie had felt special in that kind of sisterhood. At every juncture, Evelyn reinforced that she ought to. "That's what privilege gives a person, Callie. Belonging." Those words were always in her head, sometimes to the point of stinging. As Callie grew older, she found herself developing a yearning for something else, something more than perfect girls in petticoats and patent leather shoes.

Jocelyn Halfield, who stood at the other end of the line from Callie, wasn't like the other girls. Her tongue was quick and honest, and she dared to push boundaries. Jocelyn's family wasn't old money like Callie's. While Asa came from a long line of oil moguls, Jocelyn's father had made his fortune in plastics with a company he started from the ground up.

Evelyn had argued against the Halfields. "It just isn't the same kind of wealth," she said. Callie could care less what kind of circles she ran in: old money, new money, no money. Jocelyn was the best friend she'd ever had.

Once Callie took her place, she and Jocelyn exchanged a secret glance that almost threatened to turn Callie's practiced, picture-perfect smile into a smirk. If it had, and Evelyn caught her, that could have ruined everything.

The young men took their places in front of the young ladies. Callie recognized the one standing across from her, a mere boy with his pink cheeks and slick, plump pompadour. He winked at her, and Callie looked at the clock. Half past seven. *Three more hours to go.*

The band struck up the customary waltz for the first dance, one that Callie had been rehearsing for months. The young man bowed. Callie curtsied. They locked arms and began to glide across the dance floor in concert with the other couples. Callie counted the steps in her head as the air swished between her legs from the movement of her gown.

After the dance ended, the young man whispered in her ear, "Niles. My pleasure, Calista." He took her hand in his as if he were about to bring it to his lips, but he didn't.

Callie breathed a sigh of relief. "Callie," she corrected, her voice tart as a lemon. She hated the name Calista.

Niles took hold of her arm and escorted her to their seats, dictated by name cards tented on bone china plates. Jocelyn sat across from Callie, which was most certainly an oversight on Evelyn's part. Callie reveled in detecting Evelyn's misstep because she so rarely made them. A grin crossed her face, and Jocelyn knew exactly what it was for. When they both sat, at precisely the same moment, Callie's lip turned up, and Jocelyn stuck out her tongue just a tiny bit.

Callie placed the napkin on her lap and laid her folded hands on top. Her gestures scripted, Callie rolled through the rules of etiquette in her head.

"Calista." Her mother's voice pricked her from behind just before Evelyn placed her hand on the back of Callie's chair. "You look stunning, darling. How is everything?" Her hand moved through the air in a grand gesture to encompass the ambiance of the entire ballroom, as if she'd created it single-handedly. It was very like Evelyn to take all the credit, dismissing the assistance of an entire committee.

Callie winced, but her lips moved across her slippery teeth into a smile, and she turned her head to acknowledge her mother as a good girl should. Callie crossed her legs, conscious of the bare skin above her stockings, garters keeping them in place. Evelyn would not have approved.

"Lovely, Mother," Callie said.

"Yes, and finally, it was all for you."

Callie knew that comment was for the benefit of Niles and the others in earshot, the ones who judged Evelyn and would marvel at what a wonderfully doting mother she was. Callie knew the truth.

Evelyn bent, her lips close to Callie's ear, and whispered, "Your hair is mussed." With her spindly fingers, she smoothed it back in place. Evelyn couldn't see her daughter's sly eye roll.

"You've met Niles, then," Callie said.

Evelyn nodded. Of course her mother knew her escort. Even the pairings were under her control, just as surely as a Roman numeral trailed his name. Callie should have known.

With her hands on one of their shoulders, Evelyn drew Callie and Niles closer together so their shoulders touched. "You two have a splendid time tonight."

Then Evelyn excused herself as the servers took their introductory places. In choreographed style, the servers performed a dance of their own, silver trays held high on the palms of their hands while they wove in between each other. Callie's mouth hung agape at the entire show. The servers made their introductions, placed silver baskets of bread and herbed butter on their tables, then excused themselves.

Evelyn had certainly pulled out all the stops. Dancing waitstaff, champagne fountains, grand ice sculptures trimmed with floral bouquets, tall crystal centerpieces, and mints at each place setting with "Debutante Ball 1969" embossed on them in gold.

Ambient chatter filled the ballroom along with dinner music. Most of the debutantes leaned in, eager for the opportunity to get to know their escorts.

As the food was being served, Niles made small talk. "Where do you go to school?"

As if you don't know. "Briarlee."

"What is it like growing up a Sebastian?"

Really? Dull. Pretentious. "Well, it brought me here."

"What do you do for fun?"

"Hang out with friends, mostly." *Not this.* However, she'd been trained well enough to act charming when spoken to. And just as Evelyn could put on airs in public, so could her only child.

Callie didn't care about their conversation or Niles's opinion. Anyone Evelyn wanted to set her up with would never be compatible with her. She would stake her life on it.

Meanwhile, Jocelyn was engrossed in conversation with her escort. Sparkles lit her eyes. Callie turned her attention to poking at her French-cut green beans then put her fork down and repeated the napkin process while Niles prattled on and on. She nodded her head politely at just the right intervals.

Callie's mother would say that perfect etiquette was what defined the debs and kept them on their chosen path. Evelyn's perspective on life was linear. She had planned out Callie's life by day, month, year, and decade. After graduation next year, Callie would attend a prestigious college comparable to Briarlee, where she would major in home economics and secure a fiancé from an established family.

Callie tuned out Evelyn's expectations. The last kind of life she wanted to be living was one that mirrored her mother's.

As dinner dragged on, Callie considered balling up her napkin and putting it on her plate. But then she looked across the room at her father, tall and commanding, engrossed in conversation with one of the other deb-dads. For her father, Callie would do anything, including going through the motions of this rite of passage. The only reason Asa cared at all was because Evelyn did.

The committee of deb-moms trailed after their leader as Evelyn stepped to the microphone. They swarmed around her like the beautiful queen bee she was, all her dutiful worker bees trailing behind. When Callie was young, her father had told her fairytales while her mother delivered cautionary tales about not getting stung by the bees.

Evelyn stood erect, head held high, and tapped the microphone once, making loud, echoing feedback sound throughout the room. "Good evening, Georgians. The debutante committee." Her hands gestured to her right and left like graceful wings. "I would like to welcome you to the Savannah Debutante Ball, representing one hundred thirty-nine counties." Evelyn paused, drawing her hands together for a silent clap, letting her audience know they should mimic her.

Once they did, she continued. "Yes, yes. Isn't that wonderful? It's our one hundred forty-seventh year, and—I don't have to tell you, but I love saying it—we have the longest-running debutante ball in the United States." She dipped her head slightly, as if she were acknowledging something momentous. "And look at all these beautiful young women. Aren't they exquisite? An elite class of thirty-eight this year, including my own Calista Eve."

When Evelyn's face turned toward Callie's table, all eyes followed. Callie turned candy-apple red and pasted on her most well-rehearsed smile. How dare Evelyn name Callie when none of the others were named specifically? This was the kind of thing Callie hated about her mother—the way she always singled Callie out.

Stuck in the moment, with everyone staring, Callie blocked out the next several minutes of her mother's speech. Her mind fast-forwarded to the real goal of this night—Callie's goal. The palms of her hands grew sweaty just thinking about *him*. The way he looked at her like Robert Redford looked at Jane Fonda in *Barefoot in the Park*, with that foxy smirk.

Excitement bubbled inside her like the champagne in the Waterford crystal flutes that made the tables shimmer.

Another sharp whine of feedback from the microphone interrupted Callie's thoughts. Evelyn tapped at it with a momentary scowl on her face before she shook it off, curved her lips, and raised her voice. "If this year's debutantes are any indication of a charming future, we will be sparkling like diamonds. Shall we have a round of applause for this year's young ladies and their very *eligible* escorts?"

The crowd clapped and chimed their crystal glasses with silver spoons.

Callie glanced over at Niles and grimaced discreetly. Meanwhile, Evelyn's voice echoed loudly in her head. *"Look, darling, his father is on the board of..."* It could be any place, and he could be any young man with a promising inheritance in front of him. *"Very eligible. You should meet him."* Inside, Callie's blood boiled. *"Don't wait for a wealthy young man, Callie, as they get snatched up quickly... You have dowry enough to get any man you want... Remember, you want nothing*

to do with the nouveau riche." These were the mantras Evelyn sang to
Callie instead of lullabies.

From across the table, Jocelyn flailed her hands to get Callie's attention. When Jocelyn darted her head toward the powder room,
Callie understood and followed, walking with quick steps, a few
paces behind Jocelyn.

Appearing from out of nowhere, Evelyn stopped her daughter
like a traffic cop. "What do you think, darling? Niles is quite a catch."
The twinkle in her eye was unmistakable. She'd already fallen in love
with him as a possible suitor, no matter what Callie thought. "His father's on the board of directors for..."

Callie cut her off. "Mother, I have to use the ladies' room."

"You aren't feeling ill, are you, Calista?" It sounded more like an
accusation than a question. Callie knew if she were to get sick during
the event, her mother would take it as a defiant act meant to thwart
her special night—Evelyn's night, not Callie's.

"I'm fine." Callie brushed past her and quickened her pace.

Jocelyn greeted her in the powder room. "Are you sure you won't
come to the party?" she asked. "We've talked about this night since
we were eight."

"You know I can't."

Jocelyn nodded.

"You promised, Jocelyn," Callie said. "I can't do this without
you."

"Okay. Okay. You have your night, and I'll have mine." Jocelyn
reapplied her champagne lipstick then rolled her top lip over the bottom.

They walked out of the bathroom together.

"Look. Our moms are chatting. Together." Jocelyn's voice was
heavy with sarcasm.

Evelyn, wearing a rose-colored taffeta sheath and a pillbox hat to
match over an icy-blond beehive, looked down upon Wendy, who

wore a baby-blue swing dress, her whimsical black ringlets touching her shoulders. There were no pretenses where Wendy was concerned, and that was what Callie loved most about her and what Evelyn looked upon with disdain. Evelyn didn't consider Wendy as refined as the women who traveled in her own circle. She'd never actually said those words, but Callie knew her mother well enough.

Yet Evelyn had no problem sucking up every bit of praise Wendy was singing to her about that evening's ball. Evelyn shone best when she was being admired.

"Mom," Jocelyn said.

"Look," Wendy said, smiling, "our beautiful debs. I was just telling Evelyn what an honor it is to be part of this extravaganza. Isn't it?" She pulled back Jocelyn's long chestnut curls, and Jocelyn smiled warmly at her mother's touch.

"We want to talk to you about the after-party," Callie interjected, standing on her toes.

"After-party?" Judgment dripped from Evelyn's words.

Jocelyn appealed to her mother, the more sensible one. "It's at Dodie Ingalls's. We thought"—Jocelyn clasped her hands and twisted her body—"Callie might sleep over."

"This is *the* party." Evelyn turned her nose up in the air.

"All the debs are scooting out at ten, Mother," Callie said matter-of-factly.

"We'll be home by one," Jocelyn pleaded.

Wendy's face softened as she looked to Evelyn. "Well, I suppose this, too, is a rite of passage. Isn't it, Evelyn?"

Evelyn gave a stern shake of her head. "All of this preparation and money, and it isn't enough?"

Callie rolled her eyes as she walked away from her mother and back to the dance floor. She and Jocelyn melted into a crowd of debs dancing to "Wooly Bully," their crinolines making a crinkling sound beneath their dresses and their hands up in the air.

At precisely ten till ten, Callie poked Jocelyn's shoulder. A rebellious glance passed between them. No words were needed. It was time to meander through the crowd while remaining undetected.

To make their escape.

IN THE CAR, CALLIE placed a hand on Jocelyn's arm. "You are the absolute best-ever friend. I owe you." Her chest swelled with excitement that she could almost feel in her throat. Or maybe it was nerves, or a little of both.

"Oh yes, you do."

"How did we pull that off? Wendy comes through in the clutch yet again. How I wish I had a mother like yours."

"How I wish you'd change your mind and actually come to the party."

"No. *This* is happening. Now, go have fun at the party with Paul Howard Dole IV, and if anyone asks where I am, tell them I felt sick." Callie placed one hand on her stomach and the back of the other on her forehead. That part wasn't completely a lie.

"I love you," Jocelyn said, her voice cracking with worry.

"I'm happy, Joss."

"I know. And I still love you. Remember to call your parents to tell them you're sleeping at my house tonight."

"Of course. Love you too. I'll call you in the morning."

Callie scanned the street before getting out of the car, playing up the doe-eyed act as if trying to locate her destination for the very first time. But this wasn't the first time, although Jocelyn thought it was. It was, however, the first night she would be sleeping here. All night.

With the overnight bag slung over her shoulder, Callie darted clumsily across the sidewalk in her high heels and ran up the steps. She drew in a deep breath and rang the bell.

The door opened. Jon, dressed in jean shorts and a yellow polo, waved to Jocelyn. His beguiling mocha eyes widened and his dimples deepened when he took in Callie's appearance. "My gosh. You are beautiful."

Now, finally, she felt like the belle of the ball.

Callie gasped at how handsome Jon was with his mussed hair and day-old stubble. He drew her in by the waist, the bag falling loose from her hand, and shut the door behind her with conviction. He kissed her, his lips pressing hard against hers.

So much had changed over the course of six months.

During the winter session at Briarlee, Callie had been summoned to the Athletic Office to be reprimanded for stealing a fellow cheer-leader's clothes from her locker and throwing them in the trash. She'd done it after the girl had cheated off Callie's physics test and they both ended up with zeroes. The retaliation had been perfectly justified, to Callie's mind.

Callie had expected to see the stout, balding Coach Wilson, who was a notorious pushover. Instead, she found Jon Taylor, who looked like a young version of Cary Grant with a chiseled face and a cleft in his chin. However, his hair was the color of caramel, and he sported a five-o'clock shadow as if he'd meant to leave it there. Quite unconventional for a faculty member.

"I like your spunk," Mr. Taylor had said. Then he added, with a kind of forced authoritative tone, "Nonetheless, I need to hand you this demerit." And he transferred the envelope from his strong-looking, square-knuckled hand to hers.

Over the next few weeks, Callie had made it her mission to learn all she could about Mr. Taylor. He was twenty-two years old, originally an intern who was due to graduate college at the end of the year. When Coach Wilson got sick mid-term, which led to medical leave, Mr. Taylor was in the right place at the right time and "fell into the position," as he later explained to Callie.

Smitten, Callie exhausted all excuses to cross his path. What began as a mere crush led to an easy friendship. Casual conversations turned into appointments. Appointments turned into sharing root beer floats at the school cafeteria or taking walks on the school grounds. The more she got to know Jon Taylor, Callie realized he stood for everything she hadn't realized she longed for.

A young man who'd become upwardly mobile on his own merits rather than his parents', Jon helped her discover so much of what she wanted to become through what blossomed between them. Callie confided that she longed to get out of her lily-white life and do something that mattered, to work with real people when all her mother wanted for her was to marry up and secure her future. Jon shared the way he'd put himself through college, never having considered relying on his family's money. Now, that was something Callie could wrap her mind around—working toward something, earning independence.

They bonded over the Beatles and Bob Dylan, the music speaking to the freedoms they innately craved. Jon yearned to make his mark, while Callie desired anonymity. Their relationship began slowly, almost unnoticed by anyone but the two of them. It was nothing pretentious, simply a pure zest for the unexpected turns life could take. Jon was the turn Callie hadn't expected.

At first, Jocelyn found Callie's stories about Jon amusing and harmless. Then Callie confessed that they'd shared an almost-accidental kiss, and one kiss had led to another...

Callie had told Jon she wasn't a virgin—a little white lie. It was just that she'd never had these feelings before. Real, grown-up feelings. And she didn't want to do or say anything to scare him away. He was a man, for heaven's sake. A man would want a woman, not a girl. Would he recognize her innocence the first time? She worried, but if he had, he didn't say a word. That was the kind of gentleman he was, the kind of man who isn't just a boyfriend.

Each time Jon made love to Callie, everything else fell into an abyss. Callie's life as scripted by her mother. The etiquette lessons. The piano she'd never wanted to play. The rules and schedules and curfews. The social circle chosen for her and the list of the kinds of people she should shun. None of it mattered anymore. The way Jon held her so tenderly, his breath tickling her skin, the harmony they created together: that was what life was supposed to be. That was what being an adult felt like.

Standing there with him that night, she was sure of it.

"I feel bad that you left your dance," Jon began.

Callie shushed him with a finger to his lips. "Don't. *This* is the highlight of my night."

Jon backed her body against the closed front door and pressed his warm, damp lips against her neck. Callie's breath quickened. Neither Niles nor any boy her own age could make her feel this way. Only Jon.

As his soft, strong hands caressed her skin, his thumb strumming her shoulder in a gentle rhythmic motion, a wave flowed through Callie's body. Then he dotted her neck with gentle kisses. She closed her eyes and reached out to touch him, too, but he pushed her hands away.

Locking one forefinger with hers, he led her to the bedroom. Her heart began to beat faster as she walked, her dress swishing in time with the beats. She had something to tell him. Something both weighing on her mind and eager to jump from her lips.

Jon looked back at her with alluring eyes, and Callie giggled.

"Do you know what you do to me?" he asked. "That dress. Your porcelain skin. I could kiss you into eternity."

As if she were in a trance, Callie's head tilted. Now both of them stood at the foot of his bed. He turned off the lamp, and the light of the moon shone in through the window, bathing them in its glow.

He pressed against her, reaching around to unzip the back of her dress, peeling it down sleeves first and kissing her shoulders. Then he dropped the dress to her waist, exposing a lace brassiere.

Is this the time? Will he be as happy as I am? She debated with herself, suddenly feeling as if she were teetering on a tightrope. *This could be the best day of my life.* Callie turned her attention back to Jon.

She breathed in his spicy cinnamon cologne with every languid touch he lavished on her body. Kisses, caresses—each one taking her breath away more profoundly than the last. Yes, Jon was a man in every sense of the word.

"Callie," he whispered in her ear. "I need every inch of you."

"Wait, Jon."

And the mood changed like a needle scratching across a record.

Callie slipped her arms back through the sleeves of her dress and sat on the edge of the bed. She patted the vacant spot beside her. Jon sat down, a sullen expression Callie couldn't read crossing his face. She drew in a deep breath. She had to trust their love. No matter how this turned out, Callie knew two things: Jon loved her, and her news was exactly the fresh start to life they needed.

Callie reached over, taking his hand in hers and pivoting her body to face him. A slight smile curved her lips. Squeezing his hand, she said, "I'm late."

Raina
Brocton, Georgia, 2003
Chapter 3

In the rush of anticipation and secrecy, Raina Edwin tripped on something and stubbed her toe. *Doggone it.* The bag dropped out of her hand and onto the floor next to the culprit—Tina's Cinderella jewelry box, which had once been her own. It was splayed open on the floor, hair clips and ribbons left in its wake.

When Raina picked it up, the beautifully worn princess resumed spinning to the tune of "A Dream is a Wish the Heart Makes" as Raina filled it back up double-time then slammed the top of the box shut. She picked up her bag and returned the wooden box to her eight-year-old daughter's dresser.

Tina's room, which she shared with her eleven-year-old sister, represented the worlds of difference between the two girls. Tracy's bed had been neatly made while Tina's covers were wrapped in a ball in the center of the bed. Tracy's side was completely organized, a trait she inherited from her mother, which Raina acknowledged as both a blessing and a curse, whereas no one could make heads or tails of Tina's side.

Once a month, Raina sat at the center of Tina's side of the room, directing her how and where to organize her things. "She'll learn one day," Raina had said on too many occasions to Wayne, her husband. And he laughed it off because they both knew Tina wouldn't learn, because she was just like her daddy. Now, five-year-old Timothy, who had just begun kindergarten a month before, was a little like both his parents: stubborn as a mule like his mama and happy as a clam like his daddy.

Raina clutched the bag, feeling the perimeter of the container within. The box that just might change the course of her life, of all their lives. First, she listened at the top of the stairs to be sure Wayne wasn't in earshot. He worked from home on their farm, and sometimes he would pop in on Raina at the house when she wasn't aware. But all remained silent downstairs—the kind of silence that had become deafening over the past month.

With Timothy in school, Raina didn't know what to do with herself. She had no schooling or training to get a job. Sure, she worked on the farm when Wayne needed her, but filling up cartons of produce wasn't the fulfilling way she'd envisioned beginning the next chapter in her life. For the past eleven years, she'd been home with the kids who filled her house, to the point of overflowing sometimes, with beautiful, symphonic chaos. When Timothy had started school, the purpose in her days went out the door with him. She felt empty inside.

Once she was in the bathroom, Raina's hands quivered as she opened the pregnancy-test box. Raina wrestled with the plastic package inside and finally bit it apart to get to the test. She rechecked the lock on the bathroom door then balled the bottom of her sundress up in one hand to slide down her panties. Then she settled on the seat, slid the stick beneath her, took a deep breath, and peed.

The first time she'd done this, she'd been equally as nervous, perhaps more. At twenty-one, she and Wayne hadn't been married yet, nor were they technically engaged. However, it had been a sure thing they would tie the knot—it was just a question of when. Becoming pregnant with Tracy sent their nuptials into hyperspeed. It had been a happy surprise—then.

This time, unplanned and undiscussed, would be different. The possibility of another pregnancy worried Raina. *How will Wayne take the news?* Of course, Wayne knew she wanted to fill her house with children, but that didn't mean he shared her desire for more than the three they already had.

Raina didn't know what it was like to have a mother. Hers had died from ovarian cancer when she was five, leaving her alone with a father who'd grieved more than he parented. Despite that, Raina tried not to feel sorry for herself. Instead, she grew up quickly, parenting herself for most of her life and knowing she would get out of her house as quickly as she could. That first time Wayne came into the local Minimart, he'd taken her breath away from right across the counter. With his curly red hair and an Adam's apple the size of a plump strawberry, she knew he was the fire that would ignite her for the rest of her life.

Raina had married Wayne on a cool spring day when she was five months pregnant, her belly already protruding from her slight frame. Only twenty people attended. Neither Wayne nor Raina came from money—Wayne's family ran a farm that sold eggs, beef, and crops to local stores, and Wayne always envisioned himself doing the same.

Raina had continued working at the Minimart through her first pregnancy then quit when Tracy was born. Three years later, Tina came along, and three years after that, they had Timothy, the only child they'd made a concerted effort to conceive.

When the midwife had said, "It's a boy," Wayne's face lit up redder than his hair.

"Finally!" Wayne bought cigars and went to their local pub to buy a round for all his farming buddies.

Raina never worked then because she loved being a mom and Wayne earned enough to make ends meet. By the time Timothy turned three and Tina graduated from kindergarten, Raina was noticing that feeling—a void she needed to fill. Were three kids enough to keep her busy? Sure, but she wanted more like an un-scratchable itch.

From the time Raina was a little girl, she had dreamed great big dreams. First, that she would have a new mom to take care of her. Her daddy wasn't having that. Instead, he went within when her mama died, according to her Auntie Jane, who stepped in every time her dad stepped out—which was often, especially when she was little. When Raina had cried out in the middle of the night, instead of her daddy coming to her side, it had most often been Auntie Jane. Whenever Raina asked when her daddy was coming back, Auntie Jane had brushed back the bangs from her forehead and said, "Soon, Raina. Soon."

Raina always wondered where her blond hair came from. She'd only seen her mom with brown hair, and her father's was dark too. It was one of those questions she'd wished she had time to ask her mama—or that she had been brave enough to ask her daddy.

Auntie Jane suffered from cancer, too, and joined Mama in heaven when Raina was twelve. That was when she started to dream even bigger, deciding to fill her house with a husband she could count on, children, laughter, and love—everything her life had lacked.

Once she finished peeing, Raina let the test rest on the bathroom counter and washed up, then she placed the remaining evidence of the test into a paper bag to hide it. She checked the watch on her wrist. A minute to go, and there was no trace of a line.

Her heartbeat quickened, anticipating the time, as she squeezed her eyes shut, willing the anxiety to pass. When she opened them, she looked down at the pregnancy test. *Nothing.* She shook the stick and placed it back on the counter, waiting for a line to miraculously appear. It didn't.

Now what? she wondered. *This would have been, could have been, the perfect accident. Do I tell Wayne? Ask him what he thinks?* But he'd been so stressed about work lately. Usually, he didn't bring his work stressors into the house, even though Raina wished he would. She always considered it better to talk things out than keep them bottled up inside.

After Wayne's father passed, the weight of the responsibility of the farm had shifted to him. Suddenly, he wasn't only in charge of production but everything: paying bills, procuring and maintaining vendors, hiring and keeping staff. Sometimes it was all-consuming. Raina understood. She kept their home's interior going, and her bees, while Wayne handled everything else. They'd established a rhythm. But her rhythm had shifted.

She shoved the test into the bag and brought it downstairs and out to the garbage bin, pressing it down deep under the rest of the trash.

When she reentered the house through the back breezeway, she noticed the height lines of each of her kids at different stages marked with pencil on the doorframe. Of course, she walked by them every damn time, but today, of all days, they had to catch her attention.

The toilets had been cleaned, the laundry done, and even the meatloaf for dinner had been prepared and waited in the fridge to be cooked. Raina looked at her watch. It read 11:30 a.m. Three more hours. Her days consisted of checking off chores, running errands, and waiting for the kids to come home to make time elusive—the way it had been when her babies were little. Then, she would lose track of the minutes, the hours, and even the days. In the thick of their toddlerdom, she'd always lamented, *If I could just have some time to myself.* Now she had more than her share.

Knowing she was fixating on the negative test, Raina sought out a distraction. She grabbed her beekeeping suit, helmet, veil, and gloves from the back hall and headed down to her bee farm, walking the dirt path that connected the backyard to a clearing in the woods behind her house. The buzzing sound calmed her rapid breaths to a regular rhythm before she could even see the bee boxes. Then they came into view, three of them sitting on makeshift stands built by Wayne. There, she found solace—away from the home, away from the farm. When she tended to her bees, she could think.

Wayne's first reactions to Raina's big ideas were always "No" or "Are you out of your mind?" or "Raina, what goes on in that head of yours?" Then, after Raina would explain her carefully laid plan, Wayne always came around to support his wife, no matter how otherworldly the plan might sound at first, because he knew she had good instincts and a big heart.

Raina had read about bees dying off at an alarming rate and read articles on pollinator projects. "You have your farm, Wayne. I want mine. Bees are important to our ecosystem. I need to take part in saving them." She'd coaxed him over to the computer to show him the websites she'd found, full of facts and research that he couldn't deny.

Wayne had looked at Raina, his head tilted, and a big ol' smile that he couldn't conceal emerged. "My wife," he said, "always trying to save the world. In this case, one bee at a time." Before the week was up, supplies had been ordered, and the makings of a bee farm were in place.

Wayne had carved out a wooden sign that read Raina's Garden and erected it at the end of the path into the clearing. As she passed the sign, Raina reflected on the lengths Wayne had already gone to in making her dreams come true. Maybe a fourth child wouldn't be as much of a stretch as she'd thought.

The bees, they were the constant. The one thing that hadn't changed in the last month. Raina carefully lifted the grated cover on one hive and watched as thousands of worker bees surrounded their queen. It wouldn't be long before it was time to harvest the honey. First, however, came the ritual for treating the hives to protect against mites. She pulled on the trigger to release the acidic spray. It tickled her nose. Had she been wearing the mask, the way Wayne always reminded her, she wouldn't have smelled a thing.

Perhaps Raina could start a honey-selling business and make other goods, too, from her honey. That could give her purpose. Until this point, she'd simply bottled the honey in recycled baby-food jars and handed it out to friends or donated it to local church fairs to sell for charity.

As she worked, she couldn't ignore the ache for another child. *Just one more,* she told herself. A tiny miracle growing within. *Those newborn eyes, looking up at me with all the love in the world... I still have enough in me to return that love to a new baby.*

Just the other day, Raina had gotten out of the car to walk Timothy to the front door of the school, Tracy and Tina already running ahead of them. Raina took hold of Timothy's hand, and he pulled away, saying, "It's okay, Mama, I can do it all by myself."

She'd felt like she'd been punched in the gut. *Only a few weeks of school, and already he can do it by himself?* And at the same time, she'd smiled because her baby was growing up the way he was supposed to. She'd done her job. *But I'm not ready to stop being a mom, no matter what business venture lies ahead. Nothing could fill me the way another child would.*

Raina returned the covers to the bee boxes, calmed by their progress. They would be ready to keep doing what they were born to do: produce honey.

She decided to broach the baby topic with Wayne over dinner that night. She would cook the meatloaf, his favorite, and garlic mashed potatoes. She would have a glass of whiskey and a beer chaser ready for him when he came in from work, just the way he liked.

In her head, she'd made a list of pros and cons to appeal to his rational side. Wayne needed everything spelled out like that. She would start with the cons in order to take care of those right off the bat. The money, of course—it always boiled down to money. But they always managed to make ends meet. The room in the house—they would have to get creative if they had a girl. On the other hand, if the baby were a boy, Timothy could get a brother. Every boy needed a brother. Wayne always said that since he hadn't had one.

That evening, Raina fed the kids early and separately so she could lay out her argument between just the two of them. That way, Wayne could think about it without being frustrated by interruptions.

While the kids ate, Raina prepped for her special dinner, humming to herself.

"That's disgusting," Tina gasped.

"What?" Raina asked, her back to them as she whipped potatoes while they ate hot dogs and fries at the table.

"No, it's not," Timothy said.

"Stop. Mom! He's being disgusting."

Raina pivoted, mixer still running in the pot of potato chunks, garlic, and milk, to see Timothy twirling a half-eaten hot dog dripping with condiments in his sister's face.

"Timothy, stop," Raina scolded. "Please."

He laughed and shoved the hot dog into his mouth.

"Can you just eat in peace?" she asked.

"He's *gross*." Tracy ate her last bite and brought her plate and utensils to the sink. "May I go to my room? I have homework."

"Yes. Timothy can clear the table tonight." Raina turned and glared at him before resuming her humming, transferring the potatoes to a Corningware container and sticking it in the oven to keep the potatoes hot. The meatloaf was almost done, and the carrots in the boiling pot on the stove were close to tender.

Tina brought her plate to the sink while Timothy cleaned up the table. Raina caught them making faces at one another but decided it best to ignore them. Timothy pestered his sisters as if it were a legitimate sport. And Tina was sensitive.

A loud bang from outside startled both Raina and Timothy, now the only two in the kitchen. They looked at each other with quizzical eyes, then Wayne stormed into the kitchen with something in his hand.

"Tim, to your room." Wayne's voice was low and angry. Timothy, obviously recognizing that tone, scurried away.

Red in the face, Wayne waved a small brown bag in front of Raina. "What the hell is this?"

The hairs on Raina's arms stood at attention. Her heartbeat quickened. *Dammit.* Her whole plan was spiraling out of control like a tornado swooping in.

He took the test stick out of the bag. "Raina?" His voice rose.

Callie

Chapter 4

"L ate?" Jon repeated. "What does that mean?"
Callie explained it to him. She could predict her period
to the day, with exactly twenty-six days from the end of one bleed to
the beginning of another. It always started with a tiny cramp, which
Callie had felt when it was time, but while the cramp remained, her
period never came. It was three weeks late.

Jon began to pace. "We'll wait another week." Nerves distorted
his facial features.

Callie began to cry, afraid if he didn't want the pregnancy, he
would leave. She'd already convinced herself she wanted a baby. That
it was a good thing. It would solidify what they had.

As her tears started flowing, he sat back down and cradled her
face.

"Don't worry," he said. "We'll figure this out together."

That was all she needed to hear. They would figure it out together. *Together.* This was real. They lay tangled together and hugged each
other to sleep.

Early in the morning, Callie and Jon were awakened by an unexpected phone call. Jon answered. "This is Mr. Taylor."

A shiver ran through Callie as she was reminded that Jon wasn't
just her lover but also an administrator at her school. On most days,
she was able to compartmentalize that fact since he was always just
"Jon" with her in private. After their conversation last night and this

reminder of his surname and what that meant, Callie felt more desperate than ever to turn eighteen and graduate from high school so it would no longer matter that, in her life, he represented two polarizing figures.

Jon pulled at his ear and handed the phone to Callie. "Jocelyn," he said with skepticism.

"Oh fudge." Callie took the phone. "Jocelyn?"

"Your mother knows you didn't sleep here, and she is teed off." Jocelyn's voice sounded breathless.

Soon after, Jocelyn picked up Callie, and they cooked up the same story to tell. "I have your back; you have mine" had always been their promise to each other.

EVELYN'S WRATH WAS almost worse than telling Jon. And Evelyn's silence was worse than screaming. While her mother walked back and forth in the living room, pivoting on point like a soldier, Callie sat in the Queen Anne chair, head lowered, her legs crossed.

Evelyn folded her arms. "You lied to me." Her jaw clenched.

Callie watched the hemline of her mother's dress, her stockinged legs, and her black pumps as they moved in front of her.

Posture straight, Callie reminded herself. "I know, ma'am. I'm sorry."

Then Evelyn stopped and turned to Callie. "And who is this Vera whose house you stayed at? You said you were staying at Jocelyn's."

Callie had contrived Vera, a fake friend—one that couldn't be traced—with the help of Jocelyn on the car ride home from Jon's.

Careful not to make eye contact with her mother, Callie replied, "A friend from school." She remembered having read in her psychology textbook that people who lied couldn't make direct eye contact. It was best to keep her head down so her eyes didn't betray her. Instead, she paid attention to her now-intertwined fingers rubbing her knuckles.

"Have I met Vera?"

"No, ma'am."

"I sounded like a fool to Wendy. What kind of mother doesn't know where her daughter is sleeping?"

"It was a last-minute thing. Jocelyn was leaving, and I wanted to stay. I'm sorry, Mother."

"Stop saying that. You're only sorry because you were caught. You will call Wendy to apologize. I will not have you tarnish this family's name. Do you hear me?"

"Yes, ma'am."

Evelyn moved in close, lifting Callie's chin with her forefinger. "I said, do you hear me?"

For the first time, Callie made eye contact with her mother's fiery indigo orbs. Louder, Callie repeated, "Yes, ma'am."

"Now, go to your room, young lady. You're grounded."

Callie's shoulders dropped, and she asked, in the voice of her younger self, "How?"

"I haven't decided. You will be the first to know when I decide. And I'm not asking your father, because he'll let you off too easily. Now, go. I don't want to see your face."

Goosebumps crawled up Callie's arms. She walked away, humbly, until she reached the point where her mother could no longer see her. Then, about halfway up the stairs, she fist-pumped the air, considering it a win. She had hidden Jon's involvement, Jocelyn was off the hook, and Evelyn hadn't even asked for a surname or phone number for "Vera." The tradeoff was still in Callie's favor.

In her room, she lay down on her back on her yellow silk bedspread. She pulled to her nose the stuffed monkey Jon had won for her at a fair. She had sprayed it with his cologne so she could smell his cinnamon scent at will. Just then, it gave her comfort.

Rain poured down outside as Callie lay on her bed, staring out the beveled-glass arched window. She twirled a lollipop around in her mouth, hearing only the tap-tap-tapping against the panes.

She recalled a similar kind of gray day years ago when it had rained just like this in mid-July. Her breath had tightened in her throat then as she watched it, waiting impatiently for summer camp to begin. Every day back then, Evelyn had created a strict daily schedule for Stella, Callie's then-nanny, to adhere to. Idleness was something Evelyn never tolerated.

There had been a host of nannies as far back as Callie could recall, and just when they seemed to get too close, Evelyn always found a reason to fire them. But this nanny, in particular, was Callie's favorite. She'd even created an imaginary friend named after her. Stella had treated Callie like a real person, a grown-up person, even at age eight. Stella had let Callie decide what clothes she wanted to wear and what she wanted to eat and when. She'd made Callie part of every decision.

On that particular day, Callie had been pouting because the buckets of rain pouring down meant she was confined inside.

"Turn that frown upside down, little one," Stella told her. "Even on the rainiest of days, there's something to be grateful for."

Callie looked up into Stella's bright-green eyes, and Stella furrowed her brow like she was in the most fantastic conundrum. She knelt in front of Callie and said, "Callie, I need your help. I can't come up with a plan today. Can you help me?"

Callie had taken this job very seriously. She scrunched up her face and put a finger to her temple. "Let's see." She rolled her eyes to the left. She rolled them to the right. "I have just the thing. First." She underscored her enthusiasm with a pause. "We must tidy up this playroom. It's a mess. Then, we shall color a beautiful wall hanging—but a really, really big one, Stella. What are those wall ones called?"

"Murals."

Callie smiled widely. Stella always could read her mind even better than her own mother. "A mural. Yes."

"What should we draw?"

"A beautiful playground with swings and butterflies. And flowers, with one bee making its honey. One bee but not the kind that stings. Mother warned me about those. And kids playing. Lots of kids. Playing without their mommies to tell them they are playing all wrong."

"That's a wonderful plan. See, something to turn your day around. It's always there—you just have to search for it."

"And, Stella"—Callie had pointed her little finger close to Stella's face—"we can color outside the lines if we have to, okay?"

"You got it."

They got right to the plan, beginning with tidying. Callie knew where everything in her toy room belonged. Keeping things in order was one of her specialties.

When they finished, Stella rolled out a long piece of paper across the kid-sized table and placed a tub of crayons on the floor. Callie let Stella outline most of the mural because she was such a good artist. Callie watched every stroke, trying to commit them to memory so she could duplicate them. And she did, drawing her own flower next to Stella's and mirroring the billowy clouds her nanny had drawn in the sky.

Just as Callie was about to color in the squirrel brown, not gray, Evelyn had swung open the door with a distinct purpose. Dressed in a navy-blue half-swing dress, a string of pearls around her neck, Evelyn had let out a huff. "What's going on here?"

"Coloring," Callie said, not even looking up, but she noticed that Stella immediately stood at attention.

"The piano teacher canceled, and it's raining." Stella's voice trembled as it sometimes did when she spoke to Mother.

Evelyn slipped the white gloves she was holding on to her hands one finger at a time, not even looking Stella in the eye. "Has she practiced her French?"

"Yes, ma'am."

"And her multiplication tables?"

"Mother, it's summer," Callie said.

"Summer is for practice, not wasting time, Calista."

"We can practice while we finish our mural," Stella said, more like a request than a statement of fact.

Evelyn ignored her. "I'm going to the Garden Club Luncheon at the Willows. I shouldn't be long. Make good use of your time, for heaven's sake." Like the queen bee she was, Evelyn buzzed out of the playroom just as quickly as she had flown in.

And young Callie had breathed a sigh of relief.

Callie's memories scattered when her bedroom door clicked open, bringing her back to the present. Evelyn stood there, staring daggers at her. "For heaven's sake, Calista, is this how you plan on spending your day?"

"I'm grounded. What am I supposed to do?"

"You could tidy that closet, for one." She gestured to Callie's open closet door. It wasn't a mess, but anything less than perfect wasn't good enough for Evelyn. Her own closet was color-coded and arranged by item, not that Evelyn herself arranged it that way. She had servants. A maid to arrange her clothes and clean the house. A cook. A gardener. Evelyn didn't take pleasure in wifely duties—or motherly ones, for that matter. Not the way Wendy did.

Jocelyn was so damn lucky, and she didn't even know it.

The phone rang, just once, and Callie's heart leapt. Evelyn was right there, in her bedroom. No privacy. Callie suspected it was Jon, wondering if everything was okay. Months earlier, they had devised a calling plan. He would ring once and hang up. If she were in a po-

sition to speak, meaning her parents weren't at home, she was to answer on the fourth ring of the second phone call.

The phone rang a second time. Callie froze, just inches away
from the princess phone on her bed table. One ring. Two.

"For heaven's sake," Evelyn snapped. "Please answer the phone."

Three. Callie lifted the receiver off the base with trembling fingers. She heard a breath on the other end of the line, a hesitation. Of
course it was Jon. Callie slammed the handset down like it was a hot
potato. "No one there," she assured her mother.

Evelyn shrugged. "Busy yourself, Calista. Idleness is a time thief."
She pivoted and exited the room.

Callie's shoulders slumped. She wished she could have at least
heard his voice.

BY THE END OF THE NEXT week, Callie waded through conflicting thoughts. If her lateness had been a mistake, a fluke with her
body's clock, life would go on as normal. As a teenager and a senior
in high school, a big year lay ahead of her—the Sadie Hawkins dance,
the Spring Fling, graduation, college decisions—a year to make so
many plans for the future. She'd worked hard for twelve years to get
to this point, the pinnacle of her school years, the cusp of adulthood.
After all, she would soon be turning eighteen, and with that came a
certain kind of freedom, one she'd been longing for.

Of course, if she knew her body well, and her panties remained
free of blood, the following year would be a different kind of freeing
experience. A fast track to adulthood.

But she needed a plan.

Jon's only reservation, so far as she could tell, was his job. He
couldn't compromise what he'd stepped into at the school. With only two courses left to complete, he would graduate with distinction
and an administrative job in his lap. He needed that sense of secu-

rity, and Callie understood. What she did not need was her parents dictating where she would go to college or the kind of man she could marry. At some point, she had to show them what mattered to her. Convince them that this was her life, not theirs.

She and Jon would meet with her parents. Surely Evelyn and Asa would be able to see how in love they were. The first concern would be her finishing high school, which Callie had every intention of doing. Just the year before, Lanelle Ryland had become pregnant as a senior, and the school had let her work with a tutor at home to graduate. Of course Briarlee would see fit to accommodate a Sebastian.

She wouldn't tell Jon about any of this until they were face-to-face. The school wouldn't need to know who the father of Callie's baby was until after she had graduated and Jon earned his degree. By then, they would be married, living at Jon's Tudor home, figuring out how to juggle having a newborn with one parent working and one going to college. Callie had no doubt that Asa would be the most doting grandfather. Maybe Evelyn would even surprise everyone by enjoying her grandmother status.

Callie checked with frequency throughout the day. Not even a spot.

AFTER THREE CONNECTING bus rides, Callie met Jon at the location she'd suggested in the form of a note tucked into a book left in Jon's school mailbox. Callie didn't consider it a risky move but a necessary one. So far, everything had gone according to plan.

She stood beside the Summer Garden entrance, pacing. With one hand, she plucked at the petals of a daisy held in the other, whispering the words, "He loves me. He loves me not."

She heard Jon's dulcet voice before he came into her view. "Well, does he?"

Callie's face flushed as she turned and dropped the flower to the ground to run into his embrace. His strong arms held her as he dropped kisses on her forehead, moving down her cheek to her lips. His tongue slid into her mouth, so warm and sweet like wintergreen. "I love you," she said.

"God, I've missed you."

"I missed you more. Mother is serious about her groundings." Callie poked a pointer finger and thumb into his dimples and squeezed his face. Then she looked down to notice a picnic basket in his hand. Her eyes widened.

"Have you been to the Botanical Gardens before?" Jon asked.

"Many times. Mother is on the board."

Jon's eyes scanned their surroundings. A scowl crossed his face.

"It's okay. There are plenty of places to get lost here, but the Summer Garden isn't one of them." Callie took hold of his hand and squeezed. "Come on. I'll show you a place."

They walked for twenty minutes, past the Winter Garden and Bird's Nest Trail, to a path with an unmarked sign. Callie put her finger to her lips. "Shh, it's a secret garden."

"One your mother knows about?"

Callie noticed the rapid blinking of his eyes. "No. Not at all. She doesn't concern herself with anything less than pristine. She's all about the gardens with signs, the ones that are visited, the ones that are fawned over. This one, Jocelyn and I found when we were little. It isn't really even a garden, more like an off-the-beaten-path clearing. Untouched by the Garden board of directors." She added a snobbish air to her voice to mock Mother and her hoity-toity friends, and Jon laughed—one of the things she loved most, that she could be her unapologetic self with him. "Come on. It's pretty."

Leading Jon, still holding his hand, Callie pushed back the brush from the path and stepped over fallen branches. Beyond the path stretched a field of waist-high wildflowers. Extending her arm like an introduction, Callie gushed, "Isn't it beautiful? I haven't been here in years." It was a majestic sight, filled with pink queen of the prairie, delicate Queen Anne's lace, bushy blue lupines, and hearty daisies that curtsied to the radiant sun.

Jon placed the basket down and turned around, his face upturned to the sunshine. "This is something."

"I told you to trust me." Her mouth spread in a bedazzled smile, Callie stared at Jon, taking him in as he had done the landscape, before she nestled her head into his chest.

At the center of the field, he spread a blanket on which they sat so close that their sides touched. They drank orange soda pop from the same bottle and ate peanut-butter-and-jelly sandwiches. Callie wiped jelly from the corner of Jon's mouth, and he leaned in for a kiss.

He brushed back Callie's blond bangs from her face. His eyes hazed over as he stared into hers. "So, did it come?"

Jon seemed just a little too enthusiastic about the prospect of a period, and it deflated Callie like air oozing from an untied balloon. She shook her head.

He lowered his.

Callie took hold of his chin, turning him to look at her. "It's okay, right? You said we'd get through this together?"

"I know I did. But part of me..."

"Was hoping that I wasn't?" Callie tilted her head. Confusion replaced her excitement. She had thought Jon's feelings would match hers.

"A week is a long time to think. It's all too soon. If this were next year, I could get excited. But this is a big year for both of us. Having a baby is a huge responsibility."

Callie shifted away to cross her legs. She plucked at grass the way she used to when she was little, breaking it apart into confetti.

"Not to mention," he continued, "you're in your senior year. Do you know how special senior year is? I have my college studies and work at the school. I can't lose this opportunity. It doesn't come about every day." He paused. "We're young, Callie. Both of us. You have college ahead of you. How are you going to do social work with a baby at home? You can't compromise your dreams for..."

He didn't finish. He just let what he was about to say drift into the air.

"But I have this plan," Callie murmured.

"First, we need a test, right? To confirm it. We'll go to Planned Parenthood." He wasn't even listening.

She leaned in. "Jon, I have a plan."

"We shouldn't get ahead of ourselves."

"No. I suppose we shouldn't. Planned Parenthood?" Callie had never heard of that. Up until the last few weeks, even the idea of a gynecologist had been foreign to her.

"I can't take you to a real doctor. Your parents have too many connections. This is out of town. They'll never know."

A real doctor? What does that mean? This is real, Jon. That's what she wanted to say. Instead, she nodded. *He'll come around.* She'd had weeks of adjusting and dreaming before she could even share the news with Jon. He just needed time. But not too much, because it would catch up to them very soon.

GROWING UP IN A CATHOLIC household, Callie was used to church as a strict weekly ritual. Even on vacation, Evelyn found one for them to attend on Sunday mornings. Callie knew premarital sex was a sin. It was also a sin for an underage girl to engage in sex with a grown-up, established man. But she believed her God would forgive her anyway because everything she had done was out of love.

As the days passed and the dull cramps subsided, Callie grew bone-tired every day after school. Cat naps became essential.

Callie didn't need a test to confirm what she already knew, but Jon did. That was how couples worked, she supposed, by doing things for each other. One day, he picked her up at the back of the parking lot behind the maintenance building at school. She scooted into his car and laid her head down on his lap until they were far enough away.

"How are you feeling?" he asked.

"The nausea is at its worst in the morning, and I'm so tired. I could sleep on a railroad track." She looked up at him, but he kept his eyes on the road. "I'm sure, Jon."

"I need it confirmed. We need to know how far along you are and what we can do about it."

Jon hadn't alluded to *doing something* about it before. Callie feared the worst. He didn't want this child—couldn't want this child? But he'd said they would work it out. Was this what he meant?

She gave him a long, pained look. "Do about it?"

"We need to consider our options. You're seventeen."

Under her breath, she muttered, "That didn't bother you when you made this baby."

His eyes jerked away from the road. "What?"

Her skin blistered from his glare, but her strong will bubbled up inside. "You heard me."

The rest of the ride was silent. Mostly, Callie stared out the window, watching the world pass while she suddenly felt stuck. Occasionally, she looked over at Jon, who tapped the steering wheel with his thumb and sometimes bit his lip as if he wanted to say something but thought better of it.

When they arrived, Jon sat in the waiting room while Callie peed into a jar and sat in a patient gown on the examining table, legs swinging. Her hands squeezed the sides of the leather table. She could hear herself inhale then exhale deeply as the time crawled.

Our options. What did he mean? Up until this point, she'd imagined a happy little family. Callie, Jon, and baby Taylor, making a humble life for themselves.

A knock at the door jerked her into the present.

A female doctor, a tall drink of water, walked in wearing high heels and peach lipstick, with thick-rimmed glasses on the tip of her nose and a clipboard in her hands. "Good news, Mrs. Fleming." Callie looked around then remembered they'd checked in under assumed names, Mr. and Mrs. Fleming. Jon's idea. "According to your last period, you're about seven weeks along. Congratulations."

Callie's body relaxed. As the doctor rattled off a list of instructions, Callie let her hand rest on her tummy. Then the doctor handed her a bottle of vitamins. "Take these every day. They are very important for the baby's health."

Outside, Jon's body was stiff as he stood waiting, windbreaker draped over his arms.

Callie smiled ambiguously and motioned her head toward the car.

"Well?" he asked, his voice cracking, as they walked.

"Seven weeks, Jon. I'm seven weeks pregnant."

His face went white.

On the car ride back to Willow, Callie stared out the window, her mood vacillating between elation and fear. She thought about her age and all the things her parents had wanted for her. Then she thought about what she wanted for herself. She considered her own reaction compared with Jon's. All of this confliction induced a dull ache at the top of her head.

"I'll start showing soon, the doctor said. We need to make plans before that. Before I can't hide it from my parents."

"You did ask about our options, then?" he asked, his tone cautious.

Options? He wanted to talk about *options* when all she could think about was making plans for their future together? Callie cowered away. If she could have crawled into the car door, she would have.

Trying to conceal the tears sneaking from the corners of her eyes, she dabbed at them, but they continued to run free. *Why am I crying like this?* She wasn't sure. Because she was pregnant? Because suddenly Jon didn't want her to be? Because she knew, deep down, if she had this baby, there was a very good chance she could lose Jon? What her parents would do or say about it was of little consideration until she had the answers to these questions.

They drove for several minutes on the highway before Jon veered off the side of the road onto the shoulder beside a farm and a vast field filled with cows and calves lying down.

Jon turned his whole body toward Callie. She could feel the tension emitting from him, but she couldn't look. "What do you want from me?"

Callie said nothing, gazing upward as if God were there and would put the right words into her mouth.

"Look at me." He took her chin and turned her face toward him. "This is new to me too. I don't know what to do. I'm scared. Do you realize that if this gets out, my career could be over? How will we support a child if I don't have a job? We're just starting our lives. Hell, you haven't even graduated yet. What about college? Your dreams?"

She nodded. "My dreams have you in every single one of them, and now they have this." She touched her belly again, almost tangible proof of how quickly her dreams were morphing.

His head lowered. She could hear him breathe in deeply. "Give me some time, okay? To sort this all out. Can you do that?"

She knew exactly what he was asking. "Yes, I can keep it secret."

Callie

Chapter 5

For fear of her secret being discovered, Callie did everything possible to stay away from home. She had promised Jon time, and she never went back on her word. One Saturday at Jocelyn's house, she and Jocelyn lay on their backs on the floor, listening to the Beatles's *Rubber Soul* album on a loop and singing as if no one was listening. At times like that, she could almost forget her pregnancy. The cramping and nausea had subsided, and aside from her knowledge, her body didn't feel any different at all.

Wendy appeared in Jocelyn's doorway, laughing. "If Ringo could hear you now," she said. "Chicken-salad sandwiches are on the table for you two."

"On sourdough bread?"

"Yes, Jocelyn. Freshly made."

"You're the best mom."

Callie loved that Jocelyn called Wendy "Mom." She hadn't realized calling Evelyn "Mother" was an anomaly until she'd attended Jocelyn's tenth birthday party and Jocelyn asked her point-blank, "You call your mom 'Mother'? So formal."

That was the day Callie began longing for a mom like Wendy. One who was kind and spent time with her daughter—playing with Barbie dolls, taking shopping trips, and baking. One who made chicken-salad sandwiches and homemade bread instead of hiring a cook. Every time Callie visited the Halfields, a sweet or exotic aroma wafted from the kitchen. Wendy Halfield was the best baker in all of Willow. She made her house a warm home, while Callie's was a cold and lonely mansion with too much to show and not to touch.

The girls ran to the table. Callie sat down while Jocelyn poured them sweet tea. It caught Callie by surprise when the smell of the chicken made her stomach queasy. She pushed the thought out of her head and willed herself not to feel sick.

Jocelyn took a seat. "Go on," she said and took a big bite of her sandwich. "Ah, the bread is still warm."

Hesitant, Callie lifted the sandwich to her mouth and took a little bite. The minute it hit her throat, she knew she couldn't hold it down, so she dashed to the bathroom and threw up. When she looked in the mirror, she could see beads of sweat forming on her forehead. With a cold washcloth, she dabbed them away.

When Callie appeared in the kitchen doorway, Wendy looked at her. "Are you feeling ill?"

"Upset stomach." Callie tried to brush it off. "Is it okay if I skip lunch and lie down?"

Jocelyn nodded. "I'll take mine to my room."

"No," Callie said. "Finish your lunch."

When Jocelyn returned her bedroom, Callie was lying flat on her back, one knee up with the other laid across it, staring at the ceiling. "Are you all right?" Jocelyn asked.

"Fine." Callie tried to make her voice sound nonchalant, but the way Jocelyn's face wrinkled, she wasn't entirely sure she'd pulled it off. Meanwhile, her mind raced. Excuses tangled in her thoughts with the idea of telling the truth.

Confiding in Jocelyn would liberate her. Jocelyn could be a good sounding board to help her make sense of this whole situation. But how could she go back on her word to Jon? She'd promised him.

Jocelyn put both hands on her hips. "I'm not stupid."

Callie sat up. "I know." Then she lowered her head. Now she had no choice but to break her promise. And maybe it would all work out. Jocelyn could help Callie remain patient while Jon processed everything to the point that he could come to terms with it. Become excited about it, even.

"It isn't a stomach bug, is it?" Jocelyn asked.

Tears escaped from Callie's eyes. Her competing thoughts were ready to explode. She shook her head.

"Callie, you're not..."

"I am."

"How far along?"

"Almost four months."

Jocelyn's jaw hung low, and she covered her mouth with one hand. "Julie Burns had to quit school when she got pregnant."

"Shh," Callie scolded. The last thing she needed was for Wendy to overhear them and spill the secret to Evelyn. "I can probably hide for a while longer. Big sweatshirts and baby-doll tops."

"And Mr. Taylor?"

Callie's eyebrows rose. She'd scolded Jocelyn for calling him that so many times before.

Jocelyn amended her words. "I mean Jon?"

Callie shrugged.

"I told you he was a snake." Jocelyn pointed a finger.

"He's not. He's confused too. We just never thought..."

"Precisely. I hope the bastard does the right thing."

"He will." Callie projected confidence—if not at Jocelyn, at herself. "He'll come around. You'll see."

"I never thought in all the world I'd say this, but I'm going to. He'd better marry you and make an honest woman out of you."

Callie smiled. Jocelyn had always had her back since the fifth grade.

"And what about your parents?" Jocelyn asked.

"I'm putting that out of my head for now—waiting on Jon. My parents will disown me either way. I'll be a disgrace, the one thing Mother never wanted me to be." Guilt tugged at Callie for her father's sake, if nothing else, but she pushed it away. Self-preservation.

"Well, you're not." Jocelyn's mouth turned down. On several occasions, Jocelyn had told Callie she wished her parents could adopt Callie so she could know what it was like to have a normal life. Sometimes Callie wished the same, but she could never abandon her father. Evelyn would eat him alive.

"So, what are you going to do?"

"Wait. Hopefully for Jon to be okay with everything, because I'm not giving up this baby."

"God, no! Being pregnant isn't the worst thing if you and Jon really love each other. How does it feel?"

"At first, I was so tired all the time—like completely-pass-out tired. Now this. Food hasn't made me sick until now."

"Does it move?"

"Jocelyn, it's probably the size of my pinky finger."

BY THE TIME CALLIE got home, it was almost dinnertime. Normally, she could tell time by her mother's dinner routine. Every night was the same. Wearing a fancy pencil dress, Evelyn would sit and read in the library while she waited for Cookie, their live-in personal chef, to serve supper.

Tonight, however, the library was empty, although Callie thought she'd seen Evelyn's car in the drive. "Mother?" she called. Nothing.

Callie dragged herself up the stairs to her bedroom, looking forward to plopping onto her bed. Instead, she swung open the door to find Evelyn sitting there.

Callie detected *the look*—thin eyebrows in a straight line, creases outlining Mother's downturned mouth—and she felt the blood rush from the tip of her toes to the top of her head.

"Mother," Callie said, emphasizing the syllables like a question.

Evelyn took a deep breath and stood. "Sit."

Callie did so immediately, fearing where this was going.

Evelyn moved over to Callie's dresser and opened the bottom drawer, pulling out her bottle of vitamins Callie kept hidden under sweaters she no longer wore. She held them between her pointer finger and thumb the way she would show a prize at one of her benefit luncheons. "What's this?"

"They're not mine." She couldn't help it. The lie escaped.

"Calista Eve, do you think I'm a fool? All your sneaking around—is this what it's about?"

"They're not mine," Callie repeated as if saying it again might convince her mother. *But for how long?*

"To whom do they belong?"

"Vera."

"Vera? The phantom friend you lied to me about on the night of the ball? I looked her up in the school directory. Not a Vera to be found."

Callie looked down and rubbed her arms. Anything was better than making eye contact. Jocelyn came to mind, but she couldn't use Jocelyn as a scapegoat, because Evelyn would inevitably call Wendy, and then what? Their town was too small for lies like this.

Callie's head began to ache. She knew she would have to fess up or at least tell her mother enough of a truth to leave her alone.

"Mother." Callie looked up, head cocked to one side. "I'm sorry. I just found out last week." *A little white lie,* she rationalized. "I didn't mean for this to happen."

"And how did you *find out*?"

Don't you remember when you were pregnant? Evelyn had probably pushed the unsavory thought out of her mind, Callie assumed. But she felt differently. She wanted this baby. She already loved it.

Callie rested one hand on her stomach. "I did the pee test."

"At Dr. Wesson's?" Evelyn could not have sounded more mortified at the thought of Callie seeking out her pediatrician—the one everyone in their circle used.

"No, I went to Planned Parenthood."

Evelyn's shoulders relaxed, to the very small degree they could. "How far along are you?"

"Twelve weeks." Lying about a few weeks couldn't hurt her now.

Evelyn clicked her teeth with her thumbnail, something she always did when deep into thought. "Have you told anyone?"

"No." Callie told herself she needed to lie. To protect Jocelyn. To protect herself and Jon. "I'm too ashamed."

"Good. Don't tell anyone. Do you hear me? No one is to know about this."

Callie shook her head, hoping it looked convincing.

Evelyn placed the bottle on Callie's dresser, a talisman of her shame.

Callie felt beads of sweat forming at the edge of her hairline and under her arms. "Mother. Say something." Callie's heart beat so fast, she thought she could see it making her chest move. "Does Daddy know?"

Evelyn shook her head, squinting as if Callie had just asked the most ridiculous question. "This is good. We have time."

"For..."

"I'll take care of this, Calista." Her voice was pointed and stern. "Don't you worry."

Those words made Callie do just that. Worry.

"We'll have to do it as soon as possible," Evelyn went on. "Before you begin to show."

"Do... what?" Callie asked, confused.

"You don't think you're having this baby, do you?"

Callie craned her neck to look at her mother. "But I am." She'd already made the decision.

Evelyn walked over to her daughter, pushed the hair out of Callie's eyes, and let out an almost guttural laugh. "Don't be a fool, Calista. It will ruin your life."

Callie's heartbeat quickened. Her face flushed hot, and tears formed at the corners of her eyes. *Do not cry*, she willed herself. *Do not give her the satisfaction.* "Mother, I'm having this baby."

"No. You're getting rid of it, like it never existed."

"Not an abortion." Callie's thoughts darted to Jon. Even he had alluded to such a thing. *Options.* He'd never said the word, but Callie knew it was what he'd been thinking. She couldn't imagine the procedure and didn't want to explore the horrifying details.

"Yes, an abortion."

"It's not even legal."

"I know a doctor. No one will ever find out."

"You know a doctor?" Callie wrinkled her nose. She couldn't see her mother running in circles that encountered the kind of doctors who did illegal things. Then she wondered if her mother had gotten one herself. She didn't dare ask.

Evelyn nodded. "Don't worry, dear. We'll have it taken care of within a week, and you'll be back to your normal life."

Getting her life back was an enticing proposition. She would have Jon's support—of that, she was sure. Callie contemplated it for a moment, but then her stomach cramped up. *The baby.* Was it trying to tell her something? Give her a message? "I can't do it."

"You're a Sebastian. You can do anything you put your mind to. Besides, you have my blood." Evelyn pulled Callie's head to her chest and patted her hair. "Leave it to me, Callie. I'll make this go away. No one will be the wiser. Not even your father has to know."

Evelyn walked to the door then stopped and turned around. "Who's the boy?"

"Just a boy."

Evelyn's nostrils flared. "I want a name, young lady! Who did this to you?"

"It doesn't matter."

"You mean he doesn't know?"

Callie shook her head.

"Everything will be fine, then," Evelyn said. "Keep it that way."

Once her mother's footsteps faded from earshot at the bottom of the stairs, Callie shut the bedroom door, buried her head under her pillow, and sobbed.

THAT NIGHT, CALLIE tossed in her bed while her thoughts churned. One minute, she would doze off. The next, she would awaken, wondering what was reality and what wasn't. In her dreams, an empty baby carriage appeared in a long dark tunnel. Children surrounded her at a playground where she searched for her baby. She heard distant cries between the laughter of the children at play. Jon sat beside her, stroking her arm as she sobbed. Subconsciously, even during her nightmares, she wondered why everything was so illogical.

As she woke yet again, she heard Evelyn's words in her head: *I'll make this go away... Everything will be fine.* Perhaps this was Callie's destiny: a pregnancy to give her the mother's love she always craved so deeply.

Is this Mother's attempt to show me love? To get rid of my baby with no regard for my own wishes?

Across their hometown of Willow, Evelyn was known as the Queen of Bees. Not just because she carried herself like royalty or because she considered herself a monarch in Willow, but because she caught bees. People called upon Evelyn when they found a swarm of feral bees on their farms or in their yards, and she would come and snatch them up, take them to her bee garden to extract the sweet nectar from their honeycombs.

Of course, as legend had it, Evelyn did this herself in the early years of her marriage, but for as long as Callie could recollect, Evelyn had made the gardener do all the work of moving the bees while Cookie inevitably siphoned the honey into jars according to Evelyn's command. Evelyn gifted jars of honey to the neighbors who called upon her, to charity events, or to the monthly Women of Willow luncheon, giving them away the way other mothers dispensed kisses and hugs to their children, lovingly and with pride.

Callie was never permitted near Mother's bee garden.

One day, in the heat of a June that felt more like August, an eight-year-old Callie was playing outside while Stella sat reading in a lawn chair under an umbrella. Evelyn hadn't been home for hours, nor was she expected to be. Callie wandered off down the hill where wild butterfly bushes, a row of them, had begun to bloom lush lavender flowers shaped like cones. She watched a monarch butterfly dip onto a flower and perch, its orange-and-black wings fluttering. Then it sprang away and flew, gliding down low and soaring up high. Callie followed it down the dirt path where she wasn't allowed. She wasn't paying attention to where she was going, but she kept her eye on the butterfly as if it were leading her to a magical place.

If the butterfly hadn't stopped, perching itself on a leaf, Callie wouldn't have encountered the tree stump that held a strange wooden contraption, one she hadn't seen before. Inquisitive, she poked at it, shaking the box, and heard a loud buzzing from within. Callie wriggled the top, a thick wooden frame around a thin wire grate, but it stuck tight to the box it covered. She wrinkled her face and tugged hard until the top sprang free—and from behind it emerged a fountain of angry bees.

Callie let out a shrill cry.

Some time later, she awoke in her bed, confused. Her face and limbs were stiff—like giant rubber bands encased her bones. Her whole body was so wet with sweat that her clothes stuck to her limbs. She opened her eyes to Dr. Wesson standing above her with the back of his hand resting on her forehead.

"The aspirin should bring the fever down," he said.

Evelyn came into view, her lip curled. And Callie saw Stella across the room. Her nanny's face was red, her eyes swollen, and she held a tissue to her nose.

Callie's heart began to thump.

"Callie, what were you thinking?" Evelyn pinched the bridge of her nose as she stood over her.

Callie shrugged, not understanding the question and still trying to piece together what brought her here.

"She was playing." Stella sniffled.

"Stop sniveling," Callie's mother demanded. "I didn't ask you." She turned back to Callie. "I told you to never go to the bee garden. How many times do I have to tell you?"

"I'm sorry, Mother."

Evelyn sneered at Stella then said, "Sleep, Calista. When you awaken, everything will be fine."

That was the last time Callie had seen Stella. The next day, a new nanny arrived, one whose name she couldn't recall.

Callie shook off the memory, pulling the sheet tight to her chin. The stars still dotted the ebony sky outside her window. *Everything will be fine.*

"Mommy," a tiny voice called out.

Was she hearing things? But the voice was so clear. Callie jumped and sat up straight in her bed, then she heard it again.

"Mommy." The voice of a child. A little girl. Was it her own—her own voice or her own child?

Callie shook it off like a cold, wet rain. She slid down under her covers, both hands grasping them tightly, and once again, she drifted off. This time, she was at school with all her girlfriends, playing tennis. The sun beat down on them as they made plans for the weekend. Girl stuff like painting nails and doing each other's makeup before heading off to a party to flirt with boys. Callie felt young and alive. Untethered. From Jon, perhaps. Or their child. Or her mother.

Harper

Chapter 6

Harper stayed attached to her home, a cord she had no desire to cut. It took several weeks to wean herself off the Xanax. She feared the anxiety would return without it—the heaviness in her chest, like something was suffocating her. But her mother had begged her. Gabe had pleaded.

A week had passed without a single pill, without even one sign of a panic attack. Her mother's voice echoed in her head: *"You have to get back to living."* The words were meant to give her hope that life could return to normal—or at the very least, a kind of normal. She knew that cognitively, but in her heart, it made her feel more deficient.

Didn't her mother always make her feel that way? The way she couched so many statements with "Harper, you should..." as if the way she handled everything was always wrong—or, at the very least, not the way her mother would have handled it. Nonetheless, she forced herself to move forward. If not for herself, for Gabe.

The first day Harper returned to work, she scheduled showings for a young couple whose wedding was just a few months away in mid-December, so they were pressed for time.

As the couple strolled through the charming bungalow on its lovely cul-de-sac, Harper stood by the kitchen island, scanning the home. The hardwood floors were in good condition, and eclectic stone accents adorned the fireplace. The kitchen, the heart of the home, was the true selling point, though, because it had been recently updated. But as she thought about it further, she realized a house itself was a mere shell, something she hadn't considered before losing her daughter. It was the people in the house that mattered. The love and comfort and security shared from one family member to another—that was what made a home.

She remembered her own excitement when she and Gabe first toured the newly renovated Craftsman that had become their home. A realtor acquaintance had showed it to them premarket as a professional courtesy. She'd twirled in the empty living room in front of the Durango stone fireplace with the sturdy mahogany mantel. She had felt Gabe's eyes on her when she squealed, "This is the one," and he laughed. It had felt, immediately, like home. *Kismet.* The same assured feeling she had about Gabe on that Nantucket night when she realized he was the one.

Over time, they'd filled their house with carefully chosen furniture to reflect their tastes, distinct and complementary, with clean colors. They added a sprinkling of personal touches like cookbooks, tattered with use and passed on by Harper's paternal grandmother, in the kitchen nook. Blue glass bottles dug up from the yard became vases filled with flowers from the garden, some blooms planted with her own hands, some inherited from the former owners. These were the little things that filled their home with tangible items that, in Harper's mind, equated to love. Then, Harper had prided herself on being a minimalist and practical. Now, their home felt empty. Big and empty. A house that was just a shell.

She heard the young couple descending the stairs. Their eyes sparkled at one another. Harper wondered when the last time was that her eyes had sparkled at Gabe. Everything had become so heavy after losing their baby.

"What do you think?" she asked, masking her personal musings with professionalism. *"If you can't make it, fake it,"* the instructor of her real estate course had always said. In other words, if the house doesn't look appealing, find the appeal and sell it. "That kitchen, right? A great place for family."

"Harper, we love it." The young woman looked up at her fiancé, doe-eyed, for affirmation. "Don't we?"

"We do," he said. "It's a perfect fit for us."

"There's so much potential for growth too. We plan on having a big family. I could see us making the basement a playroom and putting a pool in the backyard."

Harper's muscles tensed, so she discreetly began the breathing exercises that the doctor recommended. "Yes, I see a bright future ahead for the two of you."

"I think we'd like to make an offer." The young man looked adoringly at his wife-to-be. "A new beginning."

Harper rubbed her hands together, plastering a smile on her face. *Fake it...* "Well, all right then. Let's work on getting you in your dream house. Shall we?"

GABE HAD THE TABLE set and dinner ready when Harper arrived home. She took one look, and the tension from her day drained from her shoulders down through her arms, escaping from her fingers. She sank into one of the dining room chairs as Gabe poured them glasses of wine.

"A pinot noir for my wife," he said, handing it to her. "Just a few minutes before dinner is ready." He sat across from her.

On the drive home, Harper had tried to anticipate all the questions he might ask—temperature gauges to indicate that she was better or at least moving in the right direction.

"Would you like to know the menu, madame?" Gabe leaned in toward Harper, showing his toothy grin, and she could see the perspiration on his forehead—a sign he'd been whipping something up in the kitchen for hours. In another life, Gabe was most definitely a chef. He could turn seemingly mismatched food into a feast by sheer instinct.

Harper ran a finger around the rim of her wine glass, feeling a little dazzled by him—something she'd refused to feel for a long time. "Do tell, Chef Alexander."

"Coq au vin—and, darling, when I tell you the chicken is falling off the bones, I mean you won't need a knife. Do you recall that French bistro where we first had it in the Latin Quarter? The violinist played his sweet music, and everything that night was so sexy and succulent. I want that back, *bébé*."

Harper used both of her hands to cup Gabe's. "I'm getting there. Thank you for your patience." She'd noted every gesture of his she had thwarted these past months. Every time he touched her shoulder and she wriggled away, or he tried to take her in his arms while they lay in bed and she rolled over—she remembered, even though she hadn't been able to reciprocate then. Harper's finger traced the veins on the back of Gabe's hand, snaking its way around to his forearm. "But the real test of your love isn't the coq au vin at all—it's the creme brûlée, my sweet."

Gabe's dark eyes widened, and he leaned back in his chair. Harper watched his lips as they touched the edge of the wine glass, slowly, the wine swirling against them. *He's teasing me*, she realized, and she allowed herself to become lost in the game.

It continued through dinner, one romantic innuendo following another. At one point, she took a slow bite of chicken as it dangled from the fork, teasing it with her tongue before biting. And Gabe slid his bare foot up the inside of her calf until it tickled the back of her knee.

They didn't make it to the *creme brûlée*. Dessert would have to wait until after. After they tore at each other's clothes like they'd been denied intimacy for years. After Harper felt him pressing down upon her body, squeezing all of the sadness away. After the taste of the salt from their bodies lingered on each other's tongues. After the throbbing release that made Harper scream so loudly that it was both freeing for her and validating for Gabe.

Amid the damp bedsheets, Harper pressed her face into Gabe's chest, biting her lip to hold back the tears bubbling up within, but she couldn't. She sobbed while he wrapped his arms around her, his muscles tightening as if he were literally holding her together. His silence, his patience, meant everything. Then they lay in each other's arms for some time. No words—their synergy communicated all that mattered. In the wake of their loss, they still had each other.

Harper stroked the black curls by Gabe's ears, admiring the structure of his jawline, the saucer shape of his eyes, his coffee-colored pupils that always managed to put her in some kind of trance. "I love you for giving me space," she said.

The touch of Gabe's fingertips brushing against Harper's arms made her quiver, and he pulled her closer. "I just want you to be okay."

"I want us," she said slowly, emphasizing each word, "to get to a point where we look to the future. Not the past."

Harper wanted to shed the layer of grief that had wrapped itself around her like a cocoon. Somehow, Gabe's reaction to her letting go felt like the first step.

Their smiles met each other's as if they were choreographed.

HARPER HAD TO CHECK the calendar twice to make sure the error hadn't been her own. *How long ago was that night—the one I finally broke down? Four weeks? Five?* She prided herself on never being late. Not for appointments, not for work, not for her period. Being precise about such things was what kept Harper feeling organized, on top of what was important. But it had been two weeks since her period was due.

She thought about telling Gabe, warning him, perhaps, but she thought better of it. Why get him excited if it amounted to nothing more than a fluke in her already-malfunctioning body? The doctors told her the stillbirth could have been the result of several causes, some that had more to do with the baby's genetics than her own body, but Harper would always blame herself for not keeping their baby alive.

Harper would go to the store, buy a pregnancy test—besides, she needed groceries anyway. At least that way, she would *know* instead of senselessly worrying all the time. That was what her brief experience with motherhood had done to her: made her a worrier. She grabbed a jacket, as the fall chill had begun to set in and the clouds above kept the warmth of the sun from peeking through. Before starting the car, she took a deep breath. Keeping this from Gabe felt like a betrayal, but Harper rationalized that she was protecting him. It was the least she could do to repay all the patience he'd shown through her grief.

Along the ride, she noticed the leaves already falling. It only served to remind her that her biological clock was ticking. How had she gotten to this place? During her whole upbringing, she'd watched how her mother clung to her children, particularly Harper's older brother, Ben, who was the starlight of their mother's eye. Harper had always wanted to be a woman in her own right, with no apron strings attached.

Perhaps the first time she considered fear as the cause of her lack of maternal desire was seeing Gabe's unfettered joy when she cautiously told him they were expecting. It was as if his jubilation had held up a mirror to show insecurities she hadn't recognized earlier. She'd always simply assumed her career would be the focal point of her life, unlike all her friends who anticipated having children as an integral life plan. Never once had she considered that she might be *afraid* of becoming a mother in some unconscious way until the polar opposite presented itself to her in Gabe's excitement.

The true turning point, though, had been the moment that Delilah first moved within her—that was when Harper had allowed herself to feel like a mother. When she and Gabe put the final touches on the nursery, right down to the vintage Winnie the Pooh mobile with the tiny bumblebee on the tip of his nose, she'd envisioned her daughter curled up in the crib while she and Gabe looked on lovingly.

Yes, she decided, they would make good parents, but first she needed to get past her trepidation.

As she waited at a traffic light, she noticed a trio of five-year-old faces beaming at her from the back seat of the car ahead. They waved, full of smiles and giggles. A sign, Harper, assumed, and she waved in return while tears of joy mixed with apprehension streamed down her cheeks.

Back at home, Harper sought the confines of their en suite bathroom instead of the one on the main floor. If Gabe happened to come home early, she wouldn't be able to hide fast enough. She opened the brown paper bag, pulled out the box that boasted of *Early results* and *Five days sooner*. She opened the aluminum packaging to pull out the testing stick. The first time she'd done this, Harper had been consumed with denial. This time, hope was making an appearance.

After she held the test between her legs and peed, she rested it on the counter by the sink. She set a timer for five minutes, then to keep herself busy, she read about false positives and taking the test too soon.

The timer blared. Her eyes glazed over when she looked at the very pronounced red line... and the still-shadowy one beside it. *Two lines. Two lines. Positive.*

Closing her eyes tight, Harper visualized holding a newborn in her arms. When she opened them, she stared hard at the test. Her stomach tightened. Her eyes welled up. "Two lines," she said aloud, quietly. Then she sighed and walked to the kitchen.

Harper's emotions were a roller coaster. One minute, she felt exhilarated, like standing on top of a mountain, triumphant, after a long hike. God wouldn't bless her a second time only to deliver the same devastating result. Life couldn't be so cruel.

Then, without warning, a shroud of anxiety enveloped her, every muscle tensing and knotting. The deep grief of her daughter's passing resurfaced in waves, causing Harper to doubt that she could ever get through that kind of pain again. But each time, she talked herself out of it, the way her mother suggested—*Self-talk is important, Harper. It's all about the perspective you choose to take.* Her mother always tilted her glasses when she said something profound like that.

As if on cue, she heard the sound of her mother's resonant voice calling, "Harper, Harper," as she let herself in through the front door. Harper must have left it unlocked. "Oh, here you are. I took a chance that you'd be home. And you are."

Her mother beamed at her. "I've been to the travel agent. I thought you should take a cruise. It would do the two of you so good to just get away. Dad and I would love to join you." Before her mother could even catch her breath, she was pulling out a folder full of brochures and price quotes. "This one is a cruise to the Greek Isles. Imagine it, Harper—warm beaches, hot sand, and the *food*. Gabe will love it."

"Mom," Harper said. Her mother flinched. "You always do this." Her mother's mouth fell open.

"You try to smooth everything over to make yourself feel better. You can't fix this." Harper began unpacking her groceries. "Always trying to control everything."

Her mother placed a stack of brochures on the counter. "I don't. You've been through a lot. I'm only trying to help."

"Your *help* often equates to imposing, Mother."

"Don't call me that," she snapped.

Harper rolled her eyes. Sometimes she called her that just to get under her skin.

Her mother cleared her throat. "It's my job to help you heal, Harper. Grieving takes time."

The coddling suffocated Harper, made her feel like she was about to explode. She slammed a jar of pickles on the counter. "I'm pregnant," she shouted, and not in the way an expectant mother should. *Goddammit,* she thought. *Why did I go and say that now? I wanted to tell Gabe first.*

Harper watched her mother swallow hard and her eyes shift back and forth as she processed the news. "Is it too soon?"

Of course it's too soon, Harper wanted to say. And of course her mother would go there—immediately to the negative. If it had been Ben's wife, she would be brimming with excitement. Not trying to find fault.

Harper grabbed an armful of boxes and cans, turning toward the pantry to put them away. They escaped from her grasp and fell to the floor.

"What did I say?" her mother asked in her syrupy voice, as if she were the innocent one.

They both bent down to pick up the groceries.

Normally, Harper could swallow her disdain for her mother's passive-aggressiveness when it reared its ugly head, but this time, Harper turned to her with a scowl and asked, "Can't you just be happy for me?"

Her mother's pointer finger entered the space between them. "Give me a minute here. You were just in a state of depression, and in less than six months, you're pregnant again. I'm looking out for you because it's soon. It's just soon, dear. It's not that I'm not happy for you."

"My life can't always go according to your timeline." Harper leaned against the sink with her legs crossed and arms folded.

"Believe me, it's you I'm concerned about. I'm happy. But it didn't take long at all, did it?"

"What didn't take long?" They heard Gabe's deep voice before he rounded the corner from the living room into the kitchen. Neither had realized that he'd come through the door.

Harper put both hands on her head. This wasn't how Gabe was supposed to find out at all.

IN THE DAYS AND WEEKS that followed, Harper was careful about everything. Her physical activity. What she ate. How many hours she slept. She would no longer have sex with Gabe, although her obstetrician told her it would have no effects on the pregnancy. "Just in case," Harper told Gabe. "Let's get past..." She didn't have to complete her statement because they both knew what she meant.

Every single day, she repeated a mantra to herself: "I love this baby. I want this baby. This baby will be healthy and strong." It had taken her too long to fall in love with Delilah. Not this time.

Hope ebbed and flowed, braided with fear that, even with all her conviction and all Harper's self-talk, the loss of her first child would follow her like a shadow she couldn't shake.

After the first trimester, after all tests appeared normal and the baby's heartbeat sounded strong for appointment after appointment, she allowed herself to revisit the nursery. An empty crib, a dresser, and three sealed boxes were the only evidence left that it had been Delilah's room. She pulled out the first box and lifted the lid. Inside were the comforter, fitted sheets, swaddle blankets, and crib bumpers with pastel Winnie the Poohs, plus the mobile.

She'd chosen them with her mom at Baby's World. Her mother had said then, "I love the Winnie the Pooh. It's the bee I don't like." She always found fault with the littlest of things, but it was her mother's abhorrence for bees that had sold Harper on this pattern. Seeing the model crib lined with them allowed her to form her own picture of her baby sleeping within, her tiny chest rising and falling peacefully.

Harper caressed the bed linens. She lifted them from the box and drew them to her nose to breathe in the scent of Dreft baby detergent she'd washed them with. Wishing she could take herself back to that time of preparation when sweet family-of-three thoughts swirled in her head. Only possibilities lay ahead of them then. Harper closed the lid and slid the box back into the closet.

"Hey." Gabe's voice startled her.

Harper turned around to see him standing in the doorway. She wondered how long he'd been there. "I'm okay."

"Is this the first time?"

Harper nodded. He went to her, drew her in for a long hug, and brushed his strong hands up and down her back. She felt his warmth, but she felt something else too. A little flutter from within her stomach, like a butterfly freeing itself from a cocoon. "Oh my gosh! Did you feel that?"

Gabe looked at her quizzically.

She took his hand and placed it on her slightly swollen belly. "Wait. It just moved."

They both waited but didn't feel anything.

"It did move," she said.

"I believe you." Gabe brushed her hair away from her face and kissed her forehead. "Is it still too soon to think about putting this back together?"

She wanted so desperately to give in to confident feelings, but they agreed to wait. *Two more months.*

Just shy of two months later, Harper awoke in the middle of the night with a cramping pain in her stomach below her abdomen.

She grasped her belly and managed to sit up on the edge of the bed. The pain subsided, so she lay back down. Her mind raced, trying to remember what the pain had been like the first time. *Think. Think. It wasn't a cramp. It was a stabbing feeling.* She tried to focus on Gabe's breathing pattern. Instead, memories rushed forth. The cold white room. Gabe's wounded eyes. A feeling of emptiness.

Stop it. It's just a cramp.

Harper lay there looking at the ceiling for some time, but a sharpness pierced deeply in her abdomen. Shuffling as quickly as she could while holding her stomach, she made it to the bathroom.

She heard Gabe stirring. *Should I wake him? No. I'm not going to worry him. It's probably something I ate. Self-talk.* She repeated it four times: *We're going to be okay.*

By the time she sat on the bowl, another pain—more severe than the last two—thrust from her stomach to her back, and she expelled something as if she were urinating. But it felt thick, and it gushed more than it trickled.

When she took one look down, all she could see was red.

A wave of nausea rose as she gripped the counter next to the toilet. *"Gabe!"* She wailed it so loudly the neighbors might have heard and been alarmed by such a scream. Harper's breaths quickened, and she shook her head. "No. No. No."

Gabe appeared in the doorway. The look on his face. The blood in the toilet.

Gabe raised both hands to his mouth at the same time. "I'll... call... Are you okay there?"

"It keeps coming. The blood." Harper's voice was tremulous. "Call 911."

Callie

Chapter 7

"I've called him," Evelyn said as she perused her morning paper at the other end of the dining room table.

Callie swallowed hard. She'd hoped Mother had just said she knew *a doctor* as a scare tactic. *What kind of doctor performs abortions, anyway? What kind of person knows people who perform abortions?* While she pushed eggs around her plate, Callie pictured being led to a damp, dark basement for the procedure. *How does one extract a child from someone's body?*

"Did you hear me?"

"Yes, Mother." It was all she could muster. She wanted to say, *I heard you, but I'm not doing it.* Mother's razor focus on aborting the child reinforced what Callie had known all along. She hadn't wanted to be a mother to Callie. Maybe Evelyn wished she had aborted her too. Perhaps she didn't have the means then.

"Your appointment is at eight on Friday morning. I'll drive you and call you in sick to school. You can take the weekend to recover."

What a cold word. As if one could *recover* from giving up their child in such a cruel manner.

Callie pushed back her plate, grabbed her pile of books from the bench in the foyer, and set off for school. Only, she didn't go to school. How could she when all that coursed through her thoughts were this baby, the prospect of an abortion, and Jon, who seemed merely resigned to the fact that a baby was indeed coming?

Instead, she took three buses to Planned Parenthood. She walked through the doors this time with her head down. Last time, she'd been full of hope—fantasy, perhaps. Imagining the perfect life with Jon, Callie had thought all of her dreams of family and home were about to come true. But now, everything seemed so bleak. Mother wanted her to be rid of the baby, and Jon didn't want to talk about it, as if denial would make it go away.

A woman at the receptionist desk asked how she could help Callie.

"I'm here for the reading room."

The woman smiled at her, pointing her in the right direction.

Callie made her way inside a small room with pamphlets for the taking. *Birth Control. Abstinence. Expectant Mothers. Adoption.* She took the *Expectant Mother* pamphlet with the sunny faces of mother and child on the cover. There was a book on the shelf titled *Options for Pregnant Women.* She thumbed through to the chapter on abortion that spouted facts about how unchristian it was, how dangerous and painful. Those were the parts that stuck, anyway.

Callie leafed through the *Expectant Mother* pamphlet on the bus. There were pictures of each stage of pregnancy, an inside view with a cartoonlike baby. Graphs and pie charts featured statistics about healthy pregnancies and options for birth. Once she'd read through the whole pamphlet, she folded it up and stared out the window. Jon's voice and Mother's were colliding in her head, as if they were one. She never imagined in a million years that Jon and her mother would be on the same page about anything.

"Everything will be fine," Mother's voice echoed.

"We'll figure it out," Jon's voice countered.

Maybe they were right. She should allow her mother to take care of everything, so her life could return to normal. That would make both Evelyn and Jon happy, but what about her? What did Callie want? Suddenly, she didn't feel seventeen anymore. And the debutante ball seemed years in the past. If this was what *coming out* meant, Callie had been dreaming all the wrong dreams.

THE NEXT DAY AT SCHOOL, Callie wore her lack of sleep in the dark circles under her eyes and her sloppily untucked attire. Jocelyn passed her in the hallway, but Callie was unaware, preoccupied with retrieving something from her locker, until Jocelyn doubled back.

"What happened to you? You're late."

"Shh," Callie said, and she drew Jocelyn close, leaning against the metal lockers. "Yesterday, I went to Planned Parenthood. Mother knows."

Jocelyn's eyes popped wide, her mouth an open circle. "Stop."

"Mother says she's calling a doctor to make it go away. My life will go back to normal."

"Is that what you want?"

"Joss, that's the trouble. I don't know what I want. This thing inside me has taken over. Not only my body, but my brain. I think in circles. One minute, giving up this baby is the last thing I could do. The next, I just want my life back."

"You could give it up for adoption."

"That's what Jon said. Isn't that the same but worse? The shame of me being pregnant wouldn't be any different. I'd have to carry the baby for nine months, only to let it go? I'd wonder about it for my whole life."

"Did you tell your mother you want to keep it?"

Callie shook her head.

"What about Jon? Does he know how much you want to keep it?"

Out of the corner of her eye, Callie spied Jon walking up the stairs by her locker. He paused, and Callie thought he might be circling back to talk to her, but he didn't even look her way. *What is going on in his head? Doesn't he think this is hard on me too?* Jocelyn said something that sounded like garbled words far away. Callie could only focus on Jon, who was shaking hands with a science teacher. They laughed about something. *How could he be laughing?*

"Callie. Callie!" Jocelyn turned to see what she was looking at. "Look at me. Forget about him."

"I can't." Her eyes widened as she glanced down at her stomach then looked from side to side to make sure no one caught her.

"If he loves you, he'll support you no matter what."

"He says he will. But things haven't been right. I know he doesn't think he wants this baby, but I do."

CALLIE DECIDED THE only way to avoid an abortion was to run away. If Evelyn found her at home Friday morning, she would drag Callie out of bed if she had to. But where should she go? To Jocelyn's? Surely Wendy would be understanding. The urge to go to Jon's, though far riskier, was stronger. She had to make him see that it could work for the three of them. He just needed a little reassurance.

After dinner on Wednesday night, Callie packed a small bag with only the essentials—a few outfits, her stuffed monkey, and her pregnancy vitamins.

She opened her bedroom door to peek down the hallway. Both of her parents had already retired to their bedroom. Without making a peep, she closed the door, picked up her bag, and opened the window. As she straddled the windowsill, her right foot found the slanted roof. Her heart beat so loud that she heard the thudding in her ears. Holding the bag, she dragged her left foot over and out. She stood on shaky legs for a moment then leapt to grab the thick arm of the oak tree, dropping her bag. *Don't fall. Don't fall. Don't fall.* She looked up to God when she said it, repeating it three times for good luck. The baby's life depended on it. Finally, she shimmied carefully down the trunk of the tree.

It took a good thirty minutes to walk to Jon's place. She took in a deep breath before knocking at his front door. He answered with mussed hair and a beer in his hand, wearing a cardigan and his glasses. His eyes smoldered with curiosity, and Callie's face flushed.

"Callie?" He grabbed her arm, looking down at the bag, and pulled her in. "Whatever are you doing here at this time?" There was concern in his eyes—warmth. Callie had made the right decision to come here instead of Jocelyn's.

Callie had been holding it in so tight that she nearly exploded when she said, "My mother knows."

"How?" Jon shifted his body weight away from Callie, dropping his hand from her elbow. Suddenly, the differences in their ages multiplied by a decade. He folded his arms. "I thought we agreed this is to be kept secret." He paused then softened his voice. "Until we can figure it all out."

"She found my vitamins. I tried to lie my way out of it, but she knew, Jon. She already knew. Maybe mothers have a sixth sense." Jon took a sharp breath, then Callie went on. "What you really want to ask is whether she knows about you. No. I told her it was some boy."

Jon's chest deflated. Leaning in, he put his hands on both of her shoulders, looking her in the eyes. "Are you all right? That must have been incredibly hard."

They moved into Jon's living room. Such a manly space. Dark colors, bookshelves, leather sofa. Callie sat down. "It has been."

"When did she find them?"

"Three days ago." She could feel the tension in his body ease.

"So what's your plan?" he asked, looking down at the bag.

"She scheduled an abortion on Friday. She knows someone. Who would have ever thought my mother of all people would have illegal connections? She never even mentioned adoption. Balked when I said I wanted to keep it."

Callie sat at one end of the sofa while Jon sat at the other, and he pivoted to face her.

"And you still do, after all this?"

"I want us to want this baby. It's ours. I want us to love it together."

Jon's back stiffened. "You know I love you, right, Callie?"

She nodded, but the tone of his voice made her brace herself, holding the ribbing on either side of the sofa cushion as if his words were about to catapult her off her seat.

"I could see us settling down, having a family of our own," he continued. "But you're too young, and I have too much to lose. It's too complicated right now."

Callie cleared her throat. "What if we move away? We leave Willow. You take a new job, and we'll get married. No one will look at us cross-eyed if we're married. We can make this work. I know we can."

"You live in a wonderful fantasy world. Everything has always come so easy for you."

"Don't do this. Not you."

"Hear me out." His eyebrows tented. "Your whole life, you've grown up with things working out exactly the way you want them to. That isn't real life. It isn't the life that I can give you. Not now. Not like this."

"So if I do this..." Callie looked down at her stomach. She yearned to touch it but knew she shouldn't. If he wanted her to get rid of the baby, as Evelyn did, she knew she would have to force herself to let go. "You won't leave me?"

He moved closer, pulling her in for a hug. His forehead touched hers. "I'm not going to leave you. I love you. But let's just go back to the way we were. To the plans we made before. You have so much ahead of you this year, including college. How can you be a social worker with a baby on your hip? After you graduate, I'll be established in my career, then we can get married."

"What if it hurts? What if I regret it?"

"First of all, she's your mother, Callie—she wouldn't take you to a butcher. It's a doctor. He'll take the right measures. In terms of regretting? Sure, you might. Initially. But as you live your life, you'll put it in the past and look to the future again." Jon pushed a stray hair behind her ear. He was so gentle. So sincere.

Callie should have gone home then, but she convinced Jon to let her stay the night, telling him she would face Evelyn in the morning. Even though she lay in Jon's arms, Callie's sleep was restless. At one point, she woke up in a cold sweat. The moon loomed outside his dark room. She remained stiff, trying to remember what had awakened her.

Images darted at her like a movie with frames in quick succession. Jon running away and Callie chasing him, never catching up. Evelyn shutting the door to a cold, sterile gray room. Callie lying on a hard bed covered in blue hospital paper. Monitors surrounding her. The baby's heartbeat echoing off the steel walls. "Is she pregnant? Is she giving birth? Can she ever get pregnant again?" Her mother's low, monotone voice echoed too. The doctor stared at Callie with a grave face and hollow eyes.

Only those fragments were clear. She knew they stemmed from nerves tangling and choking at once. The "procedure," as Mother referred to it, was only two days away. Callie fixated on the words, "Can she ever get pregnant again?"

Something must have gone wrong. It's a warning. She had never known anyone who had an abortion. She'd only heard horror stories about it in hushed tones from friends of friends at school, tales that made their jaws drop.

What does it feel like? What about the long-term effects? It couldn't be as easy as Mother had promised. Nothing this complicated ever was.

Callie snuck back into her house by sunrise. They would never know she had been gone.

She came downstairs, dressed in her school uniform, after her father left for work—Callie had waited until she heard his car pull away. Mother sat sipping her morning coffee and reading the newspaper, not lifting her head when Callie entered.

Callie let her head fall back slightly then sat down.

"Cookie left eggs and bacon for you," Evelyn said. "She ran to the market."

Callie nodded, playing with a button on her blouse. "I have something to tell you."

Evelyn put down her paper, open to the society page. She stared blankly, waiting.

"I can't do it," Callie said. "I'm afraid I won't be able to become pregnant again. I want a family one day."

"Don't be so silly."

"I'm not being silly, Mother. It's a real concern and one that we have no idea about."

Evelyn remained stoic. "Give me one good reason." If she was angry, she wasn't showing it.

"I just did. You can't guarantee that there isn't a long-term effect. What if they mess up? I've read about it, Mother."

"You're being dramatic, Calista."

"And because it's..." The real reason knotted in her throat. She knew her mother would dismiss it as trivial, saying that Callie was simply too young to be a mother, that it would ruin her life.

Evelyn's words had a habit of haunting her throughout her days, but she couldn't get past the way she wanted this baby. It was hers. It was her right to have it, with or without Jon.

Callie kept her head down, concentrating on twisting her button, then she squared her shoulders, mustering the courage to blurt out, "Because it's a baby. A person. You're a God-fearing Christian—how do you think God will treat me once I've done this?"

The flame of Evelyn's anger emanated heat across to Callie. Shaking her head, Evelyn said, "Don't use religion against me. There are some things you must do that no one has the power to judge. Not even God."

"That doesn't make sense!"

"You are having the procedure. Because I said so."

Callie stood up, towering over her mother. "This is my body, and you can't tell me what to do with it. My body. My baby. My future."

She picked up her books and stormed out of the house.

With a clear head, Callie marched to school, her Wellies leaving imprints in the mud. The cool air assaulted her face. Instead of going straight to class, she went to the athletic building, climbed the stairs and walked down the long corridor to Jon's office. The whole way, she practiced the words in her head. *My body. My baby. My future.*

Doing this without Jon would never be her preference, but resigning herself to becoming—no, *being*—a mother felt right. Sure, she would be trading her dreams of independence for a little while, but that would come. Later. Callie never considered a safety net once she set her mind to something. Like falling in love with Jon. Once the feelings were real, she dove headfirst. Jon needed to see how committed she was to seeing this through. Then he would come around. He had to.

Before entering his office, she removed her coat and swiped the hair out of her eyes. She swept her gaze across the corridor to make sure no one was in earshot. Then she opened the door and stood in the doorway until he looked up.

Her eyes dialed into his. For a second, she recoiled from him. Was it his smile? That look of nonchalance? *No.* She stood solidly, regaining her confidence. Once more, she looked over her shoulder both ways to be sure the hallway was clear.

Then Callie set her jaw and blurted out, "I'm having the baby. It's part of me. I already love her. Or him."

Jon's head bobbed forward slightly. The curves at the edges of his lips relaxed, but they didn't disappear entirely. Did she detect a slight gleam in his eye? Something positive for her to hang on to?

"That's all I wanted to say." Callie turned around, marched out of his office, and headed to class.

Later on in the day, when she saw Jocelyn in English class, Callie slipped her a note that read, *Meet me by the senior rock after school. Important.* Callie had underlined the last word twice.

The senior rock—an oversized boulder—was located down at the bottom of the hill behind the campus by the pond. As a Briarlee ritual, the senior students always signed the rock in permanent marker at the beginning of their school year. The park-like surroundings made it a communal gathering place in good weather, but hardly anyone went down there in the cooler months.

The wind ripped through the area, causing the trunks of the thin trees to sway. Callie paced as she waited for Jocelyn, spying where they'd both signed their names wearing shorts and tees, giggling in anticipation of all their senior year promised to hold for them. Staring at her name, written on the rock in large, curly letters, Callie realized the gulf between where she'd been at the time she'd written it and where she was today. Certainly, she would never have predicted being in this situation. But here she was. And, to her own surprise, she wouldn't have wished it away.

The crinkling of Jocelyn's shoes in the thick piles of leaves startled Callie from her thoughts.

"What on earth is so secretive that we had to come all the way down here?" Jocelyn asked, standing an arm's length from Callie.

Callie placed her hands on Jocelyn's shoulders and cleared her throat. "I've made a decision."

Jocelyn nodded. "Go on." Her teeth chattered beneath her red, red nose.

Funny, but Callie didn't feel the cold. Inside stirred just the right amount of warmth. "I told Evelyn, and I told Jon. I'm having this baby."

Jocelyn's eyes ballooned. "And..."

"I'll figure it out, with or without them. I've been doing a lot of thinking." Callie's arms fell to her sides, then she rubbed her chilled hands together. "What they never tell us is how hard growing up will be. We look forward to it all our lives because then we'll know what it's like to be happy. Why do our parents do that? Why not teach us how to appreciate life now?"

"What are you talking about?" Jocelyn crossed her eyes on purpose, a habit she knew grossed out Callie. "Hello, who has kidnapped my friend?"

"I'm still me but different. This may not be easy, but these are the cards I've been dealt, and I'm going to live in the now with whoever wants to stay by my side."

"Only thing I know is that once you set your mind to something, you do it. And you do it with grace."

"I want it all, Jocelyn. The baby, the white picket fence, and the husband I'll spend the rest of my days swooning over. I want to be happy, not stuck in a facade like my parents, who are miserable."

"Aren't you getting a little ahead of yourself? What does Jon say?"

"He didn't say no. And, I promise you, six months from now, Jon and baby"—Callie rubbed her tummy and gazed at it with glossy eyes—"and I will be a family. It's going to happen, Jocelyn. I can feel it. He'll come around. You'll see." It wasn't even that he'd said he wouldn't leave her that convinced Callie. It was the way he said it with love in his voice—just what she needed to reassure her of his love.

If he loved her, how would he ever be able to leave them?

"I have to admit, Callie—I never pegged you for a June Cleaver."

CALLIE PRACTICALLY skipped the whole way home. She anticipated tension, but she didn't care. It wasn't anything she couldn't handle. The debutante ball crept into her mind, and all the expectations Mother had set for her. For she'd assumed Callie would meet a rich young man who would sweep her off her feet and continue their courtship through college—many wealthy girls were attending these days. Then she'd be set for life. It felt right to be shunning her mother's expectations. A self-satisfied expression crossed Callie's face. For her, "coming out" meant that it was time to stand up to her mother and not back down.

She threw open the front door with fortitude, and the wind took it, slamming it shut behind her.

"Calista," Evelyn's stern voice called out from the dining room.

It's too early for dinner. She proceeded in the direction of her mother's voice. Maybe now was a good time for them to have a talk, an honest talk, so Callie could make Evelyn understand that she would keep the baby, that she was cut out to be a mother. Once she convinced Evelyn, then she and Jon could figure out the rest.

In the long dining room, she found her parents seated at opposite ends of the empty mahogany table. She looked to her father first, his eyes meeting hers. "Daddy, why are you home?"

Asa averted his gaze toward her mother.

Evelyn's expression was steel, which, after this morning, Callie had anticipated. "You're late," she said.

Asa stared down at the floor.

"Sit." Evelyn's eyes bulged like a wasp's.

Callie sat in the middle chair, mustering courage but bracing herself all the same. The tension in the air was suffocating. The silence felt like it lasted ten minutes, but it had barely been two. "I'm sorry I was late," she said. "Jocelyn and I stayed after school. For a project."

Evelyn folded her hands on top of the table. "You gave me no choice." She let those words linger in the air as Callie's feet kicked nervously under the table. "I told your father. He's very disappointed in you."

Callie looked over at her father, waiting for him to give her some kind of warm reassurance, but he didn't.

Evelyn continued. "If you refuse to get rid of it, we've made alternate plans."

Now Evelyn had Callie's attention. She gripped the edge of the table, her fingertips turning white.

"You have no idea the effect of a child on your life," Evelyn said. "You are too young. And we can't have this kind of shame fall on our family, Calista. Your father and I are pillars in this community."

The blood curdled in Callie's veins, thoughts in her head spinning on overdrive, processing the words that stung like the feral bees Evelyn kept in the yard.

"We're sending you to a school for girls like yourself."

"Like myself?" Callie asked.

"You can have the baby, but mark my words, young lady"—the glare in her mother's eyes seared through Callie—"you will put it up for adoption. You will not bring it home."

"You're taking me out of Briarlee? Daddy?" She looked at him with pleading eyes. Yet, for the first time in her life, Asa couldn't seem to look at Callie. Her father, the one who loved her unconditionally, could only shake his head, the veins in his forehead showing blue.

"Don't worry about Briarlee," Evelyn said. "I'll take care of that. No one will know."

"People will talk more if I leave." Callie's voice had become desperate.

"Rumors. I'll set them straight, and I'll make sure Jocelyn does too."

"Leave Jocelyn out of this. She doesn't know anything."

Evelyn ticked the table with her fingernail. "Please, Calista. I'm not a fool. And I'll find out about the boy too."

"You can't!" Callie blurted. She knew she needed to think fast, to protect Jon at all costs. She swallowed hard, knowing full well what she was about to say would cut Asa deeply. "I didn't even know his name," she said, head lowered.

"Well, did you hear that?" Evelyn looked at her husband, not missing this opportunity to chisel away at Asa's perception of his little girl. "Your pristine daughter."

Callie didn't look up. "How long do I have to stay away?"

"Until the baby's gone."

"I'm not giving it up." Callie stood, her voice raised. "You can't make me." She turned to her father. "Daddy, say something."

Asa let both of his hands drop onto his lap. "Please, Callie. Don't make this harder on yourself."

Seeing this as her opportunity to get to him—the only parent who understood her, who treated her like a person—Callie placed her hand on his arm. "Please, Daddy. I want this baby. I don't want to give it up." Callie's voice cracked. Tears streamed from her eyes.

He lowered his face, his chin almost touching his neck and rocking back and forth like a pendulum. She had rendered him speechless.

Callie was, without a doubt, alone. "How long before we…"

"Tonight," Evelyn said. "We've packed your things."

"Tonight? Tonight!" She lunged toward her mother, her voice growing louder as anger replaced fear. "I can't even say goodbye to my friends? You really do know people, don't you, Mother? You have connections all over the place." Callie shoved the chair hard against the table, rocking it off its legs, and it toppled to the floor.

"Asa." Evelyn's voice had never sounded so angry. "This is enough."

Her father stood and took Callie by the elbow. "Settle down, Callie. You don't have a choice."

Her eyes open wide, she stared through her father's. He'd always taken her side, especially when Mother acted unreasonably. No longer.

Asa nodded his head toward the door. "Let's go."

Callie walked ahead of him. When she reached the foyer at the bottom of the stairs, she saw the oversized bag, packed and ready to be carted off with her.

Raina

Chapter 8

Raina's body stiffened. In one fell swoop, all of her careful planning had gone for naught.

Wayne waved the test stick in front of her face. "What is this?"

"A pregnancy test."

"I know."

"It's negative."

"I see that, but were you going to tell me about it?" The veins in Wayne's forehead puffed.

Raina turned and took the plates and utensils from the counter, proceeding to set the table. "Course I was. That's why I fed the kids earlier. I wanted to have a discussion."

"About what? Did you go off the birth control?"

Her head shot up. "No, I wouldn't do that. I was just late. Could we sit? Dinner is ready."

Wayne dragged his chair out from the table, the wooden legs making a scraping noise against the floor. He plopped into the chair.

Raina pushed the glass of whiskey across the table in front of him. "Here, drink this."

"Oh, this is gonna be one of those."

Why did he have to say it like that? Raina already had her work cut out for her—now it was going to be even more difficult than she'd anticipated.

Wayne downed the whiskey in one gulp. The food's aromas permeating the room, Raina moved the meatloaf, cooked to perfection, and the garlic mashed potatoes to the table but was almost hesitant to place them in front of him, afraid he would feel like he was being duped.

She sat across from him, spooning the meal onto their plates with generous helpings for Wayne.

"I didn't tell you I was late," she began, laying a cloth napkin onto her lap, "because I thought it was nothing. Then I got to thinking, 'Well, maybe I am.' But I'm not."

Wayne dug in, heaping potatoes on top of large forkfuls of meatloaf. Raina took this as a sign. *He can't be too mad if he's still this hungry.* "But when I wasn't, it hit me. Maybe I want to be, with the kids in school and you working."

"Because you're bored? I got plenty of work to do."

"Well, yes, but no. I am bored. I know I could get a job. But I feel it inside me, Wayne. I want another baby."

"We got three. That's family enough." He shoveled down another forkful then followed it with a sip of beer.

"But it isn't enough for me. I told you, I want a houseful."

Wayne put his beer down and nodded his head. "We got a houseful. I can't afford any more mouths to feed."

"Come on. We're doing fine. I see the stock going out every day."

"What you see and what we can afford are two different things, Raina."

"What are you saying?"

He looked over at her. "We haven't taken in as much revenue as we did last year. Things are tight."

"But you know we always make it work, take what comes even if it isn't planned."

"Where is all this coming from?"

"I don't know." She shook her head. "The fact that I didn't have a mother. I didn't have siblings. I want a full life, a full home."

Wayne stopped mid-bite as if he were about to say something, but he wrinkled his face instead. Then he shoved the food in his mouth.

Raina watched him as he swallowed then scratched his head, sat up straight, and wiped his hands. "What? Say it. What were you going to say?"

"Babe, when are you going to feel satisfied? Problem is, I don't think another baby will do it. What happens when that one goes to school? You'll have another and another? We can't have six kids. We can't." He swung his head back and forth, then he took her hand into his. "You need something for yourself. It's your time now. I could put you to work on the farm, but you wouldn't like that. How about your honey and your bees? You could make it a business instead of giving the stuff away. Make yourself feel fulfilled."

Was it boredom? Emptiness was more like it. She needed something to fill her up and make her feel important again, needed, the way the kids used to need her when they were babies. It wasn't that she hadn't thought of selling her honey before, but it had always just felt nice to give it away. But maybe he was onto something—maybe she needed something all her own.

"I wouldn't know where to begin," she said.

"I could help. We'll market your products with ours."

Tina trotted into the room. "Mama, Timmy took my blankie."

Raina put her hand on Wayne's shoulder to let him know he'd been heard, then she followed Tina over to the little thief, who stood on the stairs. "Timmy, you know this belongs to Tina."

He shook his head and giggled.

Raina put her hands on her hips, trying to be diplomatic. "Timmy," she said firmly. "You have your own. Let's go find it. Tina needs hers to go to sleep."

Timmy pouted. He loved getting under the girls' skin.

Raina handed the blanket to Tina. "Now, get to bed, and I'll tuck you in."

Tina thanked her mother with a toothy grin.

Raina watched her daughter walk away, tall and satisfied, then trekked up the stairs behind Timmy to tuck him in. "Here's yours, buddy."

Timmy lay down and pulled the blanket to his chin, just as peaceful as when he was a baby. At five, he still had a chubby face, plus his father's green eyes and curly red hair. With each of her children, she fell in love with Wayne all over again. While the two girls were blondes like herself, they both had traits of Wayne's. Tracy was very practical and sensible, while Tina was sensitive with an innate passion for every single thing she did.

When Raina returned to the table, Wayne gave her a *See! I told you so* look that she didn't appreciate. Of course her kids needed her plenty, but that didn't mean she didn't have room for one more.

While Wayne's logic made practical sense, Raina couldn't figure out how to deal with the yearning she felt from inside. It was almost as if, like her menstrual cycle, her body was telling her when she was ready to get pregnant again. It wasn't a choice, not the way Wayne seemed to think. The difference between men and women was simple: it had to do with the ability to bear or not bear children. Everything else tied to that biological fact. For Raina, it was more than a fact—it was an honor and a privilege. It was also a need.

Each time she'd given birth, she'd wondered how her mother had felt when she birthed Raina, wondering if Mama would have had other children had she lived longer. Raina's father never talked about her mother, and when she'd broached the subject, he only drank more. It seemed he couldn't really live without his other half. How had her father had been different while her mother was alive? Was he different at all? Raina tried to love him because she knew Mama would have wanted that. But the truth was her life was easier without him in it. She did the dutiful daughter's chore of seeing him when he needed her, but that was seldom.

Before they fell asleep that night, Wayne turned to Raina and lifted her chin. "I know you think you want another baby, but just give your business a try. It might be the baby you didn't know you needed."

Raina closed her eyes, and full of hope, she thanked Mama in heaven for passing on her mama gene, the best gift and job she'd ever been given. But maybe this, a new purpose, could fill her up in a different way.

THE FOLLOWING WEEK, as Raina drove, one farm led to another and another for the twenty or so miles before she got into town. She'd prepared a list for the craft store. She needed material, something cute and soothing—maybe sunflowers would do—plus sticky labels and more jars, different sizes this time.

When her babies were little, Raina used empty baby food jars for her honey. Of late, she relied on donations of the jars from the PTA moms, but her stock was running low. Raina had a way of repurposing most things. Living on a budget had made her frugal in every sense. Still, they weren't exactly hurting for money the way her family had.

After a fruitful trip during which she found everything she needed, something pulled at her to visit her father in Rye. It wasn't a long drive, and questions about her mother had gnawed at her since her talk with Wayne. *Did Mama want more children? Did she feel satisfied—like her house and her heart were full?* Maybe Raina inherited all this emptiness from her mother, only she never got to ask her about it. Maybe all of this was so pressing because Raina was wondering if she would run out of time too. On automatic pilot, she drove down the forgotten, badly paved road that led to the trailer park where her father moved to downsize after she and Wayne had married.

It had seemed like a practical thing to do. Once Raina moved out, Reggie Baker couldn't keep up with the tiny bungalow they had called home, although it never felt like a home after her mother died. The house had been cold, not in temperature but in upkeep. The cracked glass in front of the photograph of the three of them, the last one taken before her mother took ill, remained in a frame on the coffee table by Reggie's armchair, along with a mess of pipe tobacco, an ashtray, and empty bottles of beer. The house stank like a dive bar. Raina had tried to clean up after her dad when she was young, when she was still too naive to realize that he had become far too depressed to care for a young child in the way she needed to be cared for—with love and empathy. Instead, she had become rebellious, staying away from home more than she was in it. The day Reggie told her he wanted to move into the trailer park, all she could think was *Good riddance*. Good riddance to the melancholy that permeated most of her life.

Raina pulled up to the front of her father's mobile home, which was couched between two others with just enough room between them for a sliver of a lawn, albeit one of burnt grass. Even that was in need of care. Next to the front stoop stood two overflowing metal trash cans and plastic bags full of empty bottles, their necks jutting out in different directions. Beside them rested a broken wooden chair, one leg cracked in half. Raina recognized it as one of the dining room chairs from their bungalow.

She picked up trash along her way to the front stoop and plopped it in one of the receptacles.

Her knock at the door was followed by a long wait. Raina looked at her watch—still two hours before the kids would come back from school. Maybe this was a bad idea. Maybe, on the very off chance he was sober enough, she could ask him the unanswered questions she had about her mama. But why did she think she would get any information from her father after all these years?

Raina always approached her father with cautious optimism. Deep inside, she knew there had been a time when he was a good father—a doting one, in fact. But the good memories of him had been replaced by those of neglect.

She knocked again, six knocks this time and louder.

The door squeaked open. "What? What?" Already looking agitated, Reggie appeared in an untucked flannel and dirty, ripped jeans. His eyes softened when they met Raina. "Oh."

"Hello, Pa."

He moved aside so she could enter through the front door. The stench of tobacco and piss-warm beer greeted her, and her nose twisted.

"What you doin' here?"

She walked a narrow clean path across a floor strewn with newspapers, clothes, and empty food boxes and bottles. "I was in the area and thought I'd stop by."

"You don't call?"

"What, do I need to announce myself?"

"You usually call is all." He moved a box from the armchair. "Sit."

Raina did. Her eyes scanned the mess of a ten-by-ten living room, which had barely enough room for a sofa, armchair, and a television blaring some game show Raina didn't recognize. Her father always needed background noise. She wondered if it was to drown out the voice of her mother in his head. Sometimes she'd caught him talking to Mama as if they were having a full-on conversation.

"How are you feeling, Pa?"

"Erm, all right. Same ol'. I got a different pain every damn day, but I'm used to it by now. My side's been hurting."

"When was the last time you saw your doctor?" She waited for an answer, but he had fixed on the television instead.

"President Hoover, you nit," he shouted.

"You should schedule a physical. Should I do it for you?"

His hand flung itself up in the air as if it were mechanical. "Doctors. They take your money and tell you nothin'. What are you out here for?"

"I had some shopping to do. I'm starting a business with my honey."

"You and those damn bees."

Raina snickered. She tidied up the end table between the sofa and chairs, arranging bills, a pack of gum, and his pipe. "Wayne's going to sell it for me, and I'll try to get it in a few local stores. Something to keep me busy. Timmy's in kindergarten."

"Oh shit, did you see that?" Reggie pointed to the television. Dollar signs and money noises splashed across the screen. "I didn't think she'd get it. Pearl Harbor. Did you know that?"

Raina stood. "Can I turn this off?"

"Sure. It's over."

She didn't have the patience to search for a remote, so she went straight to the television and pushed the power button. Silence. Her head dropped back. "I have a question for you." She sat down, finally getting his attention. "Did Mama want more kids?"

Her father's eyes narrowed. "What?"

"Did she want more kids? Did she talk about it?"

One spindly forefinger scratched at the ribbing on the sofa. "You're always wantin' to talk about your mother."

"Yeah."

He looked up. "She couldn't have 'em."

"What do you mean? She had me."

"Course she did, but then she got sick."

Talking to her father always went like this—she ended up having to solve riddles, link pieces of information together.

"She didn't get sick right away," Raina said. "Did she want one after me? Before?" Her mother had been thirty-three when she had Raina, the same age Raina was now.

"Is this why you came here? To grill me?" His voice rose. "I don't like talkin' about your mother." He stood and looked directly into her eyes, fire in his.

The hairs on Raina's arms stood at attention. This was what it had been like when she was little, which was probably why she'd stopped asking. But not this time. Raina moved to stand only a foot away from him. "I have a right to know about Mama. How can I know myself unless I know about her?"

"Pfft!" Reggie walked into the galley kitchen behind the living room. Raina heard the fridge open then the pop of a beer cap.

"All right, Pa. I'm leaving. Nice seeing you, as always. Call that doctor." Without hesitating, she picked up her purse and marched out the door.

She didn't look back. Anger and hurt churned within.

When she got in the car, the tension from her neck spidered down through her shoulders. She rolled her head in an effort to assuage the frustration. She'd known it was a mistake, but the pull she'd felt had given her hope.

RAINA DOVE HEADFIRST into the rhythm of her new business. Wayne set up a workspace in the shed beside her bee garden, moving all his tools and equipment to a different shed on the property. He built her a workstation and shelves for storage. Raina aligned the jars by size, used pinking shears to pre-cut the sunflower material into ribbons to tie around sealed jars, and bought a sunflower-yellow Sharpie to handwrite the labels.

Wayne helped her assemble the oversized bottler. She pored over the heating directions enough that when the time came, she would have the steps memorized.

Raina perched on a stool with empty jars at the ready on shelves in front of her workbench, making inventory lists ready to be filled once the goldenrods of fall appeared and it would finally be time for harvest. Now the business needed a name. Her pen tapped on her notebook as Wayne sauntered in.

"Beesy at work?" his voice bellowed behind her.

"Haha! I see what you did there."

She could feel his warm breath on the back of her neck as he peered over her shoulder. "Official."

Raina looked back and nodded. "I'm stuck on a name."

"Yes, every business needs a name. Usually that's one of the first things."

"I know, and I've been wracking my brain." She turned around. Wayne stood between her legs, took the hair from over her shoulders, and wrapped it up in his hands. His touch still sent shivers through her after all these years.

"I'm glad to see you so focused on this venture of yours. Your different kind of baby."

Raina scrunched up one side of her face. If he thought this would be a substitute for her need for a baby, he was dead wrong. But it was a distraction, and as promised, she would give it an honest try.

"Names. Let's see." He let her hair fall onto her back. She could almost see the wheels spinning in his head. "The Bee's Knees."

Raina smiled but shook her head emphatically.

"No? Hmm. The Queen's Bees."

"Too literal. I want something creative. Like a play on words."

His eyes lit up. "I got it. Bee-licious. Hyphenated to accentuate the 'bee.'"

Leave it to Wayne to make up for all that Raina felt she was missing. "I like it. I love it! Bee-licious!"

SEVERAL DAYS LATER, Raina went out to the shed after dropping off the kids at school and checking off her morning chores, ready to work on filling jars. Cup of coffee in hand, she saw one of the farmhands hanging something. Wayne was directing him, saying, "No, two inches to the right. Perfect."

"Wayne," Raina called out.

He turned around, looking startled. "You're five minutes too early."

"For?"

What the farmhand was working on was hidden by the mass of his body, then he stepped aside. Hanging before her was a wooden sign, carved and painted. It read Bee-licious! By Raina and had a cute little bee buzzing in a circle in one corner.

Raina gasped. "Oh my gosh! I love it."

Wayne stood tall beside her. "My graphics guy made it up." He handed her a box. "With some cards for distribution. Every bees-ness needs a logo."

A sense of pride filled her for the first time in a long time. A different kind of pride than she'd ever felt—something all her own. She fanned through the business cards, holding the thick paper with the whimsical design in her fingers. She would punch a hole in them and fasten them to the ribbon on each jar. Yes. Very professional.

Over the next several weeks, Raina worked on bottling and assembling her products. She established an everyday routine that began with making breakfast and helping the kids get ready for school. Of course, Tina and Tracy were very independent, while Timothy dawdled. Once she dropped them off at their respective schools, she did her household chores and errands, then she worked in the shed or down at the bee farm from noon to three most days.

Once her products were ready for distribution, Wayne added them to his menu of items to buy from the farm, while a minimal amount was sold to his grocery store vendors. Raina already had a large amount of stock to distribute. After boxing up the jars, she set out into town, determined to make her small business at least lucrative enough to justify the time she'd spent on it.

Raina started at the general store, a quaint establishment right in the center of town. As the oldest store in Brocton, it was a tourist magnet, and the proprietor, Ruthie Mae, sold an eclectic collection of regional gems from food to artwork. She had also been a good friend to Raina's mama back in the day.

As Raina approached, Ruthie Mae was crouched down, stocking blown-glass animals on a shelf. Raina called out to her.

Ruthie Mae's plump cheeks flanked a wide smile. "Why, Raina Baker, to what do I owe this honor?"

"Oh, it's Edwin now."

"You'll always be Mary Baker's girl to me." She stood up and peeked into Raina's box.

"What you got in there, girl?"

"My own little business venture. Homegrown honey. Do you have a space for it in your store? I have these tags, and the prices are on this sheet." She pulled it from the bottom of the box and handed it to Ruthie Mae. "I reckon you'll want to mark them up to take a percentage. I just ask that it be between ten to fifteen percent."

Ruthie Mae scanned the paper, which listed three sizes of honey and some honeycomb. "In honor of Mary, I'd do anything for you. I know you're starting out and all, but think about diversifying—candles, honey butter. People love that stuff."

Raina nodded. At the same time, two aisles over, a baby let out a cry. She heard the caregiver say, "Hush, hush."

"Thanks, Ruthie Mae," she said. "I'll consider it. I could use all the help I can get."

"How are those kids of yours?" The thing about Brocton was that everybody knew everybody, which was comforting and bothersome at the same time.

"The girls are getting big, and Timmy started school full-time this year." Raina set the box down on the counter. "The house is too quiet."

At the same time, a young girl holding a baby boy walked up, a diaper bag over her shoulder and a shopping basket in the other hand.

"Let me help you with that," Raina offered, taking the girl's basket and placing it on the counter.

"Daisy, will you look at that boy! Raina here was just saying her youngest is in kindergarten already. Sure goes by quick."

Even though the girl, Daisy, had dark circles under her eyes and was obviously frazzled, Raina couldn't help but feel a tinge of jealousy. She would give anything to take care of an infant instead of run a business. It wasn't fulfilling in the same kind of way, at least, not yet.

"Can I hold him while you settle up?" Raina asked.

"Please," the girl said, placing her child in Raina's arms. His newborn scent hung in the air just beneath her nose. Raina placed her pinky in his tiny, paper-smooth fingers as he slept, making a sucking noise with his lips.

"Cherish this," she said, a little swoony. "It goes by much too fast."

"Raina has three beautiful children," Ruthie Mae said. "She lives out on the Edwin farm. I recall when her husband was a little boy coming in here for five-cent candy. How he loved his candy, that little carrottop. Well, I remember Raina that young too. She was a towhead, blond as..."

Ruthie Mae chatted away, but her words evaporated as Raina focused on the feel of the baby in her arms—like a warm, soft spaghetti squash. She swayed her mama's sway to keep him soothed. Daisy looked back at her and smiled as she paid Ruthie Mae. Raina wondered who envied whom more.

Callie
Elberta, Georgia, 1969
Chapter 9

Watching live oaks towering into the sky as they drove, Callie cowered in the back seat of her parents' car, hugging her knees, feeling them press against the firmness of her belly. She wondered about the Spanish moss. She'd always thought it looked so enchanting, like a secret forest, but now it seemed to be suffocating the trees. That was much the way she herself felt, between the whizzing of cars passing them—because her father always drove his Cadillac in the slow lane—and the low, dulcet tones of the man on talk radio, his words barely decipherable.

In the front, Asa and Evelyn sat silent.

Callie wondered where they were taking her, but she was too angry to ask. Instead, she focused on the stars, imagining Jon and Jocelyn and even Wendy in them. They looked down at her. Did they sense the loss she felt inside? They watched her, and Callie convinced herself they would do more than bear witness. They would rescue her. Jocelyn would tell Jon that Callie was missing from class. She would tell Wendy, too, who would understand. The three of them would show up at whatever ghastly place her parents were taking her to, demand to have her released into their custody, and free her to live out her life the way she was supposed to.

What kind of parents shipped their child off, for God's sake? Callie decided she couldn't give in, collapse, the way they expected.

This baby needed her. The baby needed both its parents. She would hang on to that. It was all she had to hang on to.

Asa eventually pulled off the thruway onto a one-lane road, which they drove down in the dark for miles. Then his Cadillac crawled into a turn. Evelyn directed him, reading from a piece of paper held tight in her hand under the mirror light.

For miles, there hadn't been a road marker or route number for Callie to commit to memory. Callie had no idea what time it was. It seemed like they'd been driving for hours. She lost track of everything. Again, she yearned to ask, *Where am I?* but she held her tongue, not wanting to give either of them the knowledge that she cared. *Let them think I'm pleased to be away from them—out of their clutches at last.*

Old-fashioned post-top lights lined a long drive. A large white sign with archaic letters read Covenant House, illuminated by lights shining up from the ground. At the end of the curvy drive, beyond an entrance of metal gates, stood a brick building that looked like an old mansion—not at all like the dilapidated structure she'd conjured in her head.

Callie waited in the car until Asa pulled her luggage out of the trunk. By then, two women had approached Evelyn, and they appeared deep in conversation. Evelyn handed them an envelope just as Callie's car door opened. *What are they talking about?*

Her father stood outside, his shoulders slumped and his head lowered. "Callie," he said. Callie pivoted her body slowly as if giving him time to change his mind and tuck her back into the car, but he didn't. The two of them stood face-to-face, Callie's wide eyes looking into his, which looked just as vacant as Callie felt.

Asa shook his head. "Let's make the best of this, okay?"

Callie dropped her head and brushed past him.

"I'll talk to her," he whispered before she passed. One last-ditch effort to get Callie to feel sorry for *him*. *What is he thinking?* But a trace of hope stirred within. If anyone could get her out of this mess, it was her father.

Evelyn waved her arms, ushering Callie over to meet the women who now stood in front of her. Heat flushed through Callie's body as she caught herself grinding her teeth.

"Calista, this is Mrs. Goldstein, the headmaster, and Sister Jean Katherine. Mind them."

Mrs. Goldstein towered over Callie, a spindly, silver-haired woman who looked over her blue bifocals at Evelyn. "She'll mind. Not to worry." Not once did the headmaster look Callie in the eye.

Sister Jean Katherine, on the other hand, countered the chill Mrs. Goldstein sent through Callie with a lightning-quick warm gaze. Callie almost detected a hint of a smile. The woman couldn't have been more than ten years older than Callie, with her porcelain skin and flawless complexion.

"Once you get used to us," Sister Jean Katherine said, "I think you'll like it here."

Manners thrown to the wayside, Callie shot her mother an evil look, nostrils flaring and eyes bulging—a look she hoped would gnaw at Evelyn in Callie's absence.

"Sister," the spindly Mrs. Goldstein directed, "show Calista to her room."

"Of course, ma'am." And like an obedient dog, the nun took her leave.

Without a hint of a goodbye to her parents, Callie turned and followed, remaining close. It gave Callie some comfort to be greeted by a nun. She thought for a second about looking back at her parents for just one more plea, but she refused to give Mother the satisfaction.

Overtired, Callie dragged her heavy limbs up the stone steps after the nun. They made their way through the dimly lit circular foyer, which appeared like the center of a compass that jutted out into several long halls from the reception area. Callie followed Sister Jean Katherine down one hall where doors were numbered with placards and shut tight. Even the hallway was dim, and eerie shadows were cast across the floor as the two of them walked. Callie wondered how many girls were housed at this school—or prison, whatever the case may be. She must have already passed twenty doors.

Room 312. Sister Jean Katherine stopped, opening the door gingerly. "Shh, your roommate Deborah will be sleeping." Through the darkness of the room, they passed a bed with a sleeping body wrapped up like a butterfly in a thick cocoon. The glint of a nightlight led Callie to an empty twin bed. She'd been used to sleeping in a queen-sized bed.

"Your bag will be sent down by morning. There's a nightdress in the closet. Try to get a good night's sleep. Tomorrow will be a better day." Sister Jean Katherine's dimple deepened when she smiled. *Perhaps I have one ally*, Callie thought while the nun made her exit.

Callie sat on the edge of her bed. The room was small, with a partition separating her side from Deborah's. When she walked over to the other side, she noticed cluttered decorations on the corkboard and objects that Callie couldn't quite make out clumped on Deborah's dresser. She wondered how long Deborah had been a resident of Covenant House. She wondered how long she would be one. Rubbing her curved stomach, Callie felt a bit less alone.

The room looked more like a hospital room than one from any sort of home or school. Sterile white covers and sheets were tucked tightly around the bed. There was a plain, cheap closet, dresser, and desk. This was how she'd imagined a dorm room at college, but school was a thought she'd left a million miles behind her. Whether she liked it or not, college didn't appear to be in her future after all.

Callie tugged the nightdress off of the hanger in the closet. She slipped into it then went into the adjacent bathroom, splashing cold water on her face. "This is real," Callie mouthed at her reflection in the mirror as the cold water dripped down her neck.

She slipped under the covers of her stiff, narrow bed, held her hands on her belly, and cried herself to sleep.

CALLIE WOKE UP WITH an unsettled feeling in the foreign room. She scanned the small space, seeing in the daylight the white cement walls and the large wooden cross hanging above the window. The cross gave her no comfort, no matter how devoutly Christian she considered herself.

She lay still, as if her limbs couldn't or wouldn't move, wishing she had awakened to learn that all of last night was just a nightmare. But the reality remained, as did she in this stifling enclosure. She couldn't call it a bedroom. A prison stall, perhaps, a place where the involuntary were kept.

After wiggling her limbs to get feeling into them, she managed to swing her legs over the edge of the bed to face the sun beaming in through the window. She wondered how freely they would allow her to roam outside, how the routine of her day would be altered in this place. She thought about Jocelyn, who might already be looking for her at school that morning. *Where's the clock?* Not a single clock in this room.

And Jon—it could be a day or more before he caught on that she'd been sent away, unless Jocelyn reached out to him first.

Standing in front of the double window on her side of the partition, Callie gazed across the grounds, blanketed with a menagerie of fall-colored leaves. How could the outside of this place look so peaceful when the inside screamed dull oppression?

The bedroom door slammed shut, and Callie heard a huff on the other side of the room.

"I've been sent to rouse you." A tall, lanky girl with dark, straggly brown hair stood before her. She wore standard-issue uniform attire. Callie had been no stranger to school uniforms.

Callie pulled the neckline of her cotton nightgown to her chin.

"To wake you up," the girl said. "First days are hectic. There's a schedule, and you're already behind."

"How am I supposed to know?"

"That's why I'm here. Deborah. Debs for short."

She extended a hand, and Callie shook it. Debs's handshake was hardly a strong one. Of course, etiquette classes taught that a firm handshake reflected an individual's power. Callie, instead, relied on gut instinct. She prided herself on judging first impressions, and Debs's demeanor already felt like a good one. "What are you here for?"

Callie pressed the nightgown taut around her belly.

Debs scrunched the left side of her face. "There are a few of you. When are you due?"

"April thirtieth. What are you here for?"

Debs turned over one wrist to expose a jagged scar. "Dad's razor didn't do the trick. It was my second time. First time was pills."

Callie squinted, her jaw dropping, until she realized how her reaction might look to Debs and quickly adjusted her expression. *What kind of place is this?*

"No worries. I'm not suicidal now." Then Debs leaned in, like she had a secret to tell, even though the two of them were alone in the room. "This place isn't all bad. But I'll deny I said it if you ever tell anyone."

Callie crossed her heart.

"Get dressed," Debs said.

Callie looked around. No suitcase. "Where are my clothes?"

"They'll be here soon enough. They go through everything with a fine-tooth comb. Contraband is strictly prohibited. But there are clothes in your closet."

"Not last night. Just this."

"Check again."

Callie opened the closet to see a wardrobe of five standard-issue school uniforms. "These weren't here before."

Debs nodded. "Sneaky bastards. Go on. I'll wait."

Callie took one of the outfits, complete on one hanger, into the bathroom. She changed into the white blouse, which was two sizes too big, and tucked it into a black-and-white plaid skirt that hung loose at her hips, under her belly, and down to her knees.

In the cabinet above the sink, there was only one toothbrush, which she assumed belonged to Debs, but she did take a dab of toothpaste to run over her teeth with a finger to remove the stale taste from her mouth. As she leaned toward the mirror, it seemed that someone else's eyes looked back at her, bloodshot and swollen. Her makeup was probably in her bag. There was no way Evelyn wouldn't have thought to pack it—appearances and all—but the plain-Jane look would have to do for that morning.

Callie emerged from the bathroom to find Debs sitting on the edge of her bed, picking at her fingernails and humming a familiar tune.

Perplexed, Callie concentrated on the tune and blurted, "'I Feel Fine'?"

Smugly, Debs nodded. "By whom?"

Callie rolled her eyes. "The Beatles."

"We're going to get along just fine. Now, button up that shirt so you don't get into trouble on the first day. And don't let anyone see that necklace if you want to keep it. Some of the girls are kleptos."

Callie fingered the drop-pearl pendant, a debutante gift, then backed up as she dutifully fastened the top two buttons to cover it.

"I'm not going to steal it. I'm not a thief," Debs said in a joking voice, or at least, Callie hoped so. "Now, to breakfast. I'll introduce you around."

"Is this customary?" Callie asked as they walked.

Debs shrugged. "I suppose. My roommate introduced me. The one who was in the bed before you. Valerie."

"What happened to Valerie?"

"She had her baby and went home."

"Right away? After the birth? With the baby?" Callie's questions shot at Debs like bullets. She didn't care that she sounded overeager. Perhaps her parents had lied to her—tried to scare her into putting her baby up for adoption. Perhaps they would allow her to keep her baby, after all.

"Yeah to all three." Debs's brow furrowed. "Are you worried?"

"I don't know why I'm here or for how long. They told me until I have the baby."

"That sounds about right. Some girls put theirs up for adoption, but some don't."

Callie's palm pressed to her heart. "What is this place?"

"Didn't they tell you? A home for wayward girls. You'll see."

They continued walking and took a couple of turns that Callie tried to keep track of so she could find her way back. Debs pointed. "In through here is the cafetorium. Combo cafeteria and auditorium. Whole school meetings are here."

Inside the cafetorium, the noise level went from a dull hum to a cacophony of high-pitched girls' voices. "Take a tray."

Callie grabbed one. As she made her way through the line, women wearing hairnets served her food. Watery eggs on one plate. Burnt toast with jelly packets on another. A whole orange. Orange juice. And too-buttery grits.

Callie never thought she would long for Briarlee school food again, but this sloppy mess elevated Briarlee's to fine cuisine. She turned to Debs. "Coffee?"

"Oh, the machine by the door."

Callie's eyes widened. "Coffee from a machine?"

"Pop your eyes back in your head, Lily White—there are no chefs here. Only cooks."

What did she mean by *that*? Callie put her head down and went straight for the machine with Debs just a step behind her.

"Don't let them see you're a girl of means," Debs whispered into Callie's left ear.

"What?"

"The look of disgust on your face. You'll have to work on that, 'cause you'll meet all sorts here."

They settled in at a rectangular table with seats so close that everyone's shoulders touched. There were already eight girls there, clones of herself in dress, but Callie could already tell that was where the similarities ended.

"Hey," Debs said, "this is the new girl, Callie."

Each of the girls shouted out their names, but Callie lost track of them.

Callie returned a general greeting then ate in silence, taking it all in.

One girl with wide shoulders swore a lot and talked about life on the street, whatever that meant. Callie was afraid to ask. A petite, neatly kept girl remained silent—not the same way as Callie, who was learning, but more like a mouse. Her stomach swelled bigger than Callie's, and Callie wondered who the father was. Was he a man who loved the quiet girl like Jon did Callie, or just a nameless boy—like the one Callie made Evelyn believe was the father of her baby?

The last girl, the one with the big hoop earrings, dominated the conversation with her gruff, haughty voice. She appeared to be the ringleader, if there was one. "So, Callie, what are you in for?" she shouted from the other end of the table.

Callie pointed to her belly. "Four months now."

The mousy one lowered her head and giggled to herself. *What is she giggling about?* Callie opened her mouth to ask, to confront her as she would have another schoolmate at Briarlee, but closed her mouth instead. Callie had never been shy, but this was different. She was the outsider here. She didn't fit in like smooth satin the way she did at Briarlee. And she hoped she never would.

"Let's go," Debs announced, looking straight at Callie. "You're going to be late to the group."

Group? Callie couldn't imagine what that meant. Was it a code word for class? After all, Evelyn clearly called this a school. She'd promised Callie would be able to graduate on time and with her class at Briarlee at the end of June.

On their way to the next destination, Callie asked Debs what she'd been told about Callie's arrival.

"Only that you were on your way, and I'd be your big sister—that's what they call roommates here," Debs said. "I was here first, so basically, you shadow me. And right now, you're lollygagging."

"I'm taking it in. Apparently, they plan for me to be here awhile." Callie's mind drifted back home. She imagined a cold morning, her parents sitting at opposite ends of the table. Meanwhile, her father would be struggling with how best to get Callie out of this mess while placating Evelyn at the same time.

"Sounds like at least five months. It's not so bad."

Not so bad? Five months sounded like an eternity. "What's group?"

"Like therapy," Debs said so matter-of-factly that Callie feared coming off as naive or rude if she pressed her to elaborate. Therapy was something for people not quite right in the head—someone like, well, like Debs when she...

Callie couldn't even conceive of such a thing.

But Debs seemed right enough in the head, trustworthy, even. And she was right, so far, about Covenant House not being so bad. Except when Callie's thoughts led to Jon and Jocelyn, who could literally be stricken with worry right now—their minds running in a million directions, wondering where Callie could be. Inevitably, Jocelyn would let Jon know Callie was missing, and he would come for her. Callie couldn't wait to see his face at the front reception area, demanding that they release Callie to his custody.

"Okay, here we are. Group."

Callie stood at the doorway, waiting for Debs to lead her in, but Debs shook her head. "Nope, you're doing this alone. I'll come back to get you when it's over."

Callie swallowed hard and walked inside.

Five girls sat in a circle of chairs. Sister Jean Katherine, the nun she met the night before, gestured toward the one vacant chair. "Welcome, Calista. You look rested. How did your first breakfast go?" Sister's cheeks were pinker and her voice perkier than any nun Callie had ever known.

"Fine," Callie responded politely, realizing the nun was trying her best to make Callie feel not so alone. But saying the word *fine* made her heart feel hollow and ache for what had filled it yesterday—Jon and Jocelyn and her family, or at least her dad.

Callie noticed the protruding bellies of four of the girls, who were obviously pregnant. She also recognized two of them from the breakfast table.

Sister began to speak directly to Callie. "This is group for our pregnant girls." *Aha, not therapy, then? More like an extracurricular.*

"We meet twice a week. Every Wednesday and Friday morning, same time, same place."

Friday. Yes, it's Friday. Callie had almost lost track of time. She searched for a clock, but still, none were visible.

Callie placed her hand on her lap, realizing that she still had one. The others kept their hands on stomachs that looked like balls of various sizes. Callie hadn't thought that far ahead—about the way her pregnant body would take a new shape, making her trim figure unrecognizable.

"We check in and talk about the stages of our babies." Sister spoke as if she were a mother, too, but Callie knew that would never be possible in the Catholic church. She assumed the nun was Catholic from the black habit she wore, though the dress beneath was white.

Callie had attended a small Catholic elementary school and, of course, church and catechism every Sunday. Once Callie came of age as a thirteen-year-old, her religious schooling was trumped by etiquette classes, and although Callie begged to remain in school with her friends, she was transferred to a finishing school for girls. At least her parents had had the good sense to send her to Briarlee, because on the adjacent campus was an all-boys academy.

While attending Briarlee, Callie hadn't appreciated it. She thought it much too pretentious, each student more elite than the next. The competition to climb the social hierarchy was modeled by their parents, of course, who moved in the old-money circles—hardly ever the new. While the Sebastians were technically considered new money, Evelyn had them all fooled, forever alluding to their long pedigree in high society although, for as long as Callie could remember, they'd been estranged from the Sebastians for reasons she had never been privy to.

If she asked about it, Evelyn found a way to turn it on Callie, saying something like "There you go again, inserting yourself into business where you don't belong."

And Callie had no problem answering back, "My grandparents are my business," but always to no avail.

Though it surprised her, Callie longed to be back at Briarlee. To be waiting at her locker for Jocelyn and their other girlfriends to meet in the morning and plan their day. To escape to Jon's office for one excuse or another, just to lay eyes on him. If she had known she would be sent to Covenant House, she wouldn't have left him in such a sassy way, and she prayed he would forgive her, that he would look past it and come to find her.

"Ladies, let's introduce ourselves to Calista. Name and how far along we are, all right?"

"Oh," she said. "Do you mind calling me Callie?"

The girl to the left of Sister Jean Katherine raised her hand. "I'll start. Natalie, six months."

"Susan, seven months."

"Jeanine, fourteen weeks."

Next was the mousy girl from breakfast. "Kate, again! Seven and a half," she squeaked.

"Alma, nine." Alma slouched in her chair and held her hand against her back. The ankles beneath her socks were swollen.

Callie wondered if Alma was a mirror of what Callie would look in five months. Evelyn's voice spidered into her head, saying, "Don't be ridiculous, Calista. This will ruin your life... I'll make it like it never happened... I do know better. I'm your mother."

Doubt infected her—about the pregnancy, about Jon, about everything. Maybe she'd made a mistake.

"Callie... Callie." Sister's voice rose. "Tell us about yourself." Her back was poker straight against the chair. Callie wondered if the nun had been to etiquette class too. And what would have led her to the church?

More annoyed than embarrassed, Callie kept it short. "Callie. Four months."

"Anything else you'd like to share?"

Callie thought for a moment or two. She scanned the large room, which looked like a small gymnasium with hardwood floors. They sat on metal folding chairs that hurt her bottom, shooting pressure from her stomach straight through her pelvis like lightning. *Is this normal?* She wiggled in her chair to massage the pain away. It subsided. *Thank goodness.*

Why aren't there any clocks? While she wanted to ask about Covenant House's aversion to time, she simply shook her head instead. It wasn't like she would become friends with any of these girls. It was clear they had nothing in common except pregnancy.

"All right, then, let's begin. How about a physical check-in?"

The others obviously knew what this meant. Alma jumped right in. "My feet are like bowling balls, and my pelvis hurts." *Then... it doesn't go away?* "I seriously think this kid weighs fifteen pounds. I'm worried about—"

Sister cut her off. "Alma," she said, attempting a stern tone but really just sounding intimidated. "Not feelings just yet. You know the protocol."

The Mouse spoke then, nearly whispering, in her high-pitched voice. "My stomach is stretched as far as it can go."

Callie thought back to the afternoon she'd become sick at Jocelyn's—the day she let her in on the secret, as she'd known she would eventually. And, now more than ever, she was glad she had. Jocelyn might be the only savior she could have from this place. A vision of her rushing into Jon's office floated through her mind's eye while Callie pushed the voices of the pregnant girls away. She didn't want to be like any of them.

"I feel fantastic," Natalie said. "The best I've felt the whole time, but I know the third trimester is uncomfortable. Dr. Owen assured me change is just around the corner." Natalie turned to Callie. "Dr. Owen is our ob-gyn."

Callie looked around blankly.

"Oh God." Susan rolled her eyes directly at Callie. "Obstetrician and gynecologist? I thought you were supposed to be smart. Looks can be deceiving."

Callie's face turned red, and she slouched in her chair.

Sister touched Callie's arm as if to reassure her. "Respect, please. We're a team, ladies. We are here to support one another."

With arms folded and legs tucked under her chair, Callie scanned the circle of "wayward" girls. *How does pregnancy make one wayward?* That was Evelyn's skewed perception. Callie shook away the unsettled feeling the shadow of her mother gave her, always in her mind like a cloak she couldn't free herself from.

At the end of the meeting, Kate rushed up behind Callie. "We aren't that different," she whispered.

When Callie looked at her questioningly, Kate giggled and waddled away.

Debs met Callie in the hallway after group, and Callie couldn't have been more ready to move on. "Next are academics," Debs said as she walked Callie to another wing of the school.

"How many students are here?"

"I think there's eighty of us."

"All here against their will?"

Debs looked at Callie like she had a secret, but she only said, "Some are and some are not. Some of us recognize that we need help."

"Like you?"

"Yes, I came here willingly. Which is also why they paired us together. The program works, Callie. Just give it time. You won't be so resentful once you feel like you're part of this community."

Callie couldn't imagine feeling the way Debs described or ever considering herself part of the *community*. Pregnancy wasn't a mental illness or a disease. It wasn't wrong or even something people needed therapy to deal with. It was the product of an act of love between people like herself and Jon. Why did everyone act like she'd been bad?

AFTER A VERY LONG DAY, the first thing Callie saw when she entered her room was the stuffed monkey from Jon, which brought her to tears. It had been placed on her tautly made bed. She picked it up and held it close to her face, smelling Jon's fresh scent on it. Asa was responsible for packing the monkey, Callie was sure. Evelyn didn't pay much attention to items of comfort, only prestige. Of course, had either of them known where she had gotten it, surely it would not have been among her belongings. Nevertheless, Callie considered it a gift she'd been given again as she drew in a deep breath of cinnamon—of Jon—into her body and soul.

In the closet, all her own clothes had been hung beside the uniforms that were there. Her empty suitcase had been pushed beneath her bed. In the dresser were her underclothes. She opened the drawers of her desk to find loose-leaf paper, pens, and pencils.

Callie took a crisp sheet of paper, wrote the date and day of the week at the top of the page, and proceeded to write about the last twenty-four hours, like a diary. It was one way she could keep track of time. She began with dinner the night before, trying to recall the details precisely.

Debs entered the room, laughing, while Susan waited at the door. "We have to go to mass, Callie. Every night at seven. You should come with us."

They led her to a chapel in the same wing where group had been held earlier in the morning. This chapel would be dwarfed by the spacious cathedral Callie attended with her parents with its columns, gold trim, and stained-glass windows. Still, the familiar aroma of sandalwood and pungent spices filled the air from sticks of incense billowing smoke from the altar, making the unfamiliar somewhat calming. The holy table was draped with a simple white cloth embroidered with a cross, not nearly as ornate as Callie had been accustomed to. The pews, not even mahogany, were almost full. The girls from breakfast sat together, and Callie realized there were cliques even here.

The sisters, seven of them, sat on one side of the altar. When the priest, an elderly bent-over man, entered, the girls and the nuns stood. The organist played a hymn Callie didn't recognize.

The subject of the priest's sermon was forgiveness, apropos to the way she'd concluded her earlier writing, stating that she didn't think she would ever forgive her mother. Ever. As the priest spoke, Callie relived the look of sadness in her father's eyes and the smugness on her mother's face. The priest concluded with the words, "So my heavenly Father will also do to every one of you, if you do not forgive your brother or sister from your heart. Matthew 18:35."

Callie bowed her head when he signaled for the last prayer, silently saying, "I'm sorry, God. I cannot forgive her. Please bless this baby that it shall never have a mother like mine. I will love it unconditionally. Amen."

INSTEAD OF HAVING AN hour to herself after breakfast in the morning, as the schedule permitted, Callie was summoned to Mrs.

Goldstein's office. She was told it was merely protocol, an introductory meeting.

The office was up the grand staircase and through a heavy door. The staircase reminded her of the one she'd descended on her father's arm during the ball, which seemed a lifetime ago, and she wished she could go back there, not be in such a hurry for that time to end. Callie knocked at the door on which a golden plate read Headmaster in embossed letters.

"Miss Sebastian, please come in. Sit."

Callie sat in a comfortable brown-leather armchair across from Mrs. Goldstein. It reminded her of their library at home, dark wood with floor-to-ceiling bookshelves filled with gold-embossed spines of books. It was where her father went to think. On the wall of Mrs. Goldstein's office hung a grandmother clock much like the one in her dining room at home, though Evelyn's was more ornate, of course. The headmaster's clock had a cuckoo bird sitting above the twelve. The hands on it pointed to eight thirty-five, the first evidence of time since Callie had arrived.

"Good morning," Callie said.

Preoccupied, the headmaster flipped through a folder laid out on her desk. "How has your stay been so far?"

"Fine."

Still not lifting her eyes, she continued, "And I presume Deborah has been a helpful big sister."

"Yes, ma'am."

Then Mrs. Goldstein looked up, and her gray eyes dialed right into Callie's. "This is a home for wayward girls." Callie's heartbeat quickened, matching the clicking second hand of the clock. "You may have gathered a loose interpretation of that. There are some girls who have become pregnant like yourself, some who are simply of a rebellious nature—and, naturally, some who aren't quite right in their mind, some harmful to themselves."

Callie nodded. She'd already met girls in each of these categories.

"The curriculum for each of you is personally prescribed." Then she tipped her nose upward, and Callie could see it flare. "This is a very prestigious Catholic school for girls. We pride ourselves on the success rate of our graduates. Also, completion looks different for each. Are you following?"

Callie nodded. Essentially, she surmised, the birth of her child meant graduation. "Why did Mother send me here? Surely there are girls who remain at home throughout their pregnancies." Callie already knew the answer to that question, but it was important she heard it from Mrs. Goldstein.

"Sister Jean Katherine does an excellent job preparing young women for their lives as mothers or for the adoption process. Your case is somewhat dubious, I'm told. Your mother asked that we prepare you for adoption, though I gather you'd like to see yourself as a young mother. Our job is to monitor you closely. Do what is in your best interests." The headmaster's curtness reminded Callie of Mother. She wondered if they'd known each other in the past.

Mrs. Goldstein rose from behind her desk and walked around to stand in between it and Callie. In response, Callie's body closed up, mirroring how she felt. Enclosed.

"Miss Sebastian, girls your age fantasize about becoming mothers. You don't see the hardships it brings. The means from which you were raised afford you opportunity. You have no idea what you'd be sacrificing, and it's our job to educate you."

Callie sighed. So this was her mother's ulterior motive, and she'd hired Mrs. Goldstein and her flock of nuns to do what she couldn't. Evelyn's power extended far beyond Savannah.

"Your mother wants the very best for you."

Callie tried not to let Mrs. Goldstein see her sneer, but she wasn't entirely sure of her success.

"You'll continue with your maternal group work and have one-on-one sessions as needed," Mrs. Goldstein continued. "Your academics are aligned to your studies at Briarlee, so if all goes according to plan, you are on track to graduate when you return home."

There it was. The threat—according to plan. Evelyn's plan. But Debs said some girls kept their babies. *Did those girls come here with a plan too? Did it fail?* Jon had to pull through. He had to save her, because if Callie kept this baby, she knew there was no going home. Not to the home she knew before, at least. By bringing her here, Evelyn had shut that door.

Callie looked defiantly at Mrs. Goldstein. "When can I see and speak to my friends at home?"

CALLIE LOOKED FORWARD to her first phone call. She wished she could call Jon, but she didn't quite know what "monitoring" meant—the last thing she needed was to expose him. Instead, she would call Jocelyn, the only other ally she had in the whole world.

The phone rang three times, and she prayed, "Please, please, please be home." Though there wasn't a clock in sight, she had been told it was seven o'clock, a respectable evening hour to make a phone call.

"Hello." Wendy's voice sounded like a whole orchestra to Callie's ears.

Urgency escaped her voice as Callie asked, "Is Jocelyn home?"

"Callie, is that you? Jocelyn has been worried sick."

"I'm okay, Mrs. Halfield. Is she home?"

"Yes, of course, sweetheart. One minute, okay?"

Callie heard the phone dangle against the wall, then, "Are you all right?" Jocelyn's voice sounded hurried.

"My parents sent me to a Catholic school hours away. I'm not even sure what town I'm in. The headmaster said it's a school for 'wayward' girls. Covenant House."

"Wayward girls?"

Out of the corner of her eye, she saw a burly nun, her dress looking a size too small, arms glued to her sides like a soldier's as she paced the row of phones. Each handset was pressed tightly against the ear of a different wayward girl.

"Yes, apparently I'm one."

"For being pregnant? You weren't kidding. Your mother *is* crazy."

"To say the least. What did she tell you?"

"Nothing. There are rumors going around—that you've transferred schools for bigger opportunities out of state. I even heard you were in some prestigious etiquette school in France. I knew it was all a lie. You would have at least said goodbye."

"You haven't told anyone about..." Callie looked down at her belly, which no longer looked flat. "You know."

"Of course not. Not even my mother, who is concerned. She keeps trying to reassure me that you're okay, but your mother hasn't returned any of her calls."

"What about Jon?"

"Also worried. I went to him to see if he knew where you were. I thought the two of you ran away. I'll tell him you're well. He'll want to contact you. What should I say?"

The burly nun grew closer, as if she knew Callie was talking about something she shouldn't. Callie put her hand over the mouthpiece and whispered, "Tell him to come get me at Covenant House. I don't know where it is, but we drove for about three hours. Please tell him to come, Jocelyn. He'll know what to do."

"I will. I promise."

The whistle blew. Callie's body jerked like an electric current ran through it. "I have to go. I love you. See you soon."

"Callie, stay strong. Okay? Love you too." Jocelyn hung up.

Callie placed the handset on the hook. Her hand lingered on it for a moment longer. Her lifeline. This—Covenant House—was not her life. It was an obstacle Evelyn had put in her path. Jon would know exactly what to do, and on that, she depended.

Callie walked back to her room with her shoulders back and head held high. She spied Kate sitting alone in the rotunda, reading. Although she tried to avoid her by walking the other way, Kate called out her name in her meek voice.

Callie doubled back. Kate held the book *Dr. Spock Talks with Mothers,* resting it atop her taut and protruding belly. In comparison, Callie didn't feel much like a mother yet.

"I heard some of what you said on the phone," Kate said.

Callie hadn't noticed Kate in the vicinity while she was on the phone. Her expression turned to a scowl. "Were you eavesdropping on me?"

"I heard you are from Willow."

"I never said that."

"I heard some of the girls talking."

Callie's chest tightened. *Of course they're gossiping about me.*

"I'm from Cumberfield," Kate said. Callie had heard of it. An affluent town much like her own. "My parents said I'm an embarrassment too."

Callie hadn't once said that aloud the entire time she'd been here. How could Kate know?

"Do you not know your baby's father too?"

"I know him."

Kate lowered her head. "You're lucky. At least you could tell your baby where it came from."

Callie hadn't considered that luck. In her mind, it was destiny, the plan God had for her all along. One she would embrace wholeheartedly. "Are you keeping yours?"

"No. I wouldn't think of keeping it. My parents would disown me. Are you?"

"Of course I am."

"You might change your mind when you think about what you could lose." Kate placed her hand on Callie's arm. "I want you to know you aren't alone."

Callie nodded. She appreciated the gesture but questioned it at the same time. Once people knew her baby had been created out of love, they would stop ostracizing her. She wasn't anything like Kate.

When Callie got to her room, Debs was lying atop her bed, one knee up and the other leg crossed over it. She was listening to the Beatles sing about Mother Mary on her transistor radio. Callie walked past to her own bed and lay down, hugging her stuffed monkey.

After a few moments, Debs got up and pulled back the partition like an accordion. "Listen." She beckoned.

Callie wiped the tears from her eyes. "To what?" All she could hear was the song.

"To the words," Debs said. "I can't bear to hear you cry yourself to sleep again."

"You heard me?" Callie listened to the words of the song play out.

Debs scrunched her nose. "Yes. No worries. I did, too, for the whole first week."

"Why did you stop? How?"

"I resigned myself to work the program. If I'm going to get better, I need to invest in myself."

Callie wouldn't ever resign herself to "the program," whatever that meant, aside from hiding her pregnancy from Evelyn's high society. Callie didn't belong here. But she couldn't tell Debs any of this while she was still unsure of who was leaking information about her. She would have to measure her words carefully—keep track of what details she shared and with whom. Anyway, it wouldn't be long be-fore Jon came for her, to take her away to their new life. But not hav-ing had a chance to devise a plan with Jon, she could keep this all to herself. "That sounds like something Sister Jean Katherine would say."

"Yeah, well, Sister Lourdes said it. She's my group leader. The way I see it, there is no use worrying or crying over something you cannot change."

"But there isn't anything wrong with me that I need to recover from." As the words rolled off her tongue, Callie realized how they sounded—like a sharp dose of judgment. "I'm sorry. That came out wrong."

"It's okay."

"Can I tell you something that you have to keep a secret?"

Debs nodded.

"Mother wanted me to have an abortion. She said she knew a doctor who would do it. I thought she was losing her mind. First, that she'd know people like that who would intentionally break the law, and second, that she'd ever think I'd do that. She's turned my father against me. Everything is always about Mother. Her life. Her status. Her reputation. But this is my baby. I feel her."

"Her? It's impossible to know it's a girl."

"I like to think she is. I call her Stella." Callie rubbed her belly, and as she did, a warm sensation enveloped her. Just at the mention of Stella's name, Callie felt a sense of home—the kind of home her beloved nanny had created for her, even though it had been tempo-rary.

IN THE DAYS THAT FOLLOWED, each time Callie heard the click-clack of footsteps in the hallway near her room, her heartbeat quickened, and she sat up straight. Each time she walked by the reception area, she stalled, peering out the front entrance, hoping to catch Jon's approach. In group, when the door opened unexpectedly, she imagined someone calling her name—*Callie Sebastian, you're being discharged.*

Then a full week passed, and not one of the scenarios she'd played over and over in her head materialized.

The next Sunday, Callie eagerly awaited her turn for a phone call.

Her fingers shook as she dialed the number. While it rang, she scanned her surroundings, making sure the Mouse wasn't listening—or anyone else, for that matter.

When Jocelyn answered, Callie's breathing calmed at the sound of her voice.

"Joss?" Callie covered the handset just to be sure no one could read her lips. "What did he say? I expected him to come."

Silence wasn't the reaction she expected.

"Jocelyn?" she repeated, worried they had been cut off.

"I'm here," Jocelyn said. Callie could hear her take a deep breath. "He said he couldn't. Not right now."

A numb rush of fog rolled over Callie, making her legs buckle. Conscious of her own breath, she exhaled through her nose and steadied herself against the phone booth. "Can't?"

"He was questioned at school about the nature of your relationship, Callie. He's afraid it isn't the right time."

"Why? How do they know?"

"I don't know. I heard one of the secretaries said she saw you going to his office on several occasions."

"But why are they even looking into it? Surely Mother gave them some cause, if for no other reason than to protect herself."

"Jon said to tell you not to give up hope. He'll see what he can do when everything settles down. I'm sorry. I tried to call, but they wouldn't put me through."

That wasn't the end of the conversation, but it was the last Callie remembered of it. Jocelyn's words played like a broken record in her mind as she stomped back to her room.

Kate sat in the same place as last week, reading on the bench in the rotunda. She stood as Callie neared. Kate approached, mouth open like she wanted to say something, but as Callie reached her, she brushed assertively past, their shoulders touching.

Her teeth clenched and her fists balled up at her sides, Callie marched away on a mission to be alone. Once inside her room, she slammed the door shut, wanting to shut out the whole world.

Raina
Brocton, Georgia, 2004
Chapter 10

In the winter months, Raina expanded into making candles and soap, all with honey scents: honey citrus, honey cinnamon, honey basil. Orders were picking up, and she enjoyed venturing into new products.

While Bee-licious kept her busy, it still felt like a hobby. At lunchtime, she would prepare dinner, then she would watch *All My Children* for an hour. The last hour of the day was the worst, though. It seemed like forever until three o'clock arrived. As the clock ticked slowly, Raina was reminded that her thirty-third birthday was just around the corner. She wasn't getting any younger, and the older she became, the more complicated pregnancy could be.

Why tempt fate? Pregnancy has always come so easily for me. Dare I bring it up again?

Armed with a cup of warm cider just the way he liked it, with a cinnamon stick and a shot of bourbon, she went out to coax Wayne into taking an afternoon break. She found him in the barn, putting tools away, when she approached.

Raina didn't say a word. Extending the gift, or maybe bribe, she handed him the cup. "Hot," she warned.

He looked quizzically at her, took the cup, and sipped. "Can I help you?" he asked.

She simply paced back and forth with a Cheshire-cat smile. "No." She looked back at him as she walked away, arms clasped behind her back like a schoolgirl.

"Why are you walking back and forth like that?"

"Thinking is all."

"Thinking what, woman? You don't come out here and pace around without something on your mind."

She approached him, placed her hands on his chest, and breathed in the sweet scent of his sweat, something only a wife could love. She looked up at him, batting her eyes. "Now that you mention it..."

"See, you know those baby blues melt me every time."

Good. She had him just where she wanted him. After swallowing, she said, "I really think it's time. Before Timmy gets too old. I don't want our kids far apart."

He smirked at her, or maybe it was a twinkle. Either way, it wasn't a no. Wayne was definitely softening to the idea. It had been months since she broached the subject. She promised she would give the business a try, and she had—a good, honest try. It wasn't as if she didn't like making her products and selling them. It just didn't fulfill her the same way motherhood did.

"Think of all the farmhands you'll have," she said.

He laughed and kissed her hard on the lips. Even after eleven years, when they should be feeling the itch, they loved each other like the first day they'd locked eyes. "You're relentless. You know that?"

After dinner, Raina stood over Wayne as he pored over the bills, checking his spreadsheet against their income. She paced. He calculated.

Eventually, Wayne let out a big sigh and leaned against the back of his chair. "I don't see how we can manage. Crops have been down this year. It isn't the right time."

Raina bit her fingernail. "There's no such thing as the right time. You know if we have another baby, we'll make ends meet. Things like that just fall into place. And you are never gonna say, 'I regret having that kid.'"

"I could regret the deeper debt it puts us in. Kids are expensive."

"Aren't you happy?"

"I am happy, but you don't know the stress of finances, especially for a guy dependent on the right weather for his income."

After dinner and bath time, Raina went into the girls' room, where Tina was reading *Amelia Bedelia* under her night light. "Time for bed."

"Almost done, Mama."

Tina was smart as a whip, the way Raina used to be when she was little. Back then, she had loved to read. She couldn't quite put her finger on why or when she stopped. She supposed it fell away, along with so many other things, when she became a mom and put herself wholly and completely into that role.

"Tracy, you too."

Downstairs, a door slammed. Raina and her daughters jerked to attention. Then the screen door creaked open, followed by another door shutting hard. Wayne didn't make a habit of slamming doors.

Raina brushed the hair back from Tracy's eyes, reassuring her, and hurriedly tucked her in. "Make sure your sister turns in soon."

When she reached the bottom of the stairs, she saw the porch light on, so she stepped out to find Wayne leaned back in the rocker with a six-pack at his feet and a cold beer at his lips.

The chilly air prompted her to wrap her sweater tight and hold it closed. "What was that about? You startled the girls. Thank God you didn't wake up Timmy."

Wayne didn't say a word. He simply shook his head.

Raina pulled a beer out of the cardboard carton, cracking it open as she sat across from him on the wooden chair swing. "Wayne. Talk to me."

He guzzled down what was left in the can and opened another. Raina waited. The full moon shone in the sky like a big white egg.

After clearing his throat, but still not looking up at her, he said, "Belowe is selling."

Otis Belowe, owner of Belowe Markets, a staple in Brocton and beyond, was Wayne's best customer. The Belowes always treated the Edwins like kin, as Otis and Wayne's father, Big Wayne, went to grade school together. When Big Wayne passed, Otis had tipped his hat to Wayne and told him he would take care of him. "Your business will always have a place in my business." He had punctuated with a wink that was as good as a strong handshake.

Raina's jaw dropped. She knew Otis was getting on in years, but his business was a virtual dynasty. "How could he sell?"

Wayne slammed his beer on the table beside him, some of it splashing out onto his hand. "His boys don't want it, and he's ready to retire." He looked up at the starry sky, forlorn. Raina hadn't seen him in such a state since Big Wayne's passing.

"Couldn't the new owners pick us up?"

"Otis said he'd sell us hard. But no guarantees." Wayne leaned forward, elbows on his knees. Combing his hand through his hair, he let out a deep sigh.

Raina uncrossed her legs and leaned forward to put her hands on his knees. "Look. Look at me." His face turned up, the veins in his forehead purple under the porch light. "We'll get through this. In all the hard times, it always works out. I'll get a job if need be. I can find something."

"This farm is just one headache after another. I should be able to provide for you, for our family."

A knot tightened in her belly. She dared not mention it, but she couldn't help but think about the bigger family she wanted to grow. She knew she would have to put that on hold for a while—but hopefully not for too long. On the inside, her clock was ticking.

FOR THE FIRST TIME in their marriage, Christmas weighed heavy on the Edwin house. "We have to tighten our belts and cut back this year," Wayne told her.

As they waited to hear the result of Belowe's sale and determine the effect of it on their future, Wayne passed many more nights on the front porch in the cold, drinking into the wee hours of the night. Raina had never been a worrier, and Wayne had never been one to drink his troubles away. But here they both were, trying to hold everything together the best way they knew how.

Just before the new year, Wayne got word that the new owners of Belowe's were going with another distributor. Maybe this wasn't going to be the year Raina hoped for, after all. But one thing she knew about her mother, according to her Auntie Jane, was the big deal Mama made out of every New Year. Auntie Jane had said, "Your mama used to say, just when the year couldn't get any more hopeless, 'The New Year's coming 'round and will bring all the new possibilities with it.'"

Once the new year began, Raina made a habit of perusing newspaper advertisements for job openings every morning. With her own business at a standstill this time of year, she wanted to help out somehow. Wayne had given her and the kids a good life. He worked hard for it too. This had been the first time since his father's passing that his business had taken such a hit to the gut, and it had resulted in tension visible in the downturned creases beside his mouth and the shadows in his eyes. It was hard for Raina to see all the light going out of Wayne like that.

Her eyes scanned the printed page for something perfect to jump out at her. She sipped her no-longer-hot-enough coffee, tasting more milk than brew.

"Secretary wanted: small office environment, answer phones, file, experience with Microsoft." All but the computer experience sounded great. While she helped Wayne with his books, he kept only written records.

"Dog groomers wanted: nose to tail, washing, clipping & dipping, $5.15 per hour." *That won't do us a hill of beans. How do we make ends meet for five on those wages?*

Just as she drew her cold coffee to her mouth, ready to close the newspaper for the day, she saw it. A big ad screaming at the top of the next page, featuring a woman's swollen belly with her hand cupping the bottom. It read Give Life. Be a Surrogate.

After bath time that night, Raina made her rounds tucking in the kids, Timmy first. She led him in saying his prayers, then she drew him close, taking in the fresh scent of Johnson & Johnson baby shampoo. "You are getting to be such a big boy," she said and winced. Her baby, growing too fast into a little man.

By the time she reached the girls' room, the lights were off, so she stood in the doorway. "Say your prayers?"

Tina smiled her toothy grin, the front two looking monstrous next to the others, most of which were still baby teeth.

Tracy shook her head. "Mama, remember I have Girl Scouts tomorrow, and it's my turn for snacks."

Such a little lady, taking care of her own business. "Yes, I recall."

"Dunkaroos?"

"You're going to turn into a Dunkaroo, but yes. Check, check, check. Night-night, my ladies."

"Night, Mama," she heard them both say, and she returned downstairs.

On a mission, Raina headed straight to the junk drawer in the laundry room, a place Wayne never ventured, to pull out the folded-up newspaper from the morning. Then she crept up on Wayne as he sat at his office desk, poring over inventory and orders under the small lamp that lit only his desk surface while the rest of the room remained dark.

The squared paper in her hand rustled as she trembled. She stood for a moment, wondering whether to wait until she had his attention or to tell him she was there. Excitement made the decision for her, and she shoved the paper, ad showing, on top of his papers and under his nose.

He looked at it. Looked up at her. Then he wrinkled his nose.

Raina pressed her finger to his lips. "Don't say a word until you hear me out." She slid the wicker peacock-rattan chair beside him at the desk. She'd rehearsed what she would say in her head all after-noon, but that did not help one little bit, because the words felt jumbled and her breath caught in her throat, but she cleared it and point-ed to the ad. She sat quiet while he read the ad she circled. "I know what you're thinking, Wayne Edwin. 'Has this woman gone loco?' I haven't. I saw this, and I remembered that Mandy, the PTA chair, had mentioned a friend who did it."

His eyebrows tented. "You're actually thinking of..." He paused, mouth twisting.

She'd expected this, but she put both of her hands on her lap and continued. "Shush. I told you, not a word till I'm done. I called Mandy, who called her friend, the surrogate. She said she got twenty-seven thousand dollars. You know I've been looking for a job to help us out. Just till we get over the hump, which we will. I could do this—help another couple and bring us a good sum of money."

Wayne shook his head and appeared to try to stop himself from laughing, but he couldn't contain it. "The things that go on in that beautiful head." He folded his arms. "All this for a baby? You know you'll have to give it up, right? Because you'll never convince me that you could. Then what?"

Raina wriggled in her chair and went within for a moment to compose her thoughts. Anger pulsed in her veins that Wayne believed she would even consider taking on something like this if she couldn't follow through. No, she would have to set her mind on the goal by not responding with her heart but with what was in her head.

She began slowly, calmly. "You know me better than anyone else, and you know once I set my mind to something, I follow it through."

"Oh, yes, I do." He leaned back, and his eyes danced, almost as if he were entertained. "You got your bee business. You don't need another job. Focus on growing the one you have."

"I am, but you know the winter months are slow. The bees are seasonal, Wayne. And we need a lot more money than my little business can bring in."

"Not like this, we don't."

Raina's blood began to boil. "I'd be good at this. My pregnancies are easy. I have loved being pregnant every single time."

He nodded but still wore a smirk on his face.

"I know it wouldn't be ours, Wayne. I want to do this—something I know I can do—for us. Watching you walk around here like you got the weight of the world on your shoulders hasn't been easy for me. This is what I can do to feel I have purpose. For you, for the business. For our family."

"You say that, and I believe your intentions are good, but I also have to wonder... How much does this have to do with you wanting a fourth?"

He stood and crossed the room to the window. Raina watched him in the dark as he tilted his head, hitting the side of it with the palm of his hand. *Where is his faith in me?*

"We can find another way besides selling your body. That's what this is."

She held up one finger in protest. "But, Wayne..."

"How will you give it up?"

"This isn't about me wanting a fourth. It's about me wanting to help our family out of a rough patch. Don't you trust me?"

"How do you explain this to Father Sal?" Wayne stooped low bringing religion into it, knowing that was right where to get her.

"He'll understand. Don't you see that it would be helping a family who can't have children of their own—and us at the same time? If that isn't doing the work of God, I don't know what is."

"It's a job, Raina. A *job*. These people will control you for nine months. You can't believe they're going to impregnate you and relinquish you for the duration of the pregnancy."

"I am in complete control of the couple I select." She rose to her feet, strong and defiant. "I get to interview them. Me. Please let me do this. I can prove it to you."

Red in the face, Wayne brushed past her, stomping off. A few moments later, she heard the front door slam and the wheels of his truck peel out of their driveway.

FOR THE FOLLOWING FEW days, the air in the house was thick as sludge. When Wayne stomped, Raina busied herself with chores in a different room. When Wayne scowled at something mundane, she asked, "Do you feel like having meatloaf tonight?" knowing full well it was his favorite. Then she added more compromise, saying, "I'll make it just as you like, with the ham and Swiss cheese rolled in the center."

Raina had been with Wayne long enough to know he needed a cooldown period. She would walk this tightrope again, just as she had before. When Wayne avoided her, she found convenient ways to insert herself in front of him with innocuous questions like "How did the Jensen delivery go today?" The Jensens were Wayne's second-biggest customer behind the Belowes. She knew that since the Belowes contract fell through, Wayne had to keep the Jensens satisfied or they would be in serious financial trouble.

By the fourth day, she recognized the cracks in his demeanor. Instead of taking his morning coffee out to the shed, he remained with her at the kitchen table until they were both ready to begin their day.

Meanwhile, Raina continued to pursue the possibility of becoming a surrogate. After a brief telephone screening, she made an appointment to pick up an application at Give Life, scheduling it for shortly after she dropped the kids off at school so as not to raise any red flags. If Wayne asked, she would say she stopped to meet one of the other PTA moms for coffee.

When she arrived home with the packet in her bag, she scanned the farm and the shed. Not seeing Wayne or any of his employees gave her a thrill like she'd pulled off some kind of feat, the way she used to feel when she would sneak out of her house at night after her dad passed out on the couch. Reggie would still be in the same place when she arrived home in the wee hours of the morning, still snoring as she passed him on the way to her bedroom.

Once inside, Raina walked from room to room to make sure Wayne wasn't in the house before she settled in the laundry room, placing her bag on top of the washing machine. She pulled out the golden envelope like it was a prize to be savored, Willy Wonka's golden ticket.

The woman at the center had warned her the packet was thick, and when she held it in her hands, she felt the weight of the decision. Nine months. Her belly would swell early, as it had with Timothy. People would know. They would ask questions. She didn't care what they thought, but perhaps Wayne would. *Is that why he's so against it?* No, Raina knew better—his ego was a big one. He needed to get past accepting her help to support their family. Raina figured Wayne would soften to the idea over time, the way he had with most of her seemingly cockamamie ideas.

She read the fine print before she took the pen in her hand. She understood that once the procedure occurred, she would be under a contract and there would be no turning back. Her temples pulsed with pressure. *Could I give the baby up? I have to be one hundred per-cent sure.* She stared off into the backyard at the swing set Wayne had built when Tina was two. If it meant helping to hold their family and their business together, saving everything they had built, she could. She would do anything for her family.

She picked up the pen, leaned over the washing machine, and be-gan answering questions, everything from her place of birth and the quality of her childhood to the history of her own parents.

Harper
Oak Creek, Georgia, 2004
Chapter 11

Gabe found Harper weeping in front of the television. She couldn't look away from the horrors that played out like a montage. The show, *Zero Hour*, depicted the five-year anniversary of the Columbine school shootings. Of course, Harper had heard about the tragedy in the news, but she hadn't paid much attention other than to acknowledge the sadness of it. Something was different about hearing it and seeing it again.

For a short time in the ensuing years, she had briefly been a mother. Twice. Now she wavered on becoming a mother again. *Is this the world I want to bring a child into?* The thought terrified her that one day, her hypothetical children would have to fear going to school, fear being shot. *By other children.* It sent a shiver down her spine.

Gabe stood over her for a moment, dialing into the show himself. As Harper reached for another tissue, he turned it off.

"Hey!" Did he not see her staring directly at it?

"Stop. Just stop. It's sending you into a state."

"It's horrifying. All the families who lost their children..."

"Exactly. Why do you watch stuff like that?"

"Because it's real life."

Harper knew Gabe worried about her slipping into a hole again. By day, she cocooned herself in her bed, and at night, she paced

139

the house. He gave her the space she needed. All that loss—it consumed a person, turned them into someone they never wanted to be or thought they would become. Watching other tragedies helped her forget her own grief, sure, but it led to a whole new set of worries instead. Ones she hadn't considered.

"Let's do something happy today," Gabe said. "To take your mind off all of it."

Harper didn't respond. *Isn't this sad for him too?* Surely he must feel the grief that only she seemed to express. She thought back to the agreement she and Gabe had made before they got married—God, that seemed so long ago now—that there would be no children. Just the two of them. It didn't sound like such a bad idea at this point. If she hadn't become pregnant by accident, she could have avoided all this hurt, the emptiness it had caused.

Upstairs in her bedroom, the walls surrounding Harper began closing in. She noticed odd things like the wallpaper beginning to curl at the corner of a seam. A nick on a wooden windowsill. The paint had chipped there, and she hadn't noticed it before. Outside the window, the arborvitae had begun to lean to one side.

She heard the rush of the leaves rustling. Pausing, she tried to feel the same hum of her heart inside her chest. The feeling would convince her that she was still alive, even though she thought perhaps it would have been easier to die with her baby rather than feel this pain.

In her head, she knew it had been a fetus. She told herself it was. Repetitively, in fact. *Fetus*, the word, felt clinical, more like a specimen than a human being. A collection of cells and organs growing inside, evolving, until one day, it was gone. And everything shifted on that day. Not unlike the way it had shifted for the survivors of the Columbine attacks. All those parents—their children gone. Harper didn't want to begin to imagine the unfathomable void of losing children after raising them to their teens.

She got up, moved over to the window, and looked outside at the leaves cascading through the breeze. Soon the entire yard would be covered in dead leaves, the kind that smothered the earth and all the things that used to be alive.

When Harper was a little girl, she had played with dolls like they were real. Her mother had played with her that same way. Dressing her, coddling her, rocking her, sitting down on the floor for a tea party. Her mother never had another obligation that was more important. It was their "special time," Mom had told her. Why, then, did Harper feel so stifled? Suffocated? Smothered? At some point, as Harper grew older, she decided she never wanted to become that—a mother who lived wholly through her children.

"Let's do something happy," Gabe had suggested, as if ignoring the problem would make her content again.

During a recent visit, her mother had suggested, "You should look into marriage counseling. The last thing you want is this tearing you two apart. At least you have Gabe by your side, dear."

HARPER HADN'T REALIZED she was tapping her feet against the floor until Gabe steadied her knee with the palm of his hand. She gave him a passing smile, and he returned to flipping pages of a *Men's Health* magazine. Harper looked over his shoulder to find him reading an article on the ten best core exercises.

Three burning votives on a tray adorned the coffee table in front of them. Beside the tray was a sandbox and a rake—a tiny Zen garden of sorts. Harper considered swirling the sand round and round, but all she could do was look at the clock across from them on the wall, which appeared to be ticking loudly but moving slowly.

Neither she nor Gabe had been to a therapist before, and she felt somewhat paralyzed. Harper worried that she would become the center of their conversation, something she never liked to be. She attributed that characteristic to her upbringing. Her elder brother Ben had held that role in their family. Always the focus of her mother's attention, always the pinnacle she could never quite measure up to.

A broad-shouldered woman with silver hair opened the office door. Her eyes peered out from above her bifocals when she asked, "Mr. and Mrs. Alexander?"

Gabe stood first, making his way to shake the woman's hand. "Gabe. And my wife, Harper," gesturing to where she now stood behind him.

The therapist shook both their hands—a firm handshake, Harper thought, noting the strength of her grip. "Anna. Please call me Anna," she said, and she made an about-face into the office, motioning with her hand to the sofa within. "Please sit. Make yourselves comfortable."

Her office was a small room shrouded in shadows. The scents of jasmine and lime permeated the room from a billowing candle burning on her desk. The only light came in the form of a sunbeam cast across the floor from two transom windows. Beneath them was a large plush sage-colored sofa ornamented with a purple crocheted blanket and two puffy pillows decorated in feathers. Across from the sofa stood a worn red-leather wingback chair and a small round table. Dr. Devlin sat and immediately picked up a clipboard with a blank yellow legal pad from the table, placing it on her lap.

Harper sat next to the sofa's armrest, but she didn't lean on it. Instead, she perched at the edge of the seat, feet resting flat on the floor. Gabe sank down next to her. A little too close. *Is he trying to make a good first impression?* she wondered, as if it were a formality to see a therapist, that the mere act of it would put all their pieces back together. This would be the easy part.

Dr. Devlin—Anna—sat with her legs crossed. "So, what brings you here?" Her voice sounded enthusiastic, as if the therapist was ready to dig in.

Harper and Gabe began to speak at the same time, Harper saying, "We can't have children," while Gabe said, "I'm worried about my wife."

Harper's back stiffened.

Anna wrote some words on the page. "Why don't we start with you?" she suggested, nodding at Harper.

Before speaking, Harper turned a stern look on Gabe, who looked away. "I've had..." *False start.* "We've suffered two miscarriages, and it's been hard. I'm mourning the loss of two babies and also the ability to carry a baby to term."

Anna asked about a diagnosis, and Gabe promptly handed over the paperwork—placental abruption, low sperm count. *At fault.* Those were the words that that settled in Harper's mind as Anna reviewed the documents then nodded. "I see," she said.

Placing the paperwork down on the table beside her chair, Anna continued, "While not uncommon, this is certainly unfortunate and does put a strain on a marriage. Gabe, you mentioned feeling worried. What about?"

Gabe clasped his hands on his knees and took a gasp of air before beginning. "She goes into a depression each time, to a very dark place."

"I'm mourning, Gabe," Harper said. "I know you don't understand that the way I do."

Gabe's eyes glossed over with moisture.

Anna leaned in. "Harper, can you put into words what that feels like?"

Harper stared at nothing for a moment, trying to gather her words. "Empty. Sad." There was something else she wanted to say, and fiddling with the scarf that fell at her lap, she conjured up the nerve. "Guilty."

"Guilty of what?"

"Being less than..." Harper lowered her head, holding it with her left hand. "Not enough. Not being able to... not being able to carry a baby." She turned to Gabe. "You wanted a..."

Gabe closed up what little gap was between them, drawing her close. "I don't blame you."

"But you do. You want me not to feel it. You want me to just... to just move on. Make a new plan. I can't. I'm not like you."

"I don't want you not to feel it. I feel it too. I want to help you feel better. I'm trying to do what is best. For *you*."

"This is good," Anna interjected. "Productive communication is at the core of healing. Harper, how are you not like Gabe?"

Harper shifted in her seat, and Gabe dropped his arm to his side, which was what she wanted him to do. "These babies were inside me. Part of me. I know you didn't feel that connection yet. It's biology, Gabe. Each time I lost one, I lost part of myself."

Gabe's head fell forward. His fingers picked at the cord on the edge of the couch cushion. "Why does this have to be a competition over who's grieving more? I'm just as sad as you."

Anna repositioned her glasses. "It's not uncommon to feel alone in your grief, because it's often all-consuming. People grieve differently."

Harper's eyes were downcast, focusing on the pattern of her scarf—little pink and brown flowers. She'd never seen brown flowers. *Why are they brown?* "All I need is time. To process. To heal. To figure out what's next."

With a wounded look in his eyes, Gabe asked, "What do you mean?"

Anna nodded at Harper. "Can you articulate that?"

"You keep pressuring me to make a plan. To look at adoption. Or a surrogate. All the options. What if I don't want to think about any of that and just want to get back to our lives?"

Anna plucked her bifocals from her nose. "There's comfort in thinking about how life used to be before the pain, isn't there?"

Harper nodded. She didn't look to see Gabe's reaction.

"Is that something you're willing to do, Gabe? Give Harper the time she needs to heal?"

On the way home, the air between the two of them was thick with uncertainty. Harper fumbled through the radio stations to find a song that mirrored her mood, but when she couldn't, she turned the radio off.

The silence persisted in Harper's ears, ringing. She retraced the words of their session, which felt unfinished, and their relationship, which seemed more unraveled than before. Of course, she shared her truth about feeling pressure from Gabe. Pressure to focus on the next step when she wasn't sure that step would even include trying again, no matter the method. Before, she had been afraid stating her real feelings would sting too much and the words would come out all wrong. The last thing she wanted was to hurt Gabe. Why, then, did she feel safe to express herself in front of the therapist? She and Gabe had never dealt with communication problems before her pregnancy.

As Harper gazed out the window, she couldn't help but notice the young family as they walked along the leaf-covered sidewalk, swishing through the piles. A dad pushing a baby carriage and a mom walking a beagle on a leash. For a moment, Harper watched them, trying to conjure up a whole life for them. They had bought the dog first because the wife wasn't sure she wanted to be a mother. The dog had been a surprise for the husband because he wanted a baby, not a dog. But he fell in love with the puppy, babying him with toys and treats and cuddle time. When the wife became pregnant, she wasn't so afraid anymore.

That was what pulled Harper back into the car. Perhaps she should have talked about the fear. Not the fear of losing a baby again, for that was obvious, but her first fear—that she wouldn't be a good mother.

IN THE DAYS FOLLOWING their counseling, Harper couldn't get the image of that beagle walking with its family out of her mind.

While Gabe was off at work and she was preparing to leave, Harper stood in her empty house. When she walked through the foyer to the kitchen, her footsteps echoed. Had she ever noticed that before? She gazed out across the backyard, vast and empty. Even the flowers in her once-prized garden seemed bleak. She and Gabe were both minimalists when it came to decorating their home, both outside and in. Except for a few cherished items, old and new, she'd made it a point not to be a collector of things and prided herself on being more practical in nature than her mother, whose wall shelves and curio cabinet were filled with knickknacks: Lladró, old books, Austrian crystal figurines the kids had bought her for special occasions. The items not on display in the house were kept in the attic, which was full of things her mother couldn't part with—keepsakes from both of her children, including their toys, kept for her future grandchildren. Wedding gifts that had gone unused. Clothes from special occasions that she couldn't bear to give to Goodwill. The last time Harper was up there, she'd suggested having a tag sale—an idea that overtly insulted her mother.

But standing here in her own grand house, Harper homed in on the absence of cherished things that make a house a home, that exuded warmth. Even the few trinkets she had didn't cast off a ray of warmth. They were useful. Functional, not sentimental. *Why didn't I notice that before I got pregnant?*

That feeling was what led her to the pound on the way home from work. A grizzled man filled out paperwork at the front desk while a teenage girl stood beside him holding a tiny, long-haired kitten in her arms.

When Harper approached, she asked about a dog.

"We have a few dogs," the man said. "What are you looking for more specifically? Small, medium, big?"

"Oh, I don't know," Harper said. "I don't know much about dogs. But I really want a puppy."

"I ain't got no puppies here, but Greenfield, about twenty minutes away, just got a rescue litter of lab mixes."

He gave her directions, and she was out the door, humming during her drive to the Greenfield dog pound. It was the first time in a long time that she wasn't thinking about death and babies, adoption, or surrogacy. Instead, she focused on the puppies she was about to meet, the whole while imagining the glint in Gabe's eyes when she brought one home. A dog might fill the gaping hole Gabe felt and infuse their empty home with the love it was lacking. It was the least she could do.

She was led by a young man in blue coveralls to the back of the pound and a row of cages filled with barking dogs: some eager with noses pointing between the rungs of their cages, some sleeping or sulking in corners. The place smelled of wet dog and day-old urine. *These poor babies. Their innocent faces.* Harper wished they could all find homes, but she could only take one.

"Well, miss, here they are. Only four left. Three boys and a girl. The one with the little white patch on her neck is the girl." The cage rattled as the man unlocked it. "You can go right in."

Harper took a step inside. She knelt down and was almost bowled over by two black Labrador pups while their weary-looking mom lay on her side.

It had been her intention to choose the girl puppy, being partial to girls in the first place. But the girl hovered near her mom. The two boy pups at her knees yapped and looked at her with brown saucer eyes that nearly took up their whole faces.

"Go on, miss. Pick 'em up. See who you like."

She picked up the one on her right because it was slightly more playful than the other. It squirmed in her arms as she petted it, then she put him down to pick up the smaller one with a quarter-sized white patch on his chest.

"That's the runt," the man said.

She held the puppy up to her chest, and it nuzzled its little head into her neck.

"The runt?" she asked. "Is he healthy?"

"Yes, ma'am. He's a little sleepy now. He gets more playful but not as much as the other one." He gestured to the one she had just held. "The runt is a good mix of both, if you're looking for a boy."

Harper breathed in the puppy scent of the runt—vanilla malt. "I'll take this one. He seems like a cuddler."

"Oh yes, ma'am, he is."

Harper found a blanket in the trunk of her car to wrap the puppy in, and she put him on the front seat beside her. He curled up and slept the whole way home.

Once inside the foyer, she held him up to her face. "This is your new home, baby. What do you think?" She put him on the floor, where he took a few steps, his little paws slipping on the shiny tile.

For two hours until Gabe came home, Harper didn't let the puppy leave her sight. Names for him rolled around in her head. Should she name him herself or wait for Gabe to weigh in? A host of possibilities filled her head: Nico, Bailey, Reggie, Moose. She immediately crossed Nico off the list because Nicolas was among the boys' names they'd considered. With the possibility of still having a baby looming, she didn't want to omit the name because she had given it away to a dog.

She rifled through the list of names they had nixed for baby boys: Oliver, Sailor, Davis. Either she hadn't liked them or Gabe didn't. Finding a name had seemed like the most difficult part of having a child, before, when the thought of losing a child hadn't even crossed her mind.

The puppy began tugging at the corner of the oversized pillow on the floor. "Oh no, you don't. Do I have to puppy-proof for you?" She looked at him square in the face, seeing his innocence. His eyes looked stunned at her tone, locked on her. Yes, this was a good decision. It would give her a chance to determine if she had it in her to be a good mom, and it would provide Gabe with something to focus on in the interim between the present and how—and if—they would grow a family in the future.

Just then, the front door opened. Harper felt her adrenaline kick in. She scooped up the puppy in her arms, and as Gabe rounded the corner, he did a double-take. "Harper?" he asked.

"Surprise," she said. "Our new baby!"

Gabe stood, speechless, in the doorway, as she extended the puppy out to him. "Whose is that?"

"Ours."

"Ours?" His eyebrows creased, meeting in the center of his face like a unibrow.

Harper looked at him, puzzled. *How can he not fall in love with this face?* "A perfect distraction, isn't he?"

"A lot of work."

"Oh, Gabe. You wanted a baby, for God's sake."

Gabe side-eyed her, biting his lip as if he wanted to say something but was choosing not to. Instead, he rifled through the mail in his hands.

Harper looked at the puppy admiringly. "He's the runt," she said. "I took him because he's the runt. He needs love, Gabe. We have so much love to give while we're figuring all of this out."

Gabe set the mail down on the counter then shed his coat and took it to the front-hall closet. Harper waited for some kind of reaction.

"I'm going to get changed," he hollered from the foyer.

When he returned in sweatpants and a T-shirt, Harper was fixing the puppy his dinner, kibbles with a few drops of warm water to soften them. "I didn't name him yet," she said. "Any ideas? We can just call him Puppy for now. He's a lab mix. They aren't sure what he's mixed with. Boxer, they think. So he may be a bit smaller than a full-bred lab."

Gabe watched the puppy run in circles, trying to catch his tail. "So, this is your solution?"

"My solution?" Harper was taken aback.

"You don't want a baby?"

"This has nothing to do with wanting to try again—whatever we decide." *Are my reservations that transparent?* "You said we should do something happy. This is happy."

Gabe nodded and went about putting together a quick dinner of Caesar salad with some grilled shrimp.

Later, Harper suggested they set up the puppy's crate in their bedroom, but Gabe refused. Standing at the open door to what had been the nursery, Harper said, "Let's put him in here." Gabe grimaced but set it up in there anyway, next to the empty crib, as Harper stood over him with the puppy in her arms, stroking his soft fur.

As soon as the puppy realized he was to go into the crate, he stiffened his legs. When the crate door closed, he began to bark in high-pitched cries. Gabe shot Harper an I-told-you-so look, but Harper pretended she didn't see it, draping the blanket over the top and two sides. "Maybe this will comfort him."

While lying in bed, both flat on their backs, staring up at the ceiling, they listened to the puppy's shrieks.

"It will pass if we let him bark," Gabe kept saying. He knew Harper might give in at any moment.

"I know, but he's just a baby."

"It's training. Firm is good," Gabe said. "Otherwise, he'll do this every night."

"This is the reason children are meant to have two parents," Harper huffed. She pulled the blankets over her shoulder and turned away from Gabe.

Much later, while Gabe was snoring and after the puppy had settled, Harper got up and tiptoed into the nursery, just to check on him. He stirred and let out a little yelp. Compelled to comfort him, she picked the puppy up in her arms. *He must be missing his mom and siblings.* Gabe hadn't seen them all together. If he had, he might have felt differently about being so firm on the first night. She savored the feel of his warm, fluffy body, holding him close to her chest. She could feel his little heart thumping. *What harm would it be to have him sleep with us for one night?*

She tiptoed back to their bedroom and slipped quietly under the covers, tucking the puppy in the crook of her arm. They both fell soundly to sleep.

AT THE REAL ESTATE office the following day, Harper found herself busy with paperwork. She was glad for it as a distraction from worrying about her little guy at home in his crate, wondering where his new mom had gone.

She closed two lucrative deals and put in an offer on a house a middle-aged couple had bid on because they were downsizing after the last of their children moved away. Now it was up to the fate of the listing agent, who warned she had several offers.

There was one more task to accomplish before she could head home to see how the puppy had managed in his crate for four hours.

She kept looking at the clock the whole time. *Is this what it will be like to have children? A worry a minute?* If she'd learned anything about mothering from her own, the worrying never stopped—of course, Harper had always believed that to be an exaggerated characteristic unique to her mom, who went overboard in everything. Harper would never be *that* mother.

"I'm heading out to the Eton Woods then home," Harper informed the secretary, who liked to know her whereabouts at all times. "Let me know if that offer comes through," she said just before the door closed behind her.

Eton Woods was a listing she'd taken on as a favor. Normally, she didn't involve herself in companies that flipped homes, assuming the risk would be far greater than the reward. Nonetheless, she had promised, and Harper wasn't one to go back on her word.

Eton Woods was located close to the center of Oak Creek, a neighborhood of old, once-stately homes that had become rundown. The market was changing, and the neighborhood was slowly catching up. When Harper pulled up to a Federal colonial with chipped gray paint and exterior brick near the entryway, she could see the potential beyond its wounded appearance.

She dodged scaffolding and two contractors as she made her way up the cracked walkway to the house then knocked on the trim of the open doorway. "Hello," she called out.

She turned back to the contractors, but they were gone. "Hello!"

A tall man with a scruffy beard appeared. He looked to be in his late thirties. "Hey." He wiped the sawdust off his hands onto his dirty jeans and reached out to shake hers.

Harper winced and reluctantly gave him her hand, barely touching his enough to shake it. "Harper."

His head tilted.

"House Divine Real Estate," she added.

"Yes. Sorry. Cody." Harper could detect almost a blush beneath the sheen of sawdust on the man's face. "I was expecting Judy. I forgot she told me you'd be coming instead. Let me show you around."

Harper walked hesitantly over boards and nails as they toured the inside of the first floor, which had been stripped to the studs. It was a spacious twelve-room home, very charming and with plenty of potential. Cody asked if she'd worked with any flippers before, and she told him she hadn't. She'd only agreed to this because Judy was a colleague who had moved, and various agents had taken on her open projects.

"Our agency primarily deals with upscale homes that are usually turnkey," she explained. "Judy especially liked working on flipped projects."

"It can be lucrative. You need the right team," Cody said. "Look, I appreciate you taking this on to finish off where Judy started, but I'd love to establish a relationship."

Harper's head jerked up. *What is he asking?*

"This works best when a company like ours collabs with an agent who can lead us to low-priced properties and foreclosures before they hit the market. This neighborhood and its turnaround is ripe for projects like this."

Harper could see the possibilities, so she nodded but didn't know if she had any interest in such a risk. She already had enough of those, primarily of the personal nature.

"I can put together some numbers," Cody said. "If you like where this project goes, think about it. I'll be looking to replace Judy with an agent interested in partnering with us."

Harper told him she would think about it, but really what she was thinking about was getting home to her puppy, hoping he wasn't knee-deep in excrement. Gabe would have a field day with that. She shook Cody's hand, this time with a little more enthusiasm. He seemed like a nice-enough guy to work with. She would have to see how the house evolved and what kind of profit it might turn.

As she approached her front steps, she stopped before placing the key in the lock. Silence. *That's a good sign.* As she opened the front door, she could hear the puppy start to whimper and rattle his cage.

She knelt down as she opened the crate door. He almost fell out of it, clawing so much to get to her. He jumped on her lap, causing her to tumble over onto the floor, where he licked her whole face. Then she felt something hot on her shoulder. When she turned her face toward him, she saw he was peeing. Harper let out an exuberant laugh.

THE DOORBELL RANG. The puppy screeched, hiding in the middle of the table stand in the foyer. Harper chuckled over him obviously thinking he was hidden when he was still in plain sight.

The door opened before she got to it, and her mother came through with a baby-blue gift bag.

"Oh, Mom, you didn't."

"Begrudgingly, I did. Dad insisted. Do you really think this is a good idea, Harper? Adding to your stress."

Harper took the bag, peeking in. "Just the opposite. It's alleviating it." She pulled out a little stuffed lamb and some tiny puppy treats.

"Oh, he is darling, isn't he?" Her mother bent down, and the puppy trotted over to her. "What's his name?"

"Thank you, Mom. He doesn't have one yet."

"Doesn't have one yet?"

"We're taking our time. Getting to know him."

Harper could see her mother swallowing her words. She did this thing where she pursed her lips tighter than usual, willing the words not to escape.

"That's absurd," her mother finally said.

Harper picked up the puppy. "I made us some tea. Come on, little guy."

"So, your dad is thinking about retiring."

"How do you feel about that?"

"It could be wonderful. It could be awful. You know Dad, always having to be so busy. He'll drive me crazy. I take my time but adhere to a schedule of my own. How are you and Gabe doing?"

Harper bit her lip. "Um, okay."

"Just okay?"

"We had our second session with the therapist. It was hard but good to get it all out. She mediates well, I can say that."

"So?"

"So. Nothing. We're working on things."

"Did you make a decision about a baby? I know you've been going around about that."

"Or avoiding going around about it. I think he's mad I got the dog."

"You didn't tell him?"

"I wanted it to be a surprise. Surprise—he's not happy. I thought this would help get us ready until we decide."

"Decide if you're ready? Or how to go about it?"

"We have everything we need in terms of how to go about it. I just don't think we're ready. Or maybe just I'm not. I thought having the dog would give us both time." Harper stirred her tea and kept one eye on the puppy, who was gnawing at a bone held tight between cute paws that looked oversized for his body. "He wants to adopt. I don't."

"There are so many precious babies who need loving homes."

"But the laws protect the birth mother. I can't risk—"

"Why do you always go to the worst possible scenario? You are your father's daughter."

"Uh, no. Thinking the worst is *your* department."

Harper caught her mother rolling her eyes. Of course she would deny it. She denied every character flaw Harper called her out on, so most of the time, Harper kept her true thoughts to herself.

"Surrogacy is something I might consider. At least the baby would be ours biologically. Gabe's worried about the kind of surrogate we could find. He puts pamphlets around the house where they'll be under my nose, as if I don't realize he's doing it. The truth is, I'm not ready. "

Her mother put her hand on Harper's. "I know this feels like the whole world right now, but once you figure it out, you'll have a family, and this will be all part of the past."

"Anna does a good job of helping us understand each other's point of view. I didn't realize Gabe was so worried about my mental health. I think it's just sadness, and he goes right to depression."

Harper noticed her mom shifting her position in the chair then folding her arms in front of her chest, her eyes looking lost for a moment.

"Mom, have you ever been depressed?" Harper asked. "I mean, clinically? Or your mom or dad? I read that it's hereditary."

Instead of answering, her mother pushed the chair back, which made a scraping sound across the floor. "Excuse me for a moment while I use the powder room."

"Sure." Harper searched her memory for any indication of depression from her mother or her father and couldn't find a trace. When her mom returned, Harper prodded, "You didn't answer my question."

"No," her mother said matter-of-factly.

"Not once?"

"Not that I can recall." She stared at the puppy on Harper's lap.

"The sadness doesn't go away, but at least I'm not still lost in it. This little guy helps." Harper stroked the puppy's soft fur as he curled up on her lap.

Her mother reached across to pet him too. "You never asked for a pet growing up."

"That's because Ben asked and didn't get one, so I figured I never had a chance."

"Oh, stop."

"What? You always favored Ben." It was a wonder Harper still felt so close to Ben, considering her mother put him on such a pedestal her whole life.

"I never did. He was my firstborn."

"Come on, Mom. Nothing I did ever measured up."

Her mother leaned in. "That's not true. You just always felt like you needed to prove something."

Harper looked lovingly at the puppy, who was now fast asleep. "Since we've had him, he's been such a pleasant distraction that I haven't had time to worry about all my inadequacies."

Callie

Chapter 12

When Callie called Jocelyn again, as she had the past three Sundays, Jocelyn answered the phone with a solemn hello.

"What's wrong?" Callie immediately sensed something was off.

"Can you sit?"

Callie winced and looked around. Sitting wasn't possible. These booths were for standing only. *Why does Jocelyn want me to sit?* "No," she said. "You're scaring me."

"Jon was fired this week. Security walked into his office, from what I heard, made him pack his belongings then and there, and escorted him out. Rumors are flying."

Callie staggered back, and it took her a minute to catch her breath. She knew whom to blame. It had to be her mother. Evelyn must have snooped until she found him. After all, she said it herself—she knew people.

"People are saying he was having an affair with a young co-ed," Jocelyn went on. "Your name has not been mentioned. But they're painting a dirty picture of Mr. Taylor, that's for sure."

Callie's palms became so sweaty that the phone almost slipped from her hand. Her eyes teared up, but she steeled herself to channel her mounting anger. Now more than ever, she was convinced that Jon would find her and break her out of this place. What did he have left in Willow?

"When will she mind her own goddamned business?" Callie looked up and mouthed, "I'm sorry," to the girls in earshot. Then, to Jocelyn, "I hate her," Callie said through clenched teeth.

"What will you do?"

"Wait. Hope he comes here. Can you call him? I can't make any other calls tonight. It's one call per girl."

"I can try."

"He knows I'm at Covenant House?"

"I told him."

"Please ask him to come."

After she hung up, Callie spied Kate in her usual spot, reading across the room. "Kate, I need your phone call."

All smiles, Kate looked up. "I don't see how that will work."

"You can make the call, and I'll stand beside you."

"What if we are caught? They listen, you know."

"I'll take full blame. Full. I'm desperate."

Kate agreed and checked herself in with the monitor. She dialed the number Callie gave her. It rang several times with no answer. "Try again," Callie said, knowing she would have to wait a whole week before she could make another call.

Kate tried again with the same result. "I'm sorry, Callie."

Callie went straight to her room. She turned the lights off and prayed Jon was on his way.

WEEKS PASSED. CALLIE tried not to give up hope, counting on their history to convince Jon to come around, but with every day, it began to wane. Callie became sullen, opting to sit by herself at breakfast, remaining silent during group, pacing in the foyer where she could see the front steps. She waited, day in and day out, and she gave up her Sunday phone calls because she couldn't bear more bad news. Conjuring excuses for his delay only extended the inevitable realization. Jon wasn't coming, and she had no idea what might be preventing him from rescuing her except Evelyn's interference.

As Christmas neared, Callie thought for sure her parents would bring her home if for no other reason than for Evelyn to gloat. She'd taken away what Callie loved most.

Instead, her parents sent a few gifts. A sweater with Smith College embroidered on the front and SC on the back—Callie's initials, only backward, something Evelyn pointed out time and again to imply it was Callie's destiny to attend. There were underwear and brassieres and a pleated wool skirt.

The last gift Callie opened was from Asa. She could tell by the way her name had been written on the paper. She opened it up to find a musical jewelry box made of wood with a picture of Cinderella and Prince Charming on the top. Inside was a note written in her father's hand. "Dearest Callie, I miss you beyond measure and hope you find the strength and the courage to do what is best for you. That's all we've ever wanted. Love."

Callie wound up the bottom, and the tune from the film played. She remembered seeing *Cinderella* with her father when she was a little girl. He was trying to remind Callie of the dreams she'd made, only he didn't realize that a new one had taken their place.

That night after dinner, Jeanine, Susan, and Kate gathered in Debs and Callie's room. All in their pajamas, they sprawled across the two beds and between them on the floor. Kate braided Susan's hair, although Kate complained of cramps all night and retired to bed early. The others swooned over the cover of the Beatles's new album, which Debs's mom had given her earlier when she visited, but there wasn't a turntable in the room.

"We could go to the common room," Jeanine suggested.

"Nah, let's just stay here. Just us," Callie said.

Jeanine nodded. "We can sing ourselves."

So they sang a very out-of-tune "With a Little Help from My Friends," giggling and laughing when one of them messed up a word or two.

Afterward, they got quiet. Susan and Callie lay across Callie's bed, facing Jeanine and Debs on Debs's bed. They talked about what brought them to Covenant House. Callie's story seemed to pale in comparison to theirs. She hadn't quite realized the privilege she'd been born into until she measured her problems against Susan having been date-raped and Jeanine being duped into thinking the boy she'd slept with loved her. At least Callie knew Jon had loved her. And while her mother might want to disown her, she doubted her father ever could.

Callie lowered her eyes, feeling very stupid for making a big deal out of her problems like they were the only ones that mattered. "You're all very strong, and I'm fortunate to have met you." Her eyes met each of theirs, and she swallowed hard so she wouldn't cry.

"You know, Sebastian, I thought you were stuck up when you got here, but you're pretty groovy." Susan punctuated the sentiment by winking.

"Yup." Debs grinned at Callie. "She's very cool. Cool like a cu-cum-ber."

IN THE MIDDLE OF THE night, Callie heard a commotion coming from down the hall, then footsteps ran past her room.

She shook Debs awake. "Do you hear that? What is it?"

Rolling metal, frantic voices. One of the girls down the hall wailed.

Debs opened the door just a crack, wide enough for her to peek through and for Callie to get a look over her. Light shone in from the hallway, at the end of which was a gurney and one of the girls on top of it. Paramedics surrounded her, plus a few security guards and two doctors in white coats.

Callie and Debs were not the only ones peering into the hallway, as the backs of heads and bodies in night dresses could be seen down the hall. They all watched as the medical team moved swiftly. It was obvious something was very wrong.

Callie stepped out into the hall, and Debs followed. When Mrs. Goldstein, in her robe, moved aside to let the paramedics close to the gurney, Callie thought she saw bloodstained sheets. In horror, she looked at Debs. Neither could make out the identity of the girl.

One of the administrators came down the hallway, walking swiftly. "In your room, girls. Get to bed. In your room, girls. Get to bed." Her low, authoritative voice echoed off the walls.

Callie and Debs retreated, but Debs kept the door open to a crack of an undetectable degree so they could hear what was going on. Muffled voices over a radio, beeping noises, more crying, more frantic voices. Then, suddenly, it all stopped. High-heeled shoes were heard clickety-clacking down the hall until they faded away. Then, silence.

Debs shut the door and turned the light on.

"Do you think someone's dead? That was blood," Callie said, noticing the jagged scar on Debs's wrist. *Has someone tried to kill themselves?* Callie couldn't say it out loud. "I want to go into the hallway. Start knocking on doors to see who that was."

"No. We should stay here. It could be one of the girls lost her baby," Debs said.

Perhaps alarming incidents like this weren't as unfamiliar to Debs as they were to Callie. *I really do live in a glass castle, don't I?* "What if that happens to me?"

Debs moved over to sit beside Callie on the side of her bed. "Don't be silly. You'll have a healthy pregnancy, and you'll get the hell out of here like you're supposed to."

"What makes you so sure?"

"Because you're Callie Sebastian, and you're a badass for going against your parents' wishes to do what you believe in."

Callie looked down at her hands clasped in her lap. "I'm not brave. You're brave."

Debs's jaw went slack. "How so?"

"You were so low that you wanted to end your life, and instead of giving in to that feeling of nothingness, you fought back. You are fighting back every day."

"But don't you see? So are you."

"I'm waiting for Jon to come whisk me away. Take care of me. A substitute for my parents."

"But you said you love him."

"I do. But now he'll never come. My mother took care of that."

"Callie, you'll do what you do. You'll stand tall with your head up high, put one foot forward then the next. You'll make the decision. Not your parents. Not Jon. You." Debs's shoulders pushed back. "Take one day at a time. Do what feels right in your gut. Look how well you've adapted to this place. I thought you were a prim, but you're not. You're one of us. You'll find your way after you have this baby, just like you did here."

"Gosh, I never thought I'd make a friend in here. Thanks, Debs."

"Now, lie down. Get some sleep. We'll find out what happened in the morning."

Early the next morning, all the girls assembled in the cafetorium. Mrs. Goldstein, now dressed, stood at the front of the room. The sisters gathered around her. All of the girls whispered as they sat, still wearing their nightdresses, in their seats at the tables, which were already set up for morning breakfast. The sisters fanned off to the sides of the headmaster, who stepped forward and cleared her throat.

"Ladies. Ladies. Settle down, please. As all of you know, we experienced an unfortunate event in D hall last night. Kate began hemorrhaging just around two in the morning. We got the report from her roommate and sent for the doctor on call immediately. When he arrived, she had lost a lot of blood, and he could not detect the child's heartbeat."

The noise level in the room rose to a high decibel with their collective gasp. Callie's breath held tight in her throat.

Mrs. Goldstein continued, "Emergency services responded very quickly, and they were transferred to a hospital in Greenlee. I'm happy to report that Kate and her child are in stable condition. The baby was born prematurely, so he will be in ICU for a time."

A noise rose again, this time a communal sigh of relief.

Callie found herself caught between worry and fear. Kate's words from before tumbled back to her. *"We aren't that different, you and me."* Callie grabbed the edge of the metal chair with her fingers. Her muscles tightened. *Could that happen to me?* She'd never known anyone to have a baby under such alarming circumstances. Or had that been one of the perks of growing up in a bubble? Had her parents sheltered her from such realities of life?

Something deep within Callie seemed to shift. Letting go of the chair's edge, she sat, posture stiff, absorbing for the first time the weight of being a parent with every fiber of her body. Callie realized she was the only protection this baby had. With or without Jon, she needed to take care of her child.

At Mass, Callie bowed her head in prayer. She didn't pray for Kate. Instead, she prayed for herself and her baby—that the baby would be born healthy, that together they could get through anything. Inside her, the baby turned a somersault. Looking up with a smile, Callie wanted to rejoice, but all the others' heads were lowered. Instead, she focused on her belly, pulled her skirt to her sides, and she witnessed the most beautiful sight: a tiny bump extending from it. A foot? An arm? *My baby.* Maybe God was listening.

CALLIE WAS SITTING in the library, reading a book, when Debs tracked her down. The library was a quiet room with floor-to-ceiling books that reminded Callie of the library at Briarlee, though she hadn't appreciated it much then.

"I've been looking all over for you," Debs said, out of breath. "Mrs. Goldstein needs to see you."

Excitement brimmed within, and Callie closed her book and hurried to gather her stuff. "Did she say why?" *This is it. My moment. Jon's here. It must be him.* Callie shoved her book at Debs, who took it without question.

"Go. Go! I hope it's him," Debs hollered as Callie ran straight out of the library door.

She reached Mrs. Goldstein's office, straightened out her skirt, and retucked her blouse before knocking.

"Miss Sebastian, come in."

Callie entered the office, seeing a woman sitting in one of the red-leather chairs. She recognized the cowlick on the back of Mother's head. Callie made an about-face, about to retreat through the door, as so many emotions tangled inside her—betrayal that it wasn't Jon and anger that it was her mother.

"Callie," Mrs. Goldstein said sternly. "Your mother."

"I have nothing to say." She took one step out the open door.

"Miss Sebastian. Shut the door and sit down," Mrs. Goldstein commanded in her low, gravelly voice. Callie imagined running—through the door, down to the rotunda, past the clerk at the front door, down the steps... and then what? Where would she go? She didn't even know the location of Covenant House.

Instead, she turned and met her mother's gaze. Callie stood brick-stiff, staring at her mother through fiery eyes.

"Calista, dear," Evelyn said in a syrupy voice, the one she conjured to fool strangers. "Please, come in."

Callie folded her arms and shook her head but sat anyway. She looked straight ahead past Mrs. Goldstein through the window behind her, noticing the steel-gray clouds moving in.

Evelyn reached over to pat Callie's right knee the way she used to pat her head when she was a child. Two succinct pats. Callie moved her leg away from her mother's hand.

"Look at you, dear. How you've... changed." Evelyn kept her stare on Callie's protruding stomach. Three months was a long time. If there was a hint of excitement in Evelyn's voice, it was a mask for the benefit of Mrs. Goldstein. Evelyn's words poked at Callie's heart just as she had meant them to, Callie was sure.

Callie focused on the ticking clock.

"We've missed you." Evelyn's voice sounded sickeningly sweet. Sickeningly fake. "Your father wanted to be here, but he was called away on business." Lies. All lies. She most likely directed Asa to stay home or didn't bother to tell him where she was going. "You know his long trips." Her tone, as always, was condescending.

"Callie, perhaps you can tell your mother about your group sessions."

Callie clenched her teeth tight.

"Mrs. Goldstein," Evelyn said. "Will you give us a few minutes?"

"Of course, Mrs. Sebastian."

Once the door shut, Evelyn stood over Callie. "Look at me." She tilted Callie's chin with her cold, thin fingers. Callie averted her eyes. "I said look at me."

Callie looked daggers at her, her arms folded tight to her chest. "I will never forgive you."

"You'll not only forgive me, young lady—you'll thank me. Being a mother is not an easy job. You have no idea what you want."

"I want this baby. Jon's baby. And we're going to be together. I know why you sent me here. You're ashamed of me." Callie wriggled under the pressure of the fingers holding her chin.

"What were you thinking, getting involved with a... with a person like that? A junior administrator at your school, for goodness' sake."

A fire within Callie's body rose up like a dragon's wrath. "I love him. When I get out of here with our child, we'll be together, and I'll get as far away as I can from you." Her nostrils flared as she dialed in to her mother's smug look. She stood, stared straight into Evelyn's eyes. "What did you do? Mother?"

"He's long gone, Calista. You'll never see him again."

An acidic taste lodged itself in Callie's throat. Why wouldn't Evelyn say what she'd done?

"I saved you from yourself. This is the best place for you—to see what other pregnant girls are going through. I'm hoping you'll gain the good sense to decide not to keep this baby." Evelyn grabbed hold of Callie's wrist, her spindly fingers tight around it. "You have no idea what's in store, young lady."

"Tell me what you did to Jon."

"I showed him more civility than he deserved. Taking advantage of a young girl—"

"He didn't take advantage of me. We were in love. Are in love. Not even you and all your money can change that."

"We'll see, darling." She lifted Callie's chin again. "You're a beautiful little fool, Calista. This is me showing you my love."

Evelyn let go of Callie and stalked out of the office.

"Mrs. Sebastian," Mrs. Goldstein began.

"Thank you, Mrs. Goldstein," Evelyn said. "We had a very nice visit."

A FEW DAYS LATER, CALLIE was still trying to put Evelyn's visit behind her. That unwavering, self-serving tone. *Doing me a favor? She's delusional.* But Evelyn had succeeded at one thing. Jon had not made contact with Callie. He hadn't called, nor had he come for her. Evelyn had scared him away.

A glazed look came over Callie's face as she held the stuffed monkey tight in her arms. *How could I have been so foolish, thinking our love could survive anything?* Evelyn was always right, and she always got her way. Callie leaned over the side of the bed, her belly getting in the way now, and she pushed the monkey beneath it. She didn't need that reminder of her naiveté. She had a baby to think about.

Debs burst into their room, shouting, "Susan's gone into labor! Come on!" Leave it to Debs to pull Callie out of a bad mood just when she needed it most.

They sneaked into the hallway of the medical wing, hoping not to be noticed, but the minute they opened the door, they spied Sister Jean Katherine talking to a young couple. The woman rose up on her tiptoes, and the bearded man, his head balding, held her hand. Debs pulled Callie off to the side where they couldn't be seen by Sister.

"That must be the adoptive couple," Debs said, pulling on Callie's blouse. "Not old enough to be her parents, right? Well, the guy looks older than the woman does, for sure."

Callie snarled, not sure if that comment was meant as a dig at her and Jon. "He wasn't that much older than me."

"Sorry! I didn't mean it..." Callie shook her head, and Debs let it go.

Callie realized she'd spoken about Jon in the past tense. Maybe this was finally progress.

"What if Susan changes her mind?" Callie's voice rose as she began to panic.

Debs jerked her farther back. "Shush! We aren't supposed to be here. I am not getting a demerit. My program is almost done."

This took Callie by surprise. Debs hadn't shared that news with her, but she couldn't get caught up in it now, because there were too many more pressing questions. What if Susan did change her mind? What if once she held her baby, she didn't want to let it go?

Sister Jean Katherine and the other two were no longer in sight, but Callie could hear the *tap-tap-tap* of heels walking toward them. Scampering away, they searched for a place to hide, but the hall was a dead-end corridor with a locked door. They pressed themselves against the concrete wall, attempting to meld into it. Sister rounded the corner to the right, heading away. *Phew.* She hadn't seen them.

Then Sister stopped, pivoted her body, and glowered at them. "I thought I spied the two of you. What are you doing here?" Her words were pointed and stern.

Just as Callie was about to speak, about to fess up because she knew Debs had suggested this on her behalf, Sister waved her hands in front of Callie's face. "Never mind. I don't want to know. Shoo. Back to your rooms."

Callie and Debs walked double-time past the nun down the hall. They opened the door and ran down the stairs until they found themselves safely in the rotunda. Both of them let out stifled breaths.

"I'm sorry I almost got you into trouble," Callie said.

Debs laid a hand on Callie's forearm and laughed. "Don't be sorry. I love that kind of adrenaline. It makes me happy to be alive."

Callie smiled, grateful to have Debs as a friend. She couldn't have hacked it at Covenant House without her, and she wanted to tell Debs so, but something stopped her. "Do you suppose they tried to have a baby and couldn't? Or chose to adopt?" Callie asked instead.

Debs shrugged. "Who knows why people do what they do?"

"But I need to know. I need to know if Susan chose them as parents for her baby or someone else did."

Debs placed herself in front of Callie and cupped her hands around Callie's shoulders. "It doesn't matter about Susan. It doesn't matter about Kate. You're keeping this baby, right? You aren't changing your mind, are you?"

"No." On that, Callie was firm. "I'm not changing my mind, but there are so many unknowns. How will I keep her? Where will we go?"

Debs drew Callie in, patting her back while hugging her gently. "It will work out. It always does work out just the way it's supposed to."

Callie longed for a mother, but the kind of mother she'd conjured in her mind—one like Wendy. A loving, supportive parent, one who loved Callie more than herself. Asa had made his choice clear—a choice Callie knew he didn't want to make, but deep down, Callie knew why he'd chosen his wife over her. Evelyn was too strong a force to reckon with if he didn't. Of course, it could have had something to do with the Catholic religion. Asa was the force behind Callie's religious upbringing, and perhaps he was devout to a fault.

Two days after Susan's stint in the medical wing, Callie found Susan packing up her things, a teal suitcase open on her bed with her belongings all balled up such that the bed covering was no longer visible. In Callie's world, nothing was messy like that. Everything had creases and its place.

Even though the door was wide-open, Callie knocked.

"Come in," Susan said without turning around.

"So, this is it?" Callie asked. "Just like that, it's over, and you're going home."

Susan turned her head toward Callie. "Just like that." Did Callie detect a sullenness in the other girl's voice? Was she sad? Or sorry?

"Let me look at you." Callie's studying eyes scanned Susan for evidence. Yes, there was a little bump at her midsection, proof that a baby had been there.

"There's nothing to see. Girls have been dropping in all morning. To see if I've *changed*."

"Or to say goodbye. That's why I'm here." Callie stood next to Susan at the side of the bed. She picked up a black-and-white prairie skirt, holding it up in front of her. "This is pretty." She waited a second, but Susan didn't acknowledge the compliment, so Callie folded it into quarters and handed it to her. "Well, are you? Changed?"

"Still me," Susan said with a bright, fake smile.

Callie didn't believe her. Not for one second. "Are you okay with your decision?"

"Well, I made it."

Callie swallowed hard then handed Susan three rolled-up pairs of bobby socks. "Did it hurt?"

"The decision or the labor?"

"Both."

"The labor hurt like a bitch. I ripped. Down there. I have stitches."

Callie's eyes widened. Sister Jean Katherine had discussed this with their group, the possibility of tearing, but Callie had dismissed it as a scare tactic. Callie felt a sympathetic pinch in her crotch.

Susan faced her. "And the blood. I've never seen so much in my life. I don't think I'll have another..."

Sweat beads bubbled around Callie's hairline and at the base of her neck. Her stomach churned. While she knew all of that was possible from health classes at Briarlee and discussions in group, she still felt woozy. The prospect of experiencing all of it herself suddenly became very real. She bit the inside of her lip, and the thick, sweet taste of blood flooded the inside of her mouth. The room went off-kilter, turning on its side.

Callie held out her hand to Susan, who quickly grabbed her by the forearm.

"Sit. Are you all right?" Susan helped Callie sit on the edge of the bed. She took the nearest clothing item, swiping it across Callie's forehead. "Breathe in. Deep breath. And out."

Callie obeyed, repeating the process three times before her eyes lost the cloud that seemed to cover them. Then she looked up at Susan. "Can I do it?"

"The baby's coming out, one way or another. And yes, you can do it." Callie fanned her face since it still felt flushed. "All of that stuff I said didn't last long once it started—the delivery part. Before that, there were just strong cramps like a bad period." A wave flashed across Callie's abdomen. Was it a faux cramp? Did she actually feel it, or was it her imagination? "Go on, ask me anything."

"How long did it last?"

"The cramps? For"—Susan shook her head, thinking—"I don't know, about six hours."

"How did you know when it started?"

"My water broke right in the middle of class. It felt like a balloon popped, then a warm gush of water trickled down my legs. So embarrassing."

Callie rubbed her belly like it was a crystal ball. She'd never had the opportunity to talk to anyone who'd just given birth—had never needed to. But now it had become urgent. Under the palm of her hand, she felt a tender jab.

Questions darted through her mind at hyper speed. *Did you hold your child? Was it a relief to let it go? Or do you yearn for it like someone would when losing a part of their own body?*

"Did you hold it? After?"

Susan's head dropped. Her fingers fiddled with the ribbons on her blouse. Callie waited, wondering if she'd pushed too far, gotten a little too personal.

"Him," Susan said, her voice cracking. "Yes, they put him on my belly when they cut the cord. And no, I didn't feel that at all. One quick snip, and we were separated. For just a second when he was on me, and I looked at his pink-white skin—it looked like a thin layer of baby powder—I wanted to reach out and hold him, but I didn't."

Callie laid her arm over Susan's shoulder.

Susan cleared her throat. "But it's best I didn't. I couldn't give him a good life. I don't come from a family of means. I'm not like you, Callie. I know you think your parents will turn you away, but they'll come around. If you want this baby, you should fight for it."

Callie looked in Susan's lost eyes, and every doubt she ever had about keeping her baby settled like a calm after a storm.

Callie nodded. "I will," she affirmed aloud. "I will always fight for my baby."

Harper
Chapter 13

Although it turned out to be a stormy day, Harper held the first open house at Eton Woods as planned. It was never fun preparing for an open house in the rain. Despite her raincoat, she got soaked while planting the sign on the front lawn and attaching the balloons that kept tangling in the strong wind.

She had left Gabe and Puppy—the temporary name she and Gabe had taken to calling him—cuddling on the couch, watching television. "You two be good while I'm gone," she said when she left. At this point, she wished she had stayed home so she could be snuggling with them.

Cody greeted her at the front door to help her with trays of tea sandwiches and cookies and a bag full of punch ingredients—ginger ale, cranberry juice, and assorted berries. Grateful to have them unloaded, she smiled as water from her hair dripped down her forehead and into her eyes. "It's nasty. Not a good sign for a successful open house."

"They'll come," he said. "Don't you worry."

She trailed behind him, assessing the progress he'd made on the house since she last saw it. "This looks fantastic."

"I have a great stager."

"No, I mean the work you did."

"Have I impressed Ms. Alexander?"

She corrected him with a wink. "That's Mrs."

174

"Right, sorry. But have I changed your mind about a partnership?" Cody hadn't mentioned her representing future projects since the first day they met, but his offer remained in the back of her mind. And she could tell he'd used every opportunity to convince her when he shared the small milestones of the project during their brief phone conversations.

Before Harper made any decisions, she would see how quickly they could sell this property. It was in her nature to bet on a sure thing. By the looks of the house, though, there was a very good chance it would happen. His work was definitely impressive.

She walked around to investigate further while Cody laid out the sales folders near the food. Beyond the kitchen was a dining room with a long, repurposed wooden table with bench seats. A baker's rack used as a hutch stood against the far wall. At the French doors that led to a back porch hung a cascade of herbs in terracotta pots, which added to the rustic feel of the room.

The living room had large windows with transoms above them and featured a wall with a fireplace as its focus and window seats for bookends. It was decorated in soft, earthy tones to complement the old-and-new look of the place. While it was in stark contrast to her own home, which featured a much more modern, almost-crisp feel, Harper could get used to a house like this. It had a homey feel that her own didn't.

While she waited for the clock to approach noon, Harper arranged and rearranged the items on the island so they looked just perfect.

"Should we take bets?" Cody asked. "If we get an offer today that leads to a sale, you'll represent my company. If not, I'll leave you alone."

"Do you see the weather out there?" She turned her gaze to the rain pelting against the windows.

Cody bit into one of the sandwiches. "Mm, good. Did you make these?"

"Of course. Not for us, though."

"Oh, this is how you get all those real estate awards. Bribery." When Cody smiled, he had a deep dimple to the left of his mouth that looked like the hole left after poking dough. *Is he flirting with me? He knows full well I'm not available.*

"No," she replied in indignation. "Just making potential buyers feel at home."

With that, the front door opened, and both competed to greet the couple who entered. She should have talked to Cody about how this would go. *I greet the guests then introduce the contractor.* Harper made a mental note to talk to him about that when these folks left, only she never got around to it. There was a steady stream of interested and perhaps serious buyers, so instead, they worked in concert with one another. When she was with a customer, he would greet the next and bring them through the door, then they would introduce each other. They found a synergetic rhythm.

A lull came around two, and they both found themselves at the island, going through sheets of interest filled out by the visitors.

"I told you," Cody said, with no arrogance of any kind but simple confidence in his work. "My company has been at this for a few years, and we've developed a reputation."

Harper could see that. She read the comments on the paperwork and nodded. There was not one negative remark. So of course, she had to weigh the pros and cons. On the plus side, they worked well together. And projects like this would add another dimension to her career that she hadn't considered. In her work, she thrived on challenges. She worried only about timing herself out of more expensive listings where she found her expertise. Then there was the prospect of a baby. How much could she divide her time?

A knock sounded at the front door. "Hello?" came a demure voice.

"Come on in," Harper said, pulling herself from the home portfolio.

In walked a couple with two children about eight and ten years old trailing them. The husband reached out first. "Will Peterman. And my wife, Jean." A firm handshake, she noted—that equated to a serious buyer.

"So nice to meet all of you. Ready for a tour?" Harper couldn't help but notice the mismatch between parents and children. *A patchwork family*, she thought. When IVF had been ruled out as an option, Gabe had lobbied for adoption, but did she want to raise children who didn't have their biological makeup? What if the biological parents changed their minds about the adoption?

Harper shook her reservations from her mind. Work needed her attention. She had to make the sale. At one time, she'd been solely career minded, when everything she did was about building her reputation and her portfolio. Anna had suggested it would be good for her to focus on her work until her head was clear and she could make an informed decision good for both her and Gabe.

Pointing out the best features of this home was easy. Mr. Peterman latched onto the attic converted into a home office, accessible from a back-stair entrance. "I could work from home and actually get some work done," he said.

Mrs. Peterman cooed about the storage space and that the laundry room had been moved to the second floor, where the bedrooms were. "This is my dream," she said. "No more schlepping from one floor to another. Mine is in the basement now."

Speaking of, Harper showed them that this basement had had a facelift, too, offering the perfect space for a playroom.

"Don't sit on the decision too long," Harper cautioned. "This one will go fast."

"It's just beautiful," Mrs. Peterman said to Cody as Mr. Peterman filled out a form of interest.

Just then, a loud crash came from the dining room, the one room set off to the side behind French doors off the kitchen. Mrs. Peterman leapt to her feet faster than Harper. She was used to hearing sounds like this, Harper surmised.

Near the baker's rack, the boy stood over a shattered vase. Harper remembered seeing it fully intact and had thought it a nice touch by the stager—a beautiful multicolored tall mosaic vase.

"Jason!" Mr. Peterman's deep voice echoed.

While Mrs. Peterman pulled the boy away, she said to her husband, "It was just an accident."

Mr. Peterman looked at Harper, right into her eyes, and said, "Accidents follow our little guy." He ran his hand through his hair. "I don't know where that comes from. Neither she nor I have an accidental bone in our bodies."

Harper imagined a grown woman, a female version of Jason, tripping over herself. This vision led to more questions poking at her. What other things didn't the Petermans know about their own child? Did it matter? Would it matter more in the future? Did adoption complicate life even more than children did naturally?

The Petermans apologized profusely and thanked Cody and Harper for the showing. Once they left, Cody and Harper packed up what remained on the island, which wasn't much.

"See!" Cody gloated. "The rain didn't keep them away."

"Let's hope we get some offers coming in. I'll let you know tomorrow."

"You'll remember our deal?"

"I'll think about it," she said.

The truth was that she couldn't think about it. Changing or even altering her career at this stage wasn't an option until she and Gabe figured out their family situation. One little accident, the first pregnancy, had changed the course of their lives, setting their path on a different trajectory. Taking care of Puppy certainly gave her more time to work up the courage to try again. She and Gabe had found their rhythm with him. Could they do the same with a baby? She couldn't take away the one thing she knew would make Gabe happy beyond measure.

Cody carried a bag with the empty trays and some leftover plastic cups and napkins out to Harper's car. He shut the trunk and smirked at Harper. "Today was a game changer. You'll see."

On the way home, Harper couldn't get one thought in particular out of her head. If she and Gabe were to have children, she wanted to be biologically connected, somehow—at least through one of them, if not both. It hadn't occurred to her in that way before. While Mr. Peterman obviously subscribed to nurture versus nature with his earlier statement about Jason dropping the vase, it was clear to Harper that he'd inherited his clumsiness from a birth parent. She'd been so afraid of a birth parent wanting to reclaim an adopted child that Harper hadn't much focused on genetics. If her child were accident-prone, Harper wanted to know where that came from. While clumsiness would be the least of her worries, if there was something more severe like a health condition, the ability to trace the child's ancestry would be important.

Surrogacy was the better option for them. Her egg. Gabe's sperm. She made a mental note to take another look at the pamphlets Gabe kept in their office desk.

When she arrived home, Gabe was cooking dinner with Puppy, who wove in and out of Gabe's legs.

"Go see your mother," Gabe said to him.

"Come on, Puppy." She took one of Gabe's socks that had become a toy to entice the puppy away. He decided the sock meant playtime. He got down on his front legs then charged at the sock, grabbing it in his mouth, and he ran away with it into the other room. Eventually, Harper managed to grab hold of him and cradle him in her arms until he fell asleep.

"You seem to be getting used to the idea of Puppy," she said as she swayed back and forth.

Later that night, as they lay in bed with Puppy nestled between them, Harper said, "I don't think adoption is for us."

Gabe looked at the puppy.

"It's not the same as adopting a kid." She relayed her earlier experience and her rationale. "We should think about a surrogate. Besides, this guy will feel left out if we adopt, as if he wasn't enough," she joked. "At least if a baby is part of us, it will seem like it was meant to be all along."

Gabe looked at her lovingly. She could see the hope in his eyes. "This guy. Puppy. Doesn't he deserve a name?"

"You know, he does." She stared for a bit at the puppy's face. They'd already tossed around a dozen names, but one popped into her head. "How about Miles? For all the miles it took for us to get here to our happy, hopeful little family."

Gabe nodded with a peaceful grin. And as if Miles knew he'd been named, he sat up and took turns licking both of their faces profusely.

AT THEIR NEXT APPOINTMENT with Anna, Harper watched the candle flicker on the coffee table in front of them as Gabe talked about Miles and the effect he'd had on their daily routine.

"He's just easy, now—after the initial stages of house training. Miles has become part of our lives. In some ways, it feels like he's always been a part of our..." He hesitated. *What's he trying to say?* Harper looked up at him, anticipating. "Family," he finished.

Anna leaned back, crossed her right leg over her left. She looked pensive. Contemplative. Over the last several sessions, Harper had learned to brace herself in these moments.

"Do you suppose Miles has been like a trial for you to determine whether or not you still want a child of your own?"

Gabe looked at Harper, and she looked back at the candle, finding comfort in it somehow.

"Or a substitute," Gabe said very matter-of-factly.

To Harper, it felt like a gut punch. "That's not fair." Her voice rose a little more than she meant it to. When her back simultaneously stiffened, she made a point of rolling her shoulders to relax it. "I thought we needed a distraction... while we figured things out."

"Have we?"

Harper shrugged.

Gabe looked right in her eyes. He was on a mission today—she could feel it in his demeanor. What Gabe wanted to say in the comfort of their own home often waited until they were enclosed in this dim office with Anna between them as a mediator or a referee. *Since when did we stop communicating just between the two of us?*

Anna dropped her chin and raised her eyes above her bifocals in Gabe's direction. "Go on. You seem to have something to say. Say it."

Gabe shuffled in his seat, which made Harper feel uneasy. "Go on," Harper echoed.

"Do you still want a baby?" he asked.

This was it. The moment she needed to make a decision. A commitment. There were two possible answers. One led them down a path of comfort and familiarity, one in which she could have her husband and her puppy and a challenging new adventure in her career. The other was the harder choice, one that set them on a path of more uncertainty, more fear, and more trial and error, but Harper knew it was what Gabe wanted. She could see how much, in his soul, he needed to be a father. How could she deny him that after all they had been through?

"Yes," she said, hearing the hesitation in her own voice. *Could they hear it too?* "I think we should move forward with a surrogate."

THE NEXT DAY, HARPER decided to take the initiative of looking into surrogacy more in-depth than their literature at home so she could present the information to Gabe. A little surprise for the patience he'd given her over the past year since the second miscarriage. Harper chose not to share the idea with anyone else until absolutely necessary. Hearing the reservations of others might sway her again. She'd already read the criticisms of surrogacy. *How could you watch someone else carry what's yours? Wouldn't that person have a bond to your child forever? What if you don't get along with the surrogate or agree with how she conducts herself during pregnancy?*

Did she object to the reservations of others because she had them herself? There was only one way to find out.

Harper spent time on the phone with Tomorrow's Family, a surrogacy-placement office referred to her by her ob-gyn. If they were to try again, it gave her peace of mind to know the baby would be biologically theirs and the surrogate couldn't change her mind about keeping it. A bonus would be the opportunity to build a relationship with the surrogate and share in the pregnancy. These were facts reiterated to her at the other end of the phone. And still, she vacillated even after asking a host of questions.

"Would you like me to send along an application?" the woman from the service asked.

Harper hesitated.

"Mrs. Alexander?"

Yes, she needed to commit. To Gabe. To a life with a child. It was time to push her fears aside once again. She had done so before, coming to love both of her babies. "Yes," Harper said, noticing how the phone shook against her cheek from her trembling hand.

After a grueling application process and a home visit, Harper made copious notes about every step in finding the right surrogate on a notepad. She used it to inform the service of their priorities as they set up appointments with potential surrogates for the coming weeks. She felt as ready as she would ever be. Emotionally stable for the first time in a long time. Work ran nearly on autopilot with several jobs already in the contract phase. Miles was finally housebroken, and they no longer needed to puppy-proof the house. He'd been to an obedience class with both Harper and Gabe. If raising a child were a fair comparison to owning a puppy, then Harper didn't doubt herself half as much as she used to.

ON THE DAY OF THEIR first official interview, Harper woke up with a brewing headache. She rubbed her temples. *Not today*, she told herself. Her head still pulsed dully after she showered, dressed, and finished applying her makeup.

Gabe snuck up behind her while she stood in front of the mirror. "You look beautiful," he said.

"Beautiful enough that they won't say no?"

He kissed her cheeks. "You are always beautiful enough. Today could be our day."

"I know. Please stop saying that. Because what if it isn't? What if this is just one more disappointment?"

"Trust this process. Leave all our baggage in the past, and let's approach this with renewed hope."

All our baggage. Gabe's comment annoyed her. She couldn't help but read it as if she were responsible for the baggage. *Stop. I should be excited for today. I need to give myself permission to be open to this.*

To be hopeful, as Anna reminded her. *Then why do I always return to doubt?*

At Tomorrow's Family, a middle-aged woman with kind eyes sat across from them. She introduced herself as their caseworker, Ms. Wager. *The irony. If I could wager whether or not this would work... Stop.* Harper's palms were sweaty. She rubbed them on her pants legs before opening the portfolio Ms. Wager slid across the table in front of her.

"The bio, which you've already seen." Ms. Wager pointed to the tab in the binder. "Here are some additional papers she submitted, doctor's clearance, health record, birth certificate. We don't make these available until you've both agreed to meet. She should be here in just a few minutes. Here is the document I sent you already, in case you want to reference it. Basically, this is a chance for you to meet and chat. If you like one another and feel good about this, we'll proceed to signing the contract then begin next steps."

Harper looked at the caseworker. "We won't be signing a contract today. We'd like to sit with it a bit, mull it over. You understand."

"Of course."

"Is there anyone else looking at this woman as a surrogate?" Gabe asked. "We wouldn't want to lose her then ultimately decide she was the right match for us." Lines of concern creased between his eyes.

"We'd never put you in that position," Ms. Wager said. "She won't meet anyone else until she's officially off the table for you. Or a match. We pride ourselves in making the best matches for both parties."

Gabe put his arm around Harper reassuringly. She appreciated it.

A young woman floated into the room. Her hair was tied up in a ponytail, and she wore a knitted shawl in bold hues of blue. Over her shoulder, she had flung a purse that looked like patchwork denim, something she had probably made herself or bought at a thrift shop.

Harper's first impression was that she looked like a college kid, not the twenty-four years of age she had indicated in her portfolio. Out of the corner of her eye, she could see Gabe's eyes following the girl as she glided toward them.

She held out her hand, offering a limp handshake. "Hi," she said in a perky voice, chomping on a piece of gum. "I'm Gemma."

Harper was immediately skeptical.

Gabe and Harper made their introductions. Gemma sat across the table, the portfolio open between them.

Ms. Wager began the interview. "So, this is a chance to get to know each other a little and ask any questions that you have."

First impression made Harper's thoughts tangle. *What should I ask?* She'd planned out so many questions, but this girl was clearly not mature enough to carry her baby.

Gabe spoke first. "Gemma, what do you do for a living?"

She shimmied in her seat and giggled. "I'm a student. And, yeah, I work, too, if that's what you're asking. I work at an art studio. I'm an artist."

Her bio didn't say that. Not even five minutes into the interview, and Harper felt duped. "How do you manage that? What are you studying?"

"Art therapy. The studio doesn't pay near enough to put me through school and pay the rent, so I work at an art store when I'm not in class. About thirty hours a week."

"Ah." Harper nodded. "And you see being a surrogate fitting into your lifestyle... how?"

Gabe shot her a look. Harper wondered if her question came across as harsh.

"People do it all the time, have babies and work and go to school. A friend of mine is pregnant, and she takes two classes a week and waits tables. That's gotta be tough being on your feet all the time, but she says it's okay."

Gabe put his hand out on the table in Gemma's direction then pulled it back.

"I have to ask," Harper said. "Have you been pregnant before?"

Gemma moved the wad of gum inside her cheek and shook her head. "No, ma'am."

Gabe tilted his head. "There's got to be other ways to make money. Why this?"

"With all due respect, this is a lot of money. It could pay for the rest of my schooling. And I'm in pretty good shape," she said, almost as an afterthought.

Ms. Wager flipped through the paperwork, pulling out a document. "This is her medical record." Gabe studied it.

"Will it be difficult for you to let the baby go?" Harper's voice was firm.

"No. Not at all. I don't know that I want kids. I'm not in a relationship. I'm not really into guys."

Gabe bit his bottom lip and tapped the table with his finger. He looked at Harper. "Anything else?"

Harper shook her head then looked at Gemma.

The girl slid her chair back from the table and crossed her legs. "I see it as a win-win. I'm a young girl in good health. I need the money, and you need a baby. We can help each other out."

Harper rocked her head back and forth. "Do you have any questions for us?"

Gemma tilted her head, looked up at the ceiling then down again. "Nope. You seem like cool people."

After Gemma left, Ms. Wager asked, "What did you think?"

Harper had to be honest. "She seemed... wishy-washy, in flux. Not grounded enough to make a decision like this." At twenty-four, Harper had been far more mature.

"I'm going to go out on a limb here and say she wasn't at all what we expected. Is this what we can expect moving forward?" Gabe placed his hand on Harper's, and she nodded in agreement.

"We were hoping for someone more stable in her life," Harper said.

"To answer your question, yes, we get a lot of young women enticed by the money. But sometimes we get women who have families of their own and just want to give back to less-fortunate couples. Let's focus on someone like that. Shall we?"

"Look." Gabe leaned in, his chest pressing against the table. "This is a big decision, right? We don't want to waste your time. We don't want to waste ours. Our surrogate needs to be stable, grounded. Religious, perhaps. A mother herself, even better. One who isn't looking for the next quick fix to set her on a financial path. She has to be doing this for the right reason. We want someone nurturing, experienced, who can work with us. I don't have to tell you that we've been through a lot already. The less painful this process is, the better for all of us."

On the way home, Harper gazed out the window, replaying the interview in her head. "We don't just have bad luck. We have no luck."

Gabe grabbed the steering wheel even tighter. "I didn't think we needed to spell out that we want someone stable. For God's sake, isn't that part of the vetting process? If this is the kind of client we should expect from this agency, we need to consider looking elsewhere." Harper could see his face turning red, the veins starting to pulse on the sides of his head.

"I'm not mad. Don't be mad, Gabe. We didn't know just how specific we needed to be with our requests. Now we know."

"I *am* mad. She wasted our time today."

The next four appointments went similarly. Ms. Wager said it wasn't out of the ordinary to meet half a dozen people before finding the perfect match. "We do the best we can. Trust us."

Trust, and hope, was waning.

Ironically, as Gabe's frustration mounted, Harper became more calm, more resigned to a future with just the two of them. "It will work out the way it's supposed to," she kept telling Gabe, repeating something her mother had said a million times.

Callie
Elberta, Georgia, 1970
Chapter 14

As the crocuses dotted the front lawn of Covenant House, Callie still ruminated over her conversation with Susan weeks later. She couldn't get out of her head the things Susan said had transpired from the moment she felt the contractions to the way she gave her baby up.

It was Debs who talked Callie out of her preoccupation. "It won't do you any good. Keep your mind on your own path."

Each day, that became a little easier. Until Debs lost her carefree demeanor and sat Callie down for a talk.

Callie knew it was serious by the expression on Debs's face when she took both of Callie's hands into her own. "You know we're real friends, right?"

Callie nodded.

"Beyond these walls, even. You've made a friend for life in me. I am so thankful they made the two of us roommates. See, I told you—God's plan."

"What are you trying to tell me?"

"My program is over, Callie. I'm leaving today."

"Today?" This was too sudden for Callie to digest.

"Yes, Sister Lourdes released me. My mom is picking me up in a few hours."

"Are you ready? Really ready?"

"Yes, I am, thanks to you and everybody here. I'm ready to go back to real life."

Callie and Debs embraced, their arms wrapped tightly around each other. "I'm happy for you," Callie said through her tears. "Like, really happy, but I don't know how to be here without you."

"Callie Sebastian, you are one of the strongest girls I know. You can get through anything."

Callie nodded in sync with Debs's words, but it was no more than trying to convince herself of their truth.

"And when Stella comes, we'll get together so I can meet her, okay? Lafayetteville is only twenty miles from Willow."

Callie swallowed her tears. *Yes, I am strong enough to get through this.* "Can I help you pack or something?"

While the two of them put Debs's personal belongings in her suitcase, other girls stopped in to say goodbye.

"You know, Callie, they'll put another roommate in here, and you'll have to be the big sister," Debs said. "Just remember how you felt when you got here and how you feel now. That's what I did with you. She's going to need to lean on you."

Callie understood.

When Debs's mother arrived, Callie saw that Debs was a clone of her in stature and personality. Callie was grateful to meet her, even though it was a short introduction. From the front steps, she waved as Debs pulled away in her mother's old Buick.

Debs stuck her head out the window. "Remember, Callie Sebastian, everything works out the way it's supposed to!"

As the car got farther away, Callie could still see Debs's hand waving wildly out the window.

ONE NIGHT, CALLIE AWAKENED to a gush of water between her legs. Her first instinct was to use the bathroom, but then she remembered Susan explaining the warm fluid. She touched her thighs, frantic, worrying it could be blood—the incident with Kate so clear in her mind. *Not quite nine months. Will the baby be okay? It's still too early.*

Breath held tight in her throat, Callie pulled off the bedsheet and saw only a sheen of clear liquid soaking her nightgown and bottom sheet. She looked at the empty bed next to her, as she had done so many times over the three weeks since Debs graduated from the program. Callie longed for her friend. Debs would know just what to do.

What had Sister Jean Katherine said to do? She searched her memories and came up blank. Her only choice was to get up, find help. So she rose carefully out of bed, afraid that when she stood up, the baby would fall out. Although she kept her legs close together, water continued dribbling down.

The hallway was still dark, with a little light coming in from the window at the end. Callie went to the room next door and pounded on the door. She grasped her stomach as she felt what she assumed was a contraction—a sudden, sharp pain right above her uterus.

"Help," she tried to yell, breathless.

A sleepy Jeanine came to the door. She took one look at Callie, and her eyes bulged. "It's time?"

"Yes," Callie said, looking down at her soaked nightdress.

Jeanine pulled Callie inside her room to sit her down. She woke her roommate and told her to get security to contact the nuns.

Callie grabbed at her stomach again.

"Are they close?" Jeanine asked.

"Where are the damned clocks in this place?" Then Callie's stomach relaxed.

After what seemed like forever, a gurney finally appeared at the door. The on-duty nurse tried to help Callie onto it, but Callie pushed her away. Just as she did, a sharp pain attacked her like a knife while another shot down her back. *Is this what Susan meant? Or is something wrong?* Callie nearly fell from the edge of the gurney, but Jeanine and the nurse each grabbed an arm, hoisting her up onto it. Callie lay back, clutching her stomach and drawing up her knees.

The nurse asked if the baby was coming on time.

"Early," Callie managed to say through the pain. She squeezed her knees tighter to help diminish the stabbing pain. "Five weeks." The contraction disappeared as quickly as it came.

Jeanine held her hand tightly, walking down the halls with Callie as far as she could go. At the doors to the hospital wing, Jeanine smiled and said, "You're getting out of here soon. I can't wait to meet Stella."

Callie smiled back at her. Another contraction, like an electric current, traveled around her back all the way to her stomach.

In a cold gray room, Callie lay on the hospital bed, alone except for the nurse, who hustled about, doing her job. Prepping for the birth with sheets and silver tools and stainless-steel trays. An incubator was brought in by an orderly, which the nurse acknowledged.

The nurse appeared at Callie's side with a needle. "This will feel like a prick. It's for the IV."

Callie didn't even know what an IV was, and she was too afraid to ask. "Where's the doctor?"

"He's on his way. Stay calm. This baby isn't quite ready yet, but no need to panic. I'm going to give you Demerol to help the baby along."

Callie watched the nurse push the clear fluid into the IV line. Everything became a little foggy—the pain, the room. The nurse seemed to morph into a ghostlike figure. *Jon, focus on Jon.* She pictured him standing beside her with his charming smile and the dimples in his cheeks. She could almost feel the warmth of his hand wrapped around hers.

Another, much taller figure appeared in the room. Callie squinted but couldn't make out who it was. This one brushed Callie's hair from her forehead. "Everything's all right," a voice said, deep and calming.

Her body seemed to melt into the sheets, only a dull ache still apparent in her stomach. *The baby. Stella. It's almost time,* she struggled to say. Or did she think it? Aware of movement around her, Callie sank deeper and deeper into the bed.

Call my parents, she wanted to say.

Raina

Chapter 15

R aina struggled to hold two overfull grocery bags in her arms while turning the doorknob to the back entry into the kitchen. Finally she plopped them down with a huff onto the counter then shuffled back out for the remaining bags. The house was so quiet—it was almost stifling.

She proceeded to put the groceries away, jockeying around what she could in her already-overstuffed cabinets, wishing their kitchen was bigger to better accommodate a family of five. She loved her house, she really did, but with each child, it seemed to shrink. She thought back to the home she'd grown up in—half the size of this one—and reminded herself how grateful she was to have *this* house, *this* family.

With boxed and canned goods piled on the counter, she took to straightening up the cabinets to make the space she had more efficient. Then, out of the corner of her eye, she saw a figure that startled her.

"Wayne!" She expelled the breath that had caught in her throat. "I thought you were in the barn."

"Nah. Working in the office today." He scanned the countertops, covered with boxes of cereal, canned vegetables, Rice-A-Roni, and bags of snacks. "Did you buy all this today? How much did you spend?"

"I didn't buy it all. I'm just rearranging for more space."

"How much did you spend?" he repeated.

"I don't know. One forty?"

Wayne shook his head and began feeding her some of the boxes to place on shelves. "While I was doing the bills, I noticed you signed the girls up for dance. I told you, we need to cut back."

"They took dance last year. I'm not cutting out dance. They love it."

He grimaced.

It wasn't like him to question Raina's household decisions. She stopped what she was doing to look him straight in the face. "Won't you please consider letting me help in the best way I know how? Twenty-seven thousand dollars is a lot of money for nine months of work. And I enjoy it. I never minded being pregnant. Then we can go on with our lives. I can contribute with my side business. Hopefully, that will bring in more money now that I've established connections."

Wayne sighed. "You aren't giving up on this, are you?"

"No. I won't ever give up on something that will help us—help our family. Why should the girls give up what they love because our business has hit a rough patch?"

"Ugh, Raina!" His voice shook, but he was coming around. She could tell.

HOVERING OVER THE WASHING machine—her makeshift desk—with pen in hand, Raina recorded virtually her whole life history in one document. There were some sections where she skewed the truth a little, especially the ones that had to do with her parents.

Any history of terminal illness? No. *Any history of substance abuse?* No.

This was about Raina. Not her parents.

She double-checked her work and got all the documents she needed, including birth certificates for herself and for each of her children. She had the necessary blood work done. Raina slid the reports, the certificates, and the application into the envelope, then she licked it and personally took it to the post office. She wanted to see it stamped and put into the correct bin.

After two months, the phone rang on a nondescript Monday afternoon. Raina answered. "Hello?"

"Is this Mrs. Edwin?"

"Yes, ma'am."

"This is Alternative Pregnancy Methods Agency. I have a match for you if you're still interested in becoming a surrogate."

Raina's hand began to shake. After the first month of waiting daily for this phone call and being disappointed when it never came, she had allowed herself to go on with her day-to-day, put it out of her mind. But here it was. A potentially life-altering opportunity. How could she not seize it?

"You do?" she gasped, her muscles tightening.

"Yes, a lovely couple we'd like you to meet."

"I'm definitely interested!"

When Wayne came in from working, she sat him down, gave him a Jack and Coke, and opened a beer for herself. "Today was a big day." The thud of her heart beating in her chest had been ever-present since the phone call.

"I guess so," he said, looking at their drinks. "The kids?"

"No." Raina made every attempt to act calm, put on a show of composure.

"I did something, Wayne, and I want you to hear me out." Her mind flooded with words that jumbled together in one incoherent bunch. She stopped, put the beer down, and focused.

Worry lines emerged from the creases of Wayne's eyes. He started to say something.

She put her finger to his lips. "No. No. No. Listen." It was a commanding tone, especially for Raina. "I want to do something for our family. For myself too. It can't always be you bearing the brunt."

She paused, drawing in a deep breath. Wayne swallowed hard—she could tell by the way his Adam's apple rolled. "The surrogate agency called. The application, the blood work, everything is all done."

Wayne placed his glass on the table. Raina watched him get up and pace, and she waited for him to settle down. After a moment, he said, "I thought you knew how I felt."

"I do. But you haven't replaced the income from Belowe. We still need the money, and my bee business doesn't make enough of a dent."

"You don't have to do this."

Raina stood up and met Wayne where he was standing. She took both his hands in hers. "I want to. For me. For us. And I need your support."

"I'm just worried, the way you dive in headfirst. I'm worried it's gonna come back to bite you when it comes time to give the baby up."

"You underestimate me." She pointed to his glass. "Now, drink up. We're celebrating. And it might not be too much longer that I won't be able have one of these for a while."

"What are you saying?"

"They found a match for me."

Wayne scratched his head.

"Yes, a match," she squealed, dancing on her tiptoes. Then she planted her feet on the floor and pasted a serious expression on her face, looking straight into Wayne's eyes. "And this is a big ask, but I want you to come to the appointment with me."

Wayne listened intently as Raina explained everything she'd learned about being a surrogate. He asked questions about logistics.

"Is there a contract? How are doctors paid without out-of-pocket expenses?" Things men worried about. Raina, of course, was of the mind that everything would fall neatly into place because that was how everything had always felt since she'd met Wayne. Their love was a give-and-take of making things happen for the other person.

It was not what Raina had experienced growing up, and it was the very reason she knew Wayne was her forever, till-death-do-us-part person.

BEFORE OPENING THE door to the office they'd been directed to, Raina looked up at Wayne with a twinkle in her eye. "I'm silly-excited," she blurted out with the thick twang of a proper Southern belle. He squeezed her hand.

The office was comfortable, with five cushioned chairs situated around a large wooden table. Three of the chairs were taken. Raina and Wayne took their respective seats.

While Wayne shook hands and introductions were made, Raina's attention was immediately drawn to the couple, who looked both eager and worried. The wife leaned in while the husband held her hand, and a warm sensation welled up inside Raina.

The couple looked slightly younger than her but not much. She only knew that they were both professionals and were unable to conceive naturally. They dressed like city folk, especially the wife, in a cream sleeveless blouse and navy pencil skirt. Her hair was light, similar to Raina's, but her eyes were deep set and brown. She kept readjusting her position in the chair while continuing to hold on to her husband's hand as if to steady it from trembling. Attractive with short, wavy black hair and a clean-shaven face, the man was big-boned and dressed like he'd just come from the golf course. He had kind, unassuming eyes that he kept on his wife—almost as if he was trying to protect her.

Raina remembered this kind of mixed excitement she'd had as a young expectant mother.

"I brought some photographs of my family. I thought you'd get to know us better if you could see them." Raina opened a tattered manila envelope, and a slew of pictures fell out onto the table. Her finger circled around them as she decided on the perfect one to choose. "This is Christmas last year." She presented a picture of her three children dressed in complementary outfits. Timothy wore a Santa hat, while Tracy and Tina wore headbands trimmed in holly.

"They're adorable," the wife commented as she picked up some of the others that lay before her. Raina had been right to bring the photos, and as the woman looked upon them, Raina measured her spontaneous reactions of warmth and joy.

Raina had been a tinge nervous before, but the butterflies flitted away. She felt something for these two—a kind of kinship already, if that was possible. "Can I ask what you both do for a living?" Raina glanced first at the husband then to the wife, who returned her warm smile.

"Of course. I'm a realtor in Oakdale County."

Impressive homes there, Raina thought, wondering if this couple lived in one of them.

The husband cleared his throat then laid both of his hands on the table. "I'm a project manager for Courago Tech. We oversee the installation of tech systems at new sites across the state."

The wife cleared her throat. "He travels some, but my job is entirely flexible."

Raina appreciated her willingness to be flexible. Children should always come first. "My husband is a farmer, so we're both home most days. I don't work on the farm, so don't worry about physical labor or anything. I had three healthy pregnancies and pretty quick, natural deliveries, so I consider myself an expert. I'm a very involved mom, room parent, PTA member. I just love it all." Then Raina leaned in. "What are you all worried about?"

The couple looked at each other and nodded.

The husband straightened his back. "You seem like a woman who loves her children very much. How difficult will it be for you to... hand the child over to us after the birth? Will you expect to keep in touch afterward?"

Raina tucked her hand under her chin. "Oh, I hadn't thought of that as an option. The last bit. For the first, I don't think I'll have any more difficulty giving it up than any other surrogate. The way I see it, this is your child from the beginning, before it even enters my body. It's all about mindset, and I have a strong mind and will. And keeping in touch? I suppose that depends upon what we both want at the end of this journey. And it will be a journey."

"And how do you feel about this?" the husband asked Wayne.

"Look, I love my wife, and she wants to do this. She's committed to giving you the family you want. It's what I love most about her—the ability to fix on doing what she wants."

Raina was surprised the couple wasn't ready to shake on the deal right then and there, because she was. Instead, she was told she would hear from the agency within the next couple of days.

Raina stood and gathered her photographs, then she paused and pulled one out of the whole family sitting on their front porch on a summer day. Wearing a sundress, Raina held Timothy, who wasn't more than a few months old, in her arms. The girls, also in sundresses, sat on Wayne's knees, one on each.

Raina handed it to the wife. "You can hang on to this one. I want you to have it."

Between the end of the questions and the moment they were ready to depart, the husband stared at Raina for longer than made her comfortable. It wasn't a flirtatious gaze, rather a thoughtful one.

Does he think he knows me from somewhere? Raina was sure their paths had never crossed.

She shook off the awkwardness by hugging both of them because it was in her nature to be unapologetically affectionate. When she was young, her father used to scold her and say not everyone was comfortable with being hugged. She must have learned it from her mama, she was convinced.

Still, their reactions to the hug took Raina aback. The husband stood stiff as a column, arms at his sides. And the wife pursed her lips, though she tried to maintain a neutral facial expression.

Nonetheless, Raina thanked them and said, "I feel really good about this. About you. I hope you feel the same."

She left apprehensive that the couple's certainty didn't quite match her own.

Harper

Chapter 16

With the photograph in her hand, Harper nodded. "I'm sure we'll see you again." As soon as the words escaped her mouth, she wished she could take them back. It had been Gabe who was a hundred percent sure when they walked in today, but the way he peppered the surrogate candidate with questions, she wasn't so convinced they were in agreement.

And what was that look, at the end? He almost had a snarl on his face. Uncharacteristic for Gabe. *Didn't he like them?*

She supposed it was important for one of them to scrutinize the candidate. While that was normally her role, something in her gut drew her to Raina. A typical Southern mama, Raina seemed the perfect combination of sweet and fierce, the way every mother should be. In fact, Harper considered that through this *journey,* as Raina so affectionately referred to it, she could learn a thing or two about becoming a mother from her surrogate. Perhaps they could even be friends. Harper didn't question that they would at least be friendly.

The ride home was mostly silent. Harper replayed every question and response in her mind, sure Gabe was doing the same.

As they approached their front door, Harper wondered about taking their baby home for the first time. She could picture it so clearly—Gabe carrying the car seat while Harper fumbled with the lock, both amazed at the little bundle all wrapped up in a blanket. *Am I getting ahead of myself?*

When she and Gabe had first looked at this house, she had considered the possibilities, not once thinking a baby would be one of them.

After getting attacked with Miles love, Harper and Gabe set the binder out on the dining room table. While Harper let Miles into the yard, Gabe poured them two glasses of wine. He had been reticent to discuss their interview on the ride home. He said he was digesting it. And now he seemed to be making a grand gesture.

"So," he began. *Was that apprehension in his voice?*

"You go first," she said.

"Well, I liked that they are a couple. A little earthy-crunchy, though. Right?"

"I thought she was sweet. Perky. I like that she's down-to-earth. It seems like they are both on the same page. Very realistic about the process."

"Look, I know we asked for maturity, but Ms. Wager might have gone to the other extreme." He brushed his fingers through his hair while Harper reminded herself to *listen, really listen.* "They're an established couple. Three kids is a lot, and I have two concerns. Will it be too much? And how convinced were you that she'll really want to give the baby up? She seems like the quintessential mom."

Harper shook her head, feeling as if she'd experienced whiplash. "Wait! Now you're the one with reservations?" She took out the photograph Raina had left with them and placed it on the table. "As far as I'm concerned, we can check everything off. We don't even need this." She eyed the binder with Raina's history then gazed at the photo, noticing the way Raina held her baby with one hand behind his head, her expression radiant. "*This* is all I need. You told me to keep an open mind, and I did."

"But she's such a mother—she embodies it. It seems inevitable, an attachment to our baby. Doesn't that worry you?"

"I don't know. She seemed damn sure of herself, enough for both of them. Gabe, it's what we asked for. From the moment Raina walked into the room, I had a feeling. I can't explain it. It was like looking into a mirror."

"Yeah. I noticed that. Not that it matters. It'll be our baby she's carrying."

"More than the looks, though, I felt it. Like a connection. Come on. I want to do this for you."

"For us," Gabe corrected.

Harper smiled. Just then, her phone rang. She peeked at the number. "I have to take it. Work. I'm waiting for an offer."

Before Harper turned to walk into the living room, Gabe grimaced and began fanning through the binder.

The news from the office was good, and as she was returning to Gabe at the table, her phone rang again. This time, it was Cody. "Mrs. Alexander," he said, and Harper chuckled. She knew what was coming. "It seems you and I have a deal to discuss. The closing went through today."

"Well, technically..."

"Technically, a deal is a deal. Either way, it seems I may have found myself a new real estate agent." He didn't wait for her to reply. "I'll work up an offer and be in touch. Have a lovely day." He hung up his end of the line just as she was about to put the brakes on their agreement.

How on earth could she take on that role if a baby was in her relatively immediate future?

Gabe was scrutinizing the paperwork strewn about the dining room table when Harper returned.

"Well, Eton Woods closed. Cody apparently wants me to be his partner in home flipping."

Gabe seemed unfazed. "I haven't found anything out of sorts. This might be our couple."

Harper bounced from one foot to the other, adrenaline bursting loose inside. She picked up the photograph, drawn to Raina's facial structure, the same unbalanced part-oval, part-heart shape—something Harper hadn't noticed about herself until a friend once pointed it out.

They made contact with Ms. Wager before the day's end to set the process in motion. Harper felt safe enough to call her mother, but she wanted to tell her parents in person, so she invited them over for dinner. Harper would put out a spread she was sure they would enjoy. She pranced about the kitchen, singing and prepping.

"I can't recall the last time you've been this giddy," Gabe said. "We made the right choice."

Harper grabbed his chin and kissed his lips. "We sure have." She eyed the photo of Raina and her family, which she hung on the refrigerator with a magnet.

The hours sailed by as Harper set the table with her wedding china and silverware. She arranged fragrant calla lilies and poppies in a vase for the centerpiece, and she checked the Dutch apple pie baking in the oven, filling the air with the aromas of cinnamon and nutmeg.

The ringing doorbell sent anticipation through her body like an electric current. Her mother stood at the door with her father behind her, Adam's hands full of wine and salad. Harper's mom insisted on bringing something every single time she came by.

"I've invited Ben and Pam too," Harper said as they came through the door.

"Lovely," her mom said. "You didn't say so on the phone."

"An afterthought. I want all of us together."

"Having both of my children together fills my heart."

"Hi, Dad." Harper kissed her father's cheek and took the salad from him. "Wine goes to Gabe."

"Let me open that," Gabe said. He filled four glasses and handed them out, leaving two empty ones set aside for Harper's brother and sister-in-law.

They stood around the kitchen island, making small talk, until the doorbell rang again. Ben barged through the front door with his wife, his daughters Samantha and Arielle already dressed in their pajamas.

Harper's dad scooped Arielle into his arms. "Look at this princess gown."

"Papa! It's a nightgown, silly."

"You look beautiful," Harper said. "Both of you."

"Thanks, Auntie," Samantha said. "Where's Miles?"

"Oh, he must be sleeping in his favorite spot. In front of the fireplace," Gabe said. "Let's go find him."

Arielle squirmed out of her grandfather's arms, and she and her sister followed Gabe into the living room in search of the dog. Miles's little head perked up as the girls approached. Gabe fell down on the floor with the three of them and wrestled them all as the girls erupted in laughter. Harper looked on, taking it all in. *He is meant to be a father.*

She dipped back into the kitchen, grabbing wine for Ben and Pam.

"None for me, thanks," Pam said. "Seltzer?"

"Sure," Harper said, surprised. She returned with a glass of seltzer as the others continued watching the wrestling match on the floor. Even Ben joined in.

Later, they headed into the dining room to gather at the table.

"So, what is all this with the urgency? Do we have good news?" Ben asked Harper privately.

"A little bit." But she wasn't ready to tell until they were all listening.

Gabe had made a mouthwatering lemon chicken with sprigs of tarragon for garnish, Brussels sprouts oozing with a whiskey-maple glaze, and roasted-garlic mashed potatoes. Harper bustled about, filling the table as if it were a holiday.

"What is all the fuss for?" her mom asked. "It's just us."

"Nothing. I was just craving a delicious meal and family. What better excuse?"

Her mom squeezed her hand.

Conversation flowed about her mom's recent retirement and how she was filling her days. "Exercise on Tuesday, yoga on Thursday, and in between, I catch up with old friends for lunch. Sometimes I volunteer at the nursery. They love when I come in to make arrangements. Yours looks great."

Harper nodded, accepting the compliment with a smile. "Dad, Mom said you're thinking about retiring too."

"I am giving it some thought," Adam admitted. "More time with the grandkids. More time to travel."

"And golf," Ben added. They all knew golf was his favorite pastime.

Under the table, Harper tapped her fingers on her knee, wondering when was the right time to share their news. She rolled through the words she would say. *We're having a baby.* Would they object because it wasn't conventional? Express reservations that she would need to prepare herself for? *You are not less for being unable to carry one on your own.* It was Anna's voice in her head.

"Have you thought about cutting back your hours?" Ben asked their father. "I have a feeling retirement is going to get boring for you."

Adam relaxed back in his chair, a smirk on his face. "In my stately years, I've learned I have FOMO because your mother seems to be handling retirement so splendidly." They all laughed.

Harper flipped over the knife beside her plate. Two times. Three.

"Oh, I hope you won't travel too much," Pam said.

"Don't you worry—Nana and Papa will never be too far."

Pam got up abruptly from the table and dashed out of the room.

"Is she okay?" Harper asked.

Ben looked to their mother, who looked at Harper, holding both her palms up in the air.

"I guess she had to use the bathroom." Ben changed the subject quickly. "So, you are planning to travel. We'll never see you any-more."

"Are you kidding? Your mom lives for those kids," Adam said. His attention turned to the girls, sleepily watching *The Little Mermaid* on TV in the adjacent room.

Harper hoped they would love this baby, the one someone else would be carrying, as much as they did Samantha and Arielle.

Gabe was already eyeing Harper when she looked over at him. It was time. Harper ran her tongue across her lips, anticipation churning inside. Gabe grabbed her hand and nodded.

Pam came back to the table, looking steadier. "I'm sorry," she said. "A little upset stomach."

"We were talking about Mom and Dad traveling and not going far from their grandkids," Ben said.

"Speaking of grandchildren," Harper began. "We have some news."

Everyone's heads turned to her. She sat up straight and placed her hands on the table. First, she looked at Gabe, then back at her family. "We hired a surrogate. The retrieval is scheduled for next week."

Pam clapped. "Oh my gosh! We're so happy for you."

"I don't know about that," Ben said, his eyebrows furrowed. "I've heard stories about women who couldn't go through with it. Disasters."

"We have a contract," Gabe told him, coming to Harper's defense. "The couple is terrific. Checked off everything we wanted."

Harper got up preemptively and went into the kitchen. She returned with the photograph Raina had given her and placed it on the table.

Her mom picked it up. "It sounds like great news. What an attractive family. She has three children?"

"Yes, very healthy pregnancies, all of them," Harper assured her. "We even look a lot alike, Mom. We could be sisters. Not that it will affect the baby, because it will be mine and Gabe's, but if it were to affect the baby—well, her genes are good ones."

"That's great, honey," her father said. "We're so happy for you." He placed his hand over Harper's and squeezed.

Her mom studied the photograph. "She does resemble you," she said before handing the photograph to Adam.

"Please make sure your lawyer looks at that contract," Ben said.

"We have already contacted him," Gabe told him. "We've done our homework, but I appreciate your apprehension."

"It's going to be great," Harper said. "This way, we can have our own baby."

Ben nodded but with a flat smile on his face.

"Please don't burst my bubble, Ben. For the first time in two years, I really feel like we're going to have a family."

"Why not adopt?" Ben probed further. "It's clean and simple."

Harper sat up straighter. She wasn't surprised—Ben had always been a skeptical guy.

"The adoptive mother could change her mind."

"We've got it, Ben. We've done the research. Had hard conversations. Met the other couple." It was evident even Gabe had enough of Ben's questions.

"You don't have to get defensive," Ben said.

Harper placed both of her hands on the table. "I am defensive. Having a family is easy for the two of you." She was seething that Ben wouldn't allow her to have the spotlight this one time. She'd grown up with him being—needing to be—the center of attention.

"I wouldn't say easy," Pam said, looking down at her own stomach.

"We're losing sight of this," her mother said. "Ben is trying to be helpful. We couldn't be happier for you, really. All of us."

No matter their ages, Ben and Harper knew when their mom was present, she always had the last word. Still. And this time, Harper was grateful for her sensitivity to every issue. She had seen how broken Harper was after her miscarriages.

"It'll run smoothly. I feel it in my gut." Adam pointed to his stomach.

"Thanks, Dad." Harper's father always made her feel better.

"Well, on that note, I suppose we have some news to share too." Ben looked over at Pam, whose eyes darted away from him. "What?" he asked. "We can share too. Pam's expecting."

Harper swallowed hard. Time seemed to stop for a moment as she scanned the table.

"Fantastic," Gabe said.

"How far along are you?" Harper asked pointedly.

"Gosh, almost seventeen weeks now."

In one movement, Harper pushed her chair away from the table and darted toward the kitchen. She paced from the island to the sink to the refrigerator, contemplating what to do to make herself busy so she could stuff away the unhealthy feelings she was having. Of course Pam was pregnant. Shouldn't she have seen the signs? The blousy tops. No wine. Rushed trips to the bathroom.

She turned the faucet on all the way, and her eyes filled with tears.

A hand landed gently on her shoulder. When she turned her head, she saw it was Pam. Ashamed of her weeping, Harper turned back to the sink, dipping her hands in to find a dish to wash, trying to seem nonchalant about it.

"We didn't want to add to your stress," Pam said. "I'm sorry we didn't say so sooner."

Staring out the window into the darkness, Harper asked, "Did everyone else know?"

"Yes."

"I feel pathetic. You shouldn't have left me out."

"Mom didn't want to add to..."

Harper's body twisted around. "To what?"

"Well, you know. She was worried. We were all worried."

"I'm fine. I'm not going to lose it. I was mourning the death of my child... of my children, for God's sake. Not that any of you know what that's like."

Her mother walked in. "You two okay?"

"One of us would have been a lot better if you hadn't felt the need to keep secrets," Harper said. "I feel like a complete idiot for not picking up on anything. I'm happy for you. I am."

"We know you are, sweetheart." Her mom pulled Harper's hair back off her shoulders, the way she had when Harper was little. "Now you both have something to celebrate, and we couldn't be happier for both of you."

"Our babies won't be far apart. Or maybe I'm putting the cart in front of the horse," Pam said, trying to assuage the situation. She often played referee between Ben and Harper, and now she was situating herself between Harper and her mother.

At the end of the night, Ben pulled Harper aside before he left. "Don't mistake what I said for unhappiness. If it all works out, no one will be happier for you than me. Well, Gabe and Mom, maybe, but you know I'm next in line. I just don't want to see you hurt."

"Ben, I can't be more hurt than I was. This has to work. I won't accept anything less."

After Ben, Pam, and the kids left, Harper brought out the binder to share with her mother.

"Oh my goodness," she said. "They ask so many questions. Personal."

"They have to."

Harper looked at Raina's birth certificate. Something caught her eye. The birthplace was noted as Elberta, Georgia. *Elberta. Like the peach. Where have I heard that before?* Harper focused on retrieving the memory. "Mom." She handed her mother the document. "Look, Raina was born in Elberta. Where do I know that from? Have we been there?"

Callie
Savannah, Georgia, 1975
Chapter 17

In the apartment she shared with Jocelyn in Savannah, Callie pulled on her platform boots, zipping them up. "Can you help me with my dress?" she called out to Jocelyn, whom she could hear making a pot of coffee.

Jocelyn appeared, already wearing her nurse's uniform, a small apple clenched between her teeth. "Turn around. Nice pinafore."

"Is the corduroy okay? Too informal?" She could feel Jocelyn tugging the laces at her back, only stopping to hand her apple to Callie.

"Looks very professional. I like the tan turtleneck under the burgundy."

"Do you think a scarf? Or too much?"

"I like the floral one." Jocelyn finished tying the dress and took the apple back from Callie, then she watched as Callie tied the silk scarf with the pink roses around her neck.

"Why am I so nervous?" Callie wondered out loud.

"You'll do great. The first day at a new job is always intimidating."

"Says you, who has already been working for two months."

There weren't as many opportunities for social workers as there were for nurses. While Jocelyn began working immediately after graduating college, Callie had set up their quaint two-bedroom apartment with a beautiful view of Daffin Park out the front bay window, filling it with hand-me-down furniture. It felt good to finally begin their adult lives together.

Of course, Jocelyn had a boyfriend named Ernie and relentlessly tried to set up Callie on dates, but the truth was, she wasn't interested. On the few occasions she agreed to try one, it proved just how much she wasn't interested. Callie had one goal—a fresh, independent beginning. She didn't want to have to rely on anyone.

"I'm off," Jocelyn called to Callie as she made her way into their tiny living room. "Good luck." The apartment door closed behind her.

Callie stood gazing at her reflection in the mirror, taking a good, long look.

When Callie left Covenant House five years before, she hadn't looked back. The weeks that followed had become a blur of grief burdened with Evelyn's growing impatience with Callie's preoccupation over the loss of her daughter. It all seemed like one continuous day, an hourglass nailed to the table, emptied of every grain of sand. Callie didn't realize it then, but she had hit bottom.

One day, Evelyn had caught Callie on the phone, reaching out to Father Sal, the priest at their church, for counsel. Callie couldn't understand why he hadn't performed her daughter's funeral Mass, why it couldn't be in the church she had attended since she was a little girl, or why her daughter was buried two towns away.

Evelyn's wild eyes had flared as she took the receiver from Callie and slammed it onto its cradle. "What are you doing? Do you want to embarrass us? Put Father Sal on the spot? He's been so good to you. This is what I mean when I say you can't always think about yourself first. You spoiled girl." Vile spit had sprayed from her mother's mouth.

Even in the present, Callie winced. She looked into her own eyes reflected in the mirror as if they were a portal back to that time—the time she tried to bury.

She had wanted desperately to talk to someone. Anyone. But because of the lies Evelyn had built one on top of the other like a house of cards, she forbade Callie from mentioning the whole ordeal. Her pregnancy. Jon. Covenant House. Stella's death. Her memory surrounding the birth was fragmented. She wanted and needed to talk about it. But she was too weak against Evelyn, who couched every single command as if she were doing what was best *for* Callie.

"The people here believe you've been to school in France. Don't make a liar out of me." Her mother had pointed at her right between her eyes.

Of course, Callie had become so fragile while bottling all of that grief inside that Evelyn started giving her pills. At the time, she told Callie they would take the pain away. Well, they did that, and they made her numb to any kind of emotion at all.

One day, her father had come into her room to check on her.

Callie noticed the ashen look on Asa's face as he picked up the empty pill bottle beside her bed. He seemed to study the label, reading it carefully. His veins swelled under the skin on his forehead and next to his eyes.

"Let's go, Callie. Pack what you need," he directed.

She was too weak, physically and emotionally, not to obey.

In the car, Callie's body shook as her father apologized profusely. But he still made excuses for Evelyn, saying that she simply "took it too far" this time, that he hadn't known "she was capable of this" and she was "sorry." Callie had been too numb to react to his words, but to her relief, he drove her to Jocelyn's house, where she would stay until it was time to go off to college. That was his way of trying to make up for what had gone so terribly wrong.

Callie had tried to find Jon. She visited the post office to ask for a forwarding address, but there was none. She tracked down his landlord to see if he knew where Jon had gone, but he didn't. She even tried to reach out to his parents, though it was risky because she doubted he even told them about her. Still, there were so many Taylors in the phone book that they were impossible to locate.

All the dead ends made Callie realize that if a person didn't want to be found, he wouldn't. Jocelyn had reinforced this, too, with her side-eye and pitying smile. "Callie, can't you just let it be? Leave the past in the past. This has to end."

Callie's temples pulsed as she allowed her memory of that time to flow. Usually, she stuffed it away. Busied herself with something to take her mind off it. She wasn't sure why she let it creep in on this day—one of new beginnings.

"I'm not that girl anymore," she whispered to her reflection.

Callie walked about seven blocks to her new workplace. She stopped at the front door of the brownstone building, looking up, her eyes wide with anticipation.

During her interview, she had taken immediately to the woman in charge. She'd been given a tour of the floor occupied by Savannah Family and Friends, a community-outreach program for underprivileged children and families. It offered day programs for ages birth to five years, after-school programs for kids six to fifteen, and pro bono legal support, job placement, and counseling for adults. She'd been hired on the spot.

Callie waited at the front desk. She repositioned her scarf so it hung just right. A friendly older woman led Callie down the hallway to the counseling department, where she left her in a ten-foot-by-ten-foot room with a metal desk and three wooden chairs. "This one's yours," the woman said.

As Callie settled in, unpacking her cardboard box of office supplies into the desk drawers, the head of counseling, a man she hadn't met before, gave her a schedule for the day and the patient files she would need. She already had five appointments booked.

Callie put a yellow legal pad and pen on top of the blotter that covered her desk, then she took a look inside the manila folders,

studying the patient reports. Addiction, mental illness, homeless-
ness—these made Callie cringe. She had hardened herself to her own
past, focusing on helping others, convincing herself that there were
always other people who had problems bigger than her own. Swallowing hard, she readied herself for her first patient.

On her third day of work, a knock at her office door startled her
into looking up from the reports across her desk. A lanky, clean-cut
man with short brown hair mixed with gold hues stood there, looking puzzled. "You aren't Emaline," he said.

Callie looked around her small space then back at him. "No
Emaline here."

"Do you, by chance, have the Cunningham case?"

Callie rifled through her files, although the name didn't ring a
bell. She bit her lip. "Um, let me look in one more place. I'm new."

He chuckled. "Yes, I gathered." He approached her desk. "Cunningham. Short, round guy. Evicted."

Now, that sounded familiar. She had met with him on the first
day. He had three kids and a wife who had recently died. "Here it is."
She pulled the file from her drawer.

"Sorry. Adam Clarke." He reached out to shake her hand, and
she obliged. He had a firm shake, but his hands were a little sweaty.

"Callie Sebastian. Third day on the job."

He pulled his hand away, casually rubbing it against his suit
trousers, then took the file she held out to him. "I'm working on the
housing piece. Lawyer. Pro bono. I come in on Tuesdays and Thurs-
days."

"Ah." Callie nodded.

"So, since you are new. There are quite a few cases we'll work on
together. That is, if you took Emaline's case load." He raised his chin
and shook his head. "She didn't tell me she was leaving."

"Hm," Callie replied, not knowing what else to say. "Who are
some of the other cases?"

"Let's see... Jefferson, Hidalgo, Bowman, and San Angelo. I think that's it. So, you're new. Is this your first job?"

Callie determined he was five to ten years older than her by the looks of him. She nodded. "Is it that obvious?"

"Nah." He flashed a crooked smile that exposed polar-white teeth. "Emaline was old as dirt." He laughed again. Callie found him charming—a little nerdy but charming nonetheless.

"Aha. Are these jobs we work on together or clients we have in common?"

"A little of both. We try to keep everyone in the loop when they cross departments like this. Many do. I work at a law firm uptown, but I've been volunteering here since they opened three years ago."

"I didn't realize it was that new. More and more community centers are popping up. It was important for me to work with people who need the help the most."

"Me too. My firm has been flexible with my hours to accommodate me."

An awkward silence ensued.

"So, the Cunningham case..." she prompted.

"Yeah, we have a hearing on Wednesday. Poor guy. Dirt poor with three mouths to feed. After his wife died, the bills nearly put him under. I'll get this," he said, pointing to the file, "back to you after the hearing. You might want to make a note of that. Emaline used to."

"Oh." On her notepad, Callie wrote down the information and that the file was with Adam Clarke. "Nice to meet you, Mr. Clarke."

"Call me Adam." Then he disappeared down the hall.

ADAM NOT ONLY KNEW his way around the legal system, but he also helped Callie navigate their overlapping work. They became fast friends. Hardly a Tuesday or Thursday went by that they didn't have some sort of interaction. Before she realized it, Callie began to lean on him for more than collegial advice.

It was a good four months before Adam asked Callie out on an official date, but even then, it was more like a shared interest, in that he invited her to a housing benefit dinner. The city had proposed the old Arbor Manufacturers building, which had been vacant for months, to become a housing project for the homeless and those in crisis who needed temporary housing.

Callie chose a dress that wasn't too pretentious, reminded of the many benefits her mother had attended while dressed to the nines. For a split second, she'd even hesitated to accept Adam's invitation, mindful that she might see members of Evelyn's social circle at the benefit. It was certain Evelyn wouldn't be there—she'd never tried to help those less fortunate than herself, and five years later, Callie had no reason to believe she would have turned over a new leaf. *It's been five years,* Callie reminded herself even as she shuddered.

Every bit the gentleman, Adam picked her up at the precise time he had promised. They made small talk about shared clients along the way. Once they arrived, he opened the car door for her and extended his elbow, which she slipped her hand through, letting it rest comfortably on his forearm.

"I realize this is a work event, but let's try to make it about us. Our first date." The gold flecks in his eyes danced as he spoke, and that made her feel warm and tingly inside, something she hadn't felt in a very long time.

The ballroom at the Hyatt was decorated exquisitely. It shimmered with lights and candelabras. The two of them took their seats at a table of other lawyers from Adam's firm. He whispered in her ear, "I want everyone to know you're my date tonight." And with a prideful grin, he introduced her to his colleagues.

She considered, for a brief moment, how refreshing it was to be with a man who wanted to be seen with her.

Throughout dinner, conversation flowed easily among the lawyers and their wives. Only two of the other lawyers had girl-friends. *Does Adam think I'm his girlfriend?* Suddenly, being part of a couple didn't seem all that daunting.

After the charity auction, the host announced the proceeds for the Arbor project at 1.5 million dollars. The whole room erupted with applause, and something inside Callie stirred. She wanted to become involved with this project, be part of getting it off the ground.

Instead of taking her directly home, Adam suggested they stop at a diner for coffee. Callie didn't want the night to end either. The diner was all but vacant at one in the morning, and they chose a booth in the corner. Callie asked for coffee with cream and sugar, while Adam ordered his black.

"I'm mostly a tea drinker," she said.

"Well, then, why didn't you order tea?"

She shrugged then leaned forward. "I want to learn more about the Arbor project. I'd like to be involved in getting it started. Even if it's on a volunteer basis."

He took her hand in his. "I love this about you. Have you always been so benevolent?"

Callie sighed. She hadn't thought of herself that way. Perhaps seeing her parents raising so much money for causes that suited their standards had paved the way for a similar desire within her, but Callie was determined to make her life matter. Not by stuffing the pockets of the already rich but by giving to the underprivileged.

"I want to make a difference for those who can't seem to themselves," she said.

The waitress set the steaming cups in front of each of them.

"And what in your past led you to such desires?"

Callie shrugged, cupping her hands around her coffee mug. "What if I told you I don't like to talk about my past?"

"Oh, now I'm curious."

"It's a lot, Adam. Suffice it to say, I'm very different than my parents. I don't have siblings or grandparents. I really only have my friend Jocelyn and her family. A found family, if you will. Are you okay with leaving it at that?"

Adam nodded. "Well, I have enough family for both of us." He seemed to stop himself, as if he'd said something wrong.

"I'd love to hear about them."

As he shared stories of his close-knit family, with five siblings who were naturally competitive but strongly bonded, Callie let her mind wander. *Will I ever be able to tell him about my past? One day, perhaps.*

Six months later, Callie and Adam were married in a small ceremony, attended by only their witnesses, Jocelyn and Brian, one of Adam's brothers, at the town hall. She still hadn't found the courage to tell him the details of her past. The fact remained that she hardly remembered much of that time. *Why sully a perfectly good relationship with a muddy past? I'm a different person now.* Perhaps she would, one day, if they decided to have children. But the truth was, the more time that passed, the harder it became to consider sharing anything of that dreadful time.

Adam only knew that she had been estranged from a mother who wasn't capable of love. Callie rarely saw her father, but Asa met Adam one night after her wedding. She'd invited him to their home under the strict instructions that they could only talk about the present and the future, never about the past.

Harper

Chapter 18

Harper woke up to the all-too-familiar scent of bleach mixed with a hint of lemon. *The hospital room.* Groggy, she looked around to find Gabe sitting next to her in the chair, as she had too many times already.

Her throat was dry when she spoke. "Did it go all right?"

"Yes, the doctor said so. He was waiting for you to wake up before he came to talk to us."

"I thought I heard voices in here." A young nurse sauntered in. "Let me check your vitals."

Gabe moved over to the window so the nurse could have access to Harper, though he kept his eyes on Harper, as she did him.

"You are doing gestational surrogacy? So exciting!" the nurse said with well-practiced enthusiasm.

"Yes," Harper said. "How long before we know how many eggs there were?"

"When I'm done here, I'll give the doctor a call."

Harper sighed, which prompted Gabe to return to her side. She realized in those moments how lucky she was to have married the most patient man.

"Everything looks great," the nurse said. "The doctor should be in soon."

After the nurse left, Gabe took Harper's hand in both of his. "I have a good feeling about this."

"I'd like to, but I'm not allowing myself to get too excited until he tells me he retrieved some good eggs. Then I'll stop worrying."

Gabe chuckled. "Oh, you will?"

Harper never considered herself much of a worrier until her first pregnancy. She wondered if Gabe had. The realization of how much change came with bringing a child into the world was a heavy weight. Harper made a note to herself to work on coming to terms with that over the next nine months. Perhaps she was more like her mother than she'd allowed herself to see. The realization shone on her like a spotlight. *This is what motherhood does to a woman.*

The doctor walked into the room with his clipboard. He brushed a hand over Harper's leg. "All went smoothly." He nodded, and Harper waited for his next words. "You have seven eggs we can work with. They are resting right now until we can determine how many of them are mature, then we'll proceed with the fertilization."

"Seven? That's a good amount, right?"

"It's decent. Enough for us to work with. We typically like ten to fourteen, but for you, I'm happy with seven. Let's hope they are a good, ripe seven."

"And five days for the transfer, if the eggs are fertilized?"

"Yes, five days. Your surrogate is already taking fertility meds to prepare herself. We seem to be on track. You'll get a call tomorrow following up on the maturation level of the eggs. Go home. Rest for today. You may feel a little bloated. Some cramping."

She sighed. "I won't be able to rest until I know we are on the right track."

"Don't fool yourself, Harper—this could be a long road. Make sure you do what you need to stay calm and keep yourself busy. There will be a lot of waiting over the next nine months."

Gabe sat next to Harper on the bed and put his arm around her. "We will keep her in good spirits. I promise, doc."

"Listen to him." The doctor waved his thumb in Gabe's direction.

"Now we wait." At home, Gabe set Harper up on the couch under a blanket with a glass of lemonade and Miles snuggled by her side.

"TV?" he asked.

"Nah, let's just sit with this. I'm tired." The profundity of the experience and all of its implications were still sinking in.

"We've been through a lot," he said. "As Mama would say, 'We have to count the blessings we have, Gabriel.'"

What did he mean by that? Was he preparing her for bad news? Seven eggs when they'd hoped for fourteen. A fifty-fifty chance this wouldn't work. She set her glass down on the end table and shook the bleak thoughts away.

She thought back to the silent premarriage no-children contract between them that seemed like a lifetime ago. "How did you feel when I told you I didn't want children at all?"

Gabe sat at the opposite end of the couch, rubbing her feet. It helped to calm her. "Confused because I knew you'd make a fantastic mother and hopeful that you'd change your mind. I still don't know why you didn't want them."

"Mostly because of my childhood. On the outside, it looked idyllic, but my mother was so overprotective. It was almost as if she was afraid of something, but I don't know why."

"Afraid?"

"Of losing us? I don't know. Maybe that she wasn't a good-enough mom."

"But she was, right?"

Harper contemplated that before she spoke. She couldn't say her mom was a bad mother. She was never uncaring or neglectful. "She was a perfectionist. I felt suffocated—a lot."

"Oh, that's where your anxiety comes from."

"Yes, Dr. Devlin, I believe it does."

As a reaction to her sarcasm, Gabe squeezed her big toe.

The phone rang. Gabe and Harper looked at each other, and when Harper reached for the telephone, Miles groaned that she caused him to move.

"Hello. Yes, this is Harper." She concentrated on the words the nurse said. Her heart seemed to drop down to her stomach. "Only three?" She sat up straight. "Is that bad? Okay. Thank you. Yes. Thank you."

Three. But there had been seven. Pressure rose from her stomach to her chest to her throat. It strangled her for a second. *Breathe, Harper.* She closed her eyes, breathing in through her nose and out through her mouth. Then she opened them. She could feel her breaths becoming more even. In and out.

Gabe looked at her with concern on his face. "You okay?"

"Only three are viable. She said that isn't a bad number, but that we're hoping it takes the first time, as it only gives us two more options."

"For this round," Gabe reminded her in a cautious tone.

Harper didn't say so, but she'd already decided this round would be the last. She couldn't bear more loss.

Part II

Callie
Oak Creek, Georgia, 2004
Chapter 19

Every year on April twenty-third, Callie secretly celebrated Stella's birthday, the only part of her past she chose to acknowledge. She promised never to forget, and in this small way, sitting alone in silence with a cupcake, a candle, and her thoughts, she could remember what could have been. Although her life had taken a different path than she'd imagined when she gave birth, in Callie's heart, Stella would always remain her first child.

She kept these celebrations secret even from Adam, just as she had kept much of her past hidden from anyone who hadn't known her then. It was as if a chasm split her life in two—before Stella and after Stella.

Yet she held a vigil year after year for her first baby girl. By the time Harper, her youngest, was five, Callie had gotten so bogged down with balancing her job at the Arbor Outreach Center and parenting two kids that she let down her guard. Harper had been outside, playing with friends. Ben was at baseball with Adam. She'd thought it was safe.

Callie sat down at the dining room table, a single vanilla cupcake in front of her with pink frosting, sprinkles, and a sparkling candle in the center.

"Mommy, what are you doing?" Her daughter's voice made her jump. Harper's face looked wounded, as if she'd been left out of a party.

Callie made up some excuse to surprise her. "Go get your dolls and stuffed animals," she said, urging her out of the room to give her time to gather her thoughts. Harper came back with an armful and a great big toothless smile. While she was gone, Callie had conjured up a story about a little girl she knew and lost.

Year after year, she let Harper take part in her celebration, thinking it almost magical that one daughter, present and alive, could celebrate the other, whom Callie still grieved. It seemed like a gift back then. Harper's eyes would light up when her mother told the story, year after year, as if it were just a story like the ones Callie read to her at night. Then Harper outgrew her dolls and playtime, and she'd never mentioned those celebrations or the story again. Callie assumed she'd allowed it to float away in the recesses of her mind like so many other stories.

Now, more than twenty-five years later, Harper shocked her with yet another surprise when she asked Callie about Elberta, Georgia, in connection with her surrogate. Had Callie mentioned Elberta to Harper all those years ago? Why would she have? But if she didn't, how else would that town's name be familiar to Harper? In Callie's memory, the story she'd told had been so generic, so detached.

Callie had looked down at the document in Harper's hand, a birth certificate that clearly said *Elberta, Georgia*. But something else had caught her eye. In fact, that something nearly darted off the page in seemingly distorted, boldfaced type. *Birthdate: April 23, 1970.* Callie swallowed hard. A day etched in her memory forever.

Before she had left Harper's house that night, she revisited the photo hanging on Harper's refrigerator of the surrogate, hoping it seemed nonchalant. Callie had missed it at first, focusing more on the happy family than the woman. But in the oblong shape of the woman's face, her almond-shaped eyes... *She resembles me when I was young.*

Callie squeezed her eyes shut, her mouth, too, afraid to let out the gasp caught in her throat. She hoped she'd hidden her reaction well enough in front of Harper, in front of her family.

Callie didn't sleep a wink all night. When Adam asked about her sleeplessness out of concern, she attributed it to postmenopause. "Who knows the way a body changes?" she said. "Now, go back to sleep."

She tiptoed into the kitchen and poured a hot cup of tea, hoping it would warm her body, but all she felt was cold and afraid. *Will everything come tumbling back? Who is this Raina—born in Elberta on the same day as Stella? Was there a hospital in Elberta?* In her memory, it had seemed a small, desolate town. *Could someone else have delivered that same day?* No one that Callie could recall.

The next morning, after Adam left for work, Callie turned on her computer and searched *Elberta Hospital.* Nothing. Not even a similar hit. *Covenant House.* The first entry said Elberta, Georgia. *It's still there.*

The phone rang, startling Callie. Other than celebrating Stella's birthday, she never let her past into her present. "Hello?" she answered, her voice cracking.

"Mom, is everything okay?"

A chill rippled through Callie, but she shook it off. "Yes, dear, of course. How are you?"

"All right. The doctor called last night to say they retrieved three eggs."

Callie's eyes rolled up to the ceiling, and she drew in a deep breath. "That's wonderful."

"It's a little on the low side." Harper's voice sounded dejected.

"Oh, it'll be fine. Tell me more about your surrogate. Raina, is it?"

"Yes. She had three healthy pregnancies, so I'm not worried about her. I'm more worried about my eggs."

"I'd like to meet her." There, Callie had said it. If she met the woman, there was a good chance she would know for sure. She would take one look at her, and if the woman was Stella, Callie would feel the tug of her heartstrings.

"Raina? Mom, that's weird."

"It's not, not at all. I'd love to meet the person you chose to carry my grandchild." Callie rubbed her hand across her head.

"No. Let's wait and see if it even takes. Don't jinx me like that."

Harper

Chapter 20

Two days after the doctor's call, Harper woke up to the morning birds chirping outside their window. She wandered over to the blinds to lift them and let the morning sunshine stretch across the floor. She had a lot on her mind. Just two more days before Raina's procedure. Then another two weeks to wait until they could determine its success. All of this waiting made her life feel as if it was in a perpetual holding pattern.

Forward thinking, Harper reminded herself. If she were being honest, she could admit that she was cautiously excited for the transfer to work. Gabe would be such a good dad. And Harper didn't need to worry about her body failing them again.

Sometimes she allowed herself to fantasize about how being parents would change them. Cooing together over a newborn, a tiny person created out of their love. Most of the images she saw in her mind's eye were of an older child, a toddler just learning to walk, babbling and laughing, or running in the yard with Gabe and Miles chasing after him.

Why had she imagined a little boy? Was it a sign?

Also, the question her mother had asked just didn't sit right. Why would she ask to meet Raina then seem so annoyed when Harper said no? Did it have anything to do with Raina's birthplace sounding familiar? But her mother didn't seem to have a recollection of it when Harper brought it up. She honestly needed to stop letting her mother get inside her head like this.

Before going to work, Harper decided to call Cody, who'd left messages the past two days. Maybe she was reluctant to call him back because she didn't know how much of her personal life she wanted to share. Or maybe, if she was being honest with herself, this business opportunity did entice her. But she needed to quell her excitement, because this was not the time to take on a new project. She needed to rip off the Band-Aid and just let him know.

"Mrs. Alexander," he sang out, answering with optimism.

"I'm sorry for just getting back to you now. I've had a lot of personal stuff to deal with and haven't been at work."

"Everything okay?" She detected worry in his voice.

"Sure. Yes. But I'm afraid I won't be able to accept your offer." *Tempting as it may be.* She tapped a finger on the kitchen counter. "My plate is overfull at the moment." Regret pulled at her. Owning her own business was something she'd always wanted. The prospect of finding an old, battered house and watching Cody transform it sounded invigorating. But Gabe had made her see that the timing was all wrong.

"I understand."

Harper was grateful for Cody's generosity—for his faith in her—and she did enjoy working with him.

"You straighten out whatever personal business you have going on and let me know if you change your mind," he said. "We'd make a great team."

Harper chuckled. "We would. Take care of yourself, Cody. It's been great working with you."

He'd left the door open for the possibility of a future collaboration. Once everything got settled with this baby business, she would reach out to him. It was too good a prospect not to consider, even if she had to put it on the back burner for a time.

Harper trekked down to the garden to cut some fresh flowers as a way to pass the time before her first appointment. Cutting flowers always helped her put things into perspective. The hyacinths were already in full bloom and were so vibrant this spring. She clipped a bunch, placed them in her basket, and headed over to the archway, which was already covered with wisteria blossoms.

With the shears still in her hand, she spied two birds frolicking in the birdbath at the center of her garden. In her preoccupation with the birds, she accidentally swatted at a buzzing bee and felt a sting as the assailant flew away. She winced, dropping her shears. "These damn bees." *No wonder my mother hates them.* She squeezed at the back of her hand, trying to get the stinger out. The black dot, embedded, seemed to scoff at her pain.

Like the rush of a waterfall, she remembered part of a story. *My mother hated bees, and I always did what I could to ridicule her.* "The queen bee took away the little girl," her mother had said. *What little girl?*

Together, Callie and Harper had celebrated a handful of times with her dolls and stuffed animals. Her mother made a big deal of it every spring. She told Harper the story of the little girl who was lost and how it was the queen bee's fault. Hadn't this been a story? Their own secret story her mother brought to life for her with a cupcake and a candle, a magical celebration. Like a big surprise. She would set up her favorite dolls around their table and sing "Happy Birthday." Her mother said she'd lost the little girl because she went to some house in Elberta.

"Like the peach, Mommy?" Harper's childish voice echoed back to her.

"Yes," Callie had said. "Just like the peach."

But what was the name of the house? Think, Harper. Think.

Her mouth hung agape, forgetting the sting altogether. Could Raina... be the girl her mother lost? Is that why she wanted to meet her? To see for herself? But Harper was sure that wasn't the name of the lost girl in the story, though she couldn't recall what it was. Only that her mother said, "Shh, this is our little secret." Why was it such a secret that her mother lost someone?

Leaving her basket of flowers behind, Harper ran into the house. She looked around frantically for the birth certificate. It was all there. Raina Baker. Born to Mary Hudson Baker and Reginald Baker. Elberta Hospital, Elberta, Georgia.

Harper looked up Elberta Hospital on her cell phone. Not one hit. She checked her spelling, but it was right. Why would the certificate list a hospital that didn't exist? Wasn't it a legal document?

A dull ache spidered from the corners of her eyes to the back of her head. How had the little girl been connected to Mary Hudson Baker? Was that her own mother? Had her mother changed her name? Questions swirled like a tornado, creating a puzzle she needed to piece together. Something was missing. She felt it in her gut. *There was a house. What was the name of the house?*

Miles scratched at the back door. She'd left him outside. He came in huffing and puffing from the heat, so she filled his water bowl, all the while thinking. It started with a C, she remembered. *Convent?* On what occasion would her mother have been at a convent? She had never been overly religious.

Miles sauntered away and plopped into his oversize dog bed.

Hurriedly, as if in a race for time, she typed *Convent House* into her phone. A list of convents in her area popped up. She entered *Convent House and Elberta*. In tiny blue lettering, the search engine asked, *Did you mean Covenant House?*

Yes. That was it. Covenant House.

There it was, in Elberta, Georgia. When she clicked on the link, she was brought to a site that advertised the dated brick building as a home for troubled youth. As she searched deeper, she learned it was also a birthing center for displaced young women, a place they went when they were pregnant.

Harper chest constricted. *Breathe. One. Two. Three. Four. Exhale.*

Her mother had never been troubled. Had she? Perhaps one of her friends went there. Maybe Mary Baker had been a friend of Callie's. She took a couple of deep, calming breaths and dialed the number, looking around as if she were about to get caught doing something she shouldn't.

"Hello," Harper said to the woman who answered the phone. "I'm looking for some information." She made everything up as she went along, having no idea what she was looking for. She simply reacted. "I'm from the…" What was the name of the agency Raina worked with? "The Alternative Pregnancy Methods Agency, looking to verify a birth certificate I have in front of me. Yes, ma'am. The birthdate is April 23,1970."

She bit her lip while waiting then listening. "You don't have records going back that far?" Her tone became serious and her voice louder. "Well, I need this information. How can I find out if a patient gave birth on that date? It's important that you confirm it for me to move forward on this account... Okay."

She waited while the girl went to get the director, who would know the students from that time. Harper had no idea what that meant, but she was desperate, and she'd come this far.

"Deborah Vasmussen, Director of Covenant House. How can I help you?"

A knot tightened in Harper's stomach. "I'm with the APMA."

"Yes, I've been told. Your name?"

"Harper Alexander."

"Ms. Alexander, I've been told about the information you're seeking. Can I have the name of the student for which you seek verification?"

"Mary Hudson."

"No, I'm sorry."

"Or Mary Hudson Baker." There was a thirty-second silence that felt like ten minutes.

"There was no one here by that name either."

"You're certain? This birth certificate says a Mary Baker gave birth to a baby girl. Raina is her name."

"I'm not doubting what the certificate says, Ms. Alexander. I can only tell you a Mary Hudson never attended this school at that time."

"You keep saying 'school.' Is Covenant House a school or a home or a hospital?"

"Yes. It is a home and birthing center. I'm sorry I couldn't confirm your information."

Could her mother have been pregnant? Surely this woman would have known if she had. Nonetheless, Harper pulled in a deep breath. She had to know for certain. "What about Callie Sebastian? Calista Sebastian?"

There was a brief silence. "I'm sorry. I don't see anyone by that name either."

And the phone went dead. Harper held it in her hand, now more confused than before.

FROM THE FILE, HARPER had Raina's home address. She canceled her work appointment, instead driving to Brocton, where the Edwins lived.

She noticed her hands were jittery as she pulled into the farm's dirt driveway. She parked near the house, and one of the farmhands directed her to the back and down a pathway. "Miss Raina is working with her bees. Don't get too close."

As he said it, Harper realized she hadn't put anything on her sting, but she let it pass. "Raina?" she called out as she got close.

The sight of Raina in full bee gear was such an assault that Harper jumped back.

Raina did a double take, then she placed the lid on the box and met Harper at the edge of the bee garden. She removed her helmet. "Harper? Is everything okay?"

Harper rubbed her hands together as she took in the sight of Raina from head to toe.

"Oh, yeah." Raina laughed. "You've never seen this bee getup before? I promise it isn't the least bit dangerous. Are you excited for the implant? I can't lie—I'm a little nervous. Tending to my bees calms me. But I'll be fine. Don't you worry."

"That isn't why I'm here. I'm so sorry to come to your home unannounced. I know it isn't protocol."

Creased deepened across Raina's forehead.

"I noticed something odd," Harper began, then she spilled out the story. "When I mentioned it to my mother, she acted... defensively, as if I hit a nerve. Then she changed the subject. Why would my mother repeatedly mention the same place where you were born? It isn't even a hospital. I looked it up. Elberta Hospital never existed."

As Harper spoke, Raina's face changed from surprised to quizzical to angry, if Harper was reading her correctly. And Raina had every right to be all those things.

"What do you mean, Elberta Hospital never existed?" Raina asked.

"Is there a chance you could be adopted?"

"Harper, you read my whole life history in that application. Seriously. Don't you think if I were adopted, I'd say it? Why would I hide something like that?" Raina began shedding her bee gear, leaving it on the ground. "Come on," she said, voice indignant.

Raina stomped up the path. Harper followed. Raina's house was empty. She'd expected children to be running around, but of course, it was a school day. Inside, the farmhouse was decorated humbly, just like Raina herself.

So many conflicting thoughts stirred within Harper. What if she were making a big deal out of nothing but a coincidence? Perhaps there was some part of her that had created all this mystery because, deep down, she feared the implant being successful.

No, she scolded herself. *There are too many things that don't add up.*

"Wait here," Raina said as Harper stood in the kitchen. Raina disappeared into another room and came back with her birth certificate. She placed it on the counter, holding it with both hands as if it would leap up and out of her grasp. "This is mine. It's always been the same. Maybe Elberta Hospital closed."

"Does the name Covenant House ring a bell? Did your parents ever mention that?"

Raina bit her lip then shook her head. "What's that?"

"It's in Elberta. Apparently, it's a home and a hospital for at-risk girls. I called, and they didn't have any record of your mother being there—or mine."

"So you think our mothers are the same? Mine died. I went to her funeral."

"I know. It said that in your paperwork."

Suddenly Harper felt stupid for everything. For coming here, for making something out of nothing. But that still didn't explain the hospital never existing, or her mother's reaction, or the story her mother told her all those years ago. She'd thought it was make believe.

But she shrugged. Her questions were still unanswered. "Could it be a coincidence?"

"Hell if I know," Raina said. "It must. But it doesn't much matter because the transfer is the day after tomorrow." A reassuring smile spread across her face. "And I'm about to cook you a little baby."

Harper nodded. "You're right. I must have my head spinning for nothing. But we do look alike, right?"

"Listen, what I would give to have a sister. But you have your birth mother, and I have mine. They aren't the same lady. But hey, maybe by the end of this, we'll feel like sisters."

Raina

Chapter 21

Even though Harper left on what seemed a good note, Raina simmered about that visit after the woman left. *Who does she think she is, asking such questions? What is she after?*

She found Wayne in the barn to tell him about it.

"I don't know how she connected where I was born to her mother. That part sounded all jumbled. Something about a birthday party and a little girl who had been lost. She thinks I'm adopted."

"Sounds like you better rethink a business contract with her," Wayne said. "Nine months is a long time."

Raina waved her hand in the air. "She seemed so nice at our meeting. So normal. I wonder if it could be phantom hormones?"

Wayne laughed, then his expression puckered up. "Seriously, if you have a single doubt about this situation or this woman, we bail now. Before it's too late."

Raina tried to go about the rest of her day and forget about Harper, but her questions gnawed at her. The truth was that she knew nothing about where she was born.

She did a little poking on Wayne's computer, looking up Elberta Hospital for herself, and Harper was right—no such place had ever existed. Her stomach sank. Why was it on her birth certificate? Then she looked up Covenant House. The first hit displayed a beautiful stone building and an expansive lawn in Elberta, Georgia. The subtitle read, *Helping Young Women Get Ahead.*

As she read further, it seemed like a halfway house for young women who were pregnant or suffering from mental health issues. Raina shook her head. Her mother wasn't either of those.

She decided to go to the only place she could get answers.

When she killed the ignition in front of Reggie's trailer, she took a deep breath, exhaling through circled lips. Knocking hard on the front door, she called loudly, "Pa. It's me. Raina. Pa." She'd learned long ago that warning him was probably a good idea.

When he didn't answer, she took hold of the knob and turned. It was unlocked. Reggie was laid out in the recliner, snoring, with the television on an episode of *Oprah*.

"Pa," she scolded. Then she patted his arm.

He jerked as if he'd been poked. "Jesus, Raina, you scared me."

Raina shot him a dirty look for using the Lord's name in vain. He knew better, and sometimes she thought he did it just to knock the piss out of her. "Why are you sleeping?" Of course, her answer sat on the coffee table next to the chair—a half-empty bottle of Scotch. She swished the Scotch around and put it back on the table, disgusted as usual with him.

"You come all this way to give me shit about the way I live?"

Raina looked around. Stacks of newspapers, dirty dishes, empty liquor bottles—the usual mess. Nervously, she began picking up. "One day you're gonna drink yourself to death."

"And you won't miss me a stitch."

"Pa, don't say shit like that. I'm here, aren't I?"

With his thick gray brows and only a few strands of hair haphazardly crossing his predominantly bald head, Reggie seemed to have aged even more since she'd last seen him. His leathery skin highlighted the deep rivers of wrinkles punctuating his facial features.

Raina grabbed his arm to help him up to a sitting position. The smell of stale Scotch and the days-old body odor affronted her nose such that she backed away once he sat on his own.

"You need a shower, Pa."

"Don't do that," he scolded.

"You do. When was the last time you showered?"

"Where are the kids? You never bring them around."

"At school." Raina picked up newspapers and used tissues from the seat of the armchair, placing them on the coffee table, making room so she could sit down.

"I've got to ask you something." Normally, Raina tried to create peace when visiting her father, but this was no time for making nice. She had a direct question that would piss off one or both of them. "Pa, answer me honest. Am I adopted?"

He raised a hand. "Where the hell you get that idea from? Wayne put that in your head?"

"Honest."

"Don't be ridiculous." He drew his mouth into a pout.

"What's my birthday?"

"April."

"What year was I born?"

"Hell if I know, Raina." He threw up both hands and returned to staring at *Oprah*. "You've got to be thirty-something."

"Thirty-four. Where was I born?"

"Twenty questions. *Pfft*. You came here for twenty questions?"

"Where was I born?"

"At that hospital in Savannah. I don't know the name." His tone was indignant. Reggie shifted his weight, leaning on the armrest. "Did I pass the test?" He changed the channel.

"No." Heat built up behind Raina's eyelids. She pulled the birth certificate out of her pocket and showed it to him.

"Now, Pa, answer me straight. Was I adopted?"

Her father, fixed on a game show, yelled out, "Normandy! What is Normandy?"

She shook the paper, and he took hold of the corner. "Yeah, that's it. Elberta. You were born in a peach of a place." He chuckled at his own joke. "Because you're a peach of a girl."

"Stop, Pa. It's not funny. Elberta is four hours from here. Why would Ma give birth to me four hours from here?"

Reggie hit the paper still dangling from Raina's hand.

She folded it and tucked it into her pocket. "Tell me."

"Because we was visiting friends, that's why. She went into labor, and we had to take her to the closest place."

"A place that never existed?" Her eyes opened wide.

"Raina, I don't know." He looked right at her when he said it. "If I can't remember your birthday, how am I supposed to remember the name of a hospital I've never been to before or since? You were born in a hospital several hours away is all I know. What's with all these questions?"

"Because this hospital doesn't exist."

He threw his hands up in the air. "There you go, makin' problems for yourself. *Pfft.* It doesn't exist. It was thirty-four years ago. You said it yourself. Places close down. Maybe there isn't an Elberta Hospital now, but there was then."

"So you're telling me I wasn't adopted."

"No. For God's sake."

Raina lowered her head, feeling somewhat satisfied when he seemed to confirm her own theory. Perhaps the hospital shut down before the time that computers recorded everything. She believed she hadn't been adopted. She would have known something like that.

But Harper was right on two things—that the hospital didn't exist or no longer existed and about their physical similarities. So, now what? Did it mean Harper was unstable? Was Wayne right? Should she think about breaking the contract?

Nine months was a long time, indeed.

Callie

Chapter 22

Callie considered telling Adam the whole sordid story, but she should have done that years ago. First, she had to *know*. And the only person she could turn to was Jocelyn. She phoned her. Callie began with no pleasantries. "I need you."

"Oh no," Jocelyn said on the other end. "Your tone brings back haunting memories."

"Exactly." Callie sat at the table, still in her pajamas and robe, swirling a spoon in yet another cup of tea. How many had she made since last night? Three? Four? She told Jocelyn about the occasion at Harper's.

"Oh my goodness, that's wonderful."

"That's not the point."

"Way to stifle Auntie Jocelyn's excitement."

"I'm afraid what I have to tell you could have grave consequences." Callie relayed the whole conversation about the birth certificate. "When I had it in my hands, they were shaking. I mean, her *exact* birthday. I don't think anyone else at Covenant House gave birth on that day. Could it be a mistake?"

"What did you say when Harper asked you?"

"I told her she made a mistake. Tried to brush it off as something she could have seen on the news. I'm not sure she bought it."

There was a long silence on the other end. It always made Callie nervous when Jocelyn went silent. She could hear her friend take a deep breath. "Do you suppose…"

Just by the way she drew out the word, Callie knew what she was thinking. Hell, she'd thought it herself. But there was no evidence, and Asa wouldn't have been able to keep that secret for so long, especially after Evelyn's death. "I saw Stella's grave, Jocelyn. They don't just put up a grave marker for an empty coffin."

Still, could her daughter be alive? Could she be Raina?

"Evelyn had the reach and the means to do it," Jocelyn admitted.

"And an empty heart," Callie added. "How do I find out, and what do I tell Adam?"

"Let me think on it, Callie. You be happy for Harper. Maybe her curiosity will wane, and everything will work out."

"But I need to know."

The next day, Callie sat in the passenger seat, clasping her hands to stop them from trembling. Jocelyn had insisted on driving. Music played softly in the background. It was meant to be soothing to Callie, she realized, but all she could think about was the talk radio that had permeated the silence in the car the last time she'd made this drive—and Mother's smug expression, as if she had won something.

Could Evelyn have actually been capable of faking her granddaughter's death? Even that would have seemed impossible then.

Jocelyn rested her hand on Callie's knee. "No matter the outcome today, you'll get through it. You always do, Callie."

Callie rubbed her face with a cold hand and swallowed hard. "If only I had told Adam. I thought I was doing the right thing."

"You did what was right at the time. No one would fault you for that. Certainly not Adam."

"He has loved me unconditionally, as have you. The two most stable people in my life. One who knows me, while the other only thinks he does."

Jocelyn turned to look at her. "Listen, he knows you. He loves you. That other girl we're inquiring about today, she was another person back then. You came out of such trauma, Callie. When he learns that, he'll love you more, not less."

They pulled up through the long drive to the front of the brick building. It was just as Callie remembered. They walked in together and found that Covenant House was still open. It had been updated since Callie was there, with a new floor in the expansive foyer and a new reception area. Two guards stood at attention like lions.

Callie leaned over to the woman at the front desk. "Can I speak to whoever is in charge?"

"Can I ask what this is in reference to?"

"I was a student—patient—here." Callie wasn't sure how to term her status at that time. "From 1969 to 1970. I'm looking for someone who can help me with the records from that time."

"That would be the headmaster."

"Not still Mrs. Goldstein?"

"Never heard that name."

For a moment, Callie gaped. She hadn't realized just how many years had passed.

"Let me call through. It's Mrs. Vasmussen now."

As they waited, Callie paced while Jocelyn watched her. Callie thought of Harper. If what she suspected was true, this would change her life, too—perhaps she wouldn't want to go through with the surrogacy. Harper had been through too much already.

Callie pushed her worry aside. In front of her, there were too many gaps to fill, too many questions that needed answers. Callie's worst fear at this point was that she wouldn't get them.

"She'll see you now," the receptionist said. "Do you need an escort?"

"I can find it."

Callie led Jocelyn to the administrative wing. She remembered the way as if she had been there just weeks ago. The school appeared smaller, cleaner, than it was then, but the bowels, the corridors jutting off the center, were seemingly unchanged.

Callie noticed the placard on the door still read Headmaster and thought back to the first time she'd seen it, so intimidated. Then, the last time, she'd thought Jon had come to save her. What a foolish girl she had been.

"Mrs. Clarke, please have a seat. Mrs. Vasmussen will be with you shortly."

Jocelyn took hold of Callie's hand. "Are you holding up?"

Callie nodded.

The secretary led Callie to the office door and opened it. A woman with black hair, grayed at the edges, sat behind a desk but not the one that had been Mrs. Goldstein's. In fact, the whole room had a more cheerful makeover, although the same cuckoo clock hung on the wall.

When the woman lifted her head, Callie recalled the deep-set eyes, the inviting smile.

"Debs?" Callie asked.

The woman took a minute, as if she'd been transported back to the past. When recognition registered, which Callie could deduct from the glow on the woman's cheeks, she stood immediately. "Callie," she screeched as she had when they were schoolgirls, and she held Callie in a loving embrace. "Let me look at you." She stood back, sizing her up, as she nodded. "Beautiful as ever. Gosh, how I've thought about you over the years. I'm so sorry I didn't keep in touch."

"Don't be! I could have reached out too. But my life... Well, that's why I'm here. But what are you doing here?"

"First tell me what I can do for you. Come and sit." Debs gestured to a sofa that sat under the tall windows overlooking the front lawn. They both took a seat, their knees turned toward each other.

It was such a warm feeling, reconnecting with the only good thing about Covenant House, that Callie's nerves had subsided for a bit. Once she readjusted to her purpose, though, they tensed up, every muscle tight inside her.

"When I left Covenant House, I had given birth to a baby girl."

"You did? That's wonderful. Stella, right?"

Callie's head dropped. *Did I tell Debs her name? Yes, I did.* Callie continued, "I was told that she passed." She swallowed hard, her breath getting caught in her throat. "Shortly after birth. They wouldn't allow me to see her. We've uncovered some records that indicate that she might be alive."

Debs's brows furrowed. "I'm so sorry, Callie. I didn't know."

"Could you help me?"

"What do you need?"

"I don't have it with me." She relayed the long version of the story and told her she'd only seen the birth certificate, that it was in Harper's possession.

Debs nodded. "I got a phone call last week inquiring about the same incident. The woman on the other end mentioned your name, and it nearly took the wind out of me. I denied that you had been here for the sake of confidentiality."

Could it have been Harper? Callie had been afraid Harper wasn't convinced when she denied recognizing Elberta. If she'd taken it a step further, though, what could that mean?

Debs put both her hands on Callie's knees. "I can't say for sure, Callie. But if it is true, you wouldn't have been the first or the last. Covenant House had a reputation back then, I'm afraid to report."

Callie gasped, her hand covering her mouth, filled with such conflicting emotions of betrayal and tentative joy all at once. Her daughter could be alive. She couldn't find the words.

"Between me and you," Debs continued, "there was a whole behind-the-scenes scandal. It didn't make it to the papers because they didn't want to tarnish the integrity of the place or what little was left of it. Goldstein made a lot of money, along with the lawyers who were involved, in a back-market adoption scheme. Nothing was beneath them. They doctored documents, made things up. Apparently, several of the adopted children were born at a number of nonexistent hospitals. They thought it was the best way to go untraced. Sisters Lourdes and Jean Katherine fought hard to get this place back to its intended purpose—to help at-risk young women."

"Did you keep any documents that could confirm or deny such an exchange?"

"I didn't. All that's left is the paper trail they created to prove our legitimacy."

"So you know nothing about another child being born that day? Or a Mary Hudson?"

"I don't, but you and I both know there wasn't a student named Mary Hudson here then, unless she had been admitted in the interval between when I left and you gave birth."

Callie shook her head. If someone had been admitted, Callie would have been the big sister, and Debs's bed remained vacant. "How has this place not been shut down?" Her tone was desperate.

"I know, Callie. It's awful. I had no idea what I was getting into when I started. Sister Lourdes begged me to come aboard. I'm so sorry for your loss, but it seems you might have found a way back to your daughter. What a gift, Callie! I pray everything works in your favor, that she's been well brought up and will be welcoming to you."

They hugged. "Let's keep in touch," Callie said. "Really this time." She was glad to reconnect with an old friend.

Callie found Jocelyn in the waiting room, reading a magazine that she put down immediately as Callie walked swiftly past. As she descended the grand staircase for what she hoped was the last time, Jocelyn followed.

Once in the car, Callie stared dazedly out across the expanse of the grounds. "It's such a beautiful place. Where such awful things happened." Memories tumbled forth. The way she'd felt dismissed by her parents, by Jon. Hidden. Forgotten. *As if I was someone to be ashamed of.* And now she learned that babies had been bought and sold without the consent of innocent mothers. Innocent young girls and their babies. How the hell did she pull herself back together? "It's probable that Raina is Stella, but it's unconfirmed."

Jocelyn's jaw couldn't drop any lower as Callie relayed the story Debs told her. "This is good news, Callie!"

"I know. Every fiber of my being wants to go straight to Raina and tell her the whole story, but at what cost?"

"You won't tell her?" Jocelyn's lips pressed together.

"How could I disrupt everyone's life like that? Raina's, Harper's? This woman is supposed to carry her baby. Harper has been through enough."

Jocelyn left Callie alone with her thoughts for most of the remainder of the drive. Callie stared out the window as a million scenarios ran through her head, testing all the possibilities and consequences.

As they arrived back in Savannah, Callie suggested they stop at a coffee shop. Yes, she was stalling. She needed more time to arrive at a decision before getting back home. Jocelyn obliged her, as she so often did. How lucky had Callie been to have her as such a trusted friend for all these years?

"You are a lifesaver, again," Callie told Jocelyn as they sat down at a bistro table by the window overlooking River Street, bustling with working folk and passersby. "What is my move?"

"Only you can answer that."

"I need to tell Adam. Will he ever forgive me?"

"Of course he will. His love for you has never wavered."

Callie took a long sip of her chai latte, a pensive expression on her face.

"In all of this, are you thinking about... Jon?"

Callie's body responded to that question as if in that moment before a car was about to crash when a person braced themselves for impact. Her body went stiff, feet pressing on the floor. "Jon? Where did that come from?"

Jocelyn looked around, reminding Callie of her raised voice. "Shh."

"Jon doesn't deserve any of this information. He hightailed it out of here quickly."

"To be fair, he was fired."

"Since when do *you* defend Jon?"

Jocelyn looked like she'd been caught, a fish thrashing on the hook. She sipped her cappuccino, but Callie saw that her hand shook a little. "Jocelyn!"

"I'm not defending him, Callie, but he deserves to know he has a daughter. He thinks she died just as you did. He's a victim in this too."

"Who are you right now? And how does he even know that she died? For all he knows, I could have raised her alone."

Jocelyn lowered her gaze. "I told him."

"You *what?*" Callie's voice rose so that other patrons stopped their conversations to look over at the two of them.

"I changed my mind about him when you were at Covenant House. I saw how devastated he was over losing you."

"Devastated? He left. No contact. None."

"To be fair, he lost her too. He lost both of you. And his career. He was heartbroken. You didn't see him."

"And you're telling me this now? For the first time?"

"How could I tell you then? You'd just lost your baby. When you came back to us, you were so broken, Callie. We all handled you like fragile glass."

Callie's back stiffened.

"You needed to focus on rebuilding your life, getting back to yourself. I couldn't tell you that Jon reached out to me every so often to check on you."

"How often, Jocelyn?" She leaned in, her eyes wide.

"Occasionally. Months went by sometimes. Years."

"Years? *Years?*" This was too unbelievable to digest. "When was the last time you spoke to him?"

"Not for many years. He stopped getting in touch shortly after he was married."

Harper

Chapter 23

Harper looked at the clock for about the twentieth time in the last hour just as Miles began scratching at the back door. "Dammit, Miles, you were just out." With her nose flaring, she went over to the door to open it for him.

He looked at her with those bold chocolate eyes, tail tucked under his back side. He turned, sauntered past Harper, and plopped onto his bed.

Harper drew in a deep breath and expelled it with a sigh. She retraced her options. Their options. Raina had been so sure. But Harper couldn't get the doubt out of her head. How could she move forward with the transfer procedure when there were so many questions? Could Raina be her sister? Would her mother have kept that secret from her and Ben all these years? And why? Was she married before? None of it made sense.

It would be another hour before Gabe arrived home. In that hour, Harper must have walked five thousand steps throughout her first floor. She stretched her arms out and up to the ceiling. She tidied things around the house as she went. The walls felt like they were closing in then retracting. *I need to make a decision tonight. Time is running out.*

She stood at the kitchen sink but forgot why she had gone there. She blinked rapidly. *Think. Think, Harper.* She scanned the room. *The Windex.* She bent beneath the sink and retrieved it. With the

Windex and some paper towels, she moved to the back door to clean off Miles's drool. Wiping in a circular motion, Harper made the glass clear again.

How can I allow her to go through the transfer with so much uncertainty? If Raina was related to her, would she even want to be their surrogate? She and Gabe had worried about the ability of the surrogate to give up the baby. *But this... It would complicate matters exponentially.*

The front door clicked. "Harper," Gabe called, prompting Miles to eject himself from his bed to greet someone more welcoming of his attentions. Gabe knelt in the foyer to pet the dog as Miles planted sloppy kisses on his face.

Harper witnessed the entire exchange, standing over Gabe with hands on her hips, waiting for him to ask.

He stood. "How was your day?"

"How was my day? How *was* my day?" Sarcasm was thick in Harper's voice, as if Gabe was to blame or had even an inkling of what had transpired earlier.

He followed her into the kitchen, and Miles trailed close behind Gabe. Harper stood on one side of the island and Gabe on the other. He cocked his head, ready to listen.

Harper took a deep breath. She expelled her suspicions, her memories, and her visit with Raina without pausing. He shook his head more and more emphatically with each detail. Then he poured himself one shot of whiskey then a second, his hand shaky, after he downed the first.

Then Gabe placed two hands on the marble counter, gripping the edges. "So you're saying you think Raina is your sister?" Through squinted eyes, he stared straight at Harper.

She nodded.

"Because you recognized the name of a town where the hospital doesn't exist and your mother acted strangely about it?" His words were slow and measured.

"Yes."

"Do you hear how bizarre this all sounds?" Gabe tilted his head towards the ceiling then met Harper's gaze again. "Are you sure this isn't you concocting these far-fetched coincidences in your head because you're having second thoughts?"

Far-fetched? That felt like a jab to her heart. *Does he think I'm making all of this up?* "Everything I've told you is true. She could be my sister. It's too much to be coincidence."

"Not coincidence. A story you've conjured up so convincingly that you believe it. Why? Why start this if you can't follow through? Because you've had a revelation?" His face flushed like fire from his neck to his hairline.

Her chin stiffened. *How can he not see my perspective?* "Doesn't it matter to you if she is my sister and they're about to implant our baby into her? Doesn't that add a whole other level of complications? We've had so many already."

Gabe chortled out of frustration. "First, there are no facts to base this on. Not one." He clenched his jaw. "Harper, the transfer is two days from now. You need to do some soul searching before you ask that woman to go through this procedure for us."

Harper moved closer to Gabe. "What are you saying?"

"I'm saying I don't think you want this procedure. I'm not sure if you want a kid at all anymore."

"I did. I mean, I do." She moved close enough to him to reach out and grab his hand.

"What I can't understand is why you went through the retrieval in the first place. Did you change your mind because there are only three eggs?"

"No. I didn't change my mind."

He downed his second shot then vigorously loosened his tie, pulling it off and dropping it onto the counter. "I'm going to get changed." He stomped up the stairs while Harper made her way to the bottom. She heard Gabe upstairs, slamming drawers and doors. Each time, she shuddered. But she didn't cry.

She moved to the family room, where she lit the lamp and sat mostly in the dark, the tiny, faint light illuminating just part of the room. Looking up, she wanted to pray but didn't know what she even believed anymore. Perhaps she didn't believe in anything at all. Had she convinced herself of this story because she truly didn't want a baby? Could Gabe be right?

He walked slowly into the room, wearing shorts and a T-shirt. "I'm taking Miles for a run."

"Just like that? Conversation over?"

"Conversation over for now. I need to sort this all out."

"I'm going to my mother for answers. You'll see that this is not *all* in my head."

"Seems like a great idea, Harper." The tone of his voice certainly didn't match his words.

She heard Gabe putting the leash on Miles, then the front door shut so hard the whole house shook. Or, at least, it felt that way.

Their Waterford crystal vase sat on the coffee table. It had been a wedding gift, and she had loved it so much that she bought the very same one for each client on their closing day. It was as if she tried to pass on the joy she had felt as a newlywed to the clients she represented as they began a new chapter in their lives. Life had been so simple then. She and Gabe had been happy. They both had fulfilling jobs. Their dreams were easy and untethered.

As though the vase taunted her, she picked it up and slammed it onto the floor. It shattered into a million pieces. And it felt good.

Callie

Chapter 24

Callie shut the door behind her and leaned against it, nearly hyperventilating. So much of the past surged forth—a landslide. The loss. The lies. Why hadn't she demanded proof that her daughter had died? Shouldn't she have known? Felt it in her gut?

She thought back to her father's pleading voice just before she'd given birth to Harper. He had begged her to make amends with Evelyn. "She won't be here long," Asa had said. "She's your mother, after all." Had he known the extent of her mother's deceit that whole time? How could he defend her?

"She's already dead to me," Callie had replied coolly.

Two weeks later, Callie gave birth to Harper, and Evelyn died that same day. It was the first breath of fresh air she had felt in a very long time. She had Adam, Ben, and Harper, a second daughter. They were her gifts.

Adam. I have to tell him everything.

Her eyes burned. She needed to cry, to expel all of the grief that was so palpable. She couldn't. In fact, she couldn't recall the last time she had cried. Was it when she was told that Stella died? The grief that followed, then, had been unbearable. She only remembered her inability to breathe, as if all the air had constricted in her throat. The absence of tears since that time had turned into panic attacks, stifling, debilitating at times. That was how she felt now, standing against the front door as if it were keeping her upright.

Inhale. Exhale. Focus on the crack in the corner of the hallway beneath the dentil molding. She recited these words until her breathing calmed.

It would be a few hours before Adam returned from his business trip. This would be her opportunity to get all the answers she needed before having a long conversation with him.

Asa had been in an assisted-living establishment for ten years, and Callie visited him a few times a year. After he had arranged for Callie to live with Jocelyn's family, he'd bankrolled all of her expenses, including college and a car. Callie never spoke to her mother again even though Evelyn reached out on two occasions—once shortly before her marriage to Adam and once after Ben was born.

Callie used her key to enter her father's tiny apartment. Asa sat at the table in front of the window, playing solitaire, while the din of the news was on for background noise. Asa had never liked to sit in silence. Callie wondered if that had been to drown out the sound of Evelyn's voice.

"Hello, Daddy."

"Oh, Callie. You're here!" His eyes still sparkled when he saw her.

"I brought you some berry pie, the kind you like from the orchard." She bent down to kiss him.

"You always make your daddy smile. Sit. I'll make you some tea."

She watched his feeble body move at a turtle's pace toward the cabinet. His arms shook as he reached for two tea bags. Her inclination was to help him, but her father was a proud man. He would want to do it himself. Mechanically, he filled the teakettle with water and placed it on the stove.

"Come, sit." Callie patted the chair next to her at the small two-person table. "We need to discuss something."

Asa sat down.

"Daddy," she said in a low, serious tone. She wasn't sure what she hoped for—complete validation or innocence on his part. "I went to Covenant House today."

The lids of his eyes lowered in concert with his head. "Calista." He hadn't used her full name since the phone call he'd made, pleading with her to attend her mother's funeral. She had not gone. "I was afraid this day would come. Your mother was too."

"Afraid?" *Why is he using that word?*

He removed his hand from hers and put both of his on his lap, leaning in. "Whatever your mother did, it came from a place of love. She always didn't go about things properly, but her heart was in the right place. We were afraid of the truth hurting you all over again. Sometimes when you make choices—bad, awful choices—it's harder to undo them. You have to live with them."

"Undo them? All you had to do was tell me the truth."

"The truth. There had already been such a web of lies your mother caught herself up in, and I witnessed them. I didn't do anything to prevent them because I didn't want to lose her."

"But... why, Daddy?"

"There's so much you don't know about your mother, Callie. So much she never wanted you to know."

"Well, now's your chance to tell me."

Asa cleared his throat, an indication that he had plenty to say. "Her family was dirt-poor. Her mother had her out of wedlock and couldn't hold on to her. She grew up..." Asa became choked up. He took a second to fight back tears. "In an orphanage. They were awful places back then. You can't imagine how she lived."

Callie thought back to her difficulty dealing with the grief of her daughter's supposed death, how she'd felt imprisoned because she wasn't allowed to speak of it. She could well imagine the loneliness—in a different sort of way.

"I came from a very wealthy family. Something your mother did not know when I met her and not until long after we had fallen in love. I loved her grit, Callie, her untethered honesty—you are not unlike her in that way. When we announced our engagement, my parents abandoned us, for all intents and purposes. We were cut off. I had to build my way back. We were young parents, stupid ones. But we worked hard to get us there."

"What does any of this have to do with my baby?"

"In your mother's mind—and she could be a stubborn fool—your pregnancy threatened to destroy all that we had worked for. For us. For you. She didn't want to see you end up with a man of his tarnished reputation, working constantly just to make ends meet. We wanted college for you. Independence."

"But, Daddy, none of that was what I wanted."

Asa nodded his head. "I know. I know. She went about it all wrong. After she found out about your pregnancy, she did some digging at the school and found out about the athletic director. It was wrong, what he did to you."

"He was young too. We loved each other."

"Not too young to know he took advantage of you"

"That wasn't for either of you to decide."

"It was. We were your parents."

Callie wondered about Harper. *How would I have handled the same situation as a mother?*

The kettle on the stove whistled loudly. Unsteady on his feet, Asa made his way back to the stove and poured the tea. Callie sat in silence, trying to absorb it all, watching how feeble he had become. A shadow of the strong, imposing figure he'd been throughout her life.

"Why did Mother always say we were from old money if you had to make your own way?"

Asa placed two steaming teacups on the table. "Because that's the life she wanted. My name meant something in Savannah. She used it—*we* used it for the benefit of our family. She craved value, respect, from others." He bowed his head.

"When did she turn so evil?"

"She wasn't evil. She never was. She was a lot of things—stoic, desperate, reactive, self-righteous, stubborn. But don't ever mistake any of that for not loving you. She never learned how to love a child. She hadn't been loved like that."

"I never learned from Mother how to love a child, but I did... everything in my power to not be her."

"And you have two beautiful children." He drew the teacup to his lips.

"I have three."

His eyes filled with tears. Had she surprised him? He put the cup down without sipping.

"I found her, Daddy."

Asa moved his frail hand onto hers, which rested on the table. His skin felt like paper, veined and cold. "One minute." He left her alone in the small room, the size of most closets in the house where she had grown up.

Callie looked around. A worn leather recliner sat across from the television. Next to it on the table was his *Reader's Digest*, thick reading glasses, and the *Atlanta Journal-Constitution*. Throughout Callie's childhood, that same newspaper had awaited him every morning on the dining room table with his poached egg on wheat toast, grapefruit, and black tea. He had been regimented in his routines.

The sound of metal against metal made Callie suspicious. "What are you doing? Do you need help?"

"No," he hollered, rustling some papers.

Ambling back to the kitchen, Asa held out a letter with a shaking head. It was sealed in an envelope with Callie's name written on it in her mother's handwriting. "It's time to stop hating her. For you." He looked at Callie as his hand delivered the envelope to hers. "Please read this. I haven't, but before she died, she made me promise if you ever found out, I was to give this to you."

Callie grasped both ends of the envelope. Her fingers shook. She contemplated it.

"Go on," her father said.

Will this be the piece of evidence I need?

Callie gently ripped the top of the envelope and withdrew a piece of Mother's gold-embossed stationery.

February 23, 1980

Dearest Calista,

If you're reading this, you know of the awful and selfish things I've done. I hope with all my heart that you and your baby girl find one another again. When I made that decision, I was so out of my head with misplaced concern when I ought to have been thinking only about you. I tried to find a happy home where your daughter would be cared for in exchange for resurrecting your life, the life we had planned for you. Then everything spun out of control so I could keep my lie safe. I have regretted all of it. The only thing I will never regret is loving you. I cannot ask you to forgive me, for I have lived a long life of penance for what I have done, and regretfully, your father has also borne the consequences of my choices. But I do ask that you forgive me for your own sake. Put all of this in the past, Calista. Don't dwell on it, because it will color your future, and that would be another tragedy. Love your family, my beautiful daughter, better than you have learned from me.

Love Always, Mother

Callie was too angry to cry, too fixed on trying to make sense of it all.

"And you knew about this?" she asked.

Her father nodded, letting his chin hang to his chest.

"You didn't want to tell me. Why?"

He kept his gaze focused on the floor. "Your mother thought your life would be better off not being tied down at such a young age. And I didn't disagree with that."

Callie folded up the letter, placed it in the envelope, and tucked it into her purse. Perhaps Callie didn't disagree with that now either. Having Harper had changed her perspective on so many things.

When her father's eyes met hers, she saw tears leaking from them and streaming down his cheeks. She kissed the top of his head. "Thank you, Daddy."

ON THE WAY HOME, CALLIE had a missed phone call from Adam and two from Harper. Callie texted Harper back to meet her at home in two hours. She wanted time to talk to Adam first. Alone. His car was already in the garage when she pulled into the driveway.

When she walked in, he kissed her cheek. "Where have you been? I called you. I called Harper."

Callie dropped her keys and her purse on the table and nodded. "Harper will be here soon. Can we get a couple of glasses of wine and talk?"

"Oh no, this sounds serious."

Callie nodded again and moved to the living room to sit down. Adam followed her with two full glasses of chardonnay, and Callie patted the seat cushion next to her on the couch. "It's going to be a long night."

His eyes widened. "Okay, now you're scaring me. Is it your health?"

"No, nothing like that. More like my sanity. We have some time before Harper arrives, and I just want to prepare you."

Adam cocked his head. The crow's-feet beside his eyes deepened.

As Callie told her story, she could see by the way Adam's facial expressions morphed that he was trying the best he could to follow the details. His background as a lawyer had trained him to pay keen attention to details, but Callie knew even the best of lawyers would be challenged by this.

She took a breath after the part of holding her baby at Covenant House just after she was born, pink and wet and gorgeous—a groggy memory, but one she would certainly never forget.

"Cal, I gotta say, this is a lot to take in. Why didn't you ever tell me?" He stood up and walked across the room to the window. It was now pitch-black outside.

Callie watched him, measuring his every move, afraid he would flee. But she needed to continue. "I have a long way to go."

He retrieved the wine bottle from the kitchen and refilled their glasses, then he resumed his seat beside her.

"The next thing I knew, Mother was beside me, telling me my daughter had died. She took me home. We had a burial two towns away, and I don't know why I didn't question that then. Why not our church cemetery? Why not our priest? I was in shock from all of it." In the retelling, each emotion she had felt back then lived just beneath her skin, trickling out. "She basically locked me in the house for the next few weeks. Gave me medication that made me tired. Numb."

"Why? You were grieving, for God's sake."

"That's a question I've asked myself hundreds of times. Thousands." She shook the strain from her neck.

"And Asa stood for this? Why didn't he kick her the hell out?"

Callie shrugged.

Adam folded his arms and leaned back. "So, Jocelyn knew all about this." Callie could see the hurt in his eyes. "Why on earth did you think you couldn't trust me?"

Her eyes glossed over, the tears still stuck there. Perhaps this had been what she regretted the most. Not trusting Adam or the strength of their love. Maybe not at first, as that was understandable, but while they built their life? He had never once given her cause to doubt him. She shook the emotion away—there was still so much she had to tell him. "I don't know. I don't have an answer for you except that in the beginning, I didn't trust anyone. Jon and my mother did a number on me there. And as we went on, things were so good with us, and we have a beautiful family, a normal family. I can't tell you that I didn't think about it. I always just said to myself, 'What would be the sense of it?'"

He sat with that for a few minutes, then he shimmied over to her, getting close. "I don't know how you came out of this like you did." He wrapped his arms around her, and she felt his heart beating in sync with hers.

The front door opened then slammed shut. Harper entered like the wind had blown her in, all flustered. Callie didn't know what she knew, only that Harper had asked about Elberta and Callie had denied hearing of it. She needed to be the one to tell her daughter the truth.

Harper threw her arms up in the air. "Gabe is sleeping in the spare room until, I don't know, indefinitely." Her face was flushed, her head shaking. "Do you want to tell me what the fuck is going on?"

Callie began to approach Harper, but Adam gestured for her to let him hug their daughter instead. Sheepishly, she stood by, watching her husband console Harper when all she wanted to do was wrap her arms around her daughter, the only person she was concerned with right now.

"Let's get this all sorted out in the other room. Your mother was telling me—"

"Telling you what? Am I right? Is there a connection between Raina and Mom?"

"Settle down, Harper." His warm tone seemed to soften her the way it always did when she and Callie would have one of their mother-daughter screaming matches, especially through her teens. Back then, Callie had thought, *At least she loves me enough to fight with me.* For Harper's whole childhood, Callie had compared the kind of mother she was to her children—to Harper especially—against Evelyn.

Before joining them in the living room, Callie took an extra-long time getting another bottle of wine and a glass for Harper. She thought Harper might need a few of Adam's words of reassurance before Callie unleashed her whole sordid past upon her.

When she returned, Adam sat in the armchair. Callie thought he'd done that purposefully to make sure Harper sat on the couch beside her.

Looking straight into Harper's confused eyes, Callie said, "I'm sorry I lied to you. I lied to all of you."

Harper opened her mouth to say something, but Callie held up her hand. "Please, just listen. I know you have so many questions, and I will answer every one, I promise." She could see her daughter's posture relax. At least Harper seemed willing.

After a few minutes, Callie began. She started with how overbearing and pretentious her mother had been. "I was conditioned by her to be the perfect debutante. Every single thing I did was aimed toward how socially acceptable it would be and how it would play a part in the foundation of my future. Etiquette classes. Dance lessons. Private school. Handpicked friends. Everything led to those goals—her goals. As a little girl, I bought into them because they were all I knew. I had fantasies of a ball like Cinderella's. I imagined falling in love and living in a castle with my dreamy, perfect life. Do you see how unrealistic all of this is?"

Callie paused then continued.

"By the time I turned sixteen, I became rebellious. I shunned everything about my socialite parents, especially my mother. She wasn't a warm woman. I also fell in love with an administrator at Briarlee. He was five years older than me, which doesn't mean much as an adult, but then, it was a world of difference."

Harper pressed her lips together, slightly cocking her head. "He was a teacher? He took advantage of you?"

As many times as Callie had dissected why Jon had never reached out to her and why she couldn't locate him, she had never once blamed him for taking advantage of her. It had always been Evelyn where she targeted her blame. Only now, through Harper's eyes, could Callie see his culpability. She had only been a teenager. Jon should have known better.

But now was not the time to debate who was at fault, for Callie had accepted her own responsibility long ago. Callie swallowed hard and relayed the sequence of events, stopping intermittently to catch her breath. "My mother told me Stella, my daughter, had died." Saying the word aloud still sent a chill down Callie's spine, even now that she knew the death had been a lie. "I didn't have a baby and give her up. Black-market adoptions were more common than I had realized. There weren't any kinds of checks and balances back then. No paper trails. I never would have known if I hadn't seen that photograph and the birth certificate. The date was too coincidental not to send my head spinning."

Harper raised her hand to her open mouth. "Mom..."

"I know." Callie continued her story, and Harper listened intently. "When you caught me with that cupcake and candle, I had to make up something. I suppose it was recklessness that made me say Elberta. I don't even remember saying it, to be honest with you. During those early years, I was still distraught over losing her. Celebrating Stella's birthday in private was the one way I could keep the memory of her—of her existence—alive. Perhaps I'd kept the secret so bottled up inside that it was freeing somehow to offer up any details. They were safe with you because you thought all of it was just a story I made up."

Harper threw her arms around her mother. "Oh, Mom. Mom." She hugged Callie so tightly that it conveyed everything she needed. "Your mother was worse than the stories you told about her when I was young. Was she the queen bee?"

Callie nodded. "I was smothering or overprotective or paranoid—yes, I know I was all those things. I'm sorry. It was only because I didn't want to lose you." Then Callie remembered, and she pointed a finger at Harper and Adam. "Wait, my father gave me a letter from her."

Harper read the letter then passed it to Adam. Callie watched both of them as their backs stiffened in defensive mode. At least now she had her family in her corner.

"What do you think?" Adam asked. She knew he was talking about the letter. About the possibility of forgiving Evelyn.

"I'm going to have to sit with this one for a bit. I don't know that I have it in my power to forgive her." Callie turned her attention back to Harper, looking in her eyes and stroking her hair. "My beautiful daughter. I'm so lucky that you're mine. Now, what are we going to do about Gabe and about Raina?"

Harper hung her head. "I don't know. We still don't really have proof that Raina is Stella. I can't upend her life on something that's only probable."

"Oh, honey, everything will work out just the way it's supposed to. A very special friend said that to me many years ago. Go home and talk to Gabe. Make him understand. The two of you shouldn't deprive yourselves of a child if that's what you really want. And so what if Raina is your sister? That would make her all the better candidate for a surrogate."

"But we don't know. Am I supposed to lie to Raina, pretend as if you never told me any of this? She was insulted when I even suggested she'd been adopted. Adamant that she wasn't."

"We don't know. I'm not sure we ever will. So now I want you to do what's right for you. Move forward with what you know now. Dad and I will support you in whatever you decide."

With her thumbs, Callie wiped away the tears rolling down Harper's face.

Raina

Chapter 25

The white-and-gray room was chilly. In her hospital gown, Raina sat up on the bed, rubbing the goosebumps on her arms.

Wayne paced in front of the window. "Are you sure you want to go through with this? It's not too late."

"Yes, a hundred times yes. Harper's been through a lot. We're lucky, you know, Wayne."

He settled at the side of her bed and tucked a strand of hair dangling in her face behind her ear.

"They weren't kidding when they said they kept the room cool," she said.

Wayne tucked the blanket around her.

"I love you for supporting me in this."

"Well, I love you for doing this."

"Would you remember to call Ruthie Mae to tell her the honey delivery will be late? The hardest part of all of this will be staying still afterwards."

Wayne chuckled. "No one keeps Raina Edwin down."

The nurse swung open the door. "The doctor's on his way."

THE TRANSFER WENT WELL. Raina had been given strict instructions to take it easy for the first few days. It would be two weeks before a positive result could be determined.

Raina called to give Harper the news.

Harper answered immediately, as if she'd been sitting beside the phone. She sounded pleasant, calm, even. Perhaps having some time to think about the wild tale she'd concocted in her head had settled her back into a more realistic frame of mind.

Raina let it go—she always looked forward instead of back. "So I'll just be here, taking it easy. I'm so excited for you and Gabe." Should she tell her the doctor said it could take two to three attempts for the transfer to work? Raina decided not to. *Why worry her about something that hasn't even happened yet?* "Don't worry about a thing, okay?"

Harper said she wouldn't but didn't sound very convincing. Raina chalked it up to new-mother jitters, as she surely had them her first time.

On the third day, Raina resumed light housework and got back to her routine of dropping the kids off at school. The conversation between them to and from school always proved more spirited than at home. There was something about having little ones in the back seat of a car that increased their willingness to spew details about the day. Were they trying to outdo one another? It must be a sibling thing that Raina had never experienced. But as a mother, she welcomed it.

After dropping the kids off at school, Raina even managed to get some honey candles made, though not too many. She didn't want to stand on her feet for too long.

Shortly after eleven o'clock in the morning, there was a knock at her front door. She had her feet up on the sofa, as ordered, while she sewed Tina's Brownie badges to her sash.

"One minute," she called out while tucking her sewing into the basket on the floor.

When she approached the door, she peeked out the side window to see her father standing there. A man she didn't recognize was in an old beat-up Pontiac with the ignition still on in the driveway, smoke pouring from the tailpipe.

Alarmed, she opened the door. "What on earth? Pa, what are you doing here?"

He wore a thin jacket with a pilled, collared shirt underneath and too-big slacks that were cinched around his waist with a tight belt. His hair was slicked back like he'd just showered.

Raina took hold of his wrist. "Come on in. Who is that?" She motioned to the car.

"Oh. Paul." Reggie pointed at him and waved. "Friend from the park. He drove me here."

They walked in through the door, and she led him to the living room. "Go on, sit."

He remained standing instead. "I won't be here long." He brushed the side of his head. "Wayne around?"

Now Raina was definitely concerned. Her father rarely asked about Wayne.

She stepped back. "Yeah, out in the barn."

"If you would, bring him in here. I think you're going to want him to hear this."

Raina didn't take time to react, because she'd become even more alarmed. Instead, she hurried out through the back door to the barn, calling out Wayne's name. The whole while, thoughts darted at her. *Is he sick? Did he do something? Is he out of money? Why in God's good name is he scaring me like this?*

Wayne followed Raina into the house with determined steps. He greeted Reggie with a handshake. "Everything all right, there? Should you invite your friend in?"

"Nah, I told him to wait in the car. He'll be fine."

"Sit, Pa."

Reggie sat down behind where he was standing, right on the middle seat of the sofa. Raina sat next to him, and Wayne perched on the ottoman across from them.

Reggie reached into his jacket pocket and pulled out a manila envelope. "You know, I got to thinkin' after your visit, Raina..."

Her eyes shifted in Wayne's direction. *My visit.* She combed her hand through her hair, bracing herself, dialed in to the thick package shaking in her father's hand like a jittery shadow. He handed it to her.

Her hand trembled, too, as she pulled thin, coffee-stained papers from it. Raina drew in a deep breath before she began reading. Words darted out at her. *Baby Sebastian. Born April 23, 1970.*

My birthday. Me?

Delphine Goldstein. Mary and Reginald Baker. Legal and binding contract. April 24, 1970.

Raina cleared her throat and passed the document to Wayne, who read it with a snarl on his lips. She pressed her hands against her thighs, collecting her thoughts. Her father waited with

his gaze lowered.

He began slowly, picking at his finger as he spoke. "We was poor, Raina. We didn't have means to have a child, and your mama tried for years to get pregnant. So when we heard about this lawyer who set up illegal adoptions, I called him. I would have done anything for your mama."

"Who was the lawyer?"

"I don't recall. Huff-something. Hoffman, Huffman, maybe. I reached out to him. Then a few weeks later, he called early in the morning, said the baby was here and we had to pick you up at someplace three hours away. Some house, it was called."

"Covenant House?"

"Yes, that's it. In Elberta."

"Did you ask any questions?"

"We was afraid to. We handed him a bag with money. He handed us you and a doctored birth certificate and those papers, told us to lock them away, never to be seen. We ain't never looked back. Your mama loved you like she loved the rain."

"Were you ever going to tell me?"

"It would have broken your mother's heart if she knew you called someone else Mama." His voice was soft now, and it cracked. "I didn't do right by you. I knew it. I tried, Raina, but a big part of me died when your mama did. If I told, you would have flown the coop and never looked back. I couldn't have your mama sad in heaven." Tears welled in her father's eyes.

"I'm here." Raina hugged him, her hands pressing tight against his bony back.

When Reggie left, Wayne took Raina into his arms and held her with his whole body, just the way she needed him to. She could breathe in his arms because it was the one place she knew she belonged.

Wayne took her hand and led her to the sofa. He sat down and pulled her next to him, wrapping her in his arms.

A memory of grade school flashed into her mind. Her father had dropped her off as he did most days, at the beginning. He'd always felt the need to explain her mother's death. Raina never knew if he expected her teachers to pity her or if he thought she needed a mother figure and a teacher wouldn't be a bad option. One teacher had said, before her father could even deliver his ritual speech, "You must look just like your mother."

When Raina got home after school that day, she took the photograph of her mother down off the shelf. It rested next to other things Mary had especially loved, like a bronze replica of Raina's first pair of shoes and an old paperweight that had belonged to her mother. Raina imagined the photograph had been a high school graduation portrait or something that she'd posed for. Her hair was long and flowing, not blond, and her nose didn't turn up at the end, and her face looked round, not oval. A wave of disappointment had coursed through Raina, and she placed the photograph back on the shelf with a little more force than she should have. It tumbled down to the floor, cracking the glass. That was the day Raina had come to terms with the fact that she did not look like her mother.

"I don't even know what to say. Everything is just a mess." She buried her face in Wayne's chest and sobbed, her breath hitching.

Wayne wiped away her tears. "We're gonna be okay. You're going to get through this. You, me, our family." He dropped a kiss on the top of her head.

"Pa came all the way here. It must have been eating away at him since my visit."

"Now it's eating away at you. Do you want to meet her? Your biological mother?"

"I have so many questions."

"I have a big one. What about the surrogacy arrangement?"

"Harper doesn't know any of this yet. She seemed relieved when we chalked it up to coincidence. I'll have to wait to see if this transfer took. I can't even think about broaching this subject with her until we know that much." Raina let out a guffaw that expressed the irony of it all. "I have a sister. And a brother, apparently. And I just might be carrying my sister's baby."

"Well, given the results, this might make your decision a little easier. I got a new account today that could almost double what I lost with Belowe. A new chain is coming to town with stores all over Georgia."

Raina kissed Wayne's mouth long and hard then rested her head on his shoulder. "I'm so blessed to be part of *this* family."

ON A BRIGHT AND SUNNY day, Raina dropped the kids off at school. During the drive, Tina whined that Tracy didn't even acknowledge her as her sister in the hallways.

"You look the other way and laugh with all your friends," Tina admonished.

"Stop trying to copy everything I do. Get your own friends," Tracy shot back.

"Girls, girls. One day, you will cherish having a sister. I never..." Raina's thoughts took over such that she didn't finish her statement. It was no longer true. Now she had a sister, by blood. Even ten days after Reggie's confession, it didn't seem real, no matter how many times she tried to reconcile it in her head.

When Harper had called a day earlier to ask how Raina felt and what time her doctor's appointment was, Raina kept the conversation cordial and brief. Harper asked if Raina wanted her to accompany Raina for the blood work. So did Wayne. Raina declined them both. This was something she had to do on her own. Facing the results and how she felt about them needed to be on her own terms.

She walked into the doctor's office with her head held high, conjuring up all the faith she had within her. Whatever was meant to be, God would see to it, and she would accept her fate. Their fate. Over the past week and a half, her thoughts wavered like a hoverfly when she prayed they would become more calculated like her bees. She counted on the results of this test to point her in the right direction.

After the prick of the needle, she waited in the doctor's office. He came in with an indifferent expression on his face and sat across from her, behind his desk. "Well, Mrs. Edwin, the test came back negative." The rest of his words seemed muffled.

She pressed a hand to her stomach and parted her lips, nodding her head in a gentle, contemplative rhythm. Relief was what she felt, and she knew exactly what to do next.

She had written the address down on a piece of paper, and she drove there with no background music, just her thoughts. They were both as light as the breeze and as heavy as her foot pressing against the pedal.

Pulling into the long drive, she noticed the trees lining the pavement, dripping with Spanish moss, and the flower beds, pristine and vibrant, ornamenting the paver-stone walk. When she approached the front door, she drew in a deep breath and prayed to God to find the right words.

Harper opened the door, holding the collar of a black Labrador retriever at her side.

"Is he friendly?" Raina asked.

Harper nodded. "Miles." Raina petted the dog, who then welcomed her entry into the house with a wagging tail. Raina looked around—it was so spacious and bright. Everything seemed to sparkle.

"So..." Harper said with a lilt in her voice. She led Raina into the kitchen, which looked like a proper chef's kitchen, white and open. "Can I get you anything?"

Raina shook her head. They sat on stools at the island. Raina pressed her hand against the granite, then she rested her elbow on the counter, her chin in her hand, and expelled a breath. "There's so much we need to talk about."

Harper's lips pressed together in a slight grimace.

"The test came back negative." Raina's relief when Harper simply bobbed her head instead of breaking down prompted her to continue. She stuck to the facts about having two more opportunities for a transfer before getting to the caveat. Raina placed her hand on Harper's. "You were right about all of it."

Harper let out a sigh, and her eyes filled with tears. "I know. My mother told me everything, but we don't have any proof. It could still be all a coincidence."

Raina placed her oversized purse onto the counter and pulled out the paperwork that would give Harper all the proof she needed.

"So, now what?" Raina asked. "Where do we go from here? I signed a contract, and I would like to give you the child you so desperately want. But this development adds a layer of complications. I don't even know how I feel. I go back and forth from angry to hopeful and curious."

Raina took both of Harper's hands in hers. "We are half sisters. I don't know what your beliefs are, but I believe in God and fate, and I can't help wonder if all this was put in front of us to bring us together."

Harper

Chapter 26

Gabe came home from work, light on his feet, as he practically danced into the family room. Harper sat cuddled up in the corner of the sofa with Miles lying next her, resting his head on her lap while she picked at her cuticles in a daze-like state.

"Good news?" His voice was so hopeful, which made Harper's stomach churn.

She shrugged, and her cheeks puffed up in an attempt to smile. First, she scooted Miles off the couch, then she invited Gabe to sit down, patting her hand on the sofa beside her.

"I'm not sure if it's good news or not. It's overwhelming, for sure."

"Back up. Are we, or aren't we?"

Harper felt like they were on two different planes. She was so focused on a past she felt cheated out of that she hadn't given the negative test much thought, but she could tell that was all Gabe had on his mind.

She backed up, filled in the gaps of the story that Raina had completed for her. "I have a sister, and my mother has a whole past I knew nothing about. None of us did, and I'm not sure what to do with that piece of it."

"Harper, the test. Is it positive or negative?"

She felt silly for leaving that part out. "Negative."

Gabe's shoulders dropped immediately. Of course he would be sad. She should have been more sensitive to that. "So how does all of this affect us?" he asked. "Did Raina say she'd try again?"

"She said something about fate." Harper stood and walked over to the window, trying to collect her words so they came out just right. "That she thought all of this"—her hands moved in a circular motion—"is what brought out the truth, what brought us together. It got me to thinking about us. I don't usually take much stock in God and destiny, but I feel like the universe is trying to give me a message."

Gabe met Harper at the window. "What are you trying to say?"

"I know you want to be a dad, and you'll be a fabulous one. But I'm not meant to be a mother. Maybe it's something I decided when I was a little girl, feeling that love meant smothering, controlling, but I still feel it, Gabe. I know I fell in love with our babies when they were inside me. But I realized today that I wasn't sad when Raina said it didn't take. I didn't jump on her offer to try again because there is still something inside me telling me I'd be happier without children. It's a feeling I can't explain."

Something in his eyes seemed very lost at that moment. Harper stopped talking to give him time to let everything she'd said sink in. He covered his mouth with one hand and went somewhere else in his mind, even though he remained standing right there.

Harper tried to reach out, to rub his arms, but he shimmied away. Then she heard him grab his keys from the kitchen counter, and the front door slammed shut.

FOR THE NEXT FEW NIGHTS, Gabe slept in the guest bedroom. They didn't talk about the issue that stood like Gibraltar between them. Instead, they exchanged pleasantries.

"Good morning."

"Good morning."

"How was your day?"

"Fine."

On a day Gabe planned on being at the job site until late, Harper went into the nursery and surrounded herself with flat cardboard boxes and tools from the garage. Dressed in yoga pants and an over-sized T-shirt, she got right to work just after Gabe's car pulled out of the driveway.

Standing at the center of the room, Harper took in the daunting task set before her the way one might when the door closed on a dream or a long-planned goal, when all paths had been exhausted and a dead end reached. She had mustered the courage, deciding not to share her plans with Gabe because she didn't want him to find a way to talk her out of it.

Harper had never known her grandmother, but she'd craved knowing her during her formative years. Perhaps it was due to the mystery surrounding Evelyn, the grandparent rarely mentioned. She knew Grandpa Asa but not as well as she knew her paternal grand-parents. They had been part of the family in much the way her friends' grandparents were. Her mother's father felt like an adden-dum to the family, only there on big occasions—not part of their day-to-day life.

Harper did remember the house her mother had grown up in, and she was in awe of it, counting it as one of the reasons she was drawn to the real estate business. Not that she visited the big house often, but when she did, it felt like a palace. When her mother had to move her grandfather into assisted living and sell the place, Harper had wondered why it was so easy for Callie to let everything go. As sentimental as her mother was in her own house, she wasn't at all at-tached to things from her childhood. She wanted nothing from the grand house with the sprawling lawn and gardens upon gardens of flowers in bloom.

She imagined, now, that her mother had felt the same ghosts before she closed the door to her parents' home. All those years she thought Raina had died, had her mother been haunted too? So much began to make sense. The protective wing Callie had put around Harper and Ben, keeping them so close, always afraid they would disappear too. Harper looked at the empty crib, thinking about the loss that had followed her mother for the better part of her life.

Perhaps this was how it was meant to be all along—Harper experiencing her own loss so she could understand her mother's. While Harper didn't have a religious upbringing in the ritualistic sense, Callie talked about God and faith and destiny as if she had. Maybe Raina was right that Harper's purpose in seeking a surrogate wasn't to have a baby but to unravel all the secrets of the past. If their lives would become intertwined in a familial sense, Harper couldn't conceive of complicating that further with a child between them. Ending that dream was freeing in a sense, leading Harper to understand that she really didn't see herself as a mother at all, and she finally understood why.

Even though there hadn't been a tangible child for Harper to hold and bond with, there had been several imagined children that now roamed this room like ghosts. Every time she passed, every time she stepped foot into it, she felt them.

This was a day for an exorcism of ghosts by purging reminders of them. She needed desperately to close the door on this period of her life once and for all. It was the only way to free herself to move on.

She began with the elephant in the room. Armed with a screwdriver and wrench, she took to disassembling the crib backward from the way Gabe had pieced it together. That day was still clear in her mind, his excitement overflowing and overzealous, which was only apparent now. With her belly tight and round, she had stood with directions in hand, calling them out to him.

Staring at the parts of the crib now lumped in a pile on the floor, Harper experienced a release of tension that evaporated through her skin. Parts reduced to something that almost was—no longer what could be. This was a liberating revelation, for it validated what she had repressed for a long time.

Once the whole room was boxed up, not a trace left of a life they'd temporarily embraced, Harper pushed all the boxes into a pile at the center of the room.

Downstairs, in their office, she removed a folder marked *Baby* from the file cabinet. She didn't stop to peruse the documents within. Instead, she ripped them up, discarding them into the trash bin. Surrogacy and adoption pamphlets and bills from the doctor and bills from the hospital. At the back of the file were ultrasound photos, two of them, which made her only momentarily hesitate. Then she shook her head and let them drop from her fingers with the other remnants.

"This is the past," she whispered to herself and to Miles, who wagged his tail at her feet.

Harper stood, arms extended, at the center of the kitchen, and relief moved through her. She could almost see it spreading out under her skin, from her neck through her limbs, out her fingertips. They tingled.

There was one last task. Ben, the only person she'd confided in. She needed to call Ben to tell him she had finished. He was at her door by that afternoon.

The two of them stood at the bottom of the staircase. "Are you sure you want to do this?" he asked. "Sometimes when you make a decision, it's a hasty one."

Harper placed her hand on his shoulder. "I'm sure, Ben. This one is anything but hasty. I can promise you that."

"Okay." He ascended the stairs to begin the process of removing what she had packed up while Harper went into the kitchen to chop cucumbers and radishes for salad—the beginnings of a confessional dinner she'd planned with Gabe.

After several trips up and down and out the front door, Ben finished loading his truck.

Harper cracked open two cans of beer. She handed one to Ben. "Sit down, brother. I have a lot to tell you."

They sat across from one another at the island. She shared the whole story about Raina and their mother, for he'd known only bits of it already—just what their father had told him in a rushed phone call.

"Damn." He slammed the can on the counter. "So we have a half sister. Unbelievable."

"She's sweet, Ben. You and Pam will like her. Even more unbelievable is the witch that was our grandmother. How did Mom manage to keep all of that from us?"

"I always thought it was weird that we'd see Grandpa Asa but they'd never mention our grandmother."

"She must've met you. She died the day I was born. I was always a little creeped out about that. No wonder Mom was so demonstrative, so shielding. She wanted to be the exact opposite of her own mother."

Ben nodded. "I know you and Mom have had your ups and downs."

"I used to blame you. All this time, I thought Mom put you on such a pedestal that I'd never measure up. Nothing I did seemed right enough, and she kept such a tight leash on me."

"You aren't the only one. She was protective of me too."

"Protective? Suffocating, stifling, asphyxiating was more like it." She mockingly held her hand to her neck. "We were both living in the shadow of a ghost we never knew existed."

Ben's voice softened. "Harper, you've got to cut her some slack. It's amazing that she's come out of all that so sane."

Harper was just about to agree when she heard the front door shut. Her heart stopped as Gabe's footsteps grew closer.

"Why's Ben here?" he asked. "What are all the boxes in the back of his truck?"

"Hey, Gabe," Ben said, though his eyes rolled in the direction of his sister.

"You're home early." She placed her beer down on the counter.

"Ben. What's going on?" Gabe's thick brows formed a peak.

"Just helping Harper with some things."

"Things?" He cocked his head in the direction of his wife.

Harper moved around the island toward him. "Gabe," she said, her voice low and calming. She swallowed hard before speaking again. "I wanted to talk to you about it over dinner. You're early."

She could see his body stiffen. "Seems to have messed up your plan." His voice combated hers with sarcasm.

Ben interrupted. "I think this is my cue." He kissed her cheek then turned to Gabe. "Sorry, man." He left before Harper could thank him.

Once the front door closed, Gabe took a step toward Harper. She could feel anger emanating from him, or maybe it was betrayal. "So this is your decision? It's final, then?"

"Yes. We don't need it anymore," she said, not averting her focus from his glare. "Ben and Pam do."

"What does that mean?"

"They're having a baby, and we're not."

"And that's it?"

She lowered her head to take a minute to say her words in just the right way. "I can't give you what you want at the expense of my own happiness. I need to get back to myself again. My strong, driven self, the one who doesn't worry about everything. Gabe, we had a beautiful life before."

"Things change. I don't know if I can go on pretending that having kids doesn't matter to me. That's not how I see my life." The veins in his forehead were visible evidence of his conviction.

Still, Harper couldn't go back.

"I don't know where we go from here," he said as he leaned back against the wall, melding into it. "When did we stop talking? When did we stop making decisions together?"

Harper wanted to say, *With the first pregnancy*, but she didn't even know if that was the whole truth. She shrugged.

"I want a family. I do. Even after all of this. Everything we've been through. Once it happens, all of this will be a blur in our past." He leaned forward, looked Harper directly in the eyes. "I'll do everything, all the legwork. I'll find a new surrogate for us. I know things got all messed up with Raina. All of this has put an incredible strain on you, on your job. I'm sorry."

"That isn't it," she said. "You were so happy when we became pregnant the first time. I wanted to be that person for you. I even convinced myself I wanted it too. But it isn't me. It took all of this for me to understand that becoming a mother isn't what I want, Gabe. I'm happy with just us and Miles and my work."

"Harper!" His voice rose, startling her. "You're not listening to me. Listen to me. I can't be married to you if you don't want a family."

IT WASN'T OFTEN THAT Harper sought her mother's counsel, but after Callie had let Harper in, exposing her past, Harper somehow felt that they shared a connection out of a common vulnerability. But even more so, Callie put Harper first when she could have gone to Raina.

Harper turned the knob on the front door of the house where she'd grown up. She'd always regarded their life as so lily-white, stiflingly perfect. But when Harper walked through into the front hallway, it was as if a shroud had been lifted. All the pretenses were gone. "Mom," she called out.

Callie wasn't in the kitchen nor the family room. At the bottom of the stairway, Harper called up then rubbed the back of her neck as she climbed the stairs. Of course her mother was home—her car was in the driveway. Again, she called out, this time more as a question.

As she peeked into each room, her breath quickened. Her own room was left virtually intact, and Ben's too. Her mother had kept them almost as shrines.

In the spare room at the end of the hallway, she noticed the attic door left open, and relief washed over her. "Mom," she called up as she took the first step.

"Up here, honey."

Harper found her mother seated on the attic floor with items flocked around her and an empty box in front of her. "Here you are."

Callie looked questioningly at her. The light from the round window cast a glow on Callie's face. Even with the crow's feet spidering from her eyes and subtle wrinkles accentuating her mouth, Callie was a beautiful woman. A natural kind of beauty, not one put on or made up. "I'm sorry. Did I worry you?"

Harper nodded and walked closer. On Callie's lap were baby clothes and a blanket. In her hand was a stack of papers. "What are you doing?"

"Ah. Going through your and your brother's baby things. Reminiscing."

Harper nodded, wondering if today had been, perhaps, the wrong day to seek her mother's advice.

Callie patted the top of a nearby stool and pulled it closer. "Sit." Harper sat. Callie handed Harper the stack of maybe twenty pages bound in ribbon. The paper was thin and yellowed. "These are some diary entries I kept while I was at Covenant House. Go on. Read them."

Harper wet her lips and read. She took in every word, turning page after page while Callie refolded the clothes in her lap.

"Most of these were yours," her mother said of the tiny garments she held in front of her with the tips of her fingers. "I thought if Ben and Pam have a boy, I could give them the rest of his."

Tears welled in Harper's eyes as she read. She wiped them away and continued. When she finished, she put the stack in her mother's lap. "You have to let Raina read these. They're filled with such love. Such hope. How did you sustain such hope when you were locked up in that place?"

Callie shrugged. "I was determined that no matter what, we'd be okay. I refused to believe we wouldn't. Maybe out of stubbornness or sheer will. My belief in God. I can thank your grandfather for that."

Harper nodded, realizing that she'd never felt that conviction as a mother. Doubt always crept its way in. "Will you give these to Raina?"

"Maybe someday." Callie placed her hand on Harper's knee. "She hasn't even reached out. It's been almost two weeks."

"It's a lot to process. Everything she knew about her life has changed." Harper handed the pages back to her mother. "Maybe you should reach out to her."

"I don't want to scare her away now that I found her, do I? These are pretty intense." Callie took the letters and placed them in the box along with the memorabilia she'd saved from when Ben and Harper were babies—rattles, a piggy bank, envelopes with their first locks of hair, and baby books.

"Why did you save all that?"

Callie placed the top on the box. "Because it was the best part of my life, and I didn't want to forget a thing. I only wish..."

"You had more of Raina's."

"More than the trinkets. I wish I had the time. To see the little things, like her first tooth, or to hear her laugh for the first time—all the things I had with you and Ben. Those are what I treasured." Callie stood, brushing off her yoga pants. "Let's go make some tea."

Harper helped her mother replace the boxes where she had found them. "Just under the window," Callie directed. "Wait. On second thought..." Harper watched her lift the lid on the memorabilia box and slip out the diary papers. "I'll put these in the night-table drawer next to my bed. I'll at least show them to Dad now. No more secrets."

Harper smiled at her with approval.

Outside on the veranda, Harper and Callie sat in the sunlight, sipping tea and eating shortbread cookies. "Yours are the absolute best," Harper said, swallowing the flaky sweetness.

Harper scanned the backyard in all its beauty. Her mother had a place for everything. The birdbath was at the center of an island of low-growing phlox and primrose. Paver stones made a path from a circular patio down the sloping yard and around mounds of azalea, fountain grass, and lilies. "You made this a home with your love, attention, and bare hands. I'm sorry I haven't acknowledged that before."

"You made yours a home too."

Harper rocked her head left and right, stretching the kinks from her neck.

Callie put her hand over Harper's and squeezed. "Why are you really here, honey? What's on your mind?"

"Gabe and I are at an impasse. I need your wisdom." She paused and corrected herself. "Probably more so your strength."

Callie leaned in, anchoring her attention. "What is it?"

"Gabe really wants a baby. He'll do whatever I need to have one."

"Did Raina say she wouldn't go ahead with the surrogacy?"

"She said she would, but I can't. The last thing we need is a baby coming into this world with an auntie-slash-mother." Harper let a laugh escape. The levity relieved the tension crawling from her neck to her shoulders.

"So, what do *you* want?" Callie asked.

"I want to save my marriage. Without having a child."

"Why don't you want a child? Be honest. With yourself."

Harper's eyes rolled up to the sky. *How honest can I be without messing up this relationship too?* "I get it now. You lost a child. But I never knew that, and my whole life, I felt this expectation that I could never measure up to. I just always felt..."

"Go on."

"Not enough. Gosh, there were times I didn't even think you liked me. I blamed Ben for always being so perfect in your eyes."

"Goodness." Callie ran her fingers through her hair, rubbing the back of her head. "I accept that was your truth, but it wasn't mine. You and Ben have been my world. I realize, now, I might have taken the whole 'I won't be like my mother' plight to the extreme. And to your detriment." She sighed. "When I was a young mother, I suppose I didn't know how deep my loss went. I thought I did a pretty good job hiding it. But it came out in other ways. I can acknowledge that now. What I determined to be caring, you took as smothering. When I thought I was showing my love by wanting to know your every move, you understood it as mistrust. I overcompensated. I see that."

Callie looked directly into Harper's eyes, and Harper held her gaze. "I want you to know I love you. I've always loved you. I'm sorry... for so much. For not really processing my loss, which inevitably led to my shortcomings as your mom. For not being honest with Dad. For so many things."

"I'm learning that while we may be good-intentioned, we still unintentionally make mistakes in the choices we make. We are human. We are flawed. But for so long, I was afraid if I were a mom, my child would inevitably feel how I did. I told myself if I didn't become a mom, it would stop with me. I didn't want to become you. Your whole identity seemed like it was wrapped up in us. But it wasn't me or Ben, it was the ghosts—of your daughter, your mother."

Callie adjusted herself in her seat. "Thank you for being honest. All I ever wanted for you was happiness. And love. I'm truly sorry. Life is messy and unkind, but you learn to pick yourself up and move on in the best way you know how. Maybe, for you, that's without children. Maybe it's without Gabe. Only you can make that decision. Whatever it is, Harper, you can do this. You're strong, and you're smart. Dad and I will support you, no matter what."

There it was. The clarity Harper was looking for. With the solace that finally found its way into her heart and mind, she threw her arms around her mother, nearly jumped out of her seat to do so. Harper held her as tightly as she could.

Callie

Chapter 27

Harper had written out the directions for Raina's house in Brocton. She was insistent upon giving Raina a heads-up before Callie visited her the following day, a Saturday. "You can't just show up and say, 'Hey, I'm your mother,'" Harper said.

Callie knew she was right and appreciated Harper acting as her liaison. Harper had offered to take the drive with her, but Callie refused, knowing this was something she needed to do alone.

Eleven o'clock was the time Raina suggested, and the morning dragged. Callie must have looked at the clock ten times in the last ten minutes, and trying to busy herself with laundry and tidying up her house didn't help the least bit. She thought, *To hell with it. I'll be early. Better early than late. At the very least, she'll know I'm eager.*

After dropping her keys and having to kneel down to fetch them from under the car, she noticed her hands quivering. Callie stood and bent over to brush dirt off her pants. *Stop this.* In her wildest dreams, she couldn't have imagined she would be meeting the daughter she thought she'd buried thirty-four years ago. The hairs stood up on her arms.

Callie blared music on the drive, but the words in her head roared over the sweet melodies. *Hi, I'm your mother... Raina, it's so nice to meet you... You look more beautiful than your photograph...* These false starts felt cheesy. How could a mother who had been separated from her daughter for nearly thirty-four years begin? Then doubt set in.

Will she accept me? Will she be angry that I didn't know? What happened to having a mother's intuition?

Just as she glanced over at her purse, considering the contents within, the phone on the seat beside her rang. Her right hand jerked from the wheel. *Did Raina change her mind?* Callie calmed immediately when she saw Adam's number.

"I just called to wish you luck."

"Thanks. I'm on my way."

"Already?"

"Yeah, I was wearing out the floors, pacing."

He chuckled. "Listen, no matter how it goes—"

"No. No. No. Don't put negative thoughts out there. I have enough of my own already."

"We love you. That's what I wanted you to know."

"Thanks, babe. I needed to hear that."

Adam's call gave her the courage she'd needed.

As she pulled up the long drive that led to a rolling farm, acres upon acres, she heard Debs's words: *You're the strongest person I know.*

"I hope so," Callie whispered back to the memory.

The long dirt drive led to a red clapboard-and-brick farmhouse with a wide front porch, on which were two rockers and a wooden swing adorned with puffy sunflower pillows. Several barns dotted the property to the right of the house, the farthest back so far that it looked like a dwarf compared to the ones that were closer.

On the front lawn stood an old, sturdy willow tree with a canopy that almost hid a tire swing. Action figures and dolls were scattered on the ground beneath. *My grandchildren.* Callie had been so focused on meeting Raina, she'd lost sight of the children. She wondered if Raina would allow her to meet them.

A well-built, broad-shouldered man met Callie at the front porch. "Mrs. Clarke?" he asked.

"Callie," she corrected, taking it all in. The beautiful property, so green and full of life. The warmth she felt already, just being here, gave her a sense of relief that her eldest child had a blessed life.

"Wayne." He extended a hand as they drew closer to one another. Callie shuffled the bouquet of flowers she carried from her right to left hand. *Is it a cliche that I stopped to buy them?* A peace offering, perhaps. She couldn't come empty-handed. "Raina's husband." His large, rough hand gave hers a shake. "Raina wasn't expecting you un-til—"

"I know. I'm sorry."

"Raina's in the barn."

Callie turned toward the large one to the right of the house, the one she'd spied immediately from the road.

"Nope," Wayne corrected, and she circled around. "It's down the path on the other side of the house, just beyond the bee garden."

Callie winced. *A bee garden?* She hadn't seen one of those since she lived at her childhood home. Her mother and her feral bees. Closing her eyes for a second, Callie drew in a deep breath. *A sign? A connection to Mother, of all things. Raina keeps bees?* Harper would have mentioned that, knowing Callie's fear of them. Perhaps she didn't know.

Wearing pumps hadn't been a smart choice, as the dirt beneath her was full of rocks. Lovely gardens with wildflowers ornamented the backyard lined in live oaks dripping with Spanish moss. There was a worn swing set and an oversized sandbox with Tonka trucks, buckets, and shovels. Five Adirondack chairs, two adult size and three kid size, sat in a semicircle surrounding the play area. *This is a loving home, indeed.*

A small barn, more like a shed, stood to the left of what was cer-tainly the bee garden, marked by an unmistakable, worn sign that

read Raina's Garden. Beyond it, Callie recognized the familiar boxes lined up with what looked like screens atop them. A chill coursed
through her. Those did not bring good memories. The feral bees that
her mother had collected from neighbors who called in a fright represented the only altruistic task Evelyn was capable of. Aside from
being stung by them once and having had an allergic reaction, Callie
grew up hating those bees.

A large wooden sign hung crookedly over the top of the doorway, singing out Bee-licious. Perhaps Raina would change Callie's
mind and give her something to love about them.

Callie tiptoed up the wooden ramp. Raina's back was now in her
view. Long, wavy hair hung beneath her shoulders. If Harper's blond
was the color of creamy toffee, then Raina's was more like a harvest
gold. Callie's was right in the middle, which filled her with the sensation of hot tea on a cold winter's day. Though today was nothing
like winter. The sun was shining, and it cast a beam of light onto the
floor where Raina stood, barefoot and wearing a sundress, humming
a tune as she tended to something on a workbench.

Callie cleared her throat as she knocked on the opened door.

Raina jumped like a rabbit and turned around. Her eyes
widened. There was such a radiance to them. She cocked her head.

Callie anchored her feet to the floorboards beneath her because
her knees were shaking. Her stomach started to constrict. *In and out.
In and out. Breathe.* Her lips parted. All she could do was stare. She
noticed the resemblance immediately. *How did I not know my own
daughter when Harper first showed me that picture? What kind of a
mother am I?*

Raina came closer. "Mrs. Clarke, right?" Of course her voice was
sweet like honey.

Callie nodded. "Raina," she said, all airy as if expelling a long-
awaited breath. Collecting herself, she added, "Please call me... Callie." How she wished Raina might want to call her Mom, but she

couldn't be presumptuous. She didn't want to scare her away. Callie held up the bouquet of lush and colorful dahlia.

"Oh, so beautiful. I love pretty flowers." Raina exuded perkiness in both her voice and open gestures as she accepted the flowers, cradling them in her arm.

Callie flashed a Duchenne smile. "Yes, I noticed your flower garden. Lovely. My daughter..." She paused and sheepishly backstepped. "Harper does too. Something else you have in common."

"Else? Oh, besides the..."

"No. I meant in your appearance. You are strikingly similar in appearance. Can I ask..."

Callie looked around the shed. Honey jars, mason jars filled with candles, and chiseled homemade soaps were like a wall on top of stacked shelves. In the corner were large metal contraptions. One looked like an oversized water jug with temperature gauges on the face, while others were square vats with dials on the front. It looked to be quite an intricate setup. Nothing like what her mother had used.

"Oh, this. My bees. My Bee-licious business. Did you see the sign? My husband, Wayne, made it for me. Hobby-turned-part-time-job when my youngest went to school full-time. Meant to keep me beesy." She laughed at her own joke. "These are all my contraptions."

Clearly, she was as nervous as Callie, who managed to chuckle herself.

Raina held out a small round tin with stickers on top. "Try this. I'm labeling my bee balm." Raina twisted off the top and poked a finger into the container full of what looked like softened wax. "Just a dab. Try it on your hand. It's good for lips, cracked skin..."

Callie held out the back of her hand, and Raina rubbed the lotion in a circle. Seeing their hands together, Raina touching hers, made Callie realize her eyes were welling up. She swallowed hard, trying to push the visible emotions away.

"There you go. Nice, isn't it? Give it just a little sniff."

Callie smelled the hint of vanilla mixed with the honey. "Nice. You made this?"

"Sure did." Raina's smile was warm and full of light. She twisted the top back on and handed the tin to Callie. "There. A gift."

Callie held it in her hand for a moment, taking it all in. *A gift from my daughter.* "Thank you. You are very sweet."

Raina pulled the hair off her neck and fanned herself. "Let's go up to the house. I made some sweet tea and finger sandwiches. I could go for some tea. It's so stinking hot out today."

Callie followed Raina out of the shed and waited as she locked up. Callie watched her strut swiftly up the pathway as if she were rushing to something, and she wondered if Raina was eager to have a conversation or eager for it to be over. Her bare feet must be used to the pebbled ground. Callie kept up in her high heels but kept rocking such that she concentrated on walking sturdily so as not to fall and make a fool of herself.

"Come on in," Raina said. "I sent Wayne and the kids out on errands so we wouldn't be bothered."

"I met him. Very gracious."

"Oh, he's a big ol' peach in the body of a teddy bear." As they walked through the front door, Raina gasped at the sight of toys strewn about the living room. "Who doesn't listen? I did ask him to have the kids clean up their mess. Please excuse it."

"No worries. Can I help?"

"No, thanks. I've got it all ready. I just want to get these beauties in water."

Callie took in the humble surroundings. What a difference from Harper's home, where everything was simplistic, with clean lines and oversized furniture. By contrast, this house was quaint. The faded leather on the seat and headrest of the recliner looked like it would scoop a person up and snuggle them. The plaid couch was meant for a houseful of children with food stains and grime to hide. And the built-ins were surely meant to conceal buckets full of toys and stacks of games and puzzles.

Clanking sounds could be heard from the kitchen, but the wall that divided the two rooms prevented Callie from seeing what Raina was doing. "Are you sure I can't help?"

"Yes, thank you," Raina called back.

At that moment, Callie's eye met something familiar from her past, something similar to an object she'd had as a young girl. It lay open on its side, a wooden box with a faded Cinderella and Prince Charming on the cover. Callie bent to pick it up. She opened it, and there she was—Cinderella with faded, tarnished hair and dress. Callie spun the dial at the bottom of the box. And she heard the tune. *Bum, bum... bum, bum, bum... bum, bum...* Then she started mouthing the words. "A dream is a wish..." Plastic Cinderella twirled.

Raina snuck up on her with a tray in one hand and a full pitcher of sweet tea in the other. "Let me get that for you," Callie said, putting the box on the table and reaching for the glass container.

"Why, thank you very much. Everything is all set up on the porch. I hope you don't mind eating outside."

Callie followed her, and they put down what was in their hands. Raina gestured for Callie to sit at the already-set table. A large bowl of fresh fruit salad was the centerpiece.

"This is lovely."

"I hope you didn't trip on that box."

"The box?" Callie had forgotten for a second.

"My daughter's jewelry box. Timothy loves that thing. He likes to dump it and play the music."

Callie took a sip of her tea. "Mm," she said. "I used to have one just like it when I was a girl. My father took me to a screening of *Cinderella* for my birthday. He rented out the whole theater. He bought me the box later to remind me of the occasion."

Raina leaned in. She wrinkled her nose and seemed like she was about to say something but instead offered food. "I hope you like finger sandwiches. I have cucumber and mayo, dried tomato and basil, or artichoke cheese on account I didn't know what you like."

"The cucumber and the artichoke sound delicious."

Raina placed two on each of their plates with a spoonful of fruit.

"I didn't expect you to go through all this trouble."

"Callie," Raina said, looking at her with glittering eyes, "this is just as big a deal for you as it is for me. It's not every day you get to meet the birth mother you never knew you had."

They ate in awkward silence for a few minutes.

Raina daintily wiped the edges of her mouth and sat up straight. She cleared her throat such that Callie took notice. "That box you had in your hand..." Raina paused between each word, causing Callie to hang on them. "That was mine. When I was a little girl."

Callie put her hand to her mouth.

"I don't remember it being given to me. I just always had it. And I didn't know who Cinderella was until I was much older. I don't know why I kept it, but I did. I gave it to my daughters, Tracy and Tina."

Callie put her hands together as if saying a prayer. While her mother seldom gave any indication that she loved Callie, not overtly, anyway, the letter she had received from her at least opened her to the possibility that she'd wanted Callie's child to have something of hers. "Thank you for telling me that. I'd like to think it was mine—a piece of me given to you when you were adopted."

Tears streamed down Raina's face as her head bobbed up and down. "I'm so sorry. This is all just a lot. My parents—well, Mama died when I was little, so just my pa—never told me." She looked away for a second then returned her focus to Callie. "I don't know how to do this."

"Neither do I, but I want you to know if I had any inkling, even the slightest, I would have searched for you."

Raina swallowed hard. "Being here with you feels like betraying the mother who raised me."

"I'm grateful for her. That you had someone to love you."

"Thank you." Raina leaned toward her. Callie read the look on her face as tentative with the way her lip curled, but her eyes were bold. Raina blurted out, "What kind of a person did this to us?"

"Her name was Evelyn. To say we had a strained relationship would be putting it mildly. Only now can I understand that because of my father, who, God bless him, is still alive. In her twisted way, she thought she was doing the right thing. She thought she was protecting me."

"Protecting you how?"

"I was young. Not even eighteen, and your father was an administrator at the school I attended, but we fell in love. Raina, I promise you, you were conceived out of love."

"Does he know about me?"

Callie shook her head. She wanted to see how things worked out with Raina before opening *that* Pandora's box. "While I would love to announce to the world that you're my long-lost daughter, I respect that you need to do this on your terms. But we found each other, Raina. That's what's important."

Callie reached out an upturned hand across the table. While she hesitated at first, Raina placed her hand in it, and Callie squeezed. Such soft skin, Raina's fingers dainty like silver demitasse spoons.

"I do hope you and Harper can be friends, put all of this surrogacy behind you and start fresh," Callie said. "My son, Ben, is two years older than Harper. He has two children and is about to have a third himself."

"I've been an only child my whole life. It will be something, getting used to siblings. I always dreamed of having my own houseful because it was lonely being an only child."

"I know they'll welcome you with open arms."

"And your husband?"

"Adam? Oh, Adam—he is the epitome of understanding."

After lunch, Callie stood opposite Raina, absorbing her presence. Her thick brows and bouncy hair. They reminded her of her own when she was young. Her eyes were Jon's, though, dark and prominent. "Oh, Raina, we have so much ahead of us, so much learning and growing together. As mother and daughter. As families."

Instinct wanted to draw Raina in, hold her in her arms, pat her back the way she had for Ben and Harper so many times. But the understanding between them was still tentative. And, for now, that was okay. "Thank you so much for sharing this with me. I'll wait for you to be in touch."

Then Callie remembered the contents of her purse. She fumbled inside and pulled out the stack of papers tied up in a ribbon. "These might provide a little clarity on how I felt about you before you were born."

Raina took the package. "Thank you." She remained silent for a long minute, looking at the papers in her hand, her head nodding. "Give me some time. I'd like to tell my children and be sure they are settled with it before any introductions. I'm a baby-step person." She blushed a little when she said it, and Callie thought it endearing.

"Time. I'm happy to give you that." Callie smiled a little sadly. "But remember, it's precious, and it's also fleeting. We've already missed so much of it."

From the car, Callie watched Raina standing on the porch, framed by the doorway, the sunlight hitting the side of her face—a beautiful picture Callie took with her mind's eye.

As Callie drove away, she replayed every moment of the day. She didn't want to forget a thing.

Callie

Chapter 28

On the veranda out back, Callie sat waiting, watching the majestic sunset of pinks and purples as they painted the sky. On the white wrought-iron table in front of her sat a chilling bottle of champagne and charcuterie she had assembled to celebrate her breakthrough. She flitted about, readying for the occasion that was certain to end this day perfectly. It had given her a new lease on life, yes. Her secrets were revealed, and her long-lost daughter was found. She had a complete family, at last, and she couldn't feel more grateful.

Adam was at a golf outing and would be home any minute. The anticipation bubbled inside to share every detail of her visit to Raina's with him. Her cell phone buzzed on the table. Maybe it was Adam saying he would be late. When Callie held it in her hands, she realized the number was foreign, no name attached.

"Hello," she answered buoyantly.

The voice on the other end was monotone. "Calista? Calista Clarke?"

Callie's eyes narrowed. Since she'd become a mother, every time she'd been taken off guard, her mind went to the worst-case scenario. *Did something happen to Adam? One of the children?*

"This is Waterford Assisted Living." *My father.* "Your father has just been transported to Savannah General. Ms. Clarke, we believe he had a heart attack."

Everything became fuzzy and static. Callie didn't remember hanging up from the call.

She left a note for Adam and rushed to the hospital.

IN A FLURRY, CALLIE ran to the front lobby elevator, up to the fourth floor, through the hallways, noting the arrows on red-and-white signs reading Cardiac, to the nurses' station. The moment she said, "Asa Sebastian," to the nurse sitting at the desk, she knew. She was too late. He had passed.

The nurse told her in an apologetic voice—one that seemed muffled, far away. Callie held on to the desk with both hands. Everything appeared to freeze around her as she processed the news, the feeling of being untethered. Her legs wobbled.

Callie insisted on seeing him. She needed to see him.

Asa still lay in the room where he had passed. They had been preparing him for surgery, the nurse had told her. The white sheet was folded pristinely across his chest, under his arms. His skin was gray and his body thin. Had she taken note of how thin he'd become when she saw him just a couple of weeks earlier?

"Oh, Daddy." Callie picked up his hand, now cool to the touch. She examined it in hers—touched his skin like river water.

Memories of her father rushed forth in quick succession. The way he'd held her hand when she was a small girl, his so big and strong and hers hanging onto his pinky finger. He used to tickle her belly, making her giggle so much, and chase her around the playscape outside then scoop her up into his arms, which made her feel secure, as if nothing bad would or could ever happen to her in his presence.

Callie wanted to cry, felt pressure behind her eyes, but the tears wouldn't come. "I don't know how to say goodbye to you. You've been the one constant for my whole life."

Callie remembered him coloring with her in the playroom, his legs splayed out on the floor because they could never fit properly under her child-size table. She remembered standing beside him, saying, "Daddy, color the sun next... Not that yellow. This one."

The older she became, the more he taught her about life, that she should "never look down on anyone no matter their status and always help out people in need." She supposed that was one of the reasons she worked for the nonprofit for all those years and prioritized people over their bank accounts.

"You were the one who taught me all the right lessons. The ones I'd pass onto my children."

But it was the way he looked at her that told the whole story, the sparkle in his eyes on the day of the debutante ball as he escorted her down the stairs, the way she'd imagined he would at her wedding. So much had changed by then. She wished she could take back the decision to get married with only a few people in attendance, her father never on the guest list. She hadn't been able to take the chance that Mother would accompany him and ruin everything.

"I only regret the middle years that got lost, that you couldn't be as much a part of my family as I always imagined you'd be—that I couldn't let you because I was always too afraid. I'm so sorry."

She sat on the edge of his bed and studied his face, trying to memorize it, afraid she would inevitably forget the details. His knobby nose. The beauty mark above his lip. The creases in his forehead that she always equated to wisdom. Now they and the wrinkles spidering from his eyes meant something entirely different. All the secrets he carried.

"Thank you for giving me your final gift, Raina. She accepted me, Daddy. I wanted you to meet my firstborn. I wanted her to meet you."

Callie gently placed his hand down. He looked so tranquil—all the demons were gone. She put two fingers to her lips, kissed them and touched them to her father's cheek. "Please rest in peace."

FOUR DAYS LATER, CALLIE sat, stoic, in the hearse as it snaked through winding alleyways up a hill, where she spotted a tall mausoleum with an angel engraved on a cross at its peak. "Sebastian" was carved in large, looming letters on the front of the monument beneath the cross. *Of course my father bought a grand monument for my mother,* Callie thought.

Gardenias, daisies, and yellow aster trimmed the base of the marble structure. Callie was sure her father had arranged for fresh flowers to be placed there routinely. He dedicated himself wholly to those he loved.

Two runners had been placed in front of the doorway to the structure where her father's casket would lie during the gravesite ceremony. After the pallbearers transported the casket, the undertaker and his assistants placed the cascades of flowers around it.

As Callie and her family exited the hearse, she spotted Raina and Wayne standing beside the seats that had been saved for the immediate family. Callie winced. *Raina should have a place too,* she thought, and she whispered to Adam. By the time Callie's family took their seats, Raina sat beside Harper. Pam, Gabe, and Wayne stood behind their respective spouses.

The priest began with a prayer, and while everyone else bowed their heads, Callie stared at the casket, still in disbelief. Just as she'd been given her daughter, her father had been taken away. From behind her, Jocelyn reached down, her hand squeezing Callie's shoulder, and Callie looked back at her, managing a faint smile. Adam read a short eulogy Callie had written, commemorating the high points of her father's life and acknowledging how profound his loss would be to her. She feared she wouldn't have been able to get through reading it herself.

One by one, the attendees stood, plucked a flower from the arrangements, and dropped it on the casket. One by one, carnations, lilies, and roses covered the top of the mahogany box adorned in brass.

Callie watched as if it were an out-of-body experience, detached, floating above and away from the person who had anchored her since her memory could recollect. *This can't be happening. I haven't had enough time. It got away from me. So much time wasted on being angry and wounded...*

She felt a hand rest on her shoulder. *Adam.* He nodded. It was her turn to say goodbye.

But her feet were cemented to the ground. *I can't. I can't. I can't.*

Adam took hold of her hand and walked beside her to the grave. She bent down and chose a white rose. *So simple in its perfection.* She looked at it trembling in her grasp. A deafening silence enveloped her. She tried calling up how he sounded the last time he said goodbye to her. Instead, the slow trill of a red cardinal perched on a tree caught Callie's attention. It seemed to be eyeing her.

Callie turned toward the flower-draped casket. *He certainly was loved.* "Goodbye, Daddy. I'll miss you forever," she mouthed as she let the rose drop from her fingertips.

The priest invited the attendees to a small gathering at Callie's home. People congregated in small circles, exchanging sympathy and memories, and eventually, the circles dissipated. Among her three children, Callie stood and thanked the guests for attending.

Jocelyn hugged her tightly. "You'll get through this," she whispered in her ear. The longevity of their friendship, of her loyalty and sisterhood, meant the world to Callie. Jocelyn had always been her chosen sister. "I'll see you at the house," she affirmed, leaving a kiss on her cheek.

Behind her came a woman familiar to Callie, but she couldn't put her finger on exactly why. *It must be the grief,* Callie thought. *So many faces jumbled together.* "Thank you for coming," she said politely to her guest.

Just a stitch taller than Callie with midlength salt-and-pepper hair, the woman gave her a warm smile. Her eyes, the color of jade, looked so familiar. "Callie, I know how much you loved him," she said in a silvery voice.

Callie gasped. "Stella?" Her nanny—the one she named her daughter for.

"Yes."

"Oh my goodness. Stella." Callie's body melted, immediately drawn back to how Stella always made her feel. *Loved.* "It's been so many years."

"When I saw Asa's name in the paper, of course I had to pay my respects. I attended your mother's service, too, hoping to see you."

Still taking in the warmth she felt in Stella's presence, Callie shook her head. "Oh, Stella, so much happened between Evelyn and me. A story for another time. But thank you so much for coming." She took Adam's hand into hers. "Adam, this is Stella. Ben, Harper, Raina—this is Stella." They made their introductions. Callie was so proud for them to have met her. She thanked Stella profusely and promised they would get together to catch up. "Soon. Very soon," Callie said as she kissed Stella goodbye.

Callie looked up to the cloudless sky, hoping her father had something to do with this unexpected reunion. She remembered Stella's words from when she was a little girl, "Even on the rainiest days, there's always something to be grateful for, something to turn your day around. It's always there. You just have to search for it." Her Stella and Raina, one human being. Her daughter. That was what she had to be thankful for.

By now, only Callie and her immediate family remained. She returned to them after walking Stella to her car. "There's something I'd like to do before we go."

Callie reached down, plucking a lily from the remaining flowers. She walked purposefully toward the large mausoleum and opened the door. Inside was a marble sarcophagus on the left and one with a top removed on the right, where her father would be.

On the left above the top of the sarcophagus, the words "Beloved wife and mother" were etched in the wall. Callie shuddered. Beneath the words was a photograph of Evelyn encased in glass with icy-blond hair and diamond earrings—a gift from Asa, Callie presumed—and Callie recognized the dress from her own debutante ball. Evelyn had never been anything short of stunning.

Callie rubbed her arms. "Oh, Mother," she said, taking in a deep breath and releasing it. "I bet you didn't expect me to be here. I hope, in some way, you might be responsible for bringing Raina to me, that maybe you arranged for Harper to meet her from the start. Why is it only now that I know you had reasons, no matter how skewed they were? Daddy made me see that you loved me—in your own way."

Callie placed the flower down on the marble. "I forgive you because in forgiving you, I'm setting myself free. It's what you said you wanted for me all along. Please take care of Daddy. Love him deeply, the way he loved us."

Callie
Oak Creek, Georgia, 2006
Epilogue

White lights hung from tree branch to tree branch in Callie's yard. Adam stood atop a ladder, attaching the last string.

"A little to the left," Callie directed, a clipboard in her hand.

Adam rolled his eyes.

"I want it to be perfect. Adam, come on." She flexed her hands to loosen the tension.

The florist dropped off arrangements for the circular tables in the yard. *Check.* The caterer and the waitstaff hustled about, setting up the buffet table with an assortment of appetizers—charcuterie, fruits and vegetables with assorted dips, and special finger foods that were a staple when Callie was growing up. Asa had insisted on Callie taking a recipe box full of Evelyn's favorites. "Family favorites," he'd said, but Callie knew the truth. Until recently, she had kept them in the attic.

Only after the funeral, already over a year ago, did she allow herself to venture up there to rummage through some of what Asa had insisted she keep from her mother. At the time, Callie had only begrudgingly agreed. Raina made her see the importance of connecting one generation to the next, the past to the present.

Admiring the spread of food, Callie called out to the caterer, "This looks fantastic." She checked another item off her list.

Callie put the finishing touches on the tables, little terracotta pots filled with yellow dahlias adorned with alternating pink and blue ribbons at the top of each table setting. In each pot, she inserted handmaid bee sticks, an afternoon craft project, as ornaments.

"The party starts when the Clarkes arrive," Ben called out as he, Pam, and their two girls rounded the corner, Ben carrying baby Matthew.

"Oh my goodness, don't you girls look beautiful." Callie bent down to shower kisses on her granddaughters in their matching dresses. "Oh, look, Matthew's outfit matches theirs too." She touched his button nose, which evoked a smile.

"Where is everyone?" Ben asked.

"You're early. Impressive. Will you help your dad set up the gift table?"

Ben scrunched his nose.

"The table," Callie corrected. "I'll dress it. Girls, can you help me?"

Her granddaughters followed her over to the space and helped Callie spread the cloth once the table was erected.

She placed a basket on top for cards and a bouquet of flowers. "You can place your gifts here," she said.

The girls dutifully went to where Ben had put down the large pink-and-blue-decorated boxes, helping each other carry them to the table.

"Ben, could you help Dad with the sign?"

Adam took one end of the string and Ben took the other while Callie stood back to make sure the letters attached to the string were centered between the two trees.

"A sprinkle?" asked Adam. "I thought this was a shower."

"Well, it's a sprinkle," Callie said.

She tucked her clipboard, with every item checked off, on the desk in the kitchen then returned outside to admire the spectacle. *Every item in its place.*

Harper came around the side yard with Miles on a leash just seconds before Raina and her family arrived.

"This looks beautiful, Mom."

"Do you think so?"

"You know it does."

Callie squeezed Harper's hand and asked, with a concerned look on her face, "How are you?" Just two weeks before, Harper's divorce from Gabe had been finalized. Of course, they had been separated for a good six months prior, but still, divorce was never easy, even when it was mutual.

"I'm good. Really." She smiled convincingly, bending down to pet Miles.

"Hi, y'all." Raina approached, giving the whole yard a look. "Oh my. You outdid yourselves."

Callie blushed. Raina kissed her cheek.

Raina's kids tumbled to the ground to let Miles jump on them and lick their faces. Ben's two girls got into the mix.

"Look at you," Harper said to Raina. "You have a big old football in that belly. I bet it's a boy."

Wayne zipped his lips then threw away an imaginary key.

"I see how it is," Harper said.

"We may or may not be revealing what we're having today. We found out last week," Raina said.

Callie fist-pumped the air. She couldn't wait to find out.

Once Harper told Raina she had decided not to have children and that she and Gabe were separating, Raina dove back into her business and the business of getting to know her new family. Both were enough to put more purpose in her life than she had ever imagined. While the company began thriving, her adjustment to being part of a big family had taken time to navigate. But she was determined, and her new family was patient.

Then Raina found out she was pregnant when she wasn't even trying. This time, Wayne took the news in stride, eventually coming to a place of excitement, as Raina knew he would.

Yet Raina teetered on eggshells before telling Callie and, eventually, Harper, since their relationship was still somewhat tentative.

"I don't want to mess this up," Raina had said.

Callie reassured her that they were family, which meant their bond was unbreakable. To herself, though, Callie longed for the day when she no longer feared the fragility inherent in the newness of any relationship. She longed for ease and familiarity with Raina the way she felt it with her younger two. It would come, she told herself, in due time.

The guests started to arrive. Jocelyn, Debs, and their husbands, along with Stella, were already seated at the table when Callie approached. "My support table. Yet not even a hello?" She chuckled so they would know she was kidding. The host was always the center of attention no matter who the guest of honor was, especially when more guests poured in.

"You were busy. We knew you'd get around to finding us. We're calling this the anchor table. Everything looks gorgeous, Cal."

"Thanks, Joss."

"Stella and I were reacquainting ourselves. Gosh, I remember our playdates were such fun when she was there. And Debs has introduced herself."

"My sacred friend at Covenant House," Callie said. "I'm so happy we reconnected. Stella and I also caught up over lunch a few months back. Let's just say she wasn't all that surprised about the unfolding of events where it concerned Mother."

Nodding, Stella pursed her lips. Callie hugged her from behind. "I'm so glad you're here."

"Happy to have you back in my life."

Callie looked at the one vacant chair at the table then squarely at Jocelyn. "Remember to save the seat."

Jocelyn nodded.

Raina brought her father over to introduce to Callie and Adam. Reggie was older than Callie anticipated, much older than herself, or perhaps it just looked that way because his posture prompted the rounding of his shoulders. He hardly had any hair left, just a few strands combed over.

"Pleasure's all mine," he said. "You have been very good to our girl."

"Pa," Raina said, her face flushing from embarrassment as if she were still a little girl.

"She's easy to be good to," Callie said. "We have a special seat for you over here." Adam led Reggie to the family table.

Callie kept looking at the side entrance to the backyard even though most of the guests had arrived. It was time to get the festivities underway.

Laughter and conversation filled the air. Callie glanced over at the gift table, which was so buried in boxes that it could no longer be seen. Yes, this was perfect, and she still had one more surprise up her sleeve. She clanked a wine glass with a spoon, looking at Raina's table full of family.

"Can I get your attention?" The noise hushed. "Thank you, all, for coming today to celebrate Raina's sprinkle. This has been quite a year, one of endings and new beginnings. We are blessed to have gained a daughter and a sister." The radiant expression on her face was reciprocated by her three children, which filled her whole heart. "This has been a gift. And what better way to celebrate than by bringing new life into the world? Please enjoy the food and drink. And yes, we have a virgin punch in honor of the mother-to-be."

A string quartet played during brunch, and a soft breeze quelled the sticky heat. Callie relaxed, looking from one person to the next, grateful for how full her life had become. She considered the enormous weight that had been lifted, one that she hadn't always been aware of, because she'd grown used to its heaviness like a gray cloud even on a sunny day. Constantly looming and lurking until it made itself obvious again. When it did, she had learned to deal with it alone, erecting imaginary umbrellas, seeking seemingly hidden roads back to the light.

With all the secrets revealed, even with her father's death, Callie could suddenly breathe again—full, vivacious breaths. *And isn't it the best feeling?*

The transition between brunch and dessert gave everyone time to socialize. Across the yard, Callie heard Ben's throaty laughter, which caused her to turn to the best sight. Her three children were sitting together, two with their spouses and children at their feet like blossoms poking up from the ground. Harper cradled Matthew in her arms. Callie accepted that having a baby didn't work out for Harper and Gabe, realizing her children were capable of fulfilling lives even though they didn't turn out the way Callie had imagined them. Harper was happy living with Miles, her sidekick, and selling the houses that Cody flipped. She'd found joy in being part of the design process, something she hadn't ever considered before.

When Callie joined them, Ben and Wayne were talking baseball odds while Raina and Pam exchanged mommy stories. Callie sat down next to Harper, who was watching Matthew playing with her finger, holding on and letting go like it was a game.

"Everything's perfect, Mom."

"Is it, honey?"

"Yeah."

"Any regrets leaving Divine?"

"Not one. Every step is new and exciting. Cody and I work so well together."

"He's single, isn't he?" *Am I prying too much?* She'd made a conscious effort of late to let Harper take the lead, to not throw so many shoulds her way. To remind Harper how proud Callie was of her independent spirit.

"Mom!" Her reaction was light. Callie almost detected a laugh. Perhaps something was there. A mother knew these things.

Pam interjected, "I couldn't help but overhear. I told Harper to swoop him up. Men like that don't stay single long, and he's quite the catch."

A debate ensued about Cody's attributes while Harper defended her choice to remain single for the foreseeable future.

"Oh, Mom!"

Is Harper deflecting? She's definitely changing the subject on purpose. Callie nodded.

"The three of us girls are going for manis and pedis next Saturday. Would you like to come?"

"Sort of a sister bonding event," Pam added.

Raina took hold of Harper's hand and Pam's and just squeezed. "Yes, come with us," she said.

Clasping her own hands together, Callie breathed in—appreciating this moment, trying consciously to commit it to memory. "I don't think so, but thank you so much for the invite. Next time. You girls enjoy your time together."

Callie stole away, having something to check on. She wandered out to the front of the house and sat on the porch steps. Waiting. She checked her watch.

Jocelyn snuck up behind her with two drinks. "The alcoholic punch," she said as she handed it to Callie. She sat down on the step beside her. "You know, I thought this was a bad idea. Look how distracted you are. You should be enjoying this day. Yours and Raina's."

"I am." Callie kicked her legs out straight.

Two weeks ago, after stalling for days, Callie had found the nerve to call Jon. It had been eating away at her. *Should I? Shouldn't I?* She waffled back and forth so many times that she'd lost count. She had debated with Jocelyn whether it was the right thing to do, but eventually Jocelyn handed over his number, knowing full well that when Callie was determined to do anything, she did it.

Callie turned her attention back to the present, back to Jocelyn. "He said he'd be here. I wanted to give her this. One more gift."

"He must have had second thoughts, Callie. Imagine how daunting it would be to walk into something like this alone. He hasn't seen you in what? Almost forty years. And you have a whole family."

Callie's head dropped back in a fit of laughter. "Forty years ago, you warned me about him. I didn't want to believe it. I was so in love. But he was a coward then, and he's a coward now. And now you're defending him?" Callie watched the ice swirl as she swished the glass in her hand.

"I believe he wants to do the right thing. Let him figure out what that means. Let it be. Allow it to work out the way it's supposed to. You always told me that."

"Actually, I stole that from Debs."

"See, there were good things to come out of Covenant House too." Then she stopped and looked Callie squarely in the eye. "This—a relationship with you—is your gift to Raina. It's all she needs. All you need. You've raised two amazing children, who have welcomed her into the fold without so much as a doubt. You are their gift, Callie."

After not being able to cry for the better part of her life, Callie's eyes teared up. Again. She'd been doing a lot of that over the past year, thankfully from tears of joy. "Thank you. You've always been right here by my side."

Jocelyn smiled. She stood up and offered a hand to Callie, who took it. Jocelyn yanked her up. "It's getting a little harder than it used to be," she joked.

Arm in arm, they strolled back to the party.

Callie found Raina peeking at the mound of gifts on and in front of the table.

"I'm so overwhelmed. So blessed," Raina said. "I can't believe how much my life has changed in a year."

Callie gave her a warm smile. "Are you ready to open the gifts?"

"Maybe after the guests leave. That way, I could spend time with them."

"Of course," Callie agreed.

"I would like to share something with you. With everyone. If I may."

"This is your shower, Raina. Sprinkle! You can do anything you'd like."

Raina stood tall, holding the bottom of her protruding stomach, in front of the gift table. "Excuse me!" she yelled. Callie tried to give her the glass and the spoon, but Raina waved it away. "Hello. Everyone? Can I have a minute?" She put her fingers in her mouth to whistle sharply, grabbing everyone's attention.

I can't whistle like that, Callie thought, and the crowd silenced immediately. Callie stepped back, sitting in the empty chair at the anchor table, the one closest to Raina.

"Wayne, can you and the kids come up here?"

Wayne shooed their kids over to Raina's side. He stood next to her with his arm around her waist.

"Last week, we found out..." She looked down at Tracy, Tina, and Timothy then up at Wayne. "We are having a baby girl." A round of applause and hollers erupted. "Yes, we are very happy. Well, Timothy may have been hoping for a brother." The boy's freckled face flushed.

"And we would like to share," she said, her head tipped toward Callie, "that, Mom, if I may call you that..."

Tears glossed over Callie's eyes as she placed her hand over her heart. "Of course," she mouthed.

"You have been so gracious to me and my family. We are truly blessed to have this extended surprise family. Some of y'all might not know this, but when my mother had her firstborn, me!" She pointed to herself and curtsied. "She wanted to name her Stella after a very influential woman in her life."

Callie and Stella exchanged loving glances.

"As fate would have it, I became Raina instead. Thanks, Pa." Laughter broke out. "But we'd like to honor my newly found other mother by naming our daughter Stella."

Callie gasped. Aside from sharing the name Callie had in mind for her firstborn, she and Raina had never discussed it further. For her to extend this gesture meant everything.

Through the celebratory clapping, Callie gazed from her first-born to her second and third. Sure, life hadn't been perfect, but it had led to this very moment. And just then, Callie knew without doubt that this was exactly what family should be.

Raina motioned with a swoop of her hand for Callie to join her family, then she bent down and whispered something into her older daughter's ear. Tracy scurried away.

As Callie approached Raina, the tears were already flowing—a terrific release of joy spilling out like a burst of champagne. Over the years, Callie had been through so much—the betrayals, the loss, having to reinvent herself, and keeping certain parts of herself hidden. But in this one gesture, all of the pain absconded because what that seemed to matter most was the present. The warmth of their bodies was proof of a soulful synergy between them, so secure and comforting.

Tracy returned with a large bouquet of dahlias and wildflowers overflowing in her arms. Raina turned to receive them as Tracy transferred them to her mother's hands. "Mom," Raina's steady voice said. "These are for you. For everything. For us finding each other."

Callie pulled the bouquet to her nose to breathe in the sweet and pungent scents, just as she noticed a little honey bee tucked into the petals, sucking the nectar.

Acknowledgements

G rowing up, I had a short bucket list. There were two certainties on it. One, I wanted to be a mom. Two, I needed to write. Little did I know just how intertwined the two would become. Since signing my publishing contract with Red Adept Publishing, I've learned that some authors refer to a completed manuscript as a "book baby," a suitable metaphor that has been reinforced throughout my journey.

I wrote the first draft of my second book, *Of Lies and Honey*, as part of November's 2019 NaNoWriMo project. I felt meh about it; it certainly did not evoke the passion I had for my first. It wasn't until the third revision that it really started coming together, and once I worked through it with some critique partners, I really came to love it. It was like that epiphany you have when your second child is finally born, and you realize your heart absolutely has the capacity to love the second baby as much as the first.

The idea for this book came from an article I read about a debutante that was forced by her parents to give her child up for adoption. As a mom myself, I couldn't imagine being forced to give up my child, so I had to explore the notion further. With that came a whole lot of research about debutante society, social classes in the sixties, Southern culture, and the many current options for expectant mothers and those who desperately want to have a child but can't. I also decided on a bee motif early on, as the symbolism of the queen bee and the worker bees suited the characters of my novel. For that information, I relied heavily on my beekeeping brother, Michael Norman.

And I'd like to express my gratitude for the countless phone calls in which I posed different scenarios to him to see if they worked.

Much gratitude goes to my trusted critique partners, Bella Ellwood-Clayton and Linda Berlin, who were instrumental in fine-tuning this story. Thanks, also, to my early critique partners and beta readers, Diane Barnes and Michele Lugiai, who got to see the extremes of this story. And much appreciation to beta readers and trusted friends K.J. Kennedy, Cynthia Parisi Anderson, and Hope Gibbs. I would be remiss if I didn't give an additional shout-out to Hope for being my partner in many author-related things, like the Author Talking Bookish podcast we started between the releases of our debut novels, and for being my lifeline throughout this journey.

Writing this novel has made me realize how many people one needs as a support system. My thanks to my entire CHS English trust and to Ann Wellspeak and Mary Flood for their unwavering enthusiasm and support. Thank you to WFWA for being an organization that brings authors together, as I have made so many connections there. To the Bookish Road Trip crew, I am honored to have found such an amazing group of like-minded, strong, creative women with whom to work side by side, especially Grace Sammon, Mary Helen Sheriff, Barbara Conrey, and Linda Rosen—thank you for your friendship and mentorship.

None of this would be possible without Lynn McNamee having taken a chance on my first novel and now my second. Lynn works tirelessly to ensure the success of her authors at Red Adept Publishing. Thank you, Lynn, for your belief in me and the hard work you put into bringing together a Class A staff. Thanks as well to Jennifer Klepper, Jill Hannah Anderson, and Erica Lucke Dean, who always made themselves available to answer my many, many questions. And perhaps most important are my brilliant editors, who looked at my work with fresh, keen eyes and made all the suggestions to bring my story to its fullest potential. Thank you, Sara N. Gardiner and Mary Morris—this story wouldn't be what it is without you.

Last, but always first in my mind and heart, is family. My parents were teens when they had me, and I appreciate how much they struggled to give me and my siblings, Debbie and Michael, the best life possible. Thank you to my husband, who is my rock and my partner in everything. And to my children, Ryan, Tyler, and Alexa—I love you beyond measure, and you will always be at the beginning and end of everything I do.

Thank you to my readers who welcome my second book baby into their hands and hearts. I created this story to celebrate the many layers and complexities of women, to honor the bonds of mother and child and sisters, and to honor women who choose to be mothers, those who decide not to, and those for whom the choice has been taken out of their hands.

It takes a village. I'm grateful for mine.

Connect with me via my website, www.donnanormancarbone.com. Please also consider leaving a review on Amazon, Goodreads, and/or Bookbub.

Reading Guide

1. The bee motif was chosen as a symbol of motherhood. Callie, Harper, Raina, and Evelyn all have various attachments to bees. How would you characterize each of their attachments and what those attachments say about the characters themselves?
2. What are your thoughts on the way *Of Lies and Honey* addresses various choices surrounding pregnancy: abortion, adoption, surrogacy?
3. When Callie gets to Covenant House, she is annoyed about the lack of clocks there, save for the grandmother clock in the headmaster's office. Trace the mention of time throughout the novel. What importance does the time motif serve?
4. Covenant House serves as the nucleus of the secrets and lies. How authentic a point of intersection was this for the three stories to converge?
5. How do the three points of view contribute to the way you, as the reader, understand the story? For example, how would the story have been different if the entire story was told from Callie's point of view? Or Harper's? Or Raina's?
6. Given the three POVs, at what point in the story did you realize their connection?
7. With which character do you most identify, and why?
8. The relationship between Callie and Jon is a complex one given their status at Briarlee. Do you believe Jon really

loves/loved Callie? Why or why not?

9. Callie resigns herself to raising her first baby by herself. How would being a single mother in the 1970s have differed from today?

10. Each of the main characters experiences her role as a mother in a very different way from the others. How would you characterize each of them? And what is the message about the role of motherhood, generally speaking?

11. Complex mother-daughter relationships between Callie and Evelyn and Callie and Harper emerge. To what aspects of these did you most connect, and how did you feel about Raina's connection to Callie?

12. Did Callie make the right choice to invite Jon back into their lives at the end? What might have happened if he had shown up?

13. Which parts of the story made you laugh?

14. Which parts of the story were the most emotional for you?

15. To some degree, this story explores how past actions and events affect the present. Can you discuss a time when an event or a choice from the past altered the trajectory of your own life?

About the Author

Donna Norman-Carbone, the award-winning author of *All That is Sacred*, published by Red Adept Publishing, has a passion for writing women's fiction that tugs at the heartstrings. Donna is also cohost of the *Authors Talking Bookish* podcast and a tour guide for the Bookish Road Trip. Her writing affiliations include membership of WFWA, WNBA, and CAPA.

Donna is an English teacher in a small Connecticut suburb, where she and her husband have raised three children, two Labrador retrievers and a Siamese cat. In her spare time, she enjoys reading good books on a sunny Cape Cod beach (her happy place), spending quality time with family and friends, and traveling overseas.

Read more at www.donnanormancarbone.com.

About the Publisher

Dear Reader,

We hope you enjoyed this book. Please consider leaving a review on your favorite book site.

Visit https://RedAdeptPublishing.com to see our entire catalogue.

Check out our app for short stories, articles, and interviews. You'll also be notified of future releases and special sales.

Made in the USA
Las Vegas, NV
07 April 2024

88373423R00194